'The undisputed queen
of crime writing'

Erwin James

MARTINA COLE

Author of 24 novels – and counting…

15 No. 1 bestsellers

4 screen adaptations

3 stage shows

Over 15 million copies sold across the world

Celebrating 25 years of record-breaking bestsellers

Stay in touch for film and TV news,
book releases and more…

🐦 @MartinaCole
f /OfficialMartinaCole
www.martinacole.co.uk

*Martina Cole's No. 1 bestsellers – at time of press she has
spent more weeks at No. 1 than any other author

MARTINA COLE
DAMAGED

HEADLINE

First published in Great Britain in 2017 by
HEADLINE PUBLISHING GROUP

First published in Great Britain in paperback in 2018 by
HEADLINE PUBLISHING GROUP

4

Cataloguing in Publication Data is available from the British Library

ISBN 978 1 4722 0109 6 (B-format)
ISBN 978 1 4722 5620 1 (A-format)

Typeset in 11.5/15 pt ITC Galliard Std by Jouve (UK), Milton Keynes

Printed and bound in Great Britain by Clays Ltd, Elcograf S.p.A

Headline's policy is to use papers that are natural, renewable and recyclable products and made from wood grown in well-managed forests and other controlled sources. The logging and manufacturing processes are expected to conform to the environmental regulations of the country of origin.

HEADLINE PUBLISHING GROUP
An Hachette UK Company
Carmelite House
50 Victoria Embankment
London, EC4Y 0DZ

www.headline.co.uk
www.hachette.co.uk

For my beautiful girl Freddie Mary

Prologue

It was hot.

A real August day when the sun felt relentless and the air was filled with the screaming of seagulls. The landfill site in Essex was busier than ever, with the endless stream of trucks queuing up to unload their cargo. The noise of the gulls amid the constant sounds of earthmovers and lorries was so loud the ground workers had to shout to be heard above it.

But it was the stench that was the workers' main gripe. The combination of rotting vegetation, the wasted food mixed in with household chemicals and the carcasses of dead animals was even more potent in the burning heat. It never ceased to amaze the ground-force workers what people threw out without a backward glance. Dogs, cats, puppies – even the occasional exotic pet, such as a snake, and once a three-foot iguana – had been found dumped in with the household waste. One of the old-timers remembered finding a newborn baby years before, its tiny foot poking out of a Tesco carrier bag. Oh, there were plenty of gruesome tales to tell in the pubs they

1

frequented. Rubbish had a strange fascination for the people who dealt with it. They might be nicknamed 'shit shifters', among other things, but they shared a camaraderie that was well worth the ridicule.

On the plus side, many had found expensive objects over the years too; it was astounding what people inadvertently threw away. Jewellery, bundled-up money and wallets along with designer handbags and expensive electrical items – iPads, iPods, phones – the list was endless. The less scrupulous of the men would quietly pocket their finds while others took them straight to the offices in case people were looking for them.

Today was a Tuesday, a particularly busy day for them as the rubbish accumulated over two weeks in thousands of households was unloaded to be crushed and buried. Among the mass of waste, the rats were as brave as gladiators and the men had long learned to ignore them. Like the gulls they were an inescapable part of the job. Big bastards and all, some of them. Alongside them were often scavengers of the human variety – Eastern Europeans who scoured the place looking for anything of value. They were chased away regularly, but were soon inevitably back looking for stuff to sell or reuse. It was heartbreaking but the men knew they had to scare them off, especially the children – this was no place for kids. It was often a losing battle, as they continued finding them there bright and early, raking over other people's cast-offs day after day.

Micky Cartwright was one of the oldest men there; he'd been shit shovelling, as he told anyone who would listen, since he left school at fifteen, and he loved it. He had a large skull which still sported a full head of snow-white hair and, as he rolled himself a cigarette this particular morning, he sighed in exasperation. Unlike many of his workforce, Micky was a staunch Britain First supporter, which did not sit well with a lot of the other workers. Especially the men from ethnic backgrounds. There had been more than one complaint about his language and some of his remarks throughout the years. Today, the heat was getting to everyone and tempers were high. He'd thought it best to step out for a bit.

As Micky looked over the site he saw in the distance a figure climbing over the heaped rubbish and wondered how this fucker had managed to get past the others.

Walking back into the Portakabin they used to make tea, he picked up his binoculars – a wonderful find from many years before – and, stepping outside once more into the brilliant sunshine, he looked over to see who this was who'd managed to get in.

As Micky adjusted the binoculars, he wondered if he was actually seeing what he thought he saw. He was so shocked, he continued to watch the shape for a minute or two before running into the site office shouting, 'Fuck me, lads, you've got to see this!'

Putting down their mugs of tea and coffee, the men followed him outside. There was always something going on amid the bustle of a landfill site; it was one of the perks of the job. Micky handed his binoculars to a man called Jeremy Fewster who was the undisputed ganger in charge of the men and their differing duties, depending on his idea of their capabilities. Shovelling shit wasn't exactly on a par with rocket science but it was a lot more complicated than people on the outside realised.

Jeremy looked at the figure in the distance for a few minutes. Like Micky he didn't know what to make of it. It was so surreal. All the men on break were now trying to see what had captured so much attention but the sun was glaring down and it was difficult to make out anything from this distance. Jeremy started to give them a rundown on what he could see, as gradually even the men in the earthmovers stopped what they were doing to gawp at the strange sight.

A lone woman of indeterminate age dressed in a patterned sleeveless sundress and a large sunhat, her eyes hidden behind huge sunglasses and wearing a ludicrous pair of bright yellow wellington boots, was gradually making her way to the centre of the tip. She was holding what appeared to be a box or container tightly to her chest as she struggled to get to her destination. Jeremy watched, fascinated, as he could almost feel the power of her determination to do whatever it was she was there for.

When she finally stopped, she stood for a few moments looking around her at the endless sea of rubbish, wiping the sweat from her brow in a very feminine gesture, with the tips of the fingers of her free hand. He knew how difficult it was to walk through rubbish; it wasn't as easy as you'd think. He watched her steadying herself before she took the lid off the container and started to scatter what looked like ashes all over the refuse around her. He could just make out the satisfied smile on her face as she did it.

'Well, lads, she's obviously scattering her old man's ashes. All I can say is, he had to be some kind of cunt to get this treatment!'

The men were laughing, some not as heartily as others, as guilt and the thought of something like that happening to them was hammered home. But it was definitely another crazy story for the shit shifters to reminisce about as the years rolled on.

For I, the Lord your God, am a jealous God, punishing the children for the sins of the parents to the third and fourth generations of those who hate me

Exodus 20:5–6

Chapter One

'See, this is when you are glad to have a pool here. For about five weeks a fucking year it earns its upkeep!'

Patrick Kelly's voice was jovial but Kate knew that it galled him that their beautiful pool didn't get much use in Grantley. Still, they had a stunning villa in Spain if they needed the sun and they had also purchased a condo in Florida, as Patrick liked the golf courses out there. Florida was also where George Markham had died – the man who had murdered Patrick's daughter, Mandy – and she knew that he liked being close to where that evil bastard had met his end. It gave him a small sense of satisfaction. They had a very luxurious lifestyle and Kate enjoyed it more than she thought she should. She couldn't shake the feeling that it was too opulent, but it was part of Patrick's make-up. He needed to feel that people could see and admire his success and, in a way, she understood that.

After all these years together, she knew she was lucky to have him; they were growing old together these days, but they were happy. He still had it in him to give women the 'glad eye', as he called it, but his roaming days were over. At least she hoped so. She knew he still had his fingers in a lot of dirty-looking pies – Patrick Kelly was never going to be able to go completely straight – but she was retired from the force now, and she had decided that 'what couldn't be cured had to be endured'. One of her mum's old sayings; even now Kate still missed her.

Beverley Collins, their housekeeper, walked out to them where they were sitting on their terrace, smiling as usual. She was a confirmed spinster in her forties with a soft Cork accent and a face that Patrick once said was what his mother would have called 'unfortunate'. Meaning that she wasn't exactly a raving beauty, but she was wonderful at her job and that was all that mattered. Also, she had an endearing personality and wasn't even remotely intrusive. She loved her little independent flat on their property and fitted in with their set-up perfectly.

'There's a gentleman here to see you, Pat – won't give me his name.'

Patrick stood up, scowling. As he dragged on a robe, Kate followed suit. She hoped this wasn't trouble coming to their door. But after years with Patrick Kelly, Kate suspected that there'd likely be more to this than met the eye. Patrick still loved what he called 'a bit of skulduggery'.

Unfortunately, that sometimes came back to haunt him.

Chapter Two

Karen Jones was a small woman with big teeth. Her long dark hair was her best feature as she was well aware. As she cut through the alley that would eventually take her out to the high street, she heard a noise. It was low, guttural, and just the sound of it frightened her. She stopped and listened again. It was quiet now but the noise had ruffled her. She could hear the cars and the bustle of the shopping area, but here in this little alley she suddenly felt a tingling of dread.

She knew she had definitely heard something and, against her will, she started to retrace her steps. At the end of the alley, near where her council flat was, she turned left into the small woods. They were dark even in this sunny weather and, gritting her teeth, she walked carefully, keeping as near to the stone wall as she could. She was taking shallow breaths; she felt as if she had a tight band around her chest preventing her from getting enough air.

The trees were rustling in the breeze, and the sound made her feel even more uneasy, but she carried on slowly, stealthily. Then she looked in the undergrowth and saw a naked leg. That's when she started screaming.

Her shrieks soon brought her a small crowd and, as one person phoned the police and ambulance services, she was ashamed to see others taking photos with their phones of the naked girl lying there covered in blood.

Taking off her light summer jacket, Karen covered the girl as best she could till the emergency services arrived.

Chapter Three

Patrick walked into his spacious hallway and saw a man standing there. He was in his late thirties, and he had a powerful air about him, dressed in a well-cut suit and expensive shirt. He was taller than Patrick by a few inches, and he had dark hair and blue eyes. He was what Patrick would describe as 'well set up'.

In his robe and bare feet Patrick felt at a disadvantage somehow, and that came across in his voice as he barked out, 'And you are?'

Kate watched silently as the younger man held his hand out in a gesture of friendliness, a small smile on his handsome face.

Patrick ignored the hand of friendship and stood there silently, his eyebrows raised. He opened his arms and said with quiet intensity, 'Well?'

The man dropped his hand and, shrugging slightly, he said, 'Do you remember Ruby O'Loughlin?'

Patrick was perplexed at the younger man's calm tone of voice. He clearly wasn't in the least intimidated by Patrick and he found that disconcerting, as he did the question.

Kate said gently, 'Shall we go out to the patio and I'll

get us some tea?' She had a feeling that the man wasn't here to cause outright trouble exactly – but she had a sneaky suspicion he was going to cause a lot of consternation.

'Thank you. That would be lovely.'

The man smiled widely at Kate, and she felt an uneasiness rushing over her. He was smooth all right, she would give him that.

Unable to do anything else, Patrick had no option but to walk back through his opulent home and out on to the patio area. They all sat down on the terrace, and Beverley went off to make the tea.

'Look, Mr Kelly, I asked you something. Do you remember Ruby O'Loughlin?'

Patrick was bewildered by the younger man's question. Of course he remembered her – every bloke on his council estate would. 'I do. A crowd of us grew up together.'

The young man took a deep breath and said quietly, 'She died last month. Liver cancer.'

'Well, I'm sorry to hear that, son, of course. But I'm fucked if I know why you are telling me about it.' Patrick was genuinely baffled.

'I'm her son, Joseph. And before she died she told me that you were my father.'

The shocked silence was broken by Beverley's soft Irish brogue as she said hurriedly, 'I'll just put the tray here and be off out of it.'

Chapter Four

DCI Annie Carr looked down at the seriously injured girl and wondered at the terrible things people were capable of.

The doctor, a tall Indian man with soft doe eyes and a clipped British accent, was listing the girl's injuries. 'Trauma to the brain, serious head injuries. Broken ribs. Numerous burns, all over her. Genital mutilation. She is all but dead.'

Annie nodded; she had guessed as much. The girl had been pronounced brain dead a few hours earlier. The parents just needed to decide on giving her organs for donation before the machines were switched off.

The rape kit had been brought in earlier, and the swabs and other evidence sent off. Annie would make sure it got back to her ASAP.

They knew who the girl was; her parents had reported her missing two nights earlier. She was fourteen, and it looked like she had been tortured, raped and left for dead. Kylie Barlow wasn't going anywhere now, that much was for certain, and what was really worrying Annie was that she had a nasty feeling this wasn't going to be a one-off.

Whoever had done this to the child had planned it meticulously. They were evidently dealing with a dangerous predator, but she would know more after the autopsy. She ran a hand through her short greying hair and sighed heavily.

She hoped to God that she was wrong.

Chapter Five

'I beg your pardon? Is this some kind of fucking shakedown?'

Joseph O'Loughlin just looked at him calmly, and that seemed to inflame Patrick even more.

'Do I look like I've got "cunt" tattooed on my fore-head, you cheeky little fucker!' Patrick was visibly getting more and more angry.

Kate grabbed his hand and squeezed it, saying, 'Let's calm down, shall we?'

Looking at the man sitting opposite her, she had to admit that he did look a lot like Patrick – and that was making her wonder if there was some credence to this man's claim.

'Fucking calm down! He earholes his way into my house – my gaff – and tells me he's my long-lost son, and you expect me to just swallow it? No way.'

Joseph sighed and said reasonably, 'Mum said you wouldn't be too thrilled. And to be frank I'm just here because I was intrigued.'

'Intrigued, my arse!'

Patrick was staring at the younger man and Kate

knew he had to be seeing a younger, fitter version of himself. Because she was.

'Easy enough to find out.' Kate's voice was low, and both the men looked at her as she poured the tea from a silver Georgian teapot. 'DNA test.'

'If that's what you want, I have no problem with it.' Joseph produced an envelope and pulled out some pictures, which he placed on the table. 'My mum, God bless her, she was a good old girl.'

Kate saw one was a photo of an attractive woman. On her lap sat two children; both had dark hair and blue eyes like their father. But it was the little girl that Patrick was staring at – it could have been his Mandy at the same age. The same crooked smile and innocent eyes, only his Mandy had been blonder.

'That's my son, Joey Junior, and Amanda, my daughter. Bit older now, of course, but I always loved that photo of my mum with them. She doted on them.'

Amanda, *Mandy*. Patrick felt as if his head was going to explode. He picked up the picture with a shaking hand, and Kate could feel the waves of emotion coming off him.

'That could be my daughter, Mandy.' Even all these years later he still couldn't talk about her without becoming emotional.

It wasn't just her dying, but the *way* she died at the hands of the Grantley Ripper. Kate had been the detective in charge of the case and it was how they had met and eventually come together.

Joseph O'Loughlin sipped his tea; he didn't exactly know how to respond, so he said kindly, 'She's seven now, and my boy's twelve.'

Despite himself Patrick had to ask, 'What do you do? What're you into?'

Joseph puffed up as he said proudly, 'I'm a barrister. I deal with corporate stuff.'

There was a stunned silence for a few moments and then Pat laughed suddenly, saying, 'Thank fuck for that! That was all I needed – a son who's a criminal prosecutor.'

The tension broke and they laughed. Then they all became quiet once more, the incongruity of the situation making them realise that there was some serious shit to be considered with this revelation.

'Why didn't she ever tell me?'

Joseph shrugged. 'You know what she was like, self-contained to the last. I also know she could be a bit of a girl when the fancy took her.'

The last remark was said with defiance, and Patrick admired the man's loyalty to his mother.

'I wanted for nothing, and she put me through school and university by taking on any jobs she could. She was a wonderful woman – a good laugh – but, Christ, could she be determined! I think I inherited her work ethic, you know? Then, when she knew the end was coming, she told me who my father was. I asked her if she was sure and she said yes. She also said you had been married to a lovely woman called Renée and she could not have upset your home life at the time as it would have been unfair. Said your wife was a nice person who she knew slightly. So, here I am.'

Patrick was aware that Kate's eyes were boring into the back of his head and he didn't have the guts to look at her. Instead he was remembering a certain summer when his wife was first ill, and how he had been struggling to cope when Ruby had walked back into his life. It had only lasted a few weeks and he had been glad when he had ended it. The guilt had eaten away at him. That was why the name Ruby had not hit home at first. It had all been so long ago and he had wanted to forget it had ever happened. Now it seemed he had left her with more than a few hundred quid and a promise to keep in touch.

'Fucking hell.'

Joseph shrugged again. 'I don't want anything from you, Mr Kelly. Like I said, I was just intrigued.'

Patrick stared down at the photograph once more; she had aged well, had Ruby. But then she had always taken care of her appearance. She had liked a bit of the other and all, there was no denying that. But it was the children that drew him in here. They could be his flesh and blood, could be his actual family.

It was as if he was being given a second chance somehow. It was too much to take in. Patrick looked into Joseph O'Loughlin's eyes and wondered if he could really be his son – and what the consequences of such a thing would be on life as he knew it.

Chapter Six

Dana Barlow and her husband, Eric, stared down at the table. Both were in terrible shock, and Annie Carr could understand that. But she needed to talk to them straight away.

'Have you any idea where she could have gone?'

Dana, a small woman with high cheekbones and long dark hair, shook her head vehemently. 'Like I said before, she just went to school as usual.'

Annie knew that the girl had never reached the school, but that didn't mean the perpetrator had picked her up that morning. If Kylie was prone to taking days off to be with friends, that could eliminate a lot of possibilities from their enquiries. Give them a starting point, other than 'stranger danger', a term Annie loathed. It was rarer than finding a diamond growing on a Labrador. Most children were taken by people they knew and trusted, someone the child had no reason to fear. Like with most rapes, it was rarely an opportunist responsible. It was someone close – either family or family friends.

'Did Kylie ever play truant?'

They both shook their heads in absolute agreement.

'No, our Kylie is such a good girl – she's no trouble. Was no trouble . . . '

Annie heard the pain in their voices; she hated seeing people reduced to this – reduced to talking in the past tense about a loved one. Especially when it was a child.

'Was there anyone she talked about lately, someone new in her life? Maybe a friend, or even someone she might have come into contact with through you?'

Eric Barlow looked up at her then, as if the enormity of the situation was finally dawning on him. 'What are you trying to say exactly?'

Annie met his eye as she said seriously, 'I know this is hard for you both, but you must be honest with me. Have any new people come into your orbit recently? Was Kylie having trouble with anyone, or did she seem worried? I know this is hard, but I really do have to ask these questions.'

Dana Barlow shook her head in anguish. 'If we knew anything, don't you think we would tell you?' She started to cry again.

As Dana's husband comforted her, Annie sighed heavily and left the room as quietly as she had entered it.

Like most people they had no real idea what their child got up to when she was not with them. That, unfortunately, was real life.

Chapter Seven

DC Margaret Dole was busy looking through Kylie Barlow's online accounts. The girl was just fourteen but, judging by her selfie profile shot and the photographs she posted online at regular intervals, she could easily pass for eighteen or older. But that wasn't unusual these days. Girls had so much access to everything, from cheap clothes to online make-up tutorials, that they were far more sophisticated than anyone really gave them credit for. Parents who weren't computer literate couldn't police what their kids were doing. But, from what she had accessed so far, Kylie was the typical teenager, trying to be older than she was, desperate to be accepted by her peer group and obsessed with Justin Bieber and the Kardashians.

Boys were also a big priority, as was hanging out with her school friends. All in all, though, there was nothing untoward that Margaret could find. She had even looked through every deleted post and Kylie's Instagram and her Snapchat. To all intents and purposes Kylie was your average fourteen-year-old girl. Bit stupid, hated school and anything to do with homework, and she liked pictures of cute pugs and cats. In many ways she was as normal as they came.

Annie Carr listened begrudgingly as Margaret Dole updated her on the girl's online presence. There wasn't a great deal of love lost between the two of them. Margaret was still a bit of a loner among the team, with a natural ability to rub people up the wrong way. She'd been identified early on in her career as a 'computer whizz-kid' and both Kate and Annie had put her to good use over the years. The trouble was Margaret *knew* she was good – and she didn't trouble to hide it.

'Usual. Nothing. No red flags. Sorry.'

Annie had expected as much. 'I'll go and talk to her friends. While I do that, you can have a poke around on their Facebook accounts, see if there was anything interesting happening. Then I'm making my way over to see Megan McFee. Did you pull up the CCTV?'

Margaret nodded. 'Got a team going through it now. I'll call you as soon as I know anything.'

Annie nodded briskly, her glance swept around the busy office, and she wondered at the change in the place. More than ever, they were becoming reliant on the tech-savvy Margaret Doles of the world rather than old-fashioned policing and she wasn't sure how much she liked it. Grantley Police Station was still a dump but it was gradually catching up with the rest of the world.

Maybe not before time.

Chapter Eight

Joseph O'Loughlin had left, but he had let Patrick keep the photograph. Kate watched as he stared at it and she knew he was seeing his Mandy all over again. They were due to fly to Florida in a few days and she had a feeling that was now going to be put on hold. She wasn't too bothered about that – she was more concerned about the appearance of this young man, and his ready-made family. He seemed genuine enough. It was actually the knowledge that Patrick had done the dirty on the Sainted Renée that truly bothered her. She had really thought she knew him, and that little piece of information had thrown her off-kilter. Why something that happened over thirty years before – and before she'd even met him – was troubling her so much, she didn't know.

She walked to the wine fridge, took out a bottle of Sancerre and, pouring them each a glass, she sat back at the kitchen table with him. He sipped his drink gratefully as she said, 'Well, that was certainly a turn-up for the books.'

Patrick ran a hand over his face and, laughing softly, he said genuinely, 'You can fucking say that again. I can't believe it. Old Ruby, eh? I would never have believed she could keep her trap shut like that. Just shows you, don't it? You never really know anyone. Ruby could talk for England – in fact, if talking was an Olympic sport, Ruby could have taken the gold. She definitely had an eye for the lads too.'

Kate looked at him sharply. 'She seems to have done a good job with Joseph.'

Patrick smiled his agreement.

'I'll sort the DNA for you, get it done at the police lab. I'm still owed a few favours.'

Patrick nodded in acquiescence. 'Best keep it as quiet as possible till we know the score.'

He was still staring at the picture and Kate felt a prick of jealousy that the dead Ruby could have given this man something she never could. It was unreasonable and it was petty, but she couldn't help herself.

Patrick seemed to sense her discomfort and, grabbing her hand, he squeezed it tightly. 'If this is true, Kate, it's like a second chance for me, darling. These are my grandchildren, my flesh and blood.'

Kate nodded and tried to look pleased for him. But she couldn't help hoping that Ruby had a type, and that type was big, dark-haired, blue-eyed men. She had been a policewoman long enough to know the score with women like Ruby; once the child arrived, they waited to see who it looked like the most.

Well, she would arrange the DNA test tout suite. Then she would see what happened from there.

Chapter Nine

Megan McFee was thinner than ever. She was still a killer dresser, but her age was taking its toll and her fight with bulimia had left her teeth discoloured from years of vomiting up bile. Even with her problem, the former forensic pathologist was still the district coroner and her word was law. She was the best – everyone knew that.

'No rape. She was not penetrated. Cut down there but still technically a virgin. This is a new one. The sexual motive isn't clear. Of course maybe they couldn't get it up – or they satisfied themselves with the old Barclays Banking. But there's no signs of sexual penetration. This was all about pain and fear, I'm afraid. Torture. Used a blowtorch on her – she must have been in fucking agony, God love her. Do you know the worst of it for me, Annie? That a fourteen-year-old girl must have been praying for death, because it would have been a relief, I can tell you that much. Cause of death was six blows to the head. I've detected rust in the wounds and, judging by the weapon marks, I think a crowbar made these. She was brain dead. He used pliers on her as well. Toenails gone on one foot, and some of her fingernails.

I'm still examining her, so I will let you know what else I can find. Bottom line is you are looking for a sadist. Whoever did this enjoyed it.' She rubbed her eyes sleepily and, stifling a yawn, she said sadly, 'She was bound with masking tape, which was not at the scene and, for some reason, this was added after wire restraints that were also missing from where she was found. This kind of torture needs privacy.'

Annie nodded as she took in the horror of what Megan was telling her. The girl looked more like a child on the mortuary slab than she ever had in real life. Washed clean of cosmetics, and with her long hair limp and untouched by straighteners, she looked pathetic. So tiny and vulnerable.

Annie dragged her eyes away from the corpse and, looking at Megan, she shook her head. 'I have a feeling this is just the beginning.'

Megan laughed bitterly. 'Oh, I think we can guarantee that, love. Whoever did this enjoyed it far too much to stop here. Unless this was some kind of revenge. But what could a child her age do to provoke this kind of hatred?'

Annie shook her head again.

'I took some dirt and other samples which I've sent off for analysis. Might give us an idea of where she was – we can hope anyway.'

Annie left then and, once in her car, she lit a cigarette. Taking a long drag on it, she closed her eyes tightly; she had been reminded of her last big case, the one that had made her credible. It had been a serial killer, and she prayed that this was not going to be another like that. But her gut was telling her that whoever they were looking for was just getting warmed up.

She smoked her cigarette down to the butt before disposing of it. Putting her car into gear, she drove away slowly.

Chapter Ten

Beverley Collins came into the kitchen and put the TV on, saying to Kate, 'Dear Lord, would you hear what's happened.'

Kate and Patrick looked at the TV. It was on Sky News, and they both listened in morbid fascination as the newscaster filled them in on the gruesome details of a child murder in Grantley.

'The poor unfortunate! There must be a madman on the loose.'

'Turn it down, Bev.'

Picking up her mobile, Kate nearly rang Annie Carr, before placing the phone carefully back on the kitchen table. This wasn't her call any more, and she had to realise that. She had retired, and that was that.

Patrick looked at her for a moment before saying gently, 'Once a Filth, eh?'

Kate smiled at him wryly. 'Those poor parents, what must they be going through?' Then, realising what she had said, she got up and, putting her arms around Patrick's neck, she hugged him close.

He grabbed her hands and kissed them gently, saying, 'I wouldn't wish it on my worst enemy, darling.'

They stayed holding each other for a long while.

Chapter Eleven

Grantley Comprehensive was a large school with over a thousand pupils. It had been built in the sixties and was basically just a series of concrete blocks; it reminded Annie of pictures you used to see of prison camps in Eastern Europe. As she walked into the main building she was assailed by the smell of schools. Teenage sweat, musty footwear and disinfectant. School was breaking up in a few weeks for the summer holidays and she could already feel the excitement of both pupils and teachers alike.

The head teacher, Mr Yalding, and Kylie Barlow's head of year, Miss Betterway, were waiting for her patiently in the main offices. She could sense their shock and horror and knew that it was only going to get worse for them, not better. These cases were always the same; it was the violence and the newspapers' and television's love of reporting it that stopped people from moving on, or at least forgetting about it for even a short while. The shock often hit people in many different ways. That was the thing about violent crime – the shockwaves should not be underestimated.

Miss Betterway was very pretty, in a prim and proper

sort of way, and she smiled tentatively as they settled down with cups of tea.

Mr Yalding, an older man who looked like something from a Roald Dahl book, said uneasily, 'We are all still in absolute shock.'

Annie nodded and, turning to her colleague DC Ali Karim, she said gently, 'If you would kindly take the notes.'

He nodded calmly, all business as usual. Annie Carr liked him; he was a solid bloke to have on your team – dedicated, good company and an expert on gin.

'Why don't you start, Miss Betterway, by telling me a little about Kylie? Her friends and her life at school?'

The younger woman tucked a stray curl behind her ear as she said quietly, 'I don't know what to tell you. Kylie was a typical teenage girl. She was popular and her main friends were Andrea Connor and Destiny Wallace. You never saw one without the other two.' She smiled sadly. 'She might not have been the brightest of students but she was well within the mainstream. She was well liked by the other kids in the year. I suppose she could be a bit naughty at times, but then they are all capable of that, as you well know.'

The headmaster nodded his agreement, saying loudly, 'I have never once had to reprimand her, she wasn't that kind of girl. Like Miss Betterway says, she was just normal.'

'So, no fights with other girls, or feuds . . .'

Miss Betterway shrugged. 'They are teenagers, they argue, but nothing that warrants—'

'I understand that, but we have to look at every angle. Have any of the staff here mentioned anyone suspicious around or near the school?'

'We have CCTV and you are in possession of the tapes up and until just after the last time we saw Kylie. But no one had red-flagged anyone or anything. We do keep a lookout but, as you know better than me, it's almost impossible to pin these children down.'

'I want to see the names, addresses and phone numbers of everyone who works in this place and, if possible, their work records. Has anyone come to work here recently?'

Mr Yalding frowned. 'We have a new PE teacher who started this term, Duncan Watts, but he came highly recommended. I will get you all the relevant information requested. But I must stress we do vigorous background checks on everyone who works here.'

Annie smiled. 'I'm sure you do.'

Trouble was, she knew from experience that a lot of offenders never got within a cat's whisker of the registry. Too clever by half, because they had to be.

Chapter Twelve

Patrick was eating dinner on the terrace with Kate when Annie arrived at the house. He greeted her amiably and poured her a glass of white wine.

'That smells delicious!'

Kate knew that with the murder case Annie was probably living on coffee and cigarettes, so she said quietly, 'Pull up a chair, Annie, there's plenty. I'll go get Bev to make you up a plate.'

Annie sat down gratefully and smiled at Patrick. She'd grown to like him more and more over the years, though she could get flustered in his company at times. There was something about the way he looked at her – as if he was weighing her up – that made her nervous.

Patrick returned her smile and carried on eating his food. Then, when Kate came back, he nodded at her and waited while she laid the plate and cutlery in front of her friend.

Annie's mouth was watering and she felt bad because she knew that she shouldn't even want to eat, but she'd had nothing all day, and it had been a long one.

'Get that down you. I bet you haven't had time to have a pee, let alone eat.'

Annie nodded and tucked into the food, trying not to wolf it down.

'So I assume you are here about the girl from Grantley Comp?'

Annie stopped eating and said seriously, 'What else? I think we're at the beginning of a nightmare. The news cameras are already setting up outside the police station and school. I don't think the Chief Super is keen to say too much till we have something concrete to go on. This wasn't random. Strange thing is, she wasn't raped. Mutilated but no penetration. Tortured beyond belief—'

Patrick got up from the table and, picking up his plate, he said loudly, 'I'll leave you girls to talk shop, I'll eat in the kitchen.'

Annie was mortified. 'I am so sorry, Pat.'

He left the terrace, saying brightly, 'Bit too much information, as the kids say these days!'

Kate laid her hand gently on her friend's arm. 'Don't worry about it, I know what it's like. You forget the normal social niceties when you are involved with something like this. It eats you from the inside out.'

Annie was near to tears and she hastily blinked them away.

Kate's heart went out to her, so, smiling gently, she said, 'Take a deep slug of that wine and start from the beginning.'

Chapter Thirteen

While Annie was filling Kate in on the day's events, Patrick continued eating alone in his large kitchen, glad to be away from that conversation. He thought of Mandy, how she looked when she was dying, and he didn't envy that poor girl's family having to deal with such a violent death. He took the picture of Joseph's kids out of his back pocket and stared at their faces for long moments. He had never wanted anything more than to be told these kids were his flesh and blood. It must be the Irish in him, that need for blood relatives. Land and relatives, that was the Irish way; he supposed it was because they had lost so much of both over the years, the Irish needed to feel they were making up for all the lost time.

After his initial wariness, he had liked Joseph O'Loughlin a lot. In fact, he had seen himself in him. If he was telling the truth – or more to the point, if *Ruby* was telling the truth – he had a family once more. Patrick felt a prickle of excitement at the thought, and he did his best to suppress it. He knew that he had to find out the truth definitively – that until the test was done it was all pure speculation – but he had not felt this alive in years.

He stared down at the photo again and looked into the eyes of Ruby O'Loughlin. She looked happy, contented. He remembered how ashamed he had been of his affair with her and yet it could now be one of the best things that had ever happened to him. Life was strange all right – strange and fickle. They had created a child, and he was sorry in a way that he had never known the boy existed. But what could he do? Ruby, bless her, had not wanted to rock his world. Yet she had brought up his son, and he had never even given her a thought over the years. If anything, he had made himself forget her. He had disappeared from her life quicker than a bad fart. Oh, life was a bastard, always throwing things at you when you least expected or indeed deserved them.

His eyes strayed to the little girl, and he felt a rush of love. Even her name, Amanda, had to be some kind of proof that this was meant to be, surely? He was so desperate for it to be true – he wanted to shout it from the rooftops.

He picked up his mobile and phoned Danny Foster. Danny still did the day-to-day for him, and they had become close friends over the years. He decided he would have a drink with him and see what he had to say about the news. Danny shared Patrick's mindset, and he would be honest with him.

As he made the arrangements to meet in an hour, he wondered what Kate's reaction would be if this should turn out to be true. He loved her enough to make sure she would not be hurt by any of it. With Kate's daughter, Lizzy, and grandkids settled in New Zealand, and happy enough with their life there, Kate barely saw her own family once a year, if that. She could share these children with him – he had it all worked out. Now he found himself praying for it to be true. This was something he needed more than he had ever realised.

Oh, to have a family again. To have his own flesh and blood beside him. The idea was heady stuff.

Chapter Fourteen

Kate asked Annie, 'What do Kylie's friends have to say about her?'

Annie shrugged. 'Nothing untoward, usual school-girl crushes, she seems very well liked and popular. Looks much older than her age, but then so many of them do these days.'

She picked up her handbag and brought out the file that had all the relevant details. Even in this day of emails and smartphones Annie liked everything written down and in front of her eyes. It was one of the things Kate had taught her many years before.

Kate stared at the picture that had been all over the news. A beautiful young girl in school uniform, with long dark hair and a cute rosebud mouth. Then she looked at the photographs from the crime scene and had to stifle a low moan. The battered and abused body was very different to the smiling, heavily made-up girl in the previous photo. You could still see the terror on her face, and Kate swallowed down the bile that was building up in her throat. She took a deep gulp of her Montrachet and placed the photos face down on the table. Beverley came out and cleared away in her usual discreet fashion, and Kate was reminded of how lucky she was to have her.

'I made this copy for you, Kate. I hope you don't mind, but I would really value your input.'

Kate nodded slowly. She had already guessed that much; she wondered if it was Annie or the Chief Super who wanted her really, but she was too diplomatic to ask. She read through the various statements and Annie watched her as she sipped her wine. She thought the world of Kate, and they had become good friends over the years.

'Did she have a boyfriend?'

Annie shook her head. 'Not as far as we know. But her whole life was lived on social media so we would have picked up something. Margaret Dole has been through everything, Facebook, Instagram, Snapchat, you name it. There's nothing untoward. Margaret's had a look on her friends' accounts too and there's nothing there either. Nothing more than what you would expect.'

Kate was nodding as she said, 'That's what I find so strange. Whoever did this had access to her – and time. She had to have known them, I think. We both know that is the usual scenario. But we can't rule out that it was a lone man, or men, looking for someone to abduct. Fucking melon scratcher, all right. I know this is a long shot, but what did her bedroom tell you?'

Annie ran her hands through her short bobbed hair. 'Nothing of any value, definitely no diary or anything that you wouldn't want your mum and dad to see. That is the thing, Kate, there's nothing different about this girl that marks her out, except she looks a lot older than she really is. But all her friends look the same. Heavy make-up and selfies are the major content of their social media, and they all say the same thing. She was lovely. Margaret's checking on the Facebook page that's been set up as a sort of memorial to her, in case someone posts anything on that.'

Kate sighed heavily. 'Who would want to be a teenager these days, eh?'

Annie laughed but her voice was sad as she said, 'Definitely not me, Kate. Definitely not me. The pressure to fit in has been there since time began, I should imagine. But in this day and age there is this need to be validated. From what Margaret Dole says it's as if they all feel the need to look like they have perfect lives, even if it isn't true. It's part and parcel of the world today. All of them love being online and every second of their life is documented.'

Kate smiled but she felt like a dinosaur where devices were concerned. She Skyped her daughter and granddaughters, but that was as far as it went. She wasn't sure she was that interested in other people's lives. It was the level of usage these days that amazed her; she knew grown women who spent half their lives looking at their phones and posting updates of the most mundane things, and every move they made. No wonder there was a new generation of criminals out there. Cybercrime was exploding at an incredible rate, and people like Margaret Dole were now coming into their own in police stations all around the country.

'Look, if I can help in any way you just have to let me know. I will do anything I can. I agree with you that this isn't going to be a one-off. Looking at these pictures, whoever is capable of inflicting that kind of damage is a sadistic fucker. He will want to do it again.' Kate sighed then, a deep anger washing over her. It never ceased to amaze her just how low some humans were prepared to go in pursuit of their own needs. Because this had to be a need; the torture of a young girl or boy was something that riled up even the most hardened detectives inside. 'Just when you thought you had seen it all.'

Annie didn't answer her, because she didn't know what to say.

Chapter Fifteen

Joseph O'Loughlin was in his study working when his wife, Bella, brought him in a cup of coffee. He smiled his thanks as he sipped it gratefully. He needed a caffeine fix badly. Bella was a petite woman, with thick dark hair and grey eyes; her husband towered over her, and she adored him.

'How are you feeling?'

He shrugged. 'To be honest, I'm not sure. He seemed like a nice enough man. But if it turns out he's not my father I've opened up a can of worms. His daughter, who was my half-sister, died a horrific death and I could almost feel his want of grandchildren. Especially when I said the name Amanda, as his daughter was called Mandy. Like I said, it's all a bit odd. There's definitely a likeness, especially with little Amanda. She's the double of his daughter, whose pictures are all over his rather large and lavish house!'

Bella placed a hand over her husband's shoulders and hugged him to her. 'It is a bit of a mess. But your mum seemed very certain – and she would know, I suppose.'

Joseph didn't answer her; he was well aware that his mum had had more than her fair share of men over the years. Not that he would disrespect her memory by saying that too often, but facts had to be faced.

'There's a part of me that wants it to be true because I always wondered, you know? But she would never talk about it so I assumed that whoever he was had not been good to her. Plus she was always enough for me. I didn't feel hard done by, if that makes sense.'

Bella smiled at him gently. She was under no illusions about her mother-in-law. But she wasn't too impressed to be finding out that Joseph's father was a well-known criminal; although she was too tactful to say that, of course. Still, she couldn't help but imagine what effect it would have on her children, both of whom were in private schools. Bella, although she tried to pretend otherwise, was a snob.

Instead she said quietly, 'Well, you can decide what to do once you find out for definite. Sufficient to the time thereof, eh?'

Joseph patted her hand gently, and watched her walk from the room. He guessed that she wasn't exactly thrilled with his alleged father's rather dubious reputation. But that was her problem. Anyway, he wondered what her reaction would be to his father's lavish lifestyle; he had a feeling that might go a *long* way towards her accepting him into their lives.

If Patrick was his father, of course. There was definitely some connection there, even though he couldn't explain it. In fact, he knew that if anyone else had said it he would have put it down to fanciful stupidity. But he could tell that Patrick felt the same way.

He glanced at his daughter's photo on his desk and thought again about the pictures of what might turn out to be his murdered sister. Two peas in a pod they were, but time – and that DNA test – would tell.

Chapter Sixteen

Danny Foster was not at all sure how he felt about this long-lost son turning up out of the blue, and he said as much to Patrick. 'This is surely a bit suspect, though, Pat. You positive he ain't a chancer?'

Patrick smiled but it didn't reach his eyes. He suddenly realised he wanted someone to agree with him about what he saw as a fantastic stroke of luck. He had filed Ruby away many years ago, ashamed of what he had done to Renée, especially as she had been so ill at the time. But, as Kate said sympathetically, he had needed succour – a word only she would use. He had nearly had to look it up in the dictionary! Now it seemed that his little fling had borne fruit and he was equally thrilled and anxious in case it turned out to be a false alarm. Old Ruby could be economical with the truth when the fancy took her.

It was at times like this he missed his old right-hand man, Willy Gabney; he had been the best friend he had ever had, and he had never got over his death. Willy had been one of the few people, other than Kate, that Patrick had ever trusted one hundred per cent. He might not have been a contender for *Mastermind* but he had been shrewd enough in his own streetwise way.

'No, I'd lay money he ain't a chancer. Ruby, on the other hand, wasn't exactly averse to the odd porky on occasions, but this is too big a lie for anyone. Either she genuinely believed it or got her dates wrong. Anyway, Kate is sorting the DNA test so it will all be kosher.'

Danny nodded. He wanted to be pleased for Patrick, but he hated himself for wondering where all this would leave him. He had been Patrick Kelly's golden boy for a long time, and he was recognised as such. He couldn't help but question what this O'Loughlin bloke wanted. In Danny Foster's world you always had an angle, and he had a feeling he knew exactly what this cunt's angle was. He was far too shrewd to say that now, of course, especially with Pat Kelly going all weak-kneed at the thought of grandchildren. He would have to bide his time.

'Well, Pat, my advice is to get those results as quickly as possible, mate. Then you can start to make sense of it all.'

Patrick smiled a real smile this time; this was what he wanted to hear, this was what he *needed*. Action had always been his byword. He understood why Danny wasn't too thrilled, but he would make sure the lad knew that he was still as indispensable as he had always been.

If Joseph O'Loughlin was his son, he was a corporate lawyer and would not want to go within a donkey's roar of his businesses, and that suited Patrick Kelly right down to the ground. He was more or less legit, but sometimes old habits died hard. And with Danny to take the blame, he still had the luxury of a duck and a dive – and he wasn't giving that up for anyone.

Chapter Seventeen

Kate was going through the file that Annie had given her when she heard Patrick come home and she glanced at the clock, amazed to see it was gone midnight. Oh, she missed this at times; the sheer energy needed for a big investigation always set her adrenaline pumping. Like Annie she wanted this bastard caught as quickly as possible.

It was unbelievable to think that a poor child had been taken and treated so brutally by a fellow human being. But, unfortunately, it wasn't as rare as people believed; there were so many weirdos out there and, thanks to the internet, they had a forum for their particular foibles. It was almost as if they had permission to act so badly because there were like-minded individuals out there at the touch of a computer keyboard. It never ceased to amaze her how many people accessed what Margaret Dole called the darknet. A place where every depravity was accessible, and anything and anyone could be bought and paid for. It was depressing just thinking about it.

The door slammed shut and Kate guessed that

Patrick had had a few drinks. She was annoyed, because she knew he had not used his driver tonight, but she decided against saying anything until she ascertained his state of mind. This Joseph O'Loughlin business had thrown them both.

'All right, darling!'

She smiled slightly; he was definitely a bit the worse for wear. When he had a few drinks he always talked to her as if she was in another room, even though she was less than three feet away from him.

'Yes, darling, and you?'

He laughed heartily at her tone. 'Never better. I had a few with Danny and then I popped into The Oaks to see some of the old crowd. I knew you and Annie wouldn't want me around. Bad fucking business, girl. I don't know how you stomach it, darling.'

Kate's heart went out to him. She was all too aware that Mandy and her death would be haunting his dreams again. This kind of murder always brought it back; she knew that for the people who experienced such depravity the memories were never far from the surface. Christ knew, they rarely watched TV because so much of the content was about serial killers, especially on American-made shows.

'Fucking nut them all, I would. Yorkshire Ripper, fucking Rose West and that cunt Ian Brady. Wipe them off the face of the fucking earth!' He poured himself a generous brandy and slumped down on to the sofa.

She watched sadly as he lit a large cigar and, going to his side, she slipped an arm around his shoulder

51

comfortingly. 'I'm sorry, Pat. I should have gone to see Annie. I realise this just brings it all back for you, darling.'

He shook his head vehemently. 'No! It's OK. I *like* to think of you and her catching this ponce. Hopefully before he harms anyone else. It's just, you are right – it does bring it all back. But then again, to be honest, it's never that far away anyway, my love. I've just learned to keep a lid on it over the years. But there are still days when I want to howl at the moon, even though I know there's nothing to be gained. My girl, my lovely girl, is gone and she won't ever be coming back, no matter what. It's just been about learning to function without her in my life. Some days I manage that better than others, that's the truth.' He tossed back the brandy in one quick gulp and got up to replenish his glass. 'But I can't deny I lay there some nights imagining I have Markham and what I would do to him if I had the fucking chance. I frighten myself sometimes with the punishments I think up. Now that poor kid's family have to go through the same thing, and that's what makes me so fucking angry. Fourteen, her whole life in front of her, and some piece of shit decided to take her and destroy her—'

She heard the catch in his throat and tightened her arms around him and held him as he cried. This wasn't the first time, and she knew it would not be the last. But his tears made him more of a man in her eyes than he would ever know.

Chapter Eighteen

He looked at the pictures and smiled to himself. Oh, Kylie Barlow didn't look so fucking clever now, did she? Her eyes were terrified – the eyes that always looked so innocent and good in the pictures on her Facebook page. Those pictures disgusted him. Her newly developed breasts were on show even in her school uniform, she was covered in make-up, and her hair clearly coloured even at her age!

He blamed the parents. Foolish people, living useless lives, wanting to be their children's friends. How many times had he read on those Facebook posts 'my mum, and my best friend'? It was sickening; there was a cancer in this society, and he hated that no one else could see it – no one except him.

Were these people so fucking stupid that they needed the validation of their own children? They allowed them to dress and act like grown women before they had even been a child, as though they were some kind of beautiful reflection of themselves. He shook his head in abject disbelief at the sheer idiocy of these so-called adults, these parents who allowed their daughters to advertise their wares on the internet.

Well, if the invitation was there, he was going to take them up on it. It stood to reason that if he didn't, some-one else would. That was the law of the streets. More to the point, that was the law of the internet, whose streets were faceless and nameless and allowed you access to anyone's most intimate details.

He lay in his bed, admiring his photographs and smiling happily to himself.

Chapter Nineteen

Destiny Wallace was just fourteen years old but she looked at least nineteen or twenty – and that was in her school uniform. Annie couldn't help but wonder if evolution was to blame, because most of the girls in this particular group all looked like clones of each other. Well, or of Kim Kardashian or another famous person, famous for no other reason than that they were famous for basically doing fuck-all constructive.

Even now, in this basic setting, Annie noticed that this child-woman was making sure she made the correct impression on the people around her. It was fascinating to behold the lowered eyes, the hands clasped gently in her lap, and the long shapely legs crossed at the ankles demurely. Well, Annie had seen all her Facebook and Instagram pictures, and she knew this girl could project sex and promise in a selfie without even trying. She swallowed down her irritation and forced herself to smile; she had to remember that this girl had lost one of her dearest friends in terrible circumstances and, as Kate had always explained, grief took different people to different places. It was a coping mechanism, that was all.

Destiny's seemed to be acting like Mary Poppins and with a butter-wouldn't-melt look.

Destiny's mum, who was in her middle thirties, looked like a clone of her daughter, from the carefully styled hair to the perfect make-up and, as she squeezed her daughter's shoulder, Annie felt a moment's shame at how she was judging these people. There was obvious love and affection between them, especially when the girl grasped her mother's hand tightly and held on to it.

'I know we've talked to you before, Destiny, but you were very distraught at the time, and so now we would like to speak to you again. But this time in more detail, sweetheart, if that's OK?'

Destiny smiled tremulously and Annie could finally glimpse the fourteen-year-old frightened girl behind the mask, and she sighed inwardly as she said calmly, 'So, can you go through the last time you saw Kylie? And please remember that anything, no matter how insignificant, could be very useful to me and my colleagues.'

Destiny nodded and looked up at the ceiling as if really concentrating. 'After the bell – our last lesson was maths, which we all *hate*! – we collected our things from the lockers, phones and stuff, because we aren't allowed them in class for some reason. Then Kylie and me and Andrea walked home, as we always do. Me and Kylie said goodbye to Andrea at Beresford Gardens, where she lives, and then we walked to my house, but Kylie didn't come in because we were all meeting later on to go to the precinct to look in the shops. I said "see you later" and she went. We met up later, as usual, and we went to the precinct, got a Starbucks and looked around the shops. There was nothing different.'

'What about the next morning?'

Destiny shrugged. 'When she didn't knock for me, I tried ringing her but she didn't answer. I assumed she wasn't well, or had wangled the day off, you know. I didn't worry too much. Not until her mum and dad rang and said they hadn't seen her and that she had left for school. Then, obviously, I started to get worried because, you know, she *wasn't* at school, was she?'

She burst into tears then at the enormity of what had happened to her friend and Annie watched as her mother held her tightly and talked quietly to her, calming her and probably thanking God that it was Kylie and not her own child that had been murdered.

'I know you're upset but I need to ask you, Destiny, did anyone approach you while you were in the precinct? Did you see anyone watching you, or did anyone try and talk to any of you?'

Destiny wiped her eyes delicately with a tissue, careful not to smear her make-up, and once more Annie felt a glimmer of annoyance.

'No one unusual. We saw the regular people, you know – boys from our school, some of the girls in our year. There was nothing unusual about any of it.'

Andrea had said exactly the same thing. The CCTV had shown nothing untoward either. That was grainy at best, most of the time, but no one had seemed to be following the girls or taking undue interest.

Annie looked down at her notes and said casually, 'So you saw Michael Stotter, Stephen Carter and Todd Richards from the year above – is that correct?'

Destiny nodded, reddening slightly. 'Yeah, Kylie and me have known Stephen since we were kids so we hang out with him and some of the others sometimes. We all got our drinks together, some of the boys went off to the cinema, I think. It was just a normal school night in this boring dump.'

Annie sighed, she knew the girl was telling the truth; whoever had been watching Kylie had been so unobtrusive as to have been invisible to these girls, and he had taken her the next morning. There was a ten-minute walk from Kylie's house to Destiny's. In those ten minutes someone had obviously abducted her. Somehow, somebody had either forced or talked her into going with them. Kylie's parents were both in the clear, so it wasn't close to home.

Annie sighed again. No one just disappeared, not in this day and age. Did they?

Chapter Twenty

Patrick was nervous, and that was not lost on Kate – in fact, she had never seen him like this before. Joseph and his family were due to arrive any moment, and Megan McFee was ready and willing to do the DNA tests for her old friend Kate. If truth be told, she was fascinated by this whole set-up – it was like something from a book, and she was loving it! Not that she would say that, of course, but it was very intriguing.

Megan remembered when Patrick and Kate had first got together and the whole police force had been utterly astounded at the audacity and – if she was honest – admiring of how Kate had managed to get away with it all. But then she had proven herself a valuable asset in more ways than one over the years; she was what one male officer had once referred to as a 'legend in her own lunchtime'. She had shown she had her creds over the years.

As they waited, Megan sipped at her rather splendid red wine and smiled at Kate, who rolled her eyes subtly.

When the gates finally opened and Joseph's car rolled

on to the drive, Patrick was out of his seat and rushing towards the front door like a teenager about to go on his first date.

Kate followed him and watched silently as Joseph and his family exited the car and looked around them in wonder. Kate understood their awe. She had felt it herself on more than one occasion; it was a very impressive property. Kate's eyes alighted on a small woman with a very pretty face and beautiful hair. She had a strange feeling about her, as though she knew instinctively that she wasn't going to like her. She quickly told herself to stop being so fanciful and see how the day went.

The children drew her eye next. They were handsome kids and both looked to be excited by what they were experiencing. It was the boy who really caught her attention; he was like a young Patrick – even had the same unruly hair with the double crown that made him look dishevelled unless he had it tamed regularly at the barber's.

Patrick ushered them inside and, as they were all introducing themselves, Kate suddenly felt out of place, which was ridiculous as this was her own home. She blamed the feeling on Bella O'Loughlin, who barely touched her hand when introduced and immediately turned her attention to Patrick. But Patrick had eyes for no one except the children, who both apparently thought they were simply coming for a lovely day out at their daddy's friend's house.

Amanda smiled widely, saying happily, 'Is it true we can swim here? I can swim, you know, properly.'

Patrick was almost drinking her in with his eyes as he said gaily, 'Of course you can. Follow me, kids, and I'll take you to the cabana where you can get changed and I'll arrange some refreshments for us all.'

The two children followed him, excitedly taking in their surroundings, and Kate smiled at Joseph and his wife, saying neutrally, 'Please, let's go out on to the patio and I'll pour us some drinks.' As they followed her she said, 'This is my friend and colleague Megan McFee. She will be taking the tests while the children are otherwise engaged.' She smiled over her shoulder at Bella, aware that she had asserted her power.

Twenty minutes later, the joyful shrieks of Amanda filled the air, and Patrick watched greedily as the children made themselves at home. Bella was quiet, but Kate noticed that she missed nothing, especially when Bev brought out the food she had prepared that morning. Her first impressions had been spot on. This was a bitch of a woman, and Kate was sad, because if this was all going to turn out to be true, she knew they would have to find some common ground if they were to make any kind of headway towards a relationship. She saw Joseph raise his eyebrows at his tiny wife and felt inordinately pleased; it seemed she wasn't the only one who had noticed the woman's calculated indifference to her.

Megan observed it too and remarked succinctly so only Kate could hear, 'Ooh, Kate, beware short-arsed women, especially if they have snared a handsome man!'

Kate laughed with her, but she didn't really think it was very funny. She didn't like this disruption to her life – or to be made to feel second class in her own home! – and she admitted that she felt threatened by this new-found family of Patrick's. At least what she was feeling was natural – after all, she had had him to herself for so long. But if this turned out to be true, she knew her life would be changed in so many ways, and she wasn't sure she was ready for that.

She hated to admit it, but she was jealous of what these beautiful and well-behaved children would mean to Patrick, and she was ashamed of herself. But she couldn't deny her feelings; she was nothing if not honest, with herself at any rate.

Chapter Twenty-one

Annie Carr was irritated beyond measure. As Margaret Dole trawled more and more CCTV, it was becoming obvious that they were chasing what was, in effect, a ghost. The houses' CCTV seemed concentrated on their properties, not on the road outside, which made sense but was bloody frustrating. Every homeowner had given up their footage readily, and no one had refused the search teams' entry. They wouldn't; these were nice roads with nice people who only wanted to help. But there was nothing of any use.

'Have you looked at all the traffic cams?'

Margaret nodded wearily. 'If it's been on film then I've accessed it, Annie. I've even hacked a few of the private cameras along the main roads. There's nothing that stands out. After she leaves her house there's absolutely nothing.'

'For fuck's sake, this is ridiculous! All this screaming and hollering about invasion of privacy and we can't even spot the child within a ten-minute walk!'

DC Karim groaned. This was so difficult for the

team – they all felt helpless. There was literally nothing to prove the child ever existed after she left for school.

'We are missing something, people, but I'm fucked if I know what.'

No one answered; there was nothing to say.

Chapter Twenty-two

Patrick was trying to maintain a smile as he listened to Bella droning on and on about how she loved his home, and asking him questions about his life that he would rather not answer.

Joseph nodded at Kate and went to sit beside his wife, saying loudly, 'I think it's time the kids were dried and dressed, darling, don't you?'

Bella looked at her husband for long seconds before she stood up and made her way to the pool area, but anyone could see she wasn't happy about it.

Joseph grinned ruefully at Patrick and said quietly, 'It's nerves with her, believe it or not. She finds it hard to be herself, that's all.'

Patrick understood it was an apology but was not going to say a word against the pretty woman who had a voice that could crack cement. Instead he said levelly, 'This is a lot to take in, mate.'

Joseph grinned ruefully, saying, 'It's that all right. I know this sounds silly – naïve even – but I do think there is a link between us, Patrick. I know my mum was a bit of a girl, but she wouldn't lie about something so important. I felt she needed to get it off her chest before she died.'

His voice was sad and instinctively Patrick grabbed his arm and squeezed it gently. 'Well, son, we will know soon enough.'

Joseph nodded.

Suddenly the children were running back in, all noise and good-natured bantering. It broke the spell, and Kate realised in that moment that her life as she knew it was finished. She watched calmly as Bella sat down in the chair she had vacated earlier, and with a smug little smile she picked up her gin and tonic and sipped it daintily.

As she looked around her, Kate felt sure the woman was mentally calculating how much it was all worth.

Chapter Twenty-three

Stephen Carter was tall for his age and powerfully built; at fifteen he was already a man. His deep brown eyes and thick brown, unruly hair gave him the look of a Greek god – and, from what Annie had gathered, to the girls of Grantley Comprehensive that is exactly what he was. She could see the attraction; he was totally unaware of his handsome features and he had the manners of a gentleman. Coupled with the fact he could obviously look after himself, if needs be, he was quite the lethal combination.

She and Karim were back at the school interviewing the boys Destiny had said the girls saw the night before Kylie's disappearance. Mr Yalding sat discreetly at the back of the room, while Annie and Karim questioned the boys. They'd already seen Michael Stotter and Todd Richards, who'd been co-operative but really had no information of use. Now it was Stephen's turn.

'It's awful what happened to Kylie. I mean, it's something you read about in the papers, it's not something you think could happen in your own hometown to someone you actually *know*.'

Annie let Stephen speak; she knew that once he had exhausted his fear and anger he would be easier to talk to.

'I had seen her the night before, you know? I never dreamt . . . I mean, you wouldn't think that you were never going to see her again, would you?' He lowered his eyes and said quietly, 'She was flirting with me in Starbucks, but she's far too young for me. Anyway, I've known her since primary school, and I always found her vacuous. I feel terrible about that now. *All* she talked about was *TOWIE* and other reality TV rubbish . . .'

Annie nodded in sympathy. She could see the guilt was eating at him, but she knew that kids were, above all, resilient and he would get over it sooner than he thought.

'Did you notice anyone watching her, or paying her attention?'

The boy shrugged. 'Honestly, I probably wouldn't have noticed if there *was* someone. Like I said, I knew her from school, said hello, we bought our drinks and went our separate ways – there was a big crowd of us. I wish I could be of more help.'

Annie exchanged a glance with Karim and sighed heavily. They were back to square one.

Chapter Twenty-four

Patrick was pouring himself a large whisky, and Kate nodded as he pointed at another glass – his way of offering her a drink. He brought it over and they sat together companionably, each sipping the golden liquid, both immersed in their own thoughts.

Patrick suddenly swallowed down his drink in one swift gulp. 'I think it went well today. Those kids are diamonds – well spoken, well behaved. I think Joseph is a man anyone would be proud to call a son. But that fucking wife of his! Do you know she actually asked me how much this place was worth?'

Kate felt the laughter bubbling up inside her though she tried not to show it – it was such an absurd situation – but knowing that Patrick felt the same way about his new-found daughter-in-law pleased her no end.

'She is a bit of a marler, as my old mum would say, Kate. Nose that could pick a winkle, sticking it into my entire private fucking business. Cheeky mare.'

Kate smiled. 'Maybe Joseph was right saying she was just nervous, Pat.' She was trying to be fair but it wasn't easy.

Patrick laughed ruefully. 'She thought you was the hired help, I think. I saw the way she blanked you when they first arrived. I know women like her – she's just after the main chance. She was practically working out how much I had, like a human calculator. She's a fucking snob. Even her accent's false.'

He was quiet for a few seconds, so Kate said kindly, 'Well, if this is all going to turn out to be true, you'd best get used to playing Happy Families.'

Patrick put his arm around her and squeezed her to him. 'Happy Families? More like Cluedo. Bella in the library with the candlestick.'

Kate found herself laughing then; really laughing, and it felt good.

'You know something though, Kate – and I am not a sentimental old fucker – but I felt a real sense of blood there. Especially when little Mandy came and sat by me, chatting about her day. And that lad, well, he even supports West Ham. That has to be in the genes, girl.'

Kate was still laughing as she said, 'Oh well, if he supports West Ham, that clinches it.'

They were laughing together now, but in the back of her mind Kate was worried. She hated this jealousy that was rearing up inside her. It brought back painful memories of her ex-husband, Dan, and his legions of women. It also brought back memories of Patrick's affair with Danny Foster's sister, Eve, when they'd parted briefly a few years back. Luckily Eve was firmly ensconced in Majorca, having found herself a wealthy older gentleman to keep her in the style she felt she deserved. Kate was only too glad to see her out of her orbit even though she knew any allure Eve had held for Patrick was long gone. Kate knew it was beneath her – she knew that Patrick loved her – but she didn't relish the idea of sharing him with anyone – especially not *this* family, even though she liked Joseph very much, and the children were delightful.

Patrick had called the girl Mandy, only to be sharply rebuked by Bella, who had said sternly, 'It's Amanda. I do so hate shortened names.'

Patrick had let it slide, but Kate was aware it had irritated him beyond measure. There was a wasp in this particular honeypot, and Bella was out for what she could get and would likely stop at nothing to take what she wanted. At least forewarned was forearmed, something that Kate had learned many years before.

She would do a bit of digging and see what came up on Mrs Bella O'Loughlin, although for now she wisely kept this information to herself.

Chapter Twenty-five

DC Ali Karim was drinking tea in the canteen when Annie came and sat beside him. The mood in the station was sombre, but that was to be expected. A murder case was always hard on everyone, but doubly so when it was a child.

'All right, Ali?'

He nodded and they sat together in companionable silence for a while, drinking their teas, until Ali said seriously, 'Did you notice his watch?'

Annie raised her eyebrows a fraction. 'Whose watch?'

'That lad, Stephen Carter – his watch was a Tag Heuer. Not much change out of two grand. Pretty expensive for a schoolboy from Grantley Comprehensive.'

Annie let his words sink in; she had not noticed the watch, but it did seem a bit excessive for the school he was at. 'We'll make a detective of you yet, boy!'

They laughed together.

Annie liked Ali a lot. He had a great mind, very analytical. 'I think we should see if there's a reason to visit him on his own territory, eh?'

Ali nodded. 'Whatever you say, boss.'

They went back to their teas, both deep in thought.

Chapter Twenty-six

'Honestly, Bella, I despair of you at times. Why can't you just relax for once? Kate Burrows is a pretty nice woman – with impressive credentials, I might add. The children took to her. And let's face it – if this turns out to be on the level, she's going to be a part of our lives given that she lives with Patrick. You'd do well to remember that.'

Bella, when she had the petulant look on her, appeared almost ugly and it pained Joseph to see her like that. It galled him that there were times when he actually disliked her. Today was one of those days. She had deliberately set out to stake a claim, and it had backfired big time.

He could tell that Patrick Kelly had taken one look at Bella and decided she was not a person who evoked warm feelings, as he had found out himself during his marriage. She was jealous to the point of mania about him and the children, and she was also avaricious, determined to have a lifestyle that was, quite honestly, beyond him – and he didn't earn pennies. But seeing her ogling Patrick Kelly's house and picturing herself lording it over Kate had inspired a deep resentment inside him, more than ever before.

The children had enjoyed the day so much, and they had both liked Patrick and Kate, especially Joey Junior. He had sat and chatted to Kate for ages, fascinated by her past role as a detective. She had played down the more gruesome aspects of her job and had even made him laugh at times with her memories of being on the beat and dealing with drunks and other less fortunates. She had an integrity that appealed to Joseph, as well as his son; he also guessed that was what had attracted Patrick Kelly. Kate was still a beautiful woman and they were a solid couple.

He just hoped that, whatever the outcome, Bella would rein in her natural knack for putting people's backs up. The only person she had ever given the impression of liking was his mother, but he guessed that was because Ruby had known how to handle her. With people like Bella outright flattery went a long way. Plus Bella knew, if he had been asked to make a choice, his mother would have won hands down. It was the one thing Bella had been frightened of and, as she had nothing to do with her own family, his mother had been a free babysitter, plus she cooked and helped out around the house, which was something Bella relished. They had a cleaner who came every Friday, and Bella spoke to her like she was someone on *Downton Abbey*.

He sighed inwardly. That Bella loved him, he had no doubt. But his own love for her was wearing thinner by the day. Jealousy like Bella's was a disease, a canker that eventually pushed away everyone that they were close to. Bella didn't even have any friends – not real friends, anyway. She was far too competitive for that. Even the other mums at the school avoided her like the plague, and that grieved him. It wasn't healthy.

Amanda ran into his office, smelling of chlorine and with her thick dark hair still damp. 'Oh, Daddy, what a wonderful day swimming!'

She prattled on about everything, and Joseph held her on his lap and cuddled her tightly. He would be glad when this waiting was over and they knew the score, once and for all. He found that he hoped he was a blood relative, because he genuinely liked the man Patrick Kelly – not what he owned or represented or purloined. Just him as a person. He had seen a reflection of himself a few times today. Never having had a father, he was intrigued by what it would be like to suddenly acquire one at this stage of his life.

He looked at a picture of Ruby on his desk, and smiled sadly. God knew he missed her.

Chapter Twenty-seven

It really cheered him up looking at the pictures.

He loved his Polaroids, they were such vibrant colours – and, of course, no one would ever know about them but him. No trail to be found on the internet; oh no, he liked his old Polaroids.

The one of Kylie's terrified eyes was his favourite picture. He had taken it just after he had lit the blowtorch, and he smiled at the memory. She had been as meek as a lamb until then. She had struggled, of course, but not too much – a couple of well-placed punches to her abdomen had made sure of that.

The main thing for him was the fear. That was what really interested him. As much as he loved inflicting pain – and he had always enjoyed that, even as a small child – it was the fear that really set him off. He could almost smell it.

Kylie had been everything he had thought she would be – both pliable and stupid. He was still admiring his handiwork when he realised it was getting late, so he put his photos away and went for a nice long shower, humming away, wrapped up in his own happiness.

Chapter Twenty-eight

'Honestly, Kate, it's like she disappeared in a puff of smoke. I have never seen anything like this.'

Kate nodded in sympathy at Annie's words, which were filled with despair. She knew better than anyone how frustrating a case could be when it seemed as if you had hit a dead end before you had even started. She poured her friend more wine and watched as Annie lit yet another cigarette, even though she still had one burning in the ashtray.

'No one, and I mean no one, seems to have seen anything. There's no DNA to be found. Nothing.'

Kate smiled ruefully. 'That's all thanks to the internet, TV programmes and books. There's nothing you can't find out if you really want to. I read recently that, in the US, juries aren't so ready to convict because of programmes like *CSI*, where they make arrests on the slimmest of evidence. It's a fucking joke! But remember this, Annie, eventually they *all* make mistakes, it's human nature.'

Annie sipped her wine and smiled wanly. 'That is what I keep telling myself. But Christ, Kate, I just know this fucker is going to do this again.'

Kate sipped her own wine and nodded. 'Oh, without a doubt – he's got a taste for it now, darling. Did you check all other databases? See anything similar?'

'There's nothing, and we cast the net wide but fuck-all matches this fucker's MO.' Annie sighed heavily, and they were both quiet for a few moments. 'Anyway, how about you? Any news yet?'

Kate nodded wearily. 'Should know tomorrow. I shouldn't admit it, but there's a big part of me that resents Pat having a new family. I know it's selfish and wrong, but it's the truth.'

Annie raked her fingers through her hair; she looked like she hadn't slept in days, and Kate suspected that she probably hadn't. These kinds of cases ate away at you, especially when it was kids.

'I can understand that, Kate. I think that's only nat-ural. It must be like someone's dropped a bomb into your life, especially with that madam, Bella, into the bargain from what you've told me about her.'

'On the plus side, Patrick feels exactly the same! He can't bear her either. But he would put up with Katie Hopkins if those kids turn out to be his grandchildren.'

Annie actually spat her wine out and laughed genu-inely for the first time in ages. Kate laughed with her, but it wasn't funny to her really. Her world was going to change dramatically, and she wasn't sure how she would be able to cope.

Chapter Twenty-nine

Danny Foster and Patrick were in a small club Patrick had acquired in Soho a few years earlier. He had been owed a big debt and the club had been given in exchange. It was a private members' club – and the only members were those of the criminal fraternity. It was a place to meet and greet old mates just out of the Big House, or plan a meeting or do a deal. Patrick loved it there. He felt at home among his own and, as he owned the gaff, he was always welcome. He still had his creds. Though he wasn't entirely straight, he was straight enough for Kate these days. He smiled as he thought of her and he felt sad for her because he recognised how difficult it was going to be once they knew for sure that Joseph O'Loughlin was his boy. Patrick was convinced of it; in fact, he had never wanted anything so much in his life.

'So, Pat, what's the score? Any news yet?'

Patrick shook his head and sipped his whisky slowly. 'Tomorrow. I ain't a fanciful man, but I know he's my son.' Then, smiling tightly, he said sternly, 'So what have you found out about my potential offspring? I know you have been having a bit of a sniff around, so bring me up to spec, eh?'

Danny shrugged nonchalantly but he was thrown off-kilter for a few seconds. He should have known Patrick would guess what he would do. After all, he would have done the same in his position.

'He is as clean as the proverbial whistle. There's nothing on him anywhere. Not even as a youngster. Did well at school, university, he works for a big firm in the City. But I ain't telling you anything you don't already know, am I?'

Patrick smiled then, a genuine smile. ''Course you ain't. I had a little dig myself, obviously. Can't be too careful. But the reason I brought you here today is to let you know that your position will never change. I have a few ideas floating around if he *is* my boy, but I'm telling you straight – it will not affect our situation.'

Danny looked at the man he had come to love over the years, and smiled. 'I was only looking out for you, Pat.'

Patrick Kelly grinned and, squeezing the younger man's shoulder, he said seriously, 'And I appreciate that, mate. More than you know.'

Chapter Thirty

Bella had picked her daughter up from school and, as she walked into her own admittedly beautiful home, she felt a moment's irritation at the difference between her set-up and Patrick Kelly's. The fact that her husband could be related to such a character was still amazing her, but the way the man lived was what really interested her. He lived like a king! If he was Joseph's father, she was going to be willing to overlook anything to get a slice of what she saw as a *very* big pie.

The strange thing was she had found she actually liked him. That was not something she would ever have thought possible, considering his background. But that Kate! Now, she was a different kettle of fish entirely. How she had snared a man like Kelly, Bella couldn't imagine; she was an attractive woman for her age, but that didn't account for the fact that she had managed to entice and keep a man of Patrick Kelly's calibre. Criminal he might be – and Bella could overlook that, as she was under the impression he was now retired – but what she couldn't understand was what he saw in Kate Burrows.

They were a strange couple. Well, tomorrow night they would all know the score. They were due at his house for a late dinner at 9 p.m., where Patrick was going to announce the results of the DNA tests.

Bella O'Loughlin had never wanted anything so much as she wanted this man to be her father-in-law. They would be set for life. She had seen the way he had looked at the children, and how much her daughter resembled that bleached-blond monstrosity of a daughter he had lost. She shuddered as she recalled the photos of the girl – she was half-naked in most of them! No wonder that George Markham had turned his attention to her. She looked exactly what she was!

She poured a glass of milk for Amanda and a glass of chilled white wine for herself and, as she waited for her son to return from school, she sipped her wine and pictured herself as mistress of Patrick Kelly's beautiful home. That would be one in the eye for every person who had ever upset her, or looked down on her – especially her own family.

All in all, she was about as happy as it was possible for her to be.

Chapter Thirty-one

Andrea Connor's mother was getting worried. She had been waiting outside Lakeside Shopping Centre for twenty minutes and her daughter should have been out by now. It had been a week since Kylie's murder and it had been a terrible time for them all – Juliet Connor couldn't imagine what Dana and Eric Barlow were going through – and her instinct was to not let Andrea out of her sight. But life had to go on and the girls deserved a break from the emotional trauma of losing their best friend in such an unspeakable way. Lakeside with friends had seemed safe enough – the place was always packed out and covered in CCTV cameras – especially as they were to be picked up afterwards. As she scanned the faces of all the people leaving via the boulevard she breathed a deep sigh of relief. There was her Andrea, walking furiously towards her, and she instinctively put her hand to her heart to steady the beating. Andrea was a beautiful girl, and Juliet was inordinately proud of her. She could be a madam, there was no doubt about that, but what fourteen year old wasn't hard work at that age?

A part of her admitted that her daughter was spoiled

rotten, but she had waited so long for her and, when she had finally arrived after ten years of trying, it had been hard to refuse her anything. Her husband was worse; they weren't rich by any standards, but they made sure their daughter never went without – she had everything that her peer group had.

Now, as her daughter flounced into the car, all scowls and rolling eyes, Juliet said gaily, 'Did you have a nice time?'

Andrea threw her long blond hair over her shoulders, saying peevishly, 'Yes, Mummy. I had a nice time. Now, can we go home, please?'

'Where's Destiny? You know I was supposed to be picking her up too.'

Andrea shrugged. 'She ditched me almost as soon as we got here. Said she had to meet someone and just walked off. Well, she can sod off in future—'

Juliet looked at her daughter and said sternly, 'You can stop that kind of talk now, young lady. And just what am I supposed to tell her mum?'

Even Andrea picked up the underlying tension in her mother's voice, and she said quietly, 'Tell her the truth – her daughter just left me alone in the middle of Lakeside. Because that's what happened.'

Juliet took out her mobile phone and scrolled down for Destiny's mother's number. Despite herself she was starting to panic.

'You should never have split up, Andrea. The proviso was that you stayed together.'

Andrea didn't answer her mother; instead she turned away and stared at the passing cars.

Juliet wondered if there had been an argument of some kind. These girls were forever either kissing or kicking each other. There was never a happy medium.

Chapter Thirty-two

Jean Wallace was beside herself with fear and worry, and Annie Carr couldn't blame her. It was now five hours since her daughter had gone missing – that is, if she *was* missing, of course – but it wasn't looking good.

Still, young girls were often secretive, even with other friends. Kate had told her about her own daughter, all those years before, about how she had slept with any boy with a pleasing smile – or a car. How she had found her diary and nearly died of the shame and heartache. But there was nothing on Destiny's social media to suggest she was up to anything untoward. That was what worried her so much.

Kate had told her that she should keep in mind that there was always a common denominator in these cases – you just had to find out what it was. That was often the hardest part of the investigation: putting seemingly random occurrences together and making sense of them. Just like a puzzle that you had to piece together, was how Kate had described it.

'Stranger danger' was almost unheard of – most murders and rapes were carried out by people known to the victims. If these girls were communicating with someone outside their circle then how were they doing it? Certainly not on any of their devices. She might irritate the hell out of her, but Annie did believe that if Margaret Dole could find nothing then there was nothing to find, end of. So this had to be either random – which is what Annie believed – or there was a conspiracy of some kind involving these girls. It was baffling.

It would soon be getting dark, and Jean Wallace was almost hysterical. Annie wished the fucking husband would come home from searching for his daughter and help calm his wife down so Annie could get on with her job. She had never been much good at the hand-holding part. It just wasn't in her nature.

Chapter Thirty-three

Kate looked over the dining table one more time and had to admit it looked stunning. Bev had outdone herself, she couldn't deny it. The crystal glasses sparkled in the candle-light and the silver shone. Kate knew that Bev really enjoyed creating these intimate dinners, as it gave her a chance to show off her rather considerable cooking skills. Kate wondered at how she didn't look like ten-ton Tessie O'Shea, because Bev's food was spectacular.

She could hear Patrick humming as he decanted a bottle of his best claret, and she wished she had it in her to be as happy as he was. She didn't want to let this jeal-ousy consume her. But even if Bella had been like an angel, she probably wouldn't have relished the disrup-tion this revelation was bringing to their lives.

She looked around her beautiful home and imagined what her mother would have said had she been alive. She would have told her to get over herself and grow up, because there was nothing more important than blood family.

Patrick opened his arms wide as he spoke. 'I knew, Kate, I just knew when I saw the photo of that little girl.

It's like God has given me another chance at life. You make me so happy, darling, but what was all this for, if not to pass on to my own kin?' Kate felt the sting of tears as she saw the happiness in his eyes. Then, squeezing her to him, he said sneakily, 'As for that madam, Bella, she'd better watch it. I know she is a class-A cunt, but she'll be getting away with fuck-all on my watch.'

Kate found herself laughing loudly at this typical Patrick Kelly response and he laughed with her, glad to see the woman he loved finally relaxing. He had a fine line to walk, and he recognised that, but the results had confirmed what his gut knew to be true: Joseph O'Loughlin was his son and these children were his grandchildren.

He still couldn't believe it. Good old Ruby, bless her – his dirty little secret – had given him a family at this stage in his life.

Funny how life worked out.

Chapter Thirty-four

DC Ali Karim was questioning Andrea, and he wasn't getting anywhere. Her parents were hovering behind her and he had a feeling that was why she was being so close-lipped.

They had a nice house – an old Victorian semi that was decorated to within an inch of its life. He guessed that the cushions on the sofa had never once been messed up or thrown on to the expensive carpet that lay on the floor. It was like a show home. He smiled at the PC with him, and nodded.

Taking his cue, she said quietly, 'Could I talk to you both in private? Maybe we could go to the kitchen? There's a few questions I need to ask you both.'

Derek Connor looked like he was about to object but thought better of it. PC Miles followed them out to the kitchen, shutting the door firmly behind her. This was more like it. He was treading a fine line but at least now DC Karim could actually ask the girl what was needed.

'Look, Andrea, I understand there are things you might not want your mum and dad to know, but I promise you that anything you say to me will go no further, OK? I know you are annoyed at Destiny for ditching you but this is serious. Can you think of any-one that she might have gone to see? Someone who her parents might not exactly approve of?'

Andrea looked at the closed door and sighed heavily. 'Well, there's one boy in the year above us, Clinton Barber – she likes him and maybe *that's* who she left me to see. He lives on the big council estate.'

'The estate where Kylie was found?'

She nodded. 'He's always in trouble. Fighting, you know? He's part of a gang, the Bag Boys. I don't like him personally but Destiny is crazy about him. He hardly ever goes to school for a start, so she skives off occasionally to spend the day with him and his friends. But you can't ever let on I said that. She would kill me. If her mum and dad knew, she would be grounded for, like, *ever*.'

Ali nodded, as if he completely understood what she was saying, and smiled at her reassuringly. 'You did the right thing telling me. But would she stay out late to be with him, do you think?'

Andrea shrugged. 'Not that she's told me. She always said that if she broke her curfew, her parents would be worse than mine!'

'How about Kylie? Did she ever hang out with these boys?'

'Once or twice, with Destiny – we all have, at some point. Why – do you really think something's happened to Destiny too?' Andrea's eyes were suddenly wide.

Ali Karim smiled again through gritted teeth,

thinking that if these girls had mentioned this before it would have made life a whole lot easier for everyone concerned.

'Why do they call themselves the Bag Boys?'

Andrea rolled her eyes and said, as if talking to a complete imbecile, 'Because they sell weed in five-pound bags, of course!'

DC Karim answered sarcastically, 'Of course!'

Chapter Thirty-five

Bella was quiet and on her best behaviour, and Kate guessed she had been given a serious talking-to by her husband before they had arrived. She had even complimented Kate on her outfit and shoes.

They had all stood awkwardly in the hallway before Patrick said jovially, 'Well, Joseph, this is good news for me, mate. I hope you feel the same.'

Joseph had grinned and said, 'I had a feeling that first day I came here. It was like looking at myself in the mirror. Then Mandy's photos and . . . Oh, I don't know how to explain it!'

His absolute sincerity broke the ice, and Patrick shook his hand warmly. 'Come through. I think a nice glass of champagne is in order, don't you?'

He smiled at Bella as he said it, and she returned the smile nervously; it seemed she was as on edge as everyone else was. Patrick poured the champagne, and Kate invited Bella and Joseph to take their seats.

They sat together as Patrick raised a toast. 'To Ruby, God bless her.'

Joseph smiled and said genially, 'I'll second that, Pat.'

Bella sipped the cold liquid and smiled once more at Kate. She realised that this was Bella's way of trying to worm her way into her affections, but the smile never reached her eyes. Although, as Kate had to admit to herself, neither did hers. It would take a while for her to warm to this woman.

She tried small talk. 'Who has the children tonight?'

Bella seemed to relax a bit and said brightly, 'We have a wonderful girl called Caroline who is at college, and babysitting money is quite a bit these days, I can tell you! Ten pound an hour – can you imagine?'

For some reason Bella's words made Kate burst into laughter. 'Nothing is cheap these days, Bella. Is she a nice girl? Good with the children? I can't imagine little Amanda being a bother, but a twelve-year-old boy might be a different kettle of fish!'

Bella grinned, and this time her demeanour was a little warmer; whatever she was, she loved her children, that much was obvious.

'He does his homework, and we always leave him a snack. He's a good boy really. Never a minute's trouble. Amanda is in bed by seven and after a story she is gone for the night, bless her. Caroline just puts on Netflix and texts her friends, I think.'

They laughed together. The atmosphere was getting lighter by the second. Kate found she was actually enjoying herself – and that, in itself, was something she had never thought possible.

When they walked through to dinner a little while later, she actually felt that there was a chance that this might work out OK after all.

Chapter Thirty-six

Annie Carr was listening to everything that DC Karim was telling her, making sure she took the call in private. She could feel Jean Wallace's eyes boring into the back of her head and glanced at her watch. It was gone ten thirty now, and there was still no sign of Destiny.

With every minute that passed, Annie Carr felt more convinced that they were too late – that the child was already gone. There were search teams all over the woods and local waste ground. Helicopters were sweeping the surrounding areas, and there was nothing constructive coming through. It was only a matter of time before the media got wind of it.

'You go to the address and keep me informed.' She turned back to face Destiny's parents and was momentarily lost for words. But she sat them down before asking gently, 'Do you know a Clinton Barber?' She saw the hope in their eyes as she said, 'It seems he's at your daughter's school, and she may very well be with him.'

She decided to leave out the Bag Boys and drug-dealing part until they were sure what they were facing.

Although she had an idea that these people would much rather their daughter was getting stoned round some lad's house than experiencing what Kylie had gone through.

And who could blame them?

Chapter Thirty-seven

Clinton Barber had just skinned up in his bedroom; he had Bruno Mars playing on his iPhone, and he was pleasantly stoned. His older brother, Justin, was in the next room with his friends, and Clinton could hear the laughter as they watched shite on YouTube. He smiled as he lit his spliff and settled back into his bed. He was feeling good; it had been a profitable day – he had shifted a lot of puff. His dream was to get enough money to go to Jamaica and find his father, his namesake.

At nearly sixteen, Clinton was a handsome boy of mixed race. He had coffee-coloured skin and greeny-brown eyes that were his best feature. He was tall and athletic-looking, though that wouldn't last if he didn't stop smoking the weed so much. His mum worked nights at the service station on the outskirts of Grantley and had long given up on trying to control her two sons. They loved her in their own way, but she was weak, and eventually they had worn her down until now they pretty much did what they wanted – though both made a point of contributing to the household. After all, they knew she wasn't exactly rolling in it and was too proud to sign on. He admired her for that, although Justin reckoned she worked nights at the service station to get a bit of peace and quiet.

He looked down at the girl in the bed next to him; she was snoring softly, and he smiled as he climbed under the sheets beside her. He took a long draw on his joint and held it in his lungs for a while before slowly blowing it out. He looked around his bedroom at the posters and the clothes piled everywhere and decided that he would have a dung-out the next day. It was beginning to smell, and that was something he could never stand. The weed permeated the wallpaper, and the place eventually stank; coupled with his socks and discarded clothes, it wasn't a pleasant environment.

He was just about to settle down and chill to some tunes when all hell broke loose. He heard the hammering on the front door and immediately jumped out of bed. He bumped into his brother on the landing and they broke up laughing as they tripped down the stairs together. Justin assumed that it was just someone looking for a quick bag of weed. But when they opened the front door and saw all the uniforms there, they knew they were fucked.

They stalled the police as long as they could so Justin's mates could make a quick getaway, and acted the innocents as always. Justin hoped the gang had the nous to take any gear in his bedroom with them.

Chapter Thirty-eight

Kate and Patrick were sitting together on their huge sofa discussing the night's events.

'Does it feel unreal, Pat?'

He nodded. Now the waiting was over, the reality was beginning to sink in. 'I feel something for him, but more for the children, if that makes sense, Kate.'

She nodded wisely. 'I can understand that, Pat. You thought you had lost your only child and now, all these years later, you find out you have a son. It's bound to make you feel at odds with yourself. I know it's thrown me.'

He hugged her to him tightly. 'You were a fucking diamond tonight. And what the fuck Joseph said to that Bella, God knows, but she was almost human.'

Kate laughed. 'Don't forget, it's still early days, Patrick.'

He sighed. 'I know, darling, but I feel so lucky. Poor old Ruby. She did a good job with that lad and she did it on her own. I feel like I should have known, though even if I had I could never have hurt Renée. Ruby understood too. I'm ashamed to admit I probably would have blanked the kid and just paid for him. But then, who knows what I would have done after Renée died. It's all ifs and buts at the moment.'

Kate squeezed his hand. She honestly didn't know what to say.

'You know, Kate, God can be a funny fucker. I had that fling with Ruby because I was lost. I knew my Renée would never get better, and I think I just needed to forget things for a while. Instead I just felt guiltier than ever! Then, all these years later, it turns out I gave her a child, and this is the upshot.'

Kate smiled in the lamplight. He looked totally bemused. She felt a pang of jealousy again at his words, but she swallowed it down. She knew he would always love Renée and Mandy, and now he had a whole new set of people to love. And she must be the bigger person, the better person, if she was to keep him. But Christ Himself knew it was hard. 'Let's just take one day at a time, eh? The kids thoroughly enjoyed themselves in the pool the other day, and you'll see them again soon enough – that's a start.'

He smiled then, a real smile. 'You always know what to say, Kate, you always know how to make me feel better.'

She held him to her and they were both quiet, filled with their own thoughts.

Chapter Thirty-nine

Justin Barber was shouting the odds, but no one was taking any notice of him. The police just took the two lads and forced them through to the lounge area of the small first-floor maisonette.

Annie Carr was not in the mood for any histrionics so she shouted angrily, 'Oh, shut the fuck up, Justin, and tell us where Destiny Wallace is.'

DC Ali Karim came down the stairs with a young girl. She had long blond hair and smudged make-up all over her pretty face. The only thing she had on was a T-shirt that had seen better days – and was obviously Clinton's – and she had the startled look of a doe caught in headlights. It was definitely not Destiny Wallace.

'This is Michelle James. She is apparently fifteen years old and has been crashing here, as she so succinctly put it, for the last few days.'

There was an element of defeat in his voice because, like everyone else, he had hoped to find Destiny here. DC Karim then held up a few baggies full of cannabis, and Clinton said under his breath, 'Oh, for fuck's sake!'

Justin slapped him around the head then, saying in annoyance, 'How many times, bro? You're a kid. You keep your stash with me!'

Annie admired the older brother's loyalty but at this particular moment in time she didn't give two fucks about the weed.

'Listen, Clinton, have you seen Destiny Wallace today at any point?'

Clinton shook his head, and Annie saw the fear come into his eyes then. 'Why? Is she missing?'

She nodded, saying, 'Can you think of anything at all that might give us a clue as to where she might be?'

'Honestly, lady, if I knew I would tell you – especially after what happened to Kylie. Why do you think I gave Michelle a place to crash!'

Michelle was finally waking up now, and she said tremulously, 'I had a row with my mum. I've been here three days.'

Annie knew that this girl had not been reported missing by anyone, and she marvelled once more at some people's idea of parenting. But she felt sick now, because time was marching on and there was no sign of Destiny Wallace. Everyone in the room was thinking the same thing: she was missing and, until they found her body, she would stay missing.

Annie threw the baggies at the two speechless young men and said tiredly, 'Get your act together, boys, because next time I come here it will be for a full-scale raid, OK?'

Justin Barber couldn't believe his luck, and he said seriously, 'OK, but I hope you find Destiny. We both do.'

Annie motioned for the others to follow her out as she said, 'I believe you, son, I do.'

Chapter Forty

Jean Wallace had been sedated and her husband was sitting nursing a large brandy when Annie finally arrived back at their house. Desmond Wallace took one look at her dejected countenance and silent tears gathered in his eyes. He knew that his girl had no reason to run away, and had no reason to go off for such a long period without getting in touch.

He had been calling her mobile phone all night only to hear the same words over and over. *The number you are calling is unavailable.* But he still rang it at five-minute intervals; the human spirit was remarkable and hope was a powerful emotion. But it was gone 2 a.m. now, and no one was expecting Destiny Wallace to get in touch. She was like Kylie – a good enough kid who had never once given her parents any reason to doubt her. She did what she was supposed to, attended school regularly, and always kept in touch with her family.

Annie hated to admit it, but it looked like Destiny Wallace was not coming home in anything other than a body bag. If it was the same culprit who had taken Kylie Barlow then right at this moment she could be being tortured and in agony, and praying for death at fourteen years old.

Annie Carr felt so helpless and so frustrated, it took all her willpower not to scream her rage at the gods. But she was a professional, so she sat beside Desmond Wallace and tried in her own way to shoulder some of his worry and pain.

Annie squeezed his hand and, as he looked at her, the desolation in his eyes was nearly her undoing.

Chapter Forty-one

He looked down at the girl and smiled. As usual, the fear got him going. It was fascinating to behold such terror at close range. He laughed as he saw the girl fighting against her bonds. She knew she had no chance of breaking free, but the desire to live was strong – as he had found out with Kylie.

It was so easy to fool people; he knew how to talk to the girls because he just told them everything they wanted to hear! Now here she was, his little show-off, Destiny, all snug as a bug in his den. And there was nothing she could do to help herself. Her eyes kept going to the small blowtorch that stood by the tiny fireplace, and he loved the way she had finally realised that she was in the same position as Kylie Barlow. Another prick-teasing little scrubber who thought she was so fucking clever.

He kicked her viciously in the ribs. The blow was so hard she actually moved across the floor, and her muffled cries were like music to his ears. He took another Polaroid of her as she looked up at him beseechingly. All her carefully applied make-up was gone; she had cried it away earlier, when he had burned her with the cigarettes – her own cigarettes too. As if he would smoke! The taste was disgusting, and it made everything stink – even her hair stank of it. He might burn her hair off; as the thought occurred to him, he couldn't help a chuckle escaping from his throat.

This was so exciting for him. After dreaming about it and planning it for so long, the satisfaction of seeing all his hopes and wants come together was almost breathtaking in its intensity.

Destiny was nearly naked now, but that was the least of her problems.

'It's nothing personal, Destiny, I want you to know that. I hate you all equally.' His voice was low and, as the terrified girl looked into his eyes, he took another Polaroid photograph.

Destiny Wallace wasn't going anywhere. And, as he lit the blowtorch, he relished the fact that she was as aware of it as he was.

Chapter Forty-two

Joseph O'Loughlin lay beside his sleeping wife and wondered what his old mum would have made of how things were turning out. That she had wanted him to know who his father was, albeit a bit late in the day, pleased him. Luckily, things were going well so far, but it was where they went from here that worried him.

Everyone from Grantley had heard of the infamous Ripper, but it was different knowing that his half-sister had been one of the victims. Now he had learned more about it, it made it all the more real. She had died so young and so brutally that he had felt almost tearful. This was his flesh and blood, after all; he wished he'd had the opportunity to know her. He wondered how Patrick must have felt finding out that she had been raped and murdered by a psychotic maniac. He couldn't even imagine what it would have been like if it had been his Amanda. But Patrick Kelly had come through it, and now he seemed overjoyed to have another shot at family.

Joseph was well aware that Bella was over the moon too now – she'd certainly changed her tune. All she saw was the money, the lifestyle, the cars, houses and everything else. When she was told about the villa in Spain and the condominium in Florida, she had nearly had an orgasm as she pictured herself there with the children. It left a bitter taste in his mouth because Joseph didn't want anything from the man – not materially anyway; he had always worked for what he had. He suspected that Patrick would be as open-handed as possible, if he asked – which he wouldn't. It went against the grain to take anything off a man who had not even known he existed, but then he had never taken anything off anyone in his life.

He had obviously inherited the work ethic from both his parents, because his mother had worked all her life to see him do well. He still missed her so much. So did the children – even Bella claimed to, but mainly because she had been a free babysitter! He closed his eyes tightly as he thought about his mum. She had been such a big part of his life, and now she was gone he felt bereft. And Bella was never going to be enough for him – he had known that for the last few years.

Now he had a father at least – but he also had a mistress and he was in love with her. He had two children he adored and he didn't want to upset their lives in any way, but he wasn't sure he could live a lie for much longer. It was as if, when his mum had gone, he had become anchorless. She had known about his girlfriend and, although she had never said much, he knew that she understood why he needed that warmth.

Ruby had found out by accident and she had just

shrugged, saying in her usual no-nonsense way, 'It's your life, son, but madam won't be so understanding, and she has a vicious streak. So you be careful what you wish for.' Then she had never mentioned it again.

Tonight, seeing Kate and Patrick so at ease together, he had known that he would never find that peace with Bella. She wasn't built for passion, and she didn't understand that life meant more than status and possessions. She had a jealous streak but, worse than that, Bella – who, in fairness, was a wonderful mother – was cold in so many ways. After the birth of Amanda she had made it clear in no uncertain terms that she wanted no more children and that, as she had basically done her job providing him with a son and daughter, she expected to be left in what she termed 'peace'. This was from the woman who, when they were first together, had been like a sex maniac! He realised now that it had been a front to snare him.

Bella saw sex as a weapon; he was lucky if she allowed it on his birthday, and 'allowed it' was exactly how it felt. He was a virile man who needed not just sex but the closeness and intimacy of shared love and the feel of a warm body in his arms. It was all a fucking mess. As much as he cared for Bella, and he did care – she was, after all, the mother of his children – it was Christine who he felt at peace with. Christine who made him feel that the days were worth living.

In her arms he felt a contentment that he had never experienced before, and it was heady stuff. She responded to his touch, and he could feel her need of him. They talked for hours, and they laughed. Oh, how he had missed laughing with someone who shared the same sense of humour, who could articulate what they were feeling, who wasn't afraid to show tenderness and love. She had never asked him to leave his wife – she had understood from the beginning that wouldn't be an option – but now he wanted out of his marriage so badly he wondered if he was losing his mind.

Christine filled his thoughts. She was everything he had ever wanted in a woman; fortunately she was quite happy to play second fiddle to Bella, and that had been fine at first. But now, eighteen months on, it wasn't enough for *him*. He wanted to wake up with her, eat breakfast with her, he wanted to come home to her. He would *look forward* to coming home to *her*. Now he looked forward to seeing his kids, but not his wife.

Bella couldn't help how she was. It had become clear several years into their marriage, after Amanda was born, that he had not married the woman he thought he had. Bella's whole life was lived for show. She had to have the best car, the best house, the most well-behaved children. She really couldn't see that was why she couldn't make or keep friends, because she was constantly living a lie. She didn't enjoy others' success, and she couldn't ever let anyone get close enough to her because she was always frightened they would find her wanting. So she lived in a small vacuum of simply her home, her husband and her kids.

Well, that might be enough for her, but it wasn't enough for him. Tonight he had witnessed love as it should be – a couple perfectly at ease with each other – and it had made him question his own life more than ever before. Until finding out about Patrick, he had resigned himself to this loveless marriage and his wonderful children. But, as much as he adored his children, he knew now that they weren't enough to keep him in this house with a wife who showed what she thought was affection but not love. It really wasn't just about sex – though he was honest enough to admit it was a big part of it.

Seeing Patrick and Kate together, he had felt a pang of jealousy. Not of them, but because he knew that would never be him and Bella. And the thought of spending the rest of his life pretending had appalled him, because he needed more than Bella would ever be able to give to him. He needed love in all its forms, both emotional and physical – just like his mother had. He needed to feel closeness to another human being. Christine Murray gave that to him in spades, and he knew that he couldn't live without it. Not any longer.

It occurred to him suddenly that he had already made the decision. And, as guilty as he felt, he also felt a deep sense of relief. Because now he knew what he had to do, he could plan accordingly.

Chapter Forty-three

Jeanette Cole was a sprightly octogenarian, and she prided herself on her rude good health and her ability to still look after herself without the need of assistance. Her small bungalow was kept pristinely clean, and she was often to be seen in her garden weeding. Her garden was her pride and joy. Since losing her husband eight years earlier, she had lavished all her love and care on her plants. Her garden was also her way of interacting with people, and she loved to stop and have a chat with her neighbours.

Now, as she walked to the shops to pick up her *Daily Mail*, she was humming to herself happily. Mr and Mrs Patel were lovely people and always had a kind word for her; she was usually their first customer at six in the morning, and they often had a cup of tea waiting for her which she appreciated. Habitually an early riser, she loved the quiet of the early morning before the world came to life.

Though she had only been blessed with one child – a daughter who she had buried at nineteen from cancer – she still felt she had been very lucky in that she had been a mother and had married a man who she had adored. Jeanette Cole felt she had been a fortunate woman in many ways; she had experienced love and affection and she was still going strong without a real ache or pain to complain about. That was the secret of happiness she believed – remembering what you had and enjoying every day.

Today, though, she was shocked to see a distraught Mrs Patel sitting on the kerb outside her shop crying uncontrollably. Hurrying now, she went to the distressed woman and, as she put her arm around her, she heard Mr Patel shouting into the telephone that the police had to come immediately.

It wasn't until later that she found out that a young girl had been discovered on the waste ground behind their shop and she was dead. Tortured and murdered and dumped like rubbish, and poor Mr and Mrs Patel had found her as they had pulled up at the back of their shop to open it for the day.

Jeanette Cole, being the level-headed woman she was, made hot sweet tea and stayed with Mrs Patel until the police arrived, all the time wondering what kind of world they lived in where a young girl could be so brutally slain. But she also remembered the Grantley Ripper and it seemed that, once more, their little town was being stalked by a murderer. It was on days like this she hoped to meet her daughter and husband again sooner rather than later.

Chapter Forty-four

Annie Carr looked down at the body of the mutilated child and felt a sense of futility wash over her. Whoever this fucker was, he knew exactly what he was doing and where he was doing it. He was a local all right – he knew this place like the back of his hand. No CCTV images, nothing to even say he had been there – nothing except a dead girl who was barely recognisable.

He had burned her hair off, she was without finger-nails, and the blowtorch had been put to good use once again. What this child had endured was too horrific to contemplate. Her genitalia were gone; it seemed he was keeping more than a few trophies.

The back of the Patels' shop had no cameras, nothing. On either side of them were empty shops. They were situated at the end of a terrace of houses that had all seen better days and were now no more than bedsits. This fucker was far too clever by half. He was evading every camera. He had planned his dump sites like he planned everything else; with a frightening precision.

She looked out once more over the waste ground that was on the outskirts of Grantley and which was accessed by the woods where Kylie Barlow had been found. There was nothing to say a vehicle had been there, no tyre tracks, nothing.

As Megan McFee arrived, Annie looked at her, hoping against hope that she would find something – anything – that they could use to hunt this fucker down. But she was afraid she wouldn't put money on it.

Chapter Forty-five

Kate and Annie sat in Kate's kitchen, smoking and drinking whisky. Kate had a copy of everything, and, as she looked it all over, she shook her head in bafflement.

'How can he come and go without anyone even noticing anything? For fuck's sake, Annie, you can't fart these days but it's documented somewhere.'

Annie shrugged in answer. 'Your guess is as good as mine, Kate. It's like the fucker is invisible.'

Kate poured them both more Scotch and said seriously, 'He's a local. He knows the area too well. However he's transporting these girls, it's without anyone even noticing. That tells us he fits in, that he can move around without attracting attention. His dump sites are both in or around the woods, so that tells me he knows them well. I don't think he has a vehicle as such. No one has reported hearing a car, so what does he do? Park up and carry them? Neither girl weighed much.' Kate understood only too well the frustration that Annie was feeling; she had been there herself. 'Listen to me, darling – you have to keep focused. I know what it feels like to think you can't pre-empt this bastard. But believe me, he will make a mistake. They always do.'

Annie swallowed her drink down and said wearily, 'I know that, Kate, but it's so fucking hard to do nothing except wait till this fucker gets a bit too clever. He kept Kylie two days nearly, but Destiny was gone and dumped in half that time. The press are baying for blood – you can't escape those fucking cameras. And don't get me started on all the online shit.'

Kate nodded but said forcefully, 'I know it's the last thing you need on top of everything but you have to block it out, Annie, and focus on the case. He's honing his craft, darling, and he will do it again. Remember that the girls were best friends. It's like he's targeted them especially, isn't it? So whoever this is, Destiny must have felt a level of safety with him, or he abducted her somewhere he knew he was safe. It's like a puzzle, remember that. You have to find the link that will make all of this become clear. I assume there'll be memorials happening for the girls? You need to make sure there's a big presence as, chances are, he will be there in some capacity. Whoever this is, he won't want to miss out on seeing the devastation of his handiwork.'

Annie put her head in her hands; she looked so tired and so dejected that Kate put her arms around her and hugged her.

'Killers like this want to shock, they love to know that their actions have far-reaching consequences. It's why they do it. Look at George Markham. He posed those women and girls for maximum effect. This fucker is the same. He gets off on the fear, not only of his victims but also of the people around them. You just have to keep in there, girl. I guarantee you a pattern of some kind will eventually emerge, and you will see it and you will find him.'

Annie sighed heavily. She was full of Scotch and full of self-pity. 'But look at the fucking Yorkshire Ripper. The police caught him by accident—'

Kate put a hand up to silence her. 'You can't let yourself think like that. What you do now is start from the beginning, and you interview everyone again and you sift through the evidence. Don't let yourself be defeated because, believe me, Annie, this fucker is going to do this again – and sooner rather than later.'

Annie nodded. She knew that Kate was right, but seeing the destruction of that young girl had really affected her. Because, once again, it seemed there was literally nothing to go on.

Chapter Forty-six

Margaret Dole was tired out but she couldn't go home. She was once more looking through everything the girls had ever posted, no matter how obscure. There had to be something somewhere that might give them a chance of finding the man the media were calling the new Grantley Ripper. They were reminding the world of George Markham and his reign of terror and implying that this man was in some way connected to him. It was pathetic and, worse than that, she knew a lot of the people would swallow it all hook, line and sinker.

It didn't help the police in any way; every fucker with a grievance against a neighbour or workmate was ringing in, flinging accusations right, left and centre. It was always the same with these cases – people used them as a means to settle old scores. And with the added bonus of the internet, forums were popping up all over the country with amateur detectives sharing their opinions. Margaret was monitoring these, too, because the chances were the man responsible was holding forth himself, satisfied that he was anonymous.

It was the proverbial needle-in-a-haystack scenario.

She rubbed her eyes and drank some more of her cold black coffee. What she wouldn't give for a line of amphetamines now! Wake her up properly and give her that edge she so desperately needed. Like a lot of police she knew, she used recreational drugs regularly, especially when she had a weekend off.

As she trawled through the inanity of the murdered girls' social media history and read all of their friends' posts too she wondered what kind of society would produce the ruling classes of the future. True, there were some touching tributes to Kylie and Destiny, but on the whole, she had never read such banal rubbish in her life, and she had to remind herself constantly that these were young girls trying to fit in with their peer group. But there was nothing of note, just the usual schoolgirl spats, not even anything that could be classed as bullying. These all seemed like nice kids whose existence didn't raise any red flags and who seemed completely unaware that every word they wrote could be accessed by anyone with the nous to do so.

It was no wonder that a lot of women who were attacked or murdered these days had been stalked on their social media first. People checked in wherever they were, tagged who they were with, and basically gave complete strangers access to their whole lives.

One thing Margaret Dole was convinced of was that no one would ever be able to police the internet. It was an impossibility, especially for the computer literate. There were teenagers who could hack into the US Space Station without any problems whatsoever; young men and women dropped bombs on people like they were playing a computer game by controlling drones.

Privacy was a thing of the past, yet this fucker had killed twice and no one had even caught a glimpse of him. But she would find something on him. She was determined. No one, *absolutely* no one, could hide for long.

She went back to her fishing, and prayed that she would find something that would give them a lead of sorts.

Chapter Forty-seven

Patrick Kelly was at his restaurant in Brentwood, Essex, where he had arranged a lunch with Joseph. They needed to talk seriously without the women or the children about. He was excited, looking forward to forging a bond with this new son of his. Every time he thought of the word 'son', he felt a tightening in his guts.

He sipped at his glass of red wine and looked around him happily. This was a good earner, and it was regularly packed both for lunch and in the evenings. Kate had helped with the décor, which was as understated as she was, but it looked impressive – from the black granite bar top to the pristine cotton tablecloths. The menu was small but, as Kate said, too much choice could be intimidating and often made people think that a lot of the food was pre-prepared and reheated. There was a chocolate soufflé on the dessert menu which, diners were informed, would take thirty minutes to prepare. As she had predicted, it was the most-ordered item. All the food was locally sourced and of the highest quality; Patrick was proud of this place and he had every right to be.

His Kate was a shrewdie all right, and he understood

that everything going on was taking its toll on her. She was trying so hard to accommodate him and his new-found family, but he knew her better than she knew herself. He had put himself in her place, and he admitted he wouldn't be too thrilled if the boot was on the other foot. But Kate, being Kate, was doing her best to help him in any way she could, and he loved her for it. Renée would have raised the fucking roof off the house if she had known.

He wondered what his Mandy would have made of it all. One thing for sure: she wouldn't have had a minute in her day for Bella. That was one irritating cunt! He did wonder how some men ended up saddling themselves with women they should have run a fucking mile from. Patrick could see Bella pricing his life in her head, and was under no illusions that, if he didn't have so much poke, she would not have given him the time of day. She was more than capable of using the children as a ransom, and he'd have to swallow his knob and go along with whatever she wanted if he wanted to see them. It might stick in his craw but he was willing to do it for access to those kids.

The boy Joey was a Brahma, a nice lad with good manners and an easy way with him, and that little Mandy – or, as he must learn to say, Amanda – was so like his baby girl, it brought tears to his eyes just looking at her bright countenance. Bella seemed like she'd done a good job bringing them up, he had to give her that much at least.

As Joseph walked in, Patrick felt a rush of pride that

this handsome, well-set-up man was his flesh and blood. As they shook hands he could see the staff watching, and wondering what was going on. He usually did his dodgier deals well away from here, and only visited with Kate and, occasionally, a local councillor or dignitary. He couldn't help wondering if they noticed the resemblance between him and Joseph, because it was there. His sisters would have loved this, and he was sorry they were no longer around to meet this handsome man and make a fuss of him. But knowing Violet especially, she would have started World War Three with Bella and caused more harm than good.

He smiled at the thought and, as he poured Joseph a glass of wine, he said casually, 'I have to admit, this is a good day for me.'

Joseph smiled easily. 'I have been looking forward to it myself, Patrick.' He sipped the wine and raised an eyebrow in appreciation. 'Now that is a decent Merlot.'

Patrick grinned. 'Only the best, my son, only the best!'

For some reason that broke the ice and they laughed together, gathering glances from more than a few of the female diners in the restaurant.

'I can't help wondering if your mum knew this would happen? If she knew we would get on, like?'

Joseph smiled. Her passing was still raw, and he said seriously, 'I miss her every day. She worked her arse off to give me a chance in life and she was a good mother, bless her. Loving and wise in her own way. You know something, Pat? She warned me about Bella, but I couldn't see it then. She was a wise old bird. Not educated, but she had an insight that comes from life, from experience.'

Patrick was nonplussed for a moment at the man's complete honesty, and he felt he owed him the same honesty back. 'She was a good sort was Ruby. I turned to her when my wife was dying of cancer. I'm not proud of it, but I needed someone and Ruby was there. I wish she had told me about you, I really do. But I suppose she thought she was doing the right thing, and I do admire her for that.' A waitress approached the table to take their food order and he waved her away impatiently before continuing. 'All I can say is she did a fucking blinding job with you, son, and I thank God every day that she finally told you about me before it was too late.'

Joseph smiled and raised his glass. 'To Ruby – my old mum, and a fantastic lady.'

They toasted her together, and Patrick felt the pull of this man – his son, his flesh and blood – and, as he saw the tears in the other man's eyes, he felt just how big a loss Ruby had been. Once more, he wished he could have watched this young man grow up, even if it had only been from a distance. But Patrick Kelly was, above all, a realist and he knew that you couldn't change the past, no matter how much you might wish you could.

Kate said to him once that the past is a foreign country, but he had never really understood her meaning until now. She was always quoting people; she was a big reader, whereas he was happy with Ludlum and Wilbur Smith. Last book he had read was a Lee Child, and he had escaped into the world of Jack Reacher, though he did like some non-fiction stuff too. But his Kate, she really read, and she had educated him in her own way over the years.

'To Ruby O'Loughlin! God rest her soul.'

They smiled at each other then, as if they had come to some kind of understanding, but in reality they had just bonded over the only thing they had ever had in common: Ruby O'Loughlin.

Patrick waved over the young waitress and they ordered their food, completely at ease in each other's company.

Chapter Forty-eight

DC Ali Karim and Annie were impressed when they arrived at Stephen Carter's house; it was not what they had been expecting in the least.

Annie had been looking for a legitimate reason to follow up with a home visit and the tragic discovery of Destiny's body had provided that. Ali got out of the car and pressed the buzzer for the gates, announcing their arrival. As they were admitted and parked the unmarked car on the huge driveway, they raised their eyebrows at each other. It was a new build, and it had a ranch-style look that gave it a sprawling aspect. It was a big property and not exactly what you would expect a child at Grantley Comprehensive to live in.

As they approached the front door, a large man walked out, smiling welcomingly. He had a bald head and huge muscular arms covered in tattoos, and he hailed them into his home with a cockney accent that was at odds with his surroundings. 'Come inside, my old woman is just making a pot of tea. Stephen is out playing tennis with his mate, but he will be in as soon as I call him.'

Annie had no difficulty believing that; this man had

a presence about him that made her think that most people did what he told them.

They walked through a spacious hallway and into a huge state-of-the-art kitchen. A small, slim woman with thick blond hair and an easy smile was making the tea, and Annie and Ali were immediately put at their ease by the cosy domestic scene. There were about two acres of garden, including a swimming pool visible through the large kitchen window, and they were impressed despite themselves.

'You have a beautiful home, Mrs Carter.'

The woman flapped a hand, as if in denial, saying, 'Call me Sylvie – everyone does – and this is my husband, Jonny. I am a great believer in introductions! Jonny thinks I'm mad, but I think it's important.' She was as broad a cockney as her husband, which was strange because Stephen talked like a newsreader.

Jonny offered them a seat at the huge glass-and-chrome dining table and, as Sylvie poured the tea, he said conversationally, 'So why do you want to speak to Stephen?' He appeared genuinely interested and, unlike a lot of the parents they dealt with, didn't automatically assume their child was in some kind of trouble.

Annie accepted her mug of tea gratefully and said neutrally, 'We're just following up given the new developments. It's pretty routine.'

Sylvie sat down and said seriously, 'It's fucking outrageous. Those poor little girls! Don't bear thinking about, does it, Jonny?'

Her husband shook his huge head slowly. 'I can't

imagine what those parents must be going through. Especially somewhere like this. We moved this way because we thought it was a better environment for Stephen. Open fields, you know? This is the last place you would think such violent crime would occur. I was saying to Sylvie this morning that, if I hadn't invested so much money here, I would sell up and go.'

Annie smiled and said easily, 'What exactly is it you do, Mr Carter?'

He laughed suddenly. 'Call me Jonny. I own a building business. I built the new estate out Ventham Way. Do you know it? I also own a couple of places in town, in the precinct – fruit machines, games, that sort of thing – and a strip club in South London. That's where I met this one.'

Sylvie laughed in delight. 'I wasn't stripping, I was a waitress! Ooh, you do like to wind me up!'

Jonny grinned. 'Listen, one look at her in her hotpants and I was all over the place. But joking aside, we liked Grantley, still do. But this is a bad business. You any nearer finding the culprit?'

'We are looking at a few lines of enquiry – one of the reasons we are re-interviewing all the people who knew Kylie and Destiny. You never know what people see without realising the importance.'

Jonny nodded sagely. 'I admire you, I really do. My old man used to say the Old Bill couldn't catch a fever in a swamp! But he was a bit of a lad, if you get my drift. I know that if my boy can help you in any way, he will. I'll call him in for you now.'

Annie and DC Karim smiled; Jonny Carter was a genuinely nice man who spoke without thinking. He pulled himself from his chair and disappeared through the large patio doors that led out to the garden.

'That's my Jonny! What you see is what you get. I will top your teas up and you can start talking to Stephen.'

They smiled at her as she went to boil the kettle. A few seconds later, Jonny reappeared followed by a sweating Stephen Carter who strolled into the kitchen with a smaller dark-haired boy, who Annie and Ali recognised as Todd Richards.

Jonny directed Todd to the shower room and then said amiably, 'I'll leave you all to it. Got some work to catch up on.'

'OK, love – dinner at eight!' Sylvie waved him away.

Annie turned her attention to Stephen Carter, observing him in his own environment and was amazed at the young man's total aplomb. Unlike his parents he had a very offhand way with him, but she suspected being born into this kind of luxury might have a lot to do with it.

He smiled at them, showing perfect white teeth. 'You will have to excuse my attire but Todd and I had arranged a tennis match for after school.' He walked to a huge fridge and took out a can of Fanta. He held it for a few seconds to his sweating forehead before opening it and pouring it into a glass he had taken from the draining board. 'Only allowed one sweet drink a day in this house! My mum's a bit of a health nut, aren't you?' He smiled at her as she set the teapot down. 'So, DCI Carr. What can I do for you?' he asked as he sat at the table with them.

Annie and DC Karim got the distinct impression he was interviewing *them*. Annie sipped her tea before saying seriously, 'We are just going back over Kylie's last movements. Tying up any loose ends.'

Stephen looked at them blankly, not saying a word. Annie deliberately didn't say any more.

Eventually the large, athletic young man sighed and said pleasantly, 'I really don't know what to tell you. As I said before, we saw the girls in Starbucks, and that was it really. Look, I know this sounds arrogant, but those girls were just school chums, you know? People you saw out and about. I didn't really take that much particular notice of them – I've known them for ever – but I certainly never thought that anything untoward would happen to them.'

'You have a beautiful home, Stephen, rather at odds with the local school, if I might say.'

Stephen laughed then. 'My father, as you have probably already gathered, is of the opinion that if it was good enough for him it's good enough for me! I respect that. He knows that to succeed in this world, you need to strive for yourself – he has told me that since I was a baby, and I happen to agree with him. The only thing he insisted on was elocution lessons – that's for when I get to university, of course. But I think he has a good point.'

DC Karim said quietly, 'You have no presence on

social media, except for the occasional post on Face-book. That's very unusual for young people in this day and age.'

Stephen shrugged. 'I think it's childish, people's every thought put out there for the world to see. I was reading *1984* – you know, the Orwell novel? It's strange how people were once worried about Big Brother watching them, and now they are frightened no one is watching them!' He laughed. 'The girls at school especially brag about how many "likes" they get for a selfie, or some witty comment they put on their profiles. I find that inane, to be honest. As you can imagine, I do have all the latest devices as soon as they arrive in the shops, my parents see to that. But I would rather read a book or write down my thoughts and aspirations. I was born in the wrong era really, I suppose. The internet doesn't appeal to me. If I need to fact-check something, I would rather use an actual encyclopaedia. I like the feel of a book in my hands. Personal preference, I suppose. I'm also very sporty, as my mother would put it. I prefer to play tennis, the actual game, rather than on a computer console. I play football for my school and I go fencing once a week, because I like to use my energy in positive ways. I am far more at home outside in the garden reading than I am in my bedroom trawling other people's Instagram accounts or Twitterings!'

He grinned disarmingly, and Annie and Ali found themselves smiling back. They had both taken a liking to this rather unusual young man. He was like some-thing from a Famous Five book, without the lashings and lashings of ginger beer!

'I understand you are on the committee for Kylie and Destiny's memorial?'

He nodded, his face sad suddenly. 'Yes, I am. It felt like the right thing to do, didn't it, Mum? It's still sinking in. There are some sick people in the world. Another reason I prefer to keep off the internet. Some of the disgusting stuff that people share really turns my stomach. You know, you should talk to Mr Packham, the IT teacher, about something that happened last year. The school tried to keep it quiet but nothing stays secret in a school for long.'

Annie Carr was immediately interested. 'Why? What happened?'

Stephen glanced at his mother, then shrugged nonchalantly. 'It's not really my place to say and anyway I only got bits and pieces of it all, but I hear it involved quite a few of the pupils. I think you would get the full story from Mr Packham. Talk to Jennifer Andrews and her sister, Claire, too. They would know the full SP.' He was looking at them both very seriously now. 'Grantley is like an Agatha Christie novel. Nothing, and I mean nothing, is as simple as it looks. But talk to Jennie and her sister, they will give you all you need to know about that particular mess. And poor Mr Packham – well, I felt sorry for him! He's a decent bloke, you know, and he was dragged into some serious shenanigans, believe me.'

Annie looked over to see if Ali had caught all those names from Stephen's casually imparted revelations.

'Oh, by the way, do you need to talk to Todd again

too? I can go and get him. He's my best mate – we're always together.'

Annie Carr shook her head absent-mindedly. 'I think we've covered everything for now.' She was already eager to leave so she could talk to this Jennifer and her sister. It seemed the school were holding back somehow, and she was interested to know what they were hiding – and why.

Chapter Forty-nine

Christine Murray was not a classic beauty by any standards but she certainly had something about her. Tall and slim, she had long red-gold hair that was not only thick but had a natural wave to it. Coupled with blue eyes and a wide mouth she looked more sensual than beautiful. She dressed quite conservatively, and this only added to her allure.

She was a PA in a high-flying legal firm in the City and she was liked, respected and, more significantly for her, she was known for being the best at what she did. That was important to her – as a woman and as a worker. Her mother had instilled that in her from a young child. She was a grafter; coming from a council estate, she had worked her way to the top of her profession with a determination that had been inherited from her mother, a single parent of five children who had all gone out into the world and done well for themselves.

Now she was in her flat in Grantley, waiting for her lover Joseph O'Loughlin to arrive, as he did every Wednesday and Friday. And sometimes, if she was really lucky, he would turn up on a Monday night. These times were what she lived for, what kept her going through the week. She knew it was sad, but she didn't care. Joseph was her world, and always would be. There was nothing she could do about that. She had been caught from day one, although she'd never thought anything would come of it. She'd been working for one of the senior partners when Joseph joined the firm and when they realised they were both from Grantley a bond was forged. Christine knew he had a wife and children so had no expectations but around eighteen months ago, when they both found themselves working late into the night, Joseph had confided in her that his marriage was not all he'd hoped it would be and, after that, there was no turning back.

She didn't regret a second of their time together; however short it was enough. At least that is what she told herself. She hated being a mistress, but she would have this man on any terms. She had fallen hopelessly in love with him, and that was something that had never happened to her before.

At twenty-nine she knew she should be looking for a man she could settle down with, even have a child with. But without him, her life would become meaningless. Without him, she was nothing – she would rather be dead, as dramatic as that sounded. She wouldn't be able to carry on another day. That was how much Joseph had affected her, and she loved every minute of his company for as long as he could be with her. The intensity of her feelings for this man who had told her from day one he would never leave his family for her, or anyone else for that matter, frightened her sometimes. His kids were his world, and she got that. It didn't mean it didn't hurt her more as time went on.

But now she pushed that from her mind as she concentrated on her make-up – which, as always, was as subtle as she was. She fell asleep every night imagining what it would be like to be with him every day, but she knew that was all it would ever be – a dream. Yet she believed he loved her, and they had sex that was as mind-blowing as it was outrageous. She had never thought she would ever feel like this.

She walked into her tiny kitchen and turned the oven down. She had made a few of his favourite canapés to eat with their usual champagne she had chilling in the fridge. He would have to eat his evening meal when he finally arrived home and she tried her hardest not to resent this. But sometimes it was difficult, especially on lovely summer nights like this, when they should be sharing a nice meal together without having to watch the clock. Christine had already resigned herself to that when she heard his key in the door and smiled with happiness. Whatever the situation, she would rather be with him than without him.

As he stumbled into the living room, she saw to her utter amazement that he was drunk. He stood there, smiling away for a few moments, before saying loudly, 'Hello, darling, got that champagne opened yet?'

Chapter Fifty

Donald Packham was mowing his lawn when Annie Carr turned up with DC Karim. He recognised them immediately and, turning the engine off, he walked across his front lawn, cleaning his hands on a piece of rag as he walked.

Annie Carr noticed he wasn't surprised to see them; it was as if he had been expecting them at some point. He lived in a pretty semi-detached Victorian property in one of the nicer suburbs of Grantley. Annie remembered that he wasn't married.

As he smiled a welcome, he said neutrally, 'Would you like to come inside? I assume you want to talk.'

They nodded in acquiescence and followed him round the back and into a large, modern, airy kitchen that belied the outside appearance of the house. It was like something you would see on a spaceship.

He smiled at their amazed faces and said cheerily, 'My partner, David, is a chef.' It was said in such a way as to let them know he was gay and he didn't give a shit who knew about it.

As if on cue, a short Scottish man walked into the

kitchen, held out his hand and introduced himself. He was fit and, although not good-looking, he was very well presented.

'Hi. I'm David McTeer. I won't get in your way, I'm just getting myself a cold drink. It's a beautiful evening.' He proceeded to pour himself a glass of ice-cold white wine.

Annie watched enviously as he poured another for his partner. Then she smiled as he offered it to her, and she actually accepted it. DC Karim declined, explaining that he was driving. It was a good atmosphere to be in, and Annie Carr found herself envying these men their life-style, even though she had only been there for five minutes. There was an aura of calm and kindness that surrounded the two men and, as she settled down in the spacious and well-kept back garden, she relaxed. They were sitting on expensive garden furniture by a small pond that was stocked with goldfish and a few koi carp. It really was a gorgeous setting.

As they enjoyed the shade and a rather good Sauvignon Blanc, Donald Packham said, 'I have been expecting you. I told Brian – Mr Yalding – that we should have informed you, but he didn't think it had any bearing on the case. Which, in reality, it doesn't. But I said to David, "Davy, it was a bad to-do all round." '

Annie and Ali looked at him in utter bewilderment. 'We were told to talk to you by Stephen Carter. He said that something had happened, but we have no idea what it actually was. Only that it involved a Jennifer and Claire Andrews?'

Donald Packham took a deep breath and a big slug of his wine before saying wearily, 'We caught the younger girl, Claire, sexting. They were both at it. I'm an IT teacher and I couldn't find whoever it was they were involved with. Neither would talk about it. And the police, if you will forgive my bluntness, weren't that interested. The girls' parents removed them from the school and it basically blew over. I was never happy with the result – I felt that the girls were very vulnerable. The parents were flakes. The mother was absolutely terrified of her husband, and the girls were out of control. I reported my safeguarding worries to the usual agencies and never heard another word. I had to leave it at that. But there was something radically wrong with that family and the set-up. I did what I could, and had to leave it there.'

Annie nodded. She knew herself how difficult it was to get anything done these days, with everyone terrified of treading on particular toes. But she would find out who had dealt with the allegation at the police station and tear them a new one. 'That explains why we haven't got their names from the school.'

He nodded. 'I did tell Helene Betterway that she should mention it to you, but the new privacy laws make it difficult. They are now at a different school, you see.'

Annie nodded; it was a minefield all right with minors – as these all were. 'A heads-up would have been helpful.'

Donald Packham nodded. 'He's a good kid, Stephen Carter – he's like an anomaly there really. I wish there were more like him at that school. He *wants* to learn and that's refreshing. He has all the girls after him too. He doesn't seem that interested, but I think that just makes them like him more! His parents are good people. A bit rough round the edges, and I don't think I would want to fall out with his father, but they really do a lot for the school and for him. His father donated all the new equipment for my classes. Not much change out of thirty grand, but the school couldn't afford it, so he stepped in. Didn't want any recognition either, which is unusual in itself.' Donald got up and went into the kitchen.

Annie and Ali looked at each other and shrugged, both wondering what they would find out from the Andrews girls. But for now Annie accepted the top-up for her wine and continued to question Donald Packham about the sexting incident.

Chapter Fifty-one

Bella O'Loughlin was sitting at her kitchen table, drumming her fingernails in a hard tattoo. The children were both in bed and she stared out over the well-cut lawn at the summerhouse, and watched the last of the summer sun go down. She glanced at the clock and saw that it was just after nine. Never had her husband been so late home without a phone call or a text at the very least. She sipped at her iced tea and didn't bother turning on the lights in her kitchen, preferring the darkness as it closed in around her.

She knew all about his little amour, Christine, and she had wisely decided to overlook it. She was confident that he would never leave her – he loved his children too much – but Wednesdays and Fridays were particularly difficult for her. She knew she had driven him away, but she couldn't pretend feelings that she just didn't *feel*. She had no interest in sex, and she had no interest in other people. She was far too competitive to ever make any real friendships, and she didn't care.

She had convinced herself that she had all she needed with the children and Joseph. And now her new father-in-law was in the picture, she felt her life could only get better. Her eyes shone with the thought of the luxury holidays she could go on, and the expensive cars she was convinced she would be driving. Everything about her was money orientated, but she felt that was natural in a mother. After all, who wouldn't want the best for their children? She used the children as an excuse for her greed. And, boy, did she covet things! She smiled at the thought.

She wanted the best that life had to offer, and that was why she had set her cap at Joseph O'Loughlin. Even though she knew that her love was no more than tepid at best, she was married to him and her love took the form of ownership. She was the mother of his children, and that gave her leverage, because he adored them. She had observed very early on that, in order to fit in, you needed to be able to emulate emotions. As a young child she could remember trying to understand what was going on around her, understand why people acted as they did. Eventually, she had got with the programme and attempted to fit in.

But the only real emotion she had ever experienced was jealousy; it was a destructive feeling that she had gradually learned to rein in, if not to actually conquer. Even the children's school friends could arouse the beast within her. It was why she had never really had any friends to speak of; she couldn't stand to see anyone else getting on, doing better than her. She felt a raging anger at those people: how dare they? Who the fuck did they think they were? No one was better than *she* was or *her* children were. It was inconceivable; after all, she did everything that needed to be done to achieve. And she made sure *her* children did exactly what was needed. It was all she knew.

It amazed her that she had put up with her husband's infidelity for this long. But she was, above all, out for number one, and there was no way she was going to give him an excuse to leave her for that trollop. That was her biggest fear: being dumped, abandoned by her husband. While she had a wedding ring she was someone – and it was proof that she was normal, that she was wanted – needed, even. She would not give that up without a fight, and fight she would. Christine Murray would find that out, if she pushed it too far. So would Joseph. He would not know what the fuck had hit him. He had no idea about the dark places her mind could go to when she was pushed. Sometimes she shocked herself. In her fantasies, she would take him out without a second's thought. She would take her own kids out without a second's thought to punish him if he put a foot wrong – he needed to realise that.

The imagery made her smile to herself, and she cheered up momentarily. She pictured her husband looking at his children's bodies. Lifeless. Throats cut, or maybe drowned. Though young Joey might put up too much of a fight; he was a big strong lad, and she was very proud of him. He was a handsome boy, and he did so well at school – he was a clever potato, no doubt about that. So tablets, maybe. An overdose with her alongside them? Her husband would never forgive himself, and that is exactly what she wanted. For her Joseph to realise that *he* had killed them, not *her*. That his actions – his complete disregard for his marriage and his family – had caused all this upset.

That would be such a great outcome, if her husband didn't start to get what she was telling him. Idiot that he was, he thought she didn't know about Christine Murray. But she had been very good, and he would understand that when he was burying them all together, as she would request in her suicide note.

Then Miss Murray would be fucked for the rest of her days where her husband was concerned. Oh, she knew where she lived – Miss Christine Murray – she knew everything about her. She had made a point of finding out everything she could about the competition.

She could never countenance Joseph leaving her; she would bring down the wrath of God on not only him but also that red-headed whore he was bedding if he even showed signs of thinking about it. She felt her hands clawing, and she took deep breaths until she relaxed once more and her heart rate steadied. The darkness was enveloping her now and she sat wrapped in its comfort, her mind a mass of thoughts and ideas. She had to remember she was the mother of his children and that would always give her the upper hand over any whore he kept on the side. But one thing kept coming back to her: he had never been this late before without at least sending her a text or calling her. Tonight felt like a game changer, and that bothered her.

She needed a strategy in place, and that is what she

would concentrate on. She had fought to get him and she would fight to keep him. Especially now they had a rich father just waiting for a new family to spoil. She would take Patrick Kelly for every penny she could, and why not? After all, she had what he wanted, and he had what she wanted. As far as she was concerned, it was a match made in heaven.

Chapter Fifty-two

Kate heard Patrick before she saw him. He smashed through the front door, swearing as he tripped over the doormat. She smiled as she realised he was very drunk.

'Kate? Where are you?'

He was making his way through to the kitchen where she was sitting going through the files that Annie had given her and nursing a glass of Pinot. She pushed all the papers together quickly, knowing how he felt when he saw the pictures of the victims, before he stumbled into the kitchen.

She stood up quickly to help steady him. 'You're pissed!'

Patrick laughed heartily, saying, 'No shit, Sherlock! Nothing gets past you, does it?'

Kate couldn't help laughing with him. In fairness to Patrick, he was a happy drunk, and he could make her smile.

'How did the lunch go? I'm assuming by the look of you a good time was had by all?'

Patrick slumped down into a kitchen chair and said loudly, 'Fucking brilliant, lady. We got a bit squiffy, I suppose, and we talked for a long time. He is a decent bloke, Kate. But I think him and me have a good rapport somehow. It's like I've always known him, you know what I mean?'

Kate nodded but didn't speak.

'He reminds me of me. I know that sounds mental, but there's so much we have in common. After a few wines were imbibed he was very talkative, and I think that Bella might need to watch her Ps and Qs in the future. He confided in me, Kate, really *confided*.'

Kate could hear the amazement in his voice.

'It was like he had been waiting for someone to talk to all his life, and he chose me.' Patrick's voice was strangled with tears.

Kate felt a sudden rush of compassion for the man she had been with for so many years. She realised that he had been lonely for a child, much lonelier than she had ever understood.

He looked at her with those dark blue eyes that still fascinated her, and he said honestly, 'I feel so blessed, Kate, it's like I can finally look to the future again. After Mandy I would think, at times, what's all this for? But now I have a reason to graft, because I want those kids to have the best that life can offer. Even though my boy ain't doing too badly, of course. A corporate lawyer, eh? Who would have thought that!' He began to laugh.

'I think it's wonderful, Pat. Especially as you two seem to have a lot in common. I really do understand how important this is to you.'

He got up out of his seat and kissed her, a wet fume-laden kiss, and still she responded as always to him.

'Let's go to bed and have a good hard shag, lady!'

She laughed with him; it had been a while since she had heard that particular expression! Deep inside she was really pleased to know how much he still wanted her because recently she'd been worried that he might need her that little bit less now. She knew she had better swallow down these petty feelings of jealousy and sort her head out. Because this young man and his family were there for the duration and she needed to get used to that fact pronto.

As they ran up the stairs like teenagers, giggling and laughing, Kate decided that, if this was the upshot, then his finding his family could only be a good thing.

Later, as Patrick snored, she pulled on her dressing gown and went back down to the kitchen, where she poured herself a fresh glass of wine and opened up the files that Annie Carr had given her. This case was getting more and more complex, especially as whoever was responsible for these deaths was savvy enough to move about undetected.

He used lots of bleach and made sure that there was nothing to link him to these girls whatsoever. The small amount of DNA they had managed to find was anonymous.

Kate suspected that this one would be solved by accident – as so many cases were, if the police were completely honest. She yawned slightly, lit a cigarette and once more pored over the witness statements. It occurred to her that Annie Carr was probably doing exactly the same thing.

Chapter Fifty-three

Christine Murray looked down at the sleeping man beside her and felt the sting of tears. Was it the drink talking? He had been very drunk when he had arrived at her home. He'd told her he loved her and that, no matter what he'd said before, he was going to leave his wife, because he couldn't live without her. He had sounded so genuine, but she was afraid to get her hopes up as she knew that he adored his children and she was under no illusions that Bella would use them to keep him in any way she could.

Joseph didn't say much about his wife. But reading between the lines, he was clearly deeply unhappy in his marriage. He had to be – otherwise they would not be having an affair in the first place. He was quite staid in his own way and he had believed in the sanctity of marriage. Nevertheless they had carried on with this liaison, and now it was everything to her. Hearing his words tonight had really made her happy, even if it was only the drink talking. She truly believed that he loved her. She gently shook him awake, and he opened his eyes blearily, unsure exactly where he was.

She saw him look at the bedside clock, and then he groaned, 'Oh fuck! Bella will have my balls on a plate!' Then he leapt out of the bed and started to get dressed as quickly as possible.

Christine sat up in the bed and watched him.

Bending over and kissing her deeply on the lips, Joseph said quietly, 'I'm sorry, darling, but I have to go. I'll ring you tomorrow.'

She smiled sadly and watched as he crept from her bedroom, but she didn't let the tears flow until she heard his car start up and pull away. She knew then that it really had been the drink talking – nothing more. Her secret hope, though, was that his new-found father might give him a different take on the world. Patrick Kelly was well known in Grantley, and his reputation always preceded him.

She put Amy Winehouse on her iPhone and, lying back against the pillows, she wondered what her life would be if Joseph finally put his money where his mouth was. She just had to hold on to his love for her. Because it was all she had left to believe in.

Chapter Fifty-four

Jennifer and Claire Andrews were more amazed than their parents were when Annie Carr and DC Karim turned up at their council house at eight in the morning. No one was expecting them, and that is exactly what Annie depended on. Peter Andrews was so angry he looked fit to explode. His wife, Wendy, on the other hand, looked terrified, and Annie Carr concentrated on her as they walked into the council house. They didn't have enough for a warrant, so they were relying on a combination of shock tactics – and self-preservation. It never ceased to amaze her how cowardly bullies were once confronted. And she knew within three minutes that Peter Andrews was a bully of Olympian standards. Taken unawares, he was off his game, though, and that worked in her favour.

'You got a fucking warrant to come in my house?'

Annie looked at him innocently, before saying, 'Why – do we need one?'

Peter Andrews looked thrown for a few seconds, before bellowing at his wife, 'What the fuck did you let them in for?'

Wendy Andrews just stood there in her nightdress, her lips trembling with obvious fear.

Annie held her hand up and said loudly, 'We are here about the murders of two of your daughters' former school friends. It's a routine enquiry. Now, climb down off your high horse.'

Peter Andrews seemed to suddenly deflate, and Annie saw him for the jumped-up little bully he was. He wasn't a big man, nor was he particularly muscular, but what gave him the edge was the rage that seemed to be boiling inside him.

'Why don't you go and put some trousers on while my colleague and I have a chat with your daughters, Mr Andrews?'

He hesitated for a few moments, before bellowing, 'Make some tea, Wendy.' When he left the small sitting room, it was as if the air had suddenly thinned.

Wendy Andrews, a short heavyset woman, smiled tremulously, before saying quietly, 'Can I get you two a tea or a coffee?' Now she had permission to talk, she looked less frightened.

'That would be lovely.' Annie smiled at her and then turned to the two girls.

The sisters were sitting on the sofa with terrified expressions on their faces. Annie and DC Karim sat on two small dining-room chairs.

Annie fiddled with her notebook, making a big show of getting it out of her bag, and she looked down on her notes for a few seconds before saying gravely, 'We heard about the pictures. I'm assuming that's all over with now?'

Both girls dropped their eyes to concentrate on their hands that were clasped in front of them on their laps. Without their make-up and hair done they looked very young and very innocent. Jennifer, the older girl, was already well developed, and Annie could imagine what she would look like dressed up to the nines. The younger girl was clearly her sister, but in a watered-down way. She would never have the older girl's beauty, and beautiful Jennifer undoubtedly was. But then all teenagers were – it was the skin, she supposed, still so tight and crease free.

The room was shabby and the furniture had seen better days, and there was an underlying smell of cannabis that was sickening in its sweetness. The girls were both in pyjamas that had been washed until they were no more than faded rags. It depressed Annie, the way some children had to live, and the way some women allowed themselves to be intimidated to the point of no return. She had discovered that the police had been called on more than one occasion to these premises because of domestic abuse.

Sighing heavily, she said kindly, 'So, girls, when was the last time you saw either Kylie or Destiny?'

Jennifer shrugged, and Annie guessed she was the mouthpiece for the pair of them.

'Was it recently?' DC Karim's voice was gentle.

The younger girl looked at him, as if just realising he was there. They were both nervous, and that was to be expected, but Annie and Ali were both certain there was an underlying reason. And both guessed it was to do with the man whose voice was now shrieking out of the kitchen as he berated his wife. He came into the room and, as small as he was, he seemed to fill the space up.

He looked fit to burst as he shouted at the girls. 'You'd better not have been up to any fucking tricks again. Because I warn you, I'll take you apart this time!' He looked at the two police officers, then continued shouting, 'The fucking shame these two caused, sending bloody naked texts to strange men!'

The girls slumped further into the sofa, as if willing it to swallow them whole.

Annie stood up and said reasonably, 'We are not here about that. As I told you before, we are investigating the murders of Kylie Barlow and Destiny Wallace.'

'Like I told my wife, whoever did that was probably one of the perverts these two were involved with. If I get my fucking hands on them, they won't be fishing for young girls any more. I'd rip their fucking cocks off—'

DC Karim stood up and, taking the man's arm gently, he said, 'I agree with you, sir. Now let my colleague talk to the girls in here and you can fill me in on what you know out in the kitchen, OK?'

The man hesitated, as if battling with himself, before saying angrily, 'They aren't allowed phones any more, and no computer access either. I made sure of that much anyway!'

He went from the room, and Annie shut the door behind him. Then, resuming her seat, she said seriously, 'So, with no phones or computers, how do you access

Facebook et cetera, girls? Only I saw you both left messages on Kylie and Destiny's memorial pages.'

It was a shot in the dark, and it worked.

Jennifer Andrews looked at her, saying desperately, 'He can't know, he can't know. He will kill us!'

Annie smiled at the two girls reassuringly, saying, 'He won't hear it from me, I promise, but I need to know.'

Jennifer looked at her younger sister and said honestly, 'Cybercafé in town, the one by the precinct.'

'Who were the men you were messaging? Did you ever meet up with them in real life?'

Jennifer took a deep breath before answering, 'It wasn't as bad as it sounds. We sent a few pics in our underwear, that was all – nothing like what my dad's making out. The men were from a dating site we went on. It was just a bit of fun that got out of hand.'

Annie looked at these two children, because that is exactly what they were, and wondered what was happening to the next generation. 'How about you, Claire, are you still doing it?'

The girl shook her head slowly, and Annie Carr saw just how young she was.

'You do realise that those pics, as you call them, are there for ever now? Once you post something like that to other people, they have that image *for ever*. Probably shared it with their friends. Were any of the men local?'

They both shrugged. 'We don't know, but we weren't the only ones doing it. We were just the ones who got caught.'

Annie frowned. 'Were Kylie or Destiny doing it?'

Claire laughed nervously. 'Not the goody-two-shoes bitches, they were the ones who grassed us up, even though they were doing way more than us.' It was said with bitterness.

Annie said to her curiously, 'What do you mean by that?'

Claire shrugged. 'They all wear virginity rings and act like they are better than everyone else.'

'What do you mean, virginity rings?'

Jennifer rolled her eyes in frustration then, as if there was an idiot in the room and it certainly wasn't her. 'They are like promise rings. You know, when you promise to get engaged at some point? Well, these are rings that mean you will stay a virgin till your wedding day.'

Judging by the resentment in the girl's voice, Annie guessed her days of wearing a virginity ring were long gone. She was glad once more not to be a teenage girl in this climate. It was a minefield of rights and wrongs, and she didn't have a clue. Christ Himself knew how these kids were supposed to decide what was best for them.

'So what do these rings look like?' Annie was racking her brain to remember what jewellery the girls were wearing at the time of death.

Jennifer shrugged. 'Like signet rings, I guess. They get them from Argos.'

That was something that Annie was not expecting. She had heard about promise rings, of course. But this put a different complexion on things. Why had no one mentioned it? The parents or the teachers? She could hear DC Karim's voice coming from the kitchen and guessed he was once more talking Peter Andrews down.

Jennifer smiled suddenly. 'It's a load of old crap really, because they might not have gone all the way with the boys but they have done everything else!'

Claire Andrews nodded in agreement then. 'Especially that Kylie!'

The girls exchanged a look before Jennifer said seriously, 'Honestly, I just don't get how they can all wear their virginity rings but still be up for anything else. And they had the fucking cheek to look down on us and spread all that shit about me and Claire! The boys use them as well, and they can't even see the fucking irony of it. They slaughtered *us* because of the sexting thing, and they were actually giving blow jobs to boys and acting like they were better than us.'

Annie knew that she had to tread warily now, as the girls were finally opening up to her and she didn't want them to feel they couldn't speak to her about what was actually going on.

'Kylie, you say?' She looked at Claire as she spoke.

The girl nodded. 'We went on a dating site for a laugh. I mean, we sent a few pictures but we never actually met anyone. But Kylie and her mates were quite happy to go off with the boys at lunchtimes and suck them off, and they still acted like they were fucking better than everyone else. Might not have had actual sex but they were still doing stuff, you know?'

Annie nodded once more, as she wondered again

what the hell constituted being a teenager in the current climate. She was so glad she didn't have a daughter, or a son for that matter.

'Who were the boys they went off with?'

Jennifer rolled her eyes in annoyance. 'Hello! The boys in their circle – they are treated like gods because they're classed as the dog's gonads. They are the popular kids! When they called us in about the pictures, we told Miss Betterway all about their little club. Ask her. The school destroyed us over a couple of photos, but Kylie and her crowd were just as bad. But they got away with it because their parents don't know and the school didn't want its precious reputation to suffer. But everyone else knows what happened. And everyone knew that nothing was going to be done to them because they have always had a swerve. My dad might be a mug, but he knew as well as we did that we were no more than an example. The teachers were aware that there was much more going on, but the kids concerned are off limits.'

Annie Carr could hear the hurt and the humiliation in the girl's voice and knew that she was speaking the truth. 'I would appreciate it if you would explain the situation, so I can understand it properly. I am open to listening to whatever you have to tell me. I promise it won't go any further.'

The two girls exchanged glances with each other again.

Jennifer Andrews turned back to Annie and looked her in the eye, saying, 'I'm sorry Kylie and Destiny are dead but they made our lives hell. We are well out of it now at our new place. If you want my advice, you talk to Miss Betterway – she knew we were scapegoats. She was gutted, but she couldn't do anything for us. She knew what my dad was like. They all did.' She sighed heavily, before saying quietly, 'Oh, and ask her about the bracelets, and what the colours mean.'

Annie was prevented from asking what she was talking about because Peter Andrews came back into the room then, and he looked fit to be tied. For a few seconds Annie Carr could find it in her heart to pity him. It sounded like the bully had been bullied, and he had no redress. And if the girls were telling the truth, they had been served up to a man who wouldn't have fought for his daughters because he already thought the worst of them anyway. It was an interesting scenario, and Annie was determined to get to the truth. She saw the fear in the girls' eyes at the appearance of their father, and she felt a wave of pity for them too. Only now she wondered if this angry little man had been bulldozed into his daughters' downfall without even realising it.

Whatever these girls had done, she had a feeling that they were telling her the truth. She stood up and smiled at Peter Andrews as she said genuinely, 'Thank you so much for your time.'

Peter Andrews was nonplussed at her pleasant attitude. He was distrustful because he believed that his daughters, his own flesh and blood, were capable of anything. But then, after what he had already found out about them, who could blame him?

Annie left the Andrews' home with a heavy heart,

and a reminder that sometimes things really weren't as simple as you might think. Now she needed to find out if what the Andrews girls had said had any credence. Because it sounded like there was a rotten underbelly with these kids that she had to get to the bottom of. And she would.

Chapter Fifty-five

Kate wondered how she was going to deal with Bella, who had phoned her, acting like they were bosom buddies. It had been a really strange one, given that Bella had made it evident that she saw her as someone to be tolerated at best. Bella had what Patrick wanted: his grandchildren. And she would milk that for all it was worth. But thanks to Patrick's revelations the other night Kate also knew now that Joseph wasn't exactly husband of the year. Even though she hated herself for thinking it, she could understand why he might be playing away from home.

There was something decidedly strange about Bella – and not just because she had treated Kate with such scorn, as if she meant nothing – but because she seemed to genuinely think that Kate would be overjoyed to hear from her and be best friends all of a sudden. She guessed that Bella knew that she was an also-ran, and that was why she was now looking for allies. It was a shame, because Kate would have been her biggest champion if only the woman had even tried to be amenable. But Bella was the type of woman who didn't like other women – and who didn't know how to interact with them.

As Patrick had said so succinctly, Bella had a cuntish way with her, and that really did sum her up, crude as it was. But knowing about Joseph's mistress, Kate couldn't help wondering if that was the reason Bella was suddenly acting like they were bosom buddies.

Kate sighed with annoyance. She didn't want to get involved with anybody's private lives, especially when the people involved were not her flesh and blood. She would be civil and do what was required of her, for Patrick's sake, but there was no way she would ever really warm to Bella.

Kate had thought long and hard about it, and she actually admired Ruby O'Loughlin because she could have come to Patrick and been given the earth. It was a measure of the woman's decency that she had kept it to herself for so many years. Kate knew that Patrick both appreciated and resented her for keeping his son away from him. Kate understood that Ruby was fundamentally a good woman and she had done what she had thought was right at the time. Now Ruby was gone, and Joseph was here, and Patrick had another chance at having a family. She couldn't begrudge him that, because she knew how much it meant to him, but she wasn't going to like Bella O'Loughlin for anyone.

She was glad when Annie buzzed the gates. She was interested in what was happening with the case, and she smiled widely as she opened the front door. Annie was not just her friend but a contemporary – they were wired the same way. She knew that Annie looked on her as a mentor, and she relished that because, in reality, she had no one with her daughter and grandchildren living on the other side of the world. In truth, even though she loved Lizzy, it suited them both not to be living in each other's pockets. For so long, she had never really had anything other than Patrick and her job and, now that Patrick had Joseph and his new family, she felt a loneliness that she hadn't felt since her ex-husband, Dan, had abandoned her and his daughter.

Annie Carr swept into the house and they hugged, and as Kate walked her through to the kitchen she felt an urge to cry.

Chapter Fifty-six

Margaret Dole was in her element. She was pulling all the CCTV that was near or around the cybercafés in Grantley. Finally, with this new bit of information from the Andrews girls, she felt they might have something tangible that could be accessed and, hopefully, give them a clue of some description.

She was a believer in the new world order. Unlike the idiots who argued that people had a right to personal privacy, she believed that if you weren't doing anything wrong why the fuck would you care if you were caught on a camera? It was a bone of contention with a lot of her colleagues, but she didn't deviate from her stance. Why would she? She believed that in the war against crime – whatever the crime might be – the police should be able to use whatever means necessary to solve that crime. It wasn't a popular opinion, but she didn't really care.

Margaret knew far more about the dangers of cyber-space than them, and it was more important now than it had ever been. The internet was actually the greatest tool they had at their disposal. She often wondered if the people she worked with, who were so against what they saw as a breach of their privacy, were actually more worried about being seen doing something they weren't supposed to. She had been very vocal about that in the past and it had not made her a hit among her colleagues. The majority of the naysayers were older, and not as computer literate as they should be. But, as she told herself, she wasn't trying to win any popularity contests, and she was good at what she did, so she didn't give a toss what anyone thought of her.

She was happy doing her job, especially at times like this when she felt that she might be on to something. Annie Carr had given her the low-down on the cyber-cafés, and she was confident that if there was anything to find, then find it she would.

Chapter Fifty-seven

'Bella, are you all right?'

Bella turned to face her husband, and smiled gently as she said quietly, 'Of course I am, darling. I was watching the children in the garden. They seem so happy, don't you think?'

Joseph nodded, but he could sense that there had been a subtle shifting in the dynamic of their relationship and Bella was as aware of it as he was; they were both creeping around each other. Joseph wondered how he was going to resolve this dilemma because, as much as he hated what he wanted to do, he was determined to do it. Since he had confided in Patrick Kelly about his situation, he had felt a great need to put an end to this situation he was living in. It was as if, now he had said it out loud, he *had* to do something about it. Bella was his wife, and he loved her in a way – she was the mother of his children, after all. But he wasn't in love with her; that was a completely different thing altogether. Bella just wanted the trappings of love: the husband, the children, the house, and the car. She only cared about what her life looked like, how other people saw her life. She really didn't see that, in the grand scheme of things, they actually didn't have a life at all.

When she looked into his eyes, he could see the animosity that was never far from the surface these days. He knew that she was waiting for him to make the first move. He had hoped that she would be the one to do it, coward that he was; he wanted her to be the one to initiate the break. If she did it, she would at least keep her pride, and he wanted to feel less guilty.

He looked away and concentrated on the children playing in the garden; they were close, and they were good kids. Bella went to his side and tucked her arm into his: she must have felt him recoil but she didn't react at all.

Instead she said chirpily, 'How lucky are we, Joseph? We have two beautiful children and a wonderful life. So many people would give anything to be us.'

He didn't answer her.

After a few minutes she said smugly, 'Oh, by the way, I spoke to Kate today and arranged to go there tomorrow for lunch, as Joey and Amanda both have an inset day. The children are thrilled, they love the pool. I thought we could tell them the truth, darling, tonight. They really like Patrick and Kate. I mean, she's not really family, but Patrick is their grandfather, and I think they have a right to know, don't you?'

Joseph was taken aback; he wasn't expecting this attempt at normality between them.

Bella went to the fridge and took out a bottle of wine. As she poured two glasses, she continued, 'I do think that tonight is the night. After all, it's all about family, isn't it?' Her words were loaded, almost like a threat. She offered the glass of wine to him and, as she tapped his glass in a toast, she said, 'You're very quiet tonight, Joseph. Are you OK?'

He didn't answer her.

Eventually she put her finger under his chin and gently pulled his face around to hers. 'Oh, darling, I do worry about you. But remember, I will always be here beside you. Nothing could ever tear us apart, because I wouldn't allow it.'

Joseph looked into her eyes and knew that she had just delivered a real threat. And, even though she was tiny and she was smiling at him, Bella had finally thrown down the gauntlet.

He pulled away from her and, shrugging nonchalantly, he said with a pretence at calmness, 'Bella, life is a strange thing. No one knows what the future holds.'

Bella opened her eyes wide, as if she had been given a big surprise. Then, laughing, she said gaily, 'Oh, but I do, darling. I know exactly what my future holds.'

Joseph looked into her smug face and it hit him that she was more than aware of Christine Murray. He should have guessed that much. Bella was a lot of things but stupid wasn't one of them.

'For example, I know that you will never leave me, Joseph, because I won't let you. Can you imagine what would happen to the children if you did? How *hurt* they would be?' She smiled again but her words were loaded as she sipped her wine. 'I'd better get the children in for their supper. Would you set the table, darling?'

Joseph looked at his wife's retreating form with distaste. There was no going back from this for either of them. But he felt uneasy. There was a part of him that was wary of this little wife of his. She almost frightened him.

Chapter Fifty-eight

Annie Carr was tired: she had drunk a bit too much at Kate's last night and she was feeling the effects. She was so thirsty she could drink a river dry, and her head was thumping with a well-earned migraine. As she sipped a coffee and swallowed a couple of paracetamol, she wondered why she ever drank. She didn't bother to answer her own question, because she knew that she would be drinking again, and sooner rather than later. It was her escape from reality, and she actually treasured that at times like this.

She sat in her car for a while, watching the kids going into school. She couldn't really comprehend people who wanted to teach, because most of the pupils seemingly had no more interest in learning than they had in getting a hole in their vacuous heads. She saw the result of bad parenting on an almost daily basis, so she didn't envy these people their jobs. She was probably being unfair, but she didn't really care. All she saw was a swarm of kids who looked like clones of one another – the older girls especially. They all had make-up on, they all looked like they were bored and they seemed to run in packs.

She remembered how awful it had been as a teenager; she had never been part of the in-crowd. In fact, she had not really wanted to be, but she remembered how lonely it could be if you were an outsider. She had been lucky really – she had been determined to better herself, and she had known from an early age that she could only do that with an education of some kind. But she also remembered being overlooked because she wasn't pretty enough to warrant invitations to parties, and how much it hurt when everyone talked loudly about their wonderful weekends, knowing that it was for her benefit. Not being a part of a peer group, because she just wasn't good enough, had been a hard lesson. But she had learned her lesson well, and put her head down and got on with her schoolwork. Still, it had burned, even though she had convinced herself that she didn't really care about being accepted by girls she looked down on because they were completely devoid of anything that interested her. But, in truth, being pushed out by them so blatantly had hurt, and she hated that she had felt so unworthy because of their treatment. She had been devastated at the time, and all these years later she still felt the pain of not being accepted, the feeling that she wasn't good enough.

Girls could be real bitches, and she didn't envy those who happened to be teenagers in this day and age. There was so much pressure on them – to look a certain way, to dress a certain way. It had been the same when she was young to a degree, but then there hadn't been reality TV and the internet. She couldn't imagine the pressure this generation was under to conform, to fit in. As Kate had pointed out, everything they did was documented on social media. Yet the murdered girls seemed to be whiter than white, online at least. Now she was interested to know what they did offline.

She waited a while until her headache eased before she got out of the car and walked into the school. She still felt like shit, and decided she would wait till she was offered coffee before she pissed all over Miss Betterway's firework.

Chapter Fifty-nine

Bella and the children arrived on time, all smiles. Kate was waiting patiently, a fixed one on her face. But then, when young Amanda ran into her arms and hugged her, she felt a surge of affection. This was a nice child.

'Mummy said you are our step-granny, and Patrick is our granddad, our real granddad.' Kate felt the child's excitement at the news; she was almost jumping up and down with it. 'I knew you were special because I felt it when I first saw you.'

Kate looked down into the child's beautiful and trusting face and said happily, 'Well, I think you are pretty special too!'

Joey Junior just smiled and Kate could see that he was embarrassed about the whole situation, and her heart went out to him. He was looking at his mother with trepidation, and Kate realised that he worried about her and how she would react. She liked him even more for that. For now she kept her thoughts to herself and welcomed Bella like a long-lost relative, to keep the peace, even while there was a big part of her that really wanted to smack Patrick one for leaving her to deal with this alone.

He was coming 'later on', after his business meeting. She knew that meant after lunch, and she was stuck with Bella till then.

She ushered them into the house and nailed a wide smile on her face as she said to Bella, 'How lovely to see you all.'

Oh, she would make Patrick pay for his 'girlie lunch' remarks; in fact, she decided that she would have his balls on a plate. She rolled her eyes subtly at Bev, who knew exactly how she was feeling. She wondered what she would do without her, if truth be told. She was a true member of this household now, and Kate thanked God for her every day.

Chapter Sixty

Helene Betterway was not pleased to see Annie Carr, and she made the mistake of showing her annoyance. Never a good idea when Annie had a hangover – or when she felt that people were not being entirely honest with her.

'Really, Detective Carr, I do think you should have made an appointment. I am a very busy woman, you know.'

This was said with such self-importance that it took Annie a few moments to calm herself down sufficiently to answer her in a reasonably civil manner. Annie smiled snarkily at her and she could feel the woman's uneasiness as she looked across her desk at what she now saw was her antagonist.

As if offended, Annie said, 'Really? I'm here about two of your pupils who have been brutally murdered. I would have thought that took priority over a few fucking detentions?'

She knew she had the teacher on the hop, and she enjoyed it. She decided that she didn't like this woman, and she certainly didn't like that she had kept her in the dark about things that might have made a difference.

'Well, of course, Detective Carr, it's just that I thought you would have let me know you were coming in . . .'

Annie had her on the back foot now, and she used it to her advantage, saying pleasantly, 'Why don't you get me a nice coffee, and then you can tell me about the girls' bracelets, and which colour is for a blow job?'

Annie Carr had done her homework and she was extremely satisfied to see the woman's face blanch. She sat in a chair and waited patiently for Miss Betterway to enlighten her. Which she knew she would, because she had been caught out, and in the worst possible way.

Annie knew she could be a prize bitch when the moment called for it, and she was glad about it. Because sometimes it paid off. And today was one of those days.

Chapter Sixty-one

Patrick Kelly was waiting patiently for Danny Foster, and he was looking forward to seeing him. He was well aware that the lad was struggling with the arrival of Joseph on the scene, which is why he had arranged this meeting. He wanted to assure Danny Boy that he was still a valued member of this organisation. Patrick recognised the benefit of making the people who worked for you feel that they were part of the team – especially someone like Danny Foster, who he had basically given autonomy over his businesses. He trusted the boy, even though he liked to keep his hand in and he made sure he knew everything that went on. This was beneficial for Danny too because, at the end of the day, Patrick was the real name, and that was what was important in their world. In his time, he had come back from being shot, he had fucked over the Russians, and he had made sure that the people he dealt with would never forget that easily. Patrick knew the worth of the Kelly name and he had no intention of taking his eye off the ball any time soon. And, with the appearance of Joseph and his family, he had an additional excuse that he had to make sure that, if anything should happen to him, everyone in his orbit was well taken care of.

Patrick was definitely feeling the urge to indulge in a bit of skulduggery. It was in his DNA. And he couldn't resist the easy money. Kate might not like it, but she knew that as well as he did. Plus she wasn't a Filth any more – not really – and she wasn't as touchy as she had been in the past. They had a silent understanding – at least that was how he saw it anyway. She was retired, and he felt he was well within his rights to follow his natural inclinations because of that. He just didn't rub her nose in it. In any case, if Kate ever got wind of his antics, he could always blame Danny Foster.

Danny came into the office, all aftershave and bespoke suit, and Patrick had to admit he looked what he was – a very successful businessman. He had watched Patrick and he had learned well. He wore an expensive, under-stated watch – no other jewellery – and he had a receipt for everything he owned, just in case it ever came on top. It was what Patrick liked about him; he was a quick learner, and he understood the psychology of being a real Face. It wasn't about showing off the wealth, it was about being one step ahead of the Old Bill, and never giving them anything to use against you.

'All right, Danny Boy?'

Danny smiled happily and sat down opposite his boss. Patrick was proud of him – he had made a good choice when he had brought him on board. It said something for the strength of their bond that they'd survived Patrick's fleeting relationship with Danny's sister, Eve, before he went back to Kate. But that was all in the past. Danny had been the son he had never had, and he had treated him as such. Patrick had to remember that, even though Joseph was now in his life.

'I'm good, and I know you are still celebrating.'

Patrick knew that there was nothing snidey in Danny's words.

'It was a strange old experience, but I feel I have been given another chance, mate. It was hard when I lost my Renée, and then Mandy. Well, it wasn't the best of times, as you can imagine. But who would have thought I had a son out there I knew nothing about?'

Danny Foster knew the story off by heart now and he was genuinely pleased for Patrick Kelly. If anyone deserved a break, it was him. Danny had been sceptical at first, but now he accepted this change in his fortune.

He laughed, saying, 'I hope I ain't left a few Fosters about!'

They both laughed heartily at his joke. But Patrick despaired inside, because if ever a man needed to be grounded with a family it was Danny Foster.

'So, what's the latest?'

Danny smiled that easy smile he had, and then he said seriously, 'You ain't going to believe this, Pat, but Nick Christmas and his brother, Noel, want to buy the clubs.'

He watched carefully for Patrick's reaction as his words sank in. Pat had had more than a few run-ins with the Christmas brothers over the years, but they had never fallen out entirely, and that was because Nick

Christmas recognised that they were well out of their depth where Patrick Kelly was concerned. Patrick had a glint in his eye as he said, 'I think you need to sort this, Danny Boy. They obviously think that it's your call and, in reality, it is. You are my number one. What do *you* think?'

Danny grinned; he was pleased at Patrick's answer. 'I think they are taking the fucking piss! They will come in here and try to buy everything on the fucking never-never. On the fucking weekly, so to speak!'

Patrick laughed with him, because he knew the truth of that. 'Fucking muppets! Honestly, how they are still walking the streets, I don't know.' Then he said grimly, 'Unless, of course, there is someone else in the mix, who would rather stay in the background.'

Danny Foster smiled knowingly. 'My thoughts entirely, Pat, and, after a bit of a nose about, I heard from a very good source that they were apparently breaking bread with Eddie Thomas.'

Patrick rolled his eyes in annoyance. 'Please tell me this is a fucking joke?'

Danny grinned and said, 'I kid you not. It's fucking amateur hour. I was embarrassed for them, Pat.'

'So you'll sort it?' Patrick Kelly wasn't smiling any more.

That was not lost on Danny Foster, and it reminded him of just who he was dealing with. He shrugged, saying quietly, 'Already in hand, Pat. The Christmas brothers were given a serious reminder of who they were dealing with two days ago. We won't be hearing from any of them again, believe me. Fucking cheek – like we would swallow those cunts! And Eddie Thomas, it seems, has gone on an extended holiday to the Caribbean. I'm assuming that's because we know his address in Marbella.'

Patrick laughed then; that was exactly how he would have dealt with the situation. He knew that he could always depend on Danny to do the right thing. He had taught the boy well, and he thought the world of him.

'I despair at times, Danny! What the fuck would make those fucking idiots think they were in with even a minute chance?'

Danny Foster shrugged and, opening his arms wide, he said honestly, 'I couldn't even fucking begin to get the reasoning. I heard through the grapevine that Eddie Thomas was earning a serious wedge from drugs. But that doesn't mean he has made any friends, does it? He is tolerated, no more. Between the lot of them they couldn't locate each other's cocks in a urinal. Complete fucking wankers.'

Patrick laughed loudly. 'That's what I like to hear. Fucking cheek of them, thinking they have the nous to take what's mine! Fucking outrageous. So, what else is occurring?'

'Not a lot really – the usual. Everything is going well, I make sure of that.'

Patrick nodded his agreement. 'You are a good lad, Danny, and I want you to meet my boy, Joseph. I think you two will get on well. Plus I have a feeling we could put him to use somewhere.'

Danny Foster smiled his acquiescence; he had expected

this at some point. He couldn't imagine how this newcomer was going to fit into their world but he wisely thought that was something Pat would have to work out for himself. 'Whenever you want, Patrick, I'm looking forward to it.'

Patrick lit a cigar and, after he had puffed on it for a few moments, he said intently, 'I think he needs to see the score for himself, you know?'

'Of course. But do you think he will understand?'

Patrick looked at the man he trusted with his businesses and his life, and he said frankly, 'I don't know. But I want to start off as I mean to go on, and that means being honest from day one.'

Danny Foster respected what Patrick was saying, and he said as much. 'I get that, but remember, Pat, not everyone is like us.'

Patrick Kelly didn't answer for a few moments, and then he said, 'I am what I am, and I ain't apologising for it. He needs to understand the world I inhabit.'

Danny Foster admired the sentiment. 'Of course, no one wants to live a lie, Pat.'

Patrick puffed on his very expensive cigar before he answered. 'Not to family anyway.'

Chapter Sixty-two

Miss Betterway had reacted like a scalded cat, and Annie was enjoying her discomfort. She had really taken a dislike to this woman who had deliberately kept information from her and her colleagues. This was such a serious matter. She couldn't for the life of her comprehend why this woman didn't think to tell them everything that she knew about the girls in question. This sex-bracelet thing was something that should have been out there from the off. Annie had looked it up and she had been shocked at what it entailed. She was going to haul this fucker over the coals if she didn't hear what she wanted from her.

She made a point of waiting for the coffees to arrive before she said another word. She was enjoying Miss Betterway's discomfort. This woman needed a wake-up call, and she was going to get it. When the coffee arrived, Annie sipped it gratefully, despite herself; she needed it more than she had realised. She might be hung-over, but she was also angry that she had to come back here and re-interview a woman who should have been completely honest with her from the start.

She said as much. 'Well, Miss Betterway, it seems you were not entirely truthful with me about the girls in your charge. Not exactly wilting virgins by all accounts! I hear that there is some kind of sex club in this school that you knew about and didn't think to tell *me* about. Really not a good idea! Bracelets the girls wear that tell the boys what they are willing to do sexually! I understand that they are up for anything except the actual sex act. They have a ring to wear, apparently – a ring that says they won't have actual sex until they are married! How wonderful is that? I am not a happy bunny, Miss Betterway, as I am sure you have gathered. In fact, I am fucking fit to be tied. I mean, imagine if the press got hold of something like this? It would be a disaster for everyone concerned, don't you think?'

She sat back in her seat and watched the different expressions that crossed Miss Betterway's face. She knew she was at panic stations, and she was pleased about that. This woman was a disgrace to the teaching profession, because she had allowed this kind of behaviour to go on without any kind of redress. Annie Carr was working out what charges she could bring against her. Because she would not let this go without some kind of retribution. It was wrong on every level.

'I know that this sounds bad, but you have to understand—'

Annie Carr interrupted her quickly. 'Oh please, Miss Betterway, are you seriously trying to justify this kind of behaviour? I can't for the life of me understand what the fuck you were thinking of.'

Miss Betterway looked terrified, and so she should, as far as Annie Carr was concerned. This was a woman who had deliberately overlooked sexual behaviour in underage children. It was unbelievable.

'I think you should be ashamed of your actions. You are supposed to be looking after these kids.'

Helene Betterway was on the verge of tears as she said in a whisper, 'You really don't get it, do you?'

Annie Carr shook her head, saying sarcastically, 'No actually, I don't. Why don't you enlighten me?'

Helene Betterway looked at Annie and then, leaning across her desk, she said angrily, 'I reported it to the headmaster! I was as disgusted as you are. But he was the one who wanted it hushed up. You can't imagine what something like this can cause, and he decided that we should keep it in house. My hands were tied. I tried my best to make sure the girls were aware of the danger they were putting themselves in. But it's a different world now. We have to jump through hoops to keep everything on track. Most of my time is taken up with paperwork! We sorted it as best we could. As Mr Yalding pointed out, why would we destroy these girls' lives before they even had a chance to live? We corrected it as best we could. But you can't sit there and judge me – I did what I thought was best for my girls. Everything is now on record, written down for the rest of these kids' lives! Do you know that? Everything they do is documented even at their young ages. So I agreed with Mr Yalding that they didn't know how their stupid actions would impact on them, how this would follow them wherever they went.

'Can you imagine how difficult it is nowadays to be a teacher? It's a nightmare of paperwork and treading carefully in case you get sued. I was just trying to protect them, I was trying to make sure that this foolishness wouldn't follow them for all of their lives. I know that they couldn't understand the seriousness of what they were doing – they were only copying the behaviour they saw on TV or on the internet. They didn't know that everything is documented and filed away for future reference. That their behaviour could ruin a university or job application. That it could come back and destroy them in years to come. I didn't think that teenage idiocy should ruin the rest of their lives. I try and look out for my pupils.'

She stopped and gulped at her coffee. Annie didn't say a word – she had a feeling there was more to come.

Miss Betterway smiled then, a defeated smile. 'The boys were all protected, of course. They weren't classed as the perpetrators, they were without stain. It was only the girls who were actually wearing the bracelets who would have been vilified. That is why I did what I did. I protected them as best I could.'

Annie Carr was still taking in everything that she had heard. Against her better judgement she actually saw exactly what Miss Betterway was saying. This woman was genuinely only trying to give these girls a chance in life. Annie knew how hard it was for a female in the workplace, even in these days of so-called equality. That was all well and good, but it was still a different ball game in the real world. She was genuinely gobsmacked, but she was not going to let this go until she knew everything there was to know.

'I understand what you are saying, but what about the Andrews girls? If you wanted to protect all your girls' reputations, why did you let that come out? They were the ones being exploited by grown men! Yes, they went on a dating site, and sent some inappropriate pictures, but they didn't actually ever meet anyone in real life. But it seems Kylie and Destiny blew the whistle on them, even though *they* were actively involved in sexual relations with boys in this school. So it looks to me like you used the poor Andrews girls as scapegoats so you could cover up the widespread underage sexual activity among your other girls. I have to say, I find that absolutely outrageous. I get that you want to protect your pupils, but surely not at the expense of two young girls who were as vulnerable as all the others? More vulnerable in many ways, as they are living in a household where the father is a known bully and the mother is terrified to open her mouth. She won't be protecting her daughters any time soon. So explain that to me?' Miss Betterway closed her eyes in obvious distress, and Annie wondered what else this school was hiding from the world. 'Well? I'm waiting, Miss Betterway.'

'The Andrews girls left because of the father. He wasn't exactly easy to deal with. It was his decision to remove the girls from the school. I offered to help them, but he wasn't having any of it.'

Annie Carr looked into Miss Betterway's eyes as she said innocently, 'Did you discuss the other girls' behaviour with their parents? Only I have a feeling that you didn't. I think you didn't ever tell the other girls' parents about the little sex ring that was going on here. I also have a feeling that it's not on any of said girls' school records. Would I be right about that?'

Helene Betterway had the grace to look away. She couldn't look Annie in the eye, she was so ashamed of her actions. 'It was not how you think. Mr Andrews had already found out what had happened with his daughters. Our hands were tied. He came here like the Antichrist, he wanted to know everything. I don't know exactly how he found out, but it certainly didn't come from us.'

Annie believed her. She had a feeling that this woman was actually trying to do what she thought was right for the girls under her wing.

'Do you think that Kylie or one of the others involved was capable of letting him know what his daughters were up to?'

Miss Betterway sighed heavily, and Annie could see that the woman was defeated. 'Honestly? I don't know for sure. But believe me when I say I wouldn't put anything past any of them. Not any more.'

Annie could hear the sadness in the woman's voice, and she could see the abject fear at what she had been involved with and what it had caused in the long run.

Annie Carr didn't think for a second that Helene Betterway had done anything for any other reason than to help her pupils. But it seemed that her good deeds were coming back to bite her on her proverbial arse.

'You do realise that I need you to come down to the station and make a statement? I am heart-sorry for you, because I believe that you did what you thought was right. But this is serious – you and Mr Yalding deliberately kept information from us that could be relevant to our investigation. We don't know how far this so-called sex network had spread, or exactly how many people were involved. We will want all the boys' names too. I can assure you that they won't be walking away this time.'

Miss Betterway nodded, as if she had expected this. 'Actually, I did make up a file for my own purposes. I wanted to know exactly who was involved – the boys as well as the girls. It galled me that they were ignored because they weren't seen as doing anything wrong. The girls were wearing these bracelets that told the lads what they were willing to do. The boys walked away because they weren't deemed to be at fault.'

Miss Betterway stood up. Taking a bunch of keys from her handbag, she went to one of the filing cabinets and she proceeded to open up the top drawer. She looked at Annie Carr as she said sadly, 'I kept the bracelets. I put them in here for safety. I don't know why. Mr Yalding told me to destroy them, but I had a feeling that one day they might be needed.'

Annie stood up and looked into the drawer at the

tangle of nylon bracelets. They looked so innocent, so innocuous.

'The blue was for oral sex. It broke my heart, as most of the girls wore that colour. I thought they were friendship bracelets at first. Jennifer Andrews told me that when the other girls exposed her and her sister over the sexting incident. And do you know the strange thing, Detective Carr?'

Annie didn't say anything, she knew she didn't need to. Miss Betterway was now open to telling everything she knew to anyone who asked. It was as if she had been waiting for the chance, which she probably had.

'The strange thing is I still think there is something rotten in this school. Jennifer and Claire were victims of their own father. A man who was only too ready to believe that his daughters were whores, as he so succinctly put it. But I always felt that we should have told the other parents about their children's behaviour. The boys' parents as well as the girls'. It's why I kept all these bracelets, and also the notes I made when the girls spoke to me. I kept everything. Now I think it's time I gave it to you. I wanted to protect the girls because I knew they were the ones who would eventually suffer for their actions.

'It's supposed to be a different world now, but it isn't. In many ways it is a worse world where girls are concerned. They see themselves as sexual from such a young age. Mothers dress their little girls up in the latest fashions from babies. I loathe the expression "mini-me"! The girls are bombarded with images of females who are dressed provocatively. They watch TV, where they see only pretend people with pretend lives. The saddest day of my life as a teacher was when a twelve-year-old girl told me that she wanted to be a lap dancer like her big sister. So you take all this, and you tell these girls' parents what their beautiful daughters are capable of, because I couldn't do it. I didn't want to ruin everything for everyone concerned. But I ask you, how do you tell Kylie's and Destiny's families about all this now?'

Annie didn't answer. She couldn't deny there were going to be some difficult conversations ahead.

Miss Betterway shook her head sadly. 'See, it's a different ball game, isn't it, when you have to bring all this into the open? Now you know why I tried to shield these girls as best I could. My job is probably finished now, but I don't care what happens to me. I'm relieved it's all finally out in the open, because now *you* can deal with it. All I wanted to do was protect my girls from the consequences of their actions. But I failed. They aren't bad girls, Detective Carr, they are a product of their environment. They are just children who have no idea about the real world.'

Annie saw the exercise books underneath the bracelets and wondered what the hell she would have to read about these young women. She went to her handbag and took out her mobile phone to ring the station. Everything here needed to be taken in as evidence. She also needed to talk to Mr Yalding and bring him in to be interviewed.

Miss Betterway sat back at her desk, and Annie Carr saw that while the woman looked completely defeated she also appeared relieved to have finally unloaded her worries on to someone else. She was a decent person who had done what she thought was best. Annie Carr respected her for that much at least.

Chapter Sixty-three

Annie Carr might not be the flavour of the month at the station, but her discovery of the school's secrets was at least a feather in her cap in the process of the investigation. The bugbear was that the victims were now seen as not as innocent as they had been assumed to be, which put a completely different spin on things. Their main worry was the media getting wind of it; this would be absolute gold to the gutter press and it would also colour the investigation in more ways than one. But Annie Carr might have potentially discovered new evidence that could help crack the case. At least she hoped so, because she really didn't want to taint these girls' reputations unless she had to. As she read through Miss Betterway's notes she found herself wondering if these girls' parents had any idea at all of what their children were getting up to when they left their homes.

Destiny Wallace was apparently capable of giving three blow jobs in one lunchtime! And from what she had read, the girl was actually proud about that! She also wore the pink bracelet that meant she was open to having oral sex performed on her. It was the same with

Kylie Barlow. These were girls whose parents thought they were good girls, who they believed were intelligent enough to look after themselves.

She now understood Miss Betterway's reluctance to bring this out into the open. Although she had been wrong to listen to Mr Yalding, Annie could see why she had allowed herself to be talked round. No one would want to deal with this if they didn't have to. She believed that fundamentally Miss Betterway had tried to protect these girls who were too young to really understand what they were doing and how it might affect them in the future. Miss Betterway had far more experience with young girls than Annie – everybody had more experience with young girls than she did! But one thing Annie was sure of: somehow this new information had a bearing on what had happened to Kylie and Destiny and she intended to put the hard word on Mr Yalding about concealing vital information when she brought him in.

As Annie waited for Andrea Connor and her parents to arrive at the police station, she wondered for the hundredth time how she was going to approach this without World War Three starting. But it had to be done, and she was the one who would have to do it.

She wasn't relishing telling Kylie Barlow's or Destiny Wallace's parents what she had found out either. And there were still plenty more girls and boys to be interviewed. It was a fucking minefield all right, and she had uncovered it.

Chapter Sixty-four

'The Christmas brothers! You are joking.'

Kate's laughter was loud and genuine, and Patrick laughed with her.

'I know! Fucking liberty takers or what, eh?'

Kate wiped her eyes as Patrick poured them more wine.

'That has really cheered me up, Pat. Eddie Thomas! I remember him when he was a young aspiring Face. He was about as frightening as a power cut. He used to wear these fucking combat trousers, and he never changed them. They would have followed him up the road if he had taken them off. We used to call him the Weekend Warrior. Oh, listen to us! I used to hate sitting there listening to the older police talking about old cases. Used to really piss me off, and now I'm one of them!'

They laughed together again, but not as heartily as before.

Patrick sighed and, taking a gulp of his wine, he said quietly, 'When I was on my way up I used to love hearing all the stories from the old Moustache Petes. I think that's the difference with our lives, Kate. I couldn't hear enough of their stories, you know? The old London fuckers, who had their creds, were who I wanted to be, I suppose. You know, listening to them talking about the old days, about Faces long gone, about scams and robberies – I was in my fucking element! But I remember one old lag saying to me on the snide, "Remember, son, the only real villains are the ones who never get caught, and did no time." I took that on board and all!'

Kate laughed again. 'I gathered that – you always covered your arse!'

Patrick grabbed her hand and said saucily, 'Covered yours a few times and all, girl.'

Kate looked at the man she had spent the best years of her life with, and she said honestly, 'And I thank God for that every day of my life.'

They were quiet for a few moments, just enjoying each other's company.

Then Patrick said seriously, 'You are OK with all this, aren't you, Kate?'

She smiled and nodded her assent. 'I must admit that Bella is not exactly my kind of person, but then I don't think she is anyone's kind of person. But Joseph and the kids are wonderful. Especially Amanda – she's a little sweetie-pie. I think Joey Junior needs time to take everything on board, but he seems a sensible lad. All we can do is wait and see, mate. From what you have said about this Christine, I think there is going to be aggravation ahead. But you know, it's his life and he has to live it how he sees fit, I suppose. It isn't really any of our business, is it?'

Patrick Kelly shrugged and, opening his eyes wide, he said honestly, 'I can't say much, can I? Considering the relationship I had with his mother. I was a married man at the time. You know the strange thing, Kate? I had actually forgotten about it. I was so ashamed because of Renée and her being ill.'

Kate smiled sadly. If she was truthful, now she'd had time to process her feelings, she realised it gave her a hint of satisfaction that he'd been unfaithful to the Sainted Renée, even though she knew that what she felt was unfair. But it had always been so hard competing with a woman who had died and who Patrick had still been in love with. She wasn't proud of her reaction, but she was honest with herself – even if she would never voice her thoughts to the man before her.

'We are all guilty of it, Pat. None of us want to admit things we did – especially when it wasn't our finest hour, so to speak!'

Patrick smiled in agreement. 'That's why I love you, Kate. You know the score, girl. But I do worry that if Joseph goes on the trot, what that Bella is capable of. I think she's a few paving slabs short of a patio! She has a strange way about her, as you know.'

Kate didn't say anything, but she had asked Annie to have a look at Bella and her family history, and she was waiting to hear what Annie had to say before she committed herself. But, like Patrick, she had a feeling that there was something off where Bella was concerned. She had been in the game a long time, and her instincts were rarely wrong. Knowing about this Christine, she couldn't help but wonder if that was what was wrong with the woman. It was obvious she adored her husband and, if she thought he was playing away, it could explain the woman's behaviour. After being married to Dan, Kate could find it in her heart to sympathise with Bella's predicament in a way. There was nothing worse than knowing that you were suddenly an also-ran. That the man you loved was sleeping with someone else. She knew better than anybody how much *that* hurt. She should do, it had happened to her on more than one occasion.

'I think, Patrick, the best thing we can do is leave them to sort it themselves. We haven't known them that long.'

Patrick nodded, but Kate knew that his natural instinct would be to try to look out for his new-found son. Still, it was a bit too late for that, as far as she was concerned.

'We don't want to do or say something that could muddy the water in the future. We have to take a big step back, Pat.'

He knew she was right, but he hated seeing his son in such a quandary.

Kate could read his mind, and she sighed as she said, 'A couple of weeks ago you didn't even know he existed. Remember that, Patrick Kelly. This is all new to *everyone*.'

'I just want to be there for him, Kate. I know it's fucking mad but I was never there for him when he was growing up, was I?'

'Well, how could you be, Pat? Stop this now. Just be

glad you have this opportunity and enjoy it! But take my advice: *keep out* of his private life, because that's when things can get a bit messy. Be there, listen. Otherwise, unless he asks you to interfere, you keep as far away from it as possible.'

Kate watched Patrick struggle to keep his feelings under wraps. She knew him better than he would ever know himself. But she felt he had to take a step back, because this was all too raw and too new for him to be able to see what would be for the best in the long run.

Patrick filled their glasses and said lightly, 'I know you are right, darling. Anyway, let's relax and enjoy the night, eh?'

Kate smiled sadly. 'I love you, Kelly!'

Patrick grinned happily and, raising his glass, he said seriously, 'I love you too, Kate. But do me a favour, will you? Let me know what Annie comes up with about Bella's background. Only she's a bit of a mystery, ain't she?'

Kate laughed despite herself. He had sussed her out all right, and the thought made her feel good.

'I know you so well, Kate Burrows. Never forget that!'

Kate raised her glass to him as she said wryly, 'As if, you fucker!'

Chapter Sixty-five

Andrea Connor looked terrified and Annie couldn't blame her. The girl was dressed in ripped jeans, a crop top, and her hair looked like it had been professionally styled. Even her nails were perfect. Annie could see that they were false nails – they were decorated with fake diamonds. Her mother had the exact same pattern, so she assumed they had had them done together. The 'mini-me' syndrome that she was hearing about so much was in evidence here.

Juliet Connor looked worried as they settled down in the interview room, and Annie was sorry for her. The surroundings would press home the seriousness of what she wanted to find out. The woman seemed to realise that this time was completely different; until now every contact they'd had had been in friendly surroundings, where they had all felt comfortable. She saw Juliet Connor looking around the room, at the scratched table, the scuffed walls and the video equipment, with a frown.

Andrea Connor was sitting opposite her with her beautifully made-up eyes, and Annie could see the fear in them. She wondered if Miss Betterway had warned her.

She wouldn't put it past her. Miss Betterway did genuinely care about her charges.

Annie smiled at them in a friendly manner. 'Now, Andrea, something has come to our attention, and I need you to tell me the truth, OK?'

Annie opened a file and took out the bracelets that she had removed from Miss Betterway's office. Andrea nodded, but her face had lost all of its colour – even her thick foundation couldn't mask that fact. She looked ill. Her eyes were glued to the bracelets that Annie had put on to the desk in a neat pile. Annie Carr felt a huge sorrow for this little girl because, at the end of the day, that is exactly what she was – a little girl. All of the make-up, nails and clothes in the world couldn't change that fact.

'Andrea, I am not going to tape any of this unless I think what you tell me warrants being documented. You know that this is serious, and if I could avoid doing this I would. I know it is not going to be easy for you, sweetheart, especially with your mum listening. But you need to be truthful with me, OK? Do you understand what I am saying?'

Andrea Connor was still staring at her. The fear was almost palpable now. But she had been offered an alternative appropriate adult and she had refused, insisting on her mother accompanying her. Annie could tell she was regretting that decision big time.

Juliet Connor was watching her child and she had picked up on the atmosphere in the room. 'What's going on?'

Annie Carr looked at her and said honestly, 'Look,

Mrs Connor, I need to talk to Andrea because we have found out something that could be a serious line of enquiry. I understand why Andrea might have been loath to mention this when we talked before, but Miss Betterway has had to bring this out into the open. She wanted to keep this quiet – as I am sure you will – but that is not an option given the circumstances, I am afraid.' She picked up the bracelets and laid them on the desk in front of Andrea, saying softly, 'I need you to tell me, Andrea, whose idea this was, and who you, Kylie and Destiny were involved with. I also need you to tell me the names of everyone who took part and what you know about them.'

Juliet Connor looked at her daughter. When she saw her silent tears, she immediately put her arm around her daughter's shoulders, saying quietly, 'Come on, darling, be brave.'

Andrea swept the bracelets off the desk, angrily shouting at Annie, 'You fucking bitch! You rotten fucking bitch!'

Then all hell broke loose.

Chapter Sixty-six

DC Karim was sitting beside Annie Carr in the interview room, and they were both drinking tea and wondering what else this investigation was going to throw at them. They were waiting patiently for Andrea Connor and her mother to compose themselves enough to carry on the interview. Annie had made sure that DC Karim didn't come into the room until the girl's mother had understood exactly what the score was. As much as Annie felt sorry for them both, she was also losing patience with them.

'Are you telling me this is true?' Juliet Connor was obviously unable to believe what she had heard about her young daughter, and Annie could only sympathise with her. But she knew that she had to let this woman see what had actually gone on with her daughter and the other girls. Two of whom were dead.

Andrea Connor, now that it was all out in the open, was suddenly incensed that her secrets had been revealed. Far from being cowed by it, she was acting like *she* was the victim. It was a sight to see, because it showed Annie what she was really dealing with, and she was not impressed.

'Oh, do you know what, Mum? You make me sick! Well, I can tell you this. It was just a bit of fun.'

She was sitting there with her arms across her chest and her heavily made-up face was screwed up in anger and, Annie Carr knew, shame. Andrea had been caught out and she wasn't going down without a fight. She was determined to justify her behaviour, and that was the worst thing.

Juliet Connor, her own make-up streaming now with her tears, was looking at her daughter as if she had never seen her before in her life. 'A bit of fun? You did all these things with those boys and it was just a bit of *fun*?'

Andrea ran her hands through her thick hair and laughed. 'Really? Like *yes*, Mum!'

Annie Carr stood up, forcing Andrea to sit back into her chair to look up at her. 'I understand you all went on YouTube to see how a blow job is done? "Best blow job" sites, if I understand properly. You also were graded by the boys you were involved with? I understand you and Kylie and Destiny in particular were deemed quite popular.' Annie hated what she was doing, but she knew that she had to get to this girl while she was angry enough to talk honestly.

Andrea laughed nastily. 'Oh, why don't you just fuck off! It was private, nothing to do with anyone else!'

Annie sat back down and sipped her tea, then she looked at Andrea Connor and she bellowed, 'Can you hear yourself? You are just fourteen years old and you are performing sex acts on a daily basis for boys who couldn't give a shit about you. You have lost two friends, brutally murdered, and you don't even have the savvy to think that your behaviour might have had a bearing on all that. You are talking to me, a police officer, and your mother as if we are pieces of *shit* beneath your shoes. Well, do you know what, lady? I think it's time you *really* grew up, and started to act like the adult you obviously think you are.'

Juliet Connor sagged in her chair beside her daughter; she looked like a woman defeated and Annie guessed that she had been.

Andrea answered sarcastically, 'Oh, like I want to be like *you*! I liked it, we were just having fun. I don't know what the big fucking drama is.'

Juliet Connor stood up and, swinging her arm back, she slapped her daughter across the face with all her might, knocking her off her chair. As Andrea sprawled across the floor, her mother said brokenly, 'Your father will be distraught when he hears about this. Do you have *any* idea at all what you have *done*, Andrea? Do you even understand the seriousness of your actions, you *stupid* fucking girl?'

Annie helped the girl up from the floor, and she sat her back in her seat gently. Like DC Karim she wasn't going to mention the fact that Juliet Connor had assaulted her daughter. If truth be told, Annie Carr wished it had happened long before all this. If ever a girl needed a firm hand, it was Andrea Connor, along with her cohorts.

Andrea was sobbing now and, when she turned to her mother, Annie wasn't surprised when Juliet Connor physically pushed her daughter away from her. 'You, *lady*, had better spill the beans and tell the police what they need to know. Kylie and Destiny are *dead*. This is the least that you can do.'

Andrea Connor looked at her mother beseechingly. Deep down she had known for a while that it had all gone too far, and now she had been found out. There would be no going back from here. If only she had listened to Maria Walters; she had warned Andrea and she had tried to help her. But she hadn't listened, because she had been so desperate to be one of the popular girls. She had loved being important and admired. Maria Walters had refused to take part and they had all treated her like she had the plague. Andrea had loved that, if she was honest, because Maria Walters was the prettiest and the cleverest of their year.

Maria had been pushed out of their circle and she had been treated like a leper by everyone. The most annoying thing was that Maria Walters had not given a shit – she had laughed about it. Told them all that they would regret everything, and she had been right. Andrea Connor saw her whole world crashing down around her ears and she remembered her dad talking to her about hindsight, explaining to her about respecting yourself and how important that was in this day and age. She was more terrified of her father knowing what she had done than anything else. He held her in such high esteem, and she adored him. Once he knew about this, he would never look at her in the same way.

Juliet Connor had stopped crying. She was looking at

her baby girl, her daughter, with disgust. 'Whatever you know, Andrea, you had better start talking.'

Andrea Connor had no choice: she had to tell everyone what she knew, even though she was convinced that it couldn't have anything to do with what had happened to Kylie and Destiny. How could it?

Annie Carr turned on the tape and let Andrea Connor tell them everything.

Chapter Sixty-seven

Janet Cross was small for her age and she dreamt of the days when she would finally catch up with her peers. She loved clothes, music and make-up, in that order. As she walked through Grantley town centre she was smiling happily. She had been babysitting for her mum's work-mate for weeks and she was finally in a position to buy herself some decent clothes and shoes. Even better was that her mum's friend Sue let her order stuff online that she could pay off to her on the weekly, which meant she could really go to town! So of course she had. She liked Sue Border – she understood what it was like to be young and desperate to fit in. Janet liked the kids too – they were really good, and she had become fond of them. All in all, she was pleased with how her life was going.

She was determined that, by the time she went back to school after the summer holidays, she would be a new person. Better dressed and much more interesting; she was hoping that she might find herself one of the popu-lar girls. It was terrible what had happened to Kylie Barlow and Destiny Wallace, but they could be such bitches; it was hard to forget the nasty things they had said to her and the other girls at times. She remembered how they had humiliated her on more than one occasion, bullying her on a daily basis and, even though it was really awful what had happened to them, she couldn't help but feel a certain satisfaction knowing she would never have to face them again. They had been grade-A bitches, and they had made her life a misery and laughed about it to her face.

She lived in the council flats, and they never let her forget that. They had tormented her, and she had been unable to fight back. Not just because she was so small for her age but also because she didn't have the words needed to answer them. It was only much later that she would find a suitable retort but, by then, it was too late. Sue was good in that way, because she was teaching her how to stick up for herself, and that alone had given her a confidence that she had never experienced before. She was coming out of her shell and becoming a different person, and it was all thanks to Sue and her advice. Because she didn't have the latest phone or the latest clothes, she had been open to the ridicule of girls like Kylie and Destiny and that bitch Andrea! But now she was gradually making sure that she was going to get these things. And, if she kept on working, she would have everything that was necessary to be accepted. That was Janet's dream anyway.

Miss Betterway had been so good to her, and she was doing very well at school. She was reading everything that Miss Betterway told her to. And in her spare time she was also going online and teaching herself how to apply make-up from the tutorials on YouTube, and that had been an education in itself. Who knew how many tricks there were to change the way you looked? She was pleased with her new outfit, and she now understood what Sue meant when she said that clothes were important; she had explained how clothes had to be what suited you and your body shape, *not* just what was fashionable. Thanks to Sue she felt like a million dollars. On top of all that, she had also gone up a cup size so she actually had breasts that were noticeable – finally! Sue had explained that some girls were late bloomers, and that wasn't a bad thing. Oh, she loved Sue. She had been so good to her, and she had helped her in so many ways.

Janet was so lost in her own thoughts she forgot that she was meant to avoid her usual shortcut to Sue's through the woods and go the long way round. It was a beautiful summer evening and she had blow-dried her hair and carefully applied her make-up. Sue was absolutely right. She said that if you felt good about yourself then everyone else would follow suit and she knew that she looked lovely. She had seen that people from school, especially the boys, had begun to notice her, take an interest in her. It was heady stuff, because it was what she had wanted more than anything else. Sue had explained that anyone could change if they really wanted to, and she had done just that! With Sue's help she had reinvented herself!

She was smiling happily to herself when she felt the blow to the back of her head. As she dropped to her knees instinct told her that she had to try to get back up on her feet, to keep her wits about her. She tried to pull herself up off the ground. She didn't want her new clothes getting dirty. She had worked so hard for them.

The second blow caught her off guard, and she collapsed on to the ground. Her head was bleeding profusely and she could feel the warmth of her blood as it trickled down her neck.

Chapter Sixty-eight

Elaine Cross was watching the ten o'clock news when she took the call from her workmate Sue Border, asking her what had happened to Janet and if she was on her way.

Elaine told her that Janet had left over two hours earlier, and she should have been there ages ago. She looked out of her front-room window and saw that the night was starting to draw in, and she felt a sudden fear as she realised that her daughter was not where she was supposed to be.

She put the phone down and immediately rang her daughter's new phone, the phone she was so proud of. But it went straight to voicemail.

She rang Sue back and, as the panic rose inside her, she started to cry.

It was Sue Border who phoned the police because, as she said, poor Elaine was in no fit state.

Chapter Sixty-nine

Sue Border was feeling guiltier by the hour. She had not known that Janet was coming to her earlier than arranged, but she should have guessed, because the girl treasured their time together. She loved asking her about make-up and boys and life in general, and Sue had relished acting the big sister instead of the mum. Janet had been fabulous with the kids, and they had cherished her being with them. And it had been a bit of company for Sue too. Janet had been interested in what she had to say and had looked up to her, and she had really enjoyed that as much as she enjoyed Janet's company. Because she was good company, bless her little heart.

She had really liked Janet, and now it seemed she was missing. And given what had been happening recently, that did not augur well.

Elaine Cross was terrified at what might have befallen her only child, and she chain-smoked and said little unless spoken to directly. She had aged ten years in a few hours, and that fact wasn't lost on the police or Sue Border.

As Annie Carr walked into the tiny front room of

Elaine Cross's council flat she was already convinced that this was abduction. The knowledge depressed her, because there was nothing she could have done to prevent it. The girl had been taken in broad daylight, and that was a daring act. Whoever was responsible had a lot of front, and wasn't afraid of being seen, which told her that she was dealing with somebody who believed they were beyond capture. That in itself was a frightening thought. She knew they were clever, as there had been literally no evidence left on the two girls' bodies. The clean-up operation was really first class, as the pathologist had so succinctly put it. Whoever this was had planned everything, down to the last detail, and Annie couldn't help wondering if he had some kind of agenda, if these girls were being taken in some kind of significant order.

The spanner in the works was that this young girl, Janet Cross, was not a part of the other girls' social circle. In fact, she was completely different to the two previous victims. She was small for her age and, from the pictures spattered about the room, she actually looked like what she was: a young thirteen-year-old girl. Somehow this just didn't fit the profile, as the other girls were a particular type. Even though Annie didn't like to think that, she knew that it was true.

Miss Betterway had given her a list of the girls involved in the 'sex circle', as she insisted on calling it, and Janet's name was nowhere to be seen. Annie was aware that she might have to rethink her earlier thoughts about the girls and the bracelets. The other alternative was, of course, that this girl's disappearance had nothing to do with Kylie or Destiny – which would mean that there was not one but two fucking nutbags out there.

She hoped she was wrong and that Janet Cross was just being a typical teenager, and gone on the trot for the night with some friends and would turn up later on, shamefaced and frightened of the scare she had given everybody, especially her mum. But it was seeming less and less likely, and they all knew it.

Elaine Cross looked like she was going to collapse at any second, and Annie wished she could tell the woman something she wanted to hear, but there were no words. Instead she sat down with her and sensitively tried to find out what she could about Janet, her friends and her life, all the time waiting and praying that someone somewhere was going to find her alive and well.

She didn't hold out much hope.

Chapter Seventy

Bella O'Loughlin was watching her husband closely. She could tell that he had something on his mind, and she had a feeling she knew what that something was. She could feel the anger rising up inside her and she swallowed it down. When he got up and poured out two glasses of red wine she took hers with a half-smile, determined that she would not give him any cause to doubt her devotion. She had to tread warily, because knowing he'd been to see his paramour tonight was very hard for her. She could feel him slipping further and further away from her with each passing day.

She had always believed that his children would keep him by her side, but now she wasn't so sure. Divorce was commonplace nowadays and, even though she had never believed her husband would have contemplated it, she was beginning to doubt whether she could hold on to him. This Christine was a fucking home-wrecking bitch, and it seemed to Bella that her husband had been mesmerised by her and sex. Oh, she knew that this was all about sex – it was all it could be. She honestly wondered what all the fuss was about, as she had never really understood the attraction. She had found the whole thing distasteful, but she had never let on about that. Well, not at first anyway. But they had two children and a wonderful life, so why the hell should she have to endure the nightly assaults on her body? It wasn't something that she could ever find enjoyable. And surely, after so long, she shouldn't be expected to do something she hated? And hate it she did, every sweaty messy second of it. She shuddered inwardly at the thought. And, as always, she blamed Joseph for wanting what she felt was something that should be put away like last year's clothes.

It was everywhere she looked – in the papers, on the television, on the internet! It was like everyone was suddenly obsessed with the sex act, and she despaired of how humanity was evolving. Young girls walking about like trollops, their whole body on show for everyone to see. Like the girls in Grantley who had been murdered. If they weren't asking for it, she didn't know who was! Suddenly she realised that her husband was talking to her, and she looked at him in confusion.

'Are you OK, Bella? I've been talking to you for five minutes and you were miles away.'

She could hear the consternation in his voice, and she took deep breaths to calm herself down. This was happening more and more lately; she lost time, immersed in her own head, and it was something that she had to hide from everyone around her. She knew that young Joey had already started to worry about her, and that should have sounded her warning bells. The last thing that had set her off had been that creature Kate asking her why Joseph Junior could be called Joey and yet Amanda had to be called Amanda. Oh, she had not forgotten or forgiven that! Sneaky two-faced fucking bitch that she was. Now she was swearing in her head again, and she knew that her husband was trying to talk to her and she had to concentrate.

She looked at Joseph and tried to smile. 'I'm sorry, darling, I was miles away. You know what it's like when you are thinking!'

She gulped at her wine and tried to look interested in what her husband was saying to her, but it was difficult. She was alert enough now to realise that he was worried about her, and she knew that she had to allay his fears, so she said seriously, 'I have a lot on my mind, darling. You know me, I take things too much to heart.' She saw Joseph close those beautiful blue eyes of his and she carried on talking to drown out the voice in her head. 'It's Kate. I worry that she doesn't like me. I try with her, darling, but you know she isn't really my kind of woman. A bit too full of herself. And the hold she has over Patrick . . .'

Joseph had been hearing this since day one and, against his better judgement, he snapped at his wife suddenly. 'Oh, for fuck's sake, Bella, she has been with him for years. She has made us very welcome, and I'm sorry to say this but it's *you* who is the problem, not Kate.'

Joseph had drunk a bit too much this evening. It had been a wrench to leave Christine after their usual Friday-night tryst and come back to this unhappy home, and he wasn't in the mood for games. Because that is exactly what they were, *games*. Mind games! The same games that his wife had been playing ever since he had first clapped eyes on her. He only wished he had realised earlier that his mother had been right, and if he had listened to her he might not be in the position he was in now. But he had not wanted to hear anything against Bella, because he had seen her as this tiny girl who needed looking after. Well, he now knew that she could more than look after herself.

His mother had questioned why she had nothing to do with her parents, and why she seemed to have no female friends. But he had not listened to her, because he had been so enamoured of Bella and her complete reliance on him. How had he not seen that she was sucking the life from him? His mother had understood that from the start; she had worked out how to deal with Bella, and that had stood her in good stead, because she had kowtowed to his wife and told her everything she needed to hear. He had done the same, but he had not understood that until recently. She was not just odd – Bella was seriously damaged, and he was beginning to realise the truth of that.

Suddenly he felt guilty and asked, 'Are you OK, Bella?' He was frightened for her in his own way.

Bella sipped at her wine once more and, grinning, she said nastily, 'Oh, I might have known you would take darling *Kate's* part! I mean, since the moment you met her you have been in her corner.'

Joseph looked at his wife as if he had never really seen her before. That she had taken against Kate from the beginning had been obvious to everyone, including Kate. Her 'girlie lunch' had fooled no one, and it seemed that even Bella had recognised that much. He sighed in annoyance, all sympathy lost.

'Listen to yourself, Bella. Kate is a nice woman, and she and my father have been together for years. Do you honestly think that you could ever come between them? And, more to the fucking point, why would you want to? It's not like she has ever done anything except be nice to you, is it? But you, being you, have to ruin it all, not just for yourself but for everyone else concerned.'

He knew that he should shut up, but he couldn't stop himself. For the first time in years he was saying what he really thought, and that felt good. In the past, his mother had been the mediator, the voice of reason. But that was by the by now. He was sick of Bella, and he was sick of listening to her and her negativity. He was looking for an out. He wanted to be with Christine, and even his children weren't enough to keep him in this sham of a marriage.

Bella felt like she had been slapped. Oh, if only this man would see what was in front of his face for once! 'You think that Kate has welcomed me? *Us*? I can't believe you are that naïve, Joseph! She doesn't want us interfering in her life with Patrick Kelly! Think about it: she and her daughter were in the running to inherit everything, until you arrived. Do you think that she will be happy about that?'

Joseph shook his head in disbelief at her words, and she knew deep inside that she should stop talking, but she couldn't. She had to explain to him the truth of their situation, because it was obvious that he couldn't see what was really going on.

'Can you hear what you are saying, Bella? Can you really justify what you are accusing Kate of?'

Bella could hear the sadness and the disgust in her husband's voice, and she wondered at a man who was that stupid. This was his inheritance he was talking about, and Kate and her daughter had no right to any of it. *Her* children should be the beneficiaries, not some stranger who lived on the other side of the world!

'Oh, Joseph, I knew you were weak! I have always had to be the strong one in this relationship. You are like your mother – you let people take advantage of you. I think you should be asking yourself whether you want your kids to get what is rightfully theirs.'

Joseph looked at his wife and saw what he should have seen years before. He didn't love her, and he never had. He had been in love with the woman he had thought she was, not the real Bella. She wasn't just toxic – she was also vicious and underhanded.

'But, Bella, my mother could have told me who my father was at any time, and I believe she did what she thought was for the best. He had a life, a family, and I respect her for understanding that. Surely you, as a mother, have to see that too?'

Bella laughed, unable to believe the stupidity of the man she had deigned to marry. 'You would know all about that, wouldn't you, Joseph? Know about fucking around while married? I mean, what about you and

Christine, eh? You are your mother's son all right. Oh God, you both disgust me. I loathed good old Ruby, whore that she was. The only good thing to come out of it was she finally fucked someone who could do something for us all!'

Somewhere in her mind Bella knew that she had gone too far, but she was incapable of stopping herself. It was as if she was deliberately trying to cause a massive upset and that was exactly what she wanted. She had wanted her husband to choose her and her children over his slut. Now she had a terrible feeling that he wouldn't.

'Do you know what, Bella? If I needed a reason to walk away from you, this was it. That you could ever talk to me about my mum like that! She was worth a hundred of you, lady. She didn't like you, Bella, she warned me about you, and she was right. You are a bitter pill, and I know now that I should have listened to her. She saw through you like a pane of glass, and she tried to warn me. But I was so taken in with your "poor little me" act. Well, not any more. You can hang as you grow – another one of Mum's sayings. It means, basically, *fuck you*, Bella.'

They looked at each other for long moments and, as Bella started to cry, he pushed her away from him with all the strength he could muster, sending her sprawling on to the floor. He knew that, whatever happened, he was finished with her. He only hoped she knew it too.

Chapter Seventy-one

Kate was in the kitchen looking through all the files that Annie had given her; she had been saddened when Annie had called to tell her that yet another girl had gone missing, especially as this girl was the complete antithesis of the other two. She wasn't involved in this so-called sex circle, and she looked like what she was – a little girl. Annie had emailed her the girl's picture and the relevant information. The fact that she had also gone missing without trace was the only common denominator.

It seemed that Margaret Dole had traced the girl on CCTV to the outskirts of the woods, which again was in keeping with the Kylie Barlow case. It was where she had been found, and it was also in the frame for Destiny Wallace's disappearance. It was obvious that the woods were this man's hunting ground, but it appeared that no one ever saw him. Or, if they did, they didn't really take much notice of him. She looked over the pictures of the dead girls and wondered at a person who could inflict that kind of damage without care. She sighed and took a sip of her coffee and wished she was drinking something stronger, because these pictures were not for the faint-hearted.

According to the pathologist, the blades used varied in size and make; there was something almost random about that. There would also be copious amounts of blood, which meant that wherever this was taking place would look like an abattoir. It was also secluded enough for the girls' screams to go unheard, because anyone could see that these girls would have been screaming in fear and pain.

There was no evidence that they had ever been gagged, so whoever was responsible either knew the girls very well, or he had subdued them somehow. Yet there were no drugs in their systems, although Kate knew that no one could rule out a new type of Rohypnol or other drug. There was a new fucking drug on the streets every few months, and it wasn't until someone died that the police would be made aware of them. That was the sad fact for a lot of the new so-called designer drugs. And with so many people now making their own recipes, and the increase in 'legal highs', more people were dying than ever before. It was a different world all right, and it was getting more dangerous every week, if truth be told.

She could hear the muted sound of the football on the TV and envied Patrick his ability to lose himself in sport. She sat back and rubbed her eyes and wondered how Annie was getting on. If only the girl were found unharmed; but, like Annie, she didn't hold out much hope.

She looked down at the lists she had made and screwed her eyes up in concentration as she tried to link any two things together, find something that might give her an insight into where these girls might have been, or how they had come to the notice of the man who had murdered them. If that one link could be established, it would give them something to go on. Because the main factor, as she saw it, was finding out how this man had decided that these particular girls were his victims.

The sex circle, she felt, might be muddying the waters, but it couldn't be ruled out completely. Annie seemed to think that it was something to do with the murders, along with the way the girls had dressed and acted. It seemed they were not what anyone had thought they were, but Kate knew from experience that that wasn't unusual where teenage girls were concerned. In fact, it seemed to be a part of their DNA to lie and be evasive to get what they wanted. It was hard, looking like a woman and being treated like a child.

She looked through the statements once more, and hoped that something might jump out at her. Annie was liable to turn up later, but she had asked her to ring first although she'd said that she didn't care what time it was. She had told Bev to make up one of the spare rooms so Annie could stay the night if she needed to. It would give them extra time to talk everything through. Like Annie Carr, Kate wanted whoever was responsible for this carnage caught, and the sooner that was done the better for all concerned.

When the gate buzzed, she assumed it was Annie, and she was surprised to hear Pat's son's voice on the intercom. She buzzed him in and called out to Patrick that Joseph had arrived. It was nearly midnight. She guessed that this wasn't going to be good news.

She knew she was right when she heard him slam his car door loudly.

As Joseph walked into the house, he looked at them both standing in the large hallway and he said sadly, 'I didn't know where else to go, I hope you don't mind.'

Patrick smiled easily, saying, 'Kate's working in the kitchen, mate, and, believe me, you do not want to see what she has out there. Come through to the lounge and I'll pour you a drink, OK?'

Kate watched them go and wondered what had happened to bring Joseph O'Loughlin to their home so late at night. She had a feeling it was something to do with Bella. She would know what had happened soon enough; they didn't need her with them, and it would probably be easier for them to talk without her there. But she was intrigued, there was no getting away from that fact. As she went back into the kitchen she poured herself a glass of Chablis and sipped it thoughtfully while she looked over the files and statements once more.

Chapter Seventy-two

'I'm not seeing anything, Annie. I've scanned every-thing, even Janet's Facebook page which, I have to say, is sad for this day and age. Hardly any friends, and noth-ing even remotely interesting posted. This was a nice little girl who acted a lot younger than her age for a change and who didn't seem to court any kind of con-troversy. Even her YouTube history is all cats and animals. Unless, like the others, she was sensible enough to not use her own device for any incriminating stuff! But I don't think so somehow. I think this is a girl who was just growing up. Have you seen the photos Sue Bor-der showed us of her though? They were taken when she was giving her make-up lessons apparently.'

Annie looked at the pictures with wonderment, because they were completely different to the picture her mother had given to the police. She looked at little Janet Cross in her make-up and with her hair all done, and she saw immediately that *this* was what had attracted the man who was murdering these poor unfortunates.

She looked like a different person. Picking up the pictures, she walked through the police station to show the rest of the team. Because this wasn't the little girl they thought they were looking for. This was a different girl altogether.

Chapter Seventy-three

Janet Cross was frightened but she felt calm, and that surprised her, because she had never seen herself as brave before. She looked around and saw that she was in a small space – like a cell, she supposed. But there was a candle alight and she could smell it burning. Her eyes were watering and she blinked away the tears, determined that she wasn't going to lose it, at least not until she knew exactly what was going on.

It was suddenly important to her that she knew who had done this to her and asked them why. She guessed that she had been taken by the same person who had taken Kylie Barlow and Destiny Wallace. This was the last thing they had seen in their brief lives, and she knew that this would be the last thing she saw too.

The knowledge disturbed her, but there was absolutely nothing she could do about it. Her biggest fear was how her mother would react. She loved her mum, she had been a diamond always. She had been on her own with her since she got pregnant, and Janet's father had gone on the trot. But she had never felt she had lost out because of that – if anything, she felt that she had

232

been lucky to have her mum's undying love and devotion. They had been all right together, and they had a good life, as such. She just couldn't understand why this person had decided to rob her of it – she had never done anything to anyone. But she had seen enough TV programmes to know that, in the grand scheme of things, that didn't really matter.

It was such a small space, and she could see the blood of the other dead girls all over the walls and even on the mattress she was lying on. She swallowed down a scream, determined that she would face the inevitable with as much courage as she could. She just wished she could have said goodbye to her mum, because she knew that this would really affect her, and that was her biggest regret. The room she was in looked so sinister, and she wondered where she could be.

She didn't remember anything, except being knocked unconscious, and that was too frightening to contemplate. She wondered why she was feeling so accepting of her situation; she would not have believed she could be so stoic. She was such a coward in real life, and she was proud at how she was coping with this. She only hoped she could keep it up until the end, because she knew that there would be an end, and it wouldn't be an easy one. Whoever had taken her would not let her off lightly. The newspapers had not held back where their reporting of the details of Kylie's and Destiny's murders were concerned, and she knew to expect the very worst. That was why she didn't understand why she wasn't in bits. She looked around her once more and wondered how she had ended up in such a precarious position, wishing that she had never taken that shortcut through Grantley woods, but of course that was neither here nor there now. She was caught, and she had to wait and see what was going to happen to her.

She didn't realise that her captor was watching her, documenting her reactions. She didn't know that he was smiling as he watched the different expressions flitting across her face, that he enjoyed this as much as he enjoyed the pain he would eventually inflict. He liked to let them wait a while so he could observe them while they were unaware.

He was amazed that little Janet Cross was being so brave, and he felt a sudden rush of affection for her – all the more unexpected because seeing her tonight had really enraged him. Plastered in make-up and dressed like a slut, she was turning into the kind of girl that angered him, that made him disgusted.

He was humming as he loaded his Polaroid camera. He was going to document this, as he documented everything. This was his pet project, and he had to admit that he really was enjoying it.

Chapter Seventy-four

Annie Carr was counting on Margaret Dole to find something somewhere that might give them an idea of what tied the three girls together. But they were having no luck; they didn't mix in school, and certainly not outside of the school. Miss Betterway had been at pains to explain that Janet Cross had been a good girl who had never done anything to draw attention to herself. Whereas Kylie Barlow and Destiny Wallace had been the leaders of their peers, and had been looked up to by everyone around them, Janet had never once done anything to even get herself noticed. She wasn't that kind of girl.

As she looked once more at Janet Cross's new pictures, Annie knew in her heart that these and the young girl's new look were what had brought her to the attention of the man who had stolen her. Because he *had* stolen her, he had *stolen* her life, and that was something that Annie had such a difficult time processing. These young women were being cut down before they had even had a real chance to live.

Margaret Dole was still searching through all the

girls' and their friends' various social media accounts, but it was another dead end; she believed that, whoever this man was, he did not stalk them online first. This man was watching them physically and, as she had said to Annie Carr, she believed that he was hiding in plain sight. She was trawling through every CCTV camera she could to try to find *someone* who was in the vicinity of each girl's abduction.

Being the tech head that she was, she couldn't accept that this man was walking about without his image being seen anywhere. Whoever he was, he was somewhere, and she just had to find him. She was *determined* to find him. She couldn't comprehend that in a town as small as Grantley there was no evidence of anyone near or following the girls who had gone missing. It was like the perpetrator was invisible.

Annie was convinced that whoever they were looking for had some kind of relationship with the girls concerned. So far, everyone they had spoken to had an alibi, so Margaret knew that it had to be someone that had not come to their attention yet. But she would lay money, *serious* money, that whoever they were looking for had already come into their orbit at some point.

She was going to find this fucker. It was getting personal now; there was *nothing* she could not find out if she wanted to, and yet she could not collate one thing that put these girls' abductions together.

But she would, if it was the last thing she did. She would find the link needed to find the man who was doing this.

Chapter Seventy-five

Christine Murray was not really sure what to say about the latest developments in her love life. While she had dreamt of Joseph leaving his wife, she had never actually thought he would do it. And now overnight it seemed he had. While a large part of her was pleased there was another, smaller part of her that felt ashamed, frightened of the consequences. She knew how much he loved his children – they were everything to him – so she couldn't believe that he had truly left them. From what she could understand, it had all become too much for him.

It seemed to her that in the short time since he had found his father he had changed, and changed for the better. He was braver, he had become more outgoing and, best of all, he appeared to have found in Patrick Kelly the strength that he so desperately needed. They had talked long and hard during the course of their relationship about Bella and her behaviour. Christine was convinced she needed some kind of medical assistance. Joseph had loved Bella once and still did, in a way, because she was the mother of his children. For so long Joseph's hands had been tied because Bella acted the part of a loving wife, even though he felt she was doing just that – acting.

There was something cold and calculating about her, even in the way she parented their children. Joseph had once said that he couldn't fault her as a mother, yet there was a big part of him that didn't trust her entirely. Bella had what Joseph termed a 'different take' on the world around her. She had a screw loose somewhere and, at times, she worried him; she had a strange kink in her nature, and sometimes her behaviour could be seriously unpredictable.

Now that it was all out in the open, Christine had to expect some kind of backlash at some point, and she hoped she was strong enough to cope with it. Joseph O'Loughlin was the big love of her life, and it seemed that a future with him was now within her grasp. So she couldn't understand why this knowledge frightened her.

Her doorbell rang and she went through the hallway to answer it. As soon as she opened the front door, she saw Bella O'Loughlin standing there and, before she could react, Bella had thrown something in her face, and it was burning her. Christine felt as if her skin was melting. She had attempted to slam the door closed when she had seen Bella, and so the acid only hit part of her face, head and shoulder, but it was painful and she could smell burning.

Her agonised screams alerted her neighbours to the fact that there was something unpleasant happening, so they immediately called the police.

When they arrived, Bella O'Loughlin was long gone.

Chapter Seventy-six

Amelia Johnson was exhausted. She hated working shifts and, now that she actually had a day off, she was too tired to do all the things she had planned. But the one thing Amelia always did when she had time off was go to her son's grave and place fresh flowers on it. She still missed him, even after all these years. And, even though she had only had him for a few weeks, she cherished that time every day of her life. Her son's death had broken up her marriage – not that it had been that stable to start with. They had both been so young, too young really, but she often wondered if things might have worked out between them if Charlie hadn't died in his sleep. After that they didn't have a chance.

So now, thirteen years later, Amelia lived alone, she worked and, when she got home, she watched TV and she drank. It wasn't the life she had envisaged for herself, but it was a life of sorts. It was the life she had anyway, and it suited her in many respects.

As she walked into the cemetery, she looked around her at the familiar surroundings. There were a few graves she liked to look at, old graves that held other young babies like her Charlie. Amelia was comforted thinking that they were all near to each other, that there were other babies close by to keep him company. She strolled through the sunshine and, as she approached her son's small grave, she smiled. Amelia talked to him in her head, and she told him all about what was going on in her life. She knew it wasn't the most exciting news, as nothing much happened to her, but it was still contact, and that was what she felt was important. Little Charlie was the only thing that she had ever accomplished of note – he was the only thing that she had ever been remotely proud of. She still kept his photos all over her flat, and she prayed for the repose of his soul every Sunday at mass. All things considered, Amelia felt that she had been very lucky to have had her son as long as she had. It had taken a long time for her to come to that realisation, but now she accepted his death and she didn't blame herself any more.

Amelia knelt down and placed the flowers she had purchased at her local Asda supermarket and stroked the grass that covered him like a blanket. It was cut neatly once a week. All Charlie had was a small cross with his name and a picture on, but it was perfection to her. His image was still so much a part of her life, even if he wasn't. She opened her bag up and took out her rosary; she always said a quick decade, and it was always the Joyful Mysteries because she loved them so much. There was so much hope there, and she appreciated that.

When Amelia opened her eyes once more, she heard a sound. Her son's grave was near the copse of trees where the old gate was situated – perfect, really, if any mourners wanted to walk through the woodland. The woods were beautiful any time of the year; she had walked them many times herself, especially at the beginning, when it had still been raw and she had been coming to terms with her son's death. In the spring the whole place was blanketed in bluebells. She would pick a couple of bunches and place some on Charlie's grave and take the others home with her to remind her of her son.

Amelia stood up and looked towards the trees and, frowning, she walked slowly towards what she first thought was a bundle of rubbish. It was only when she was nearer that she realised it was a young girl, and that she had been laid on some old newspapers. And that was the noise she had heard when the wind blew.

Putting her hand across her mouth to stop herself from vomiting, she looked down at the destroyed body on the ground. As she stumbled away from the gruesome sight she saw a young family and, calling out to them, she tried to stop herself from collapsing on the ground. Starting to throw up, Amelia felt the tears that were never far away when she was near her son's grave. But this time they weren't for her son, they were for the naked girl who looked like she had been through a meat grinder.

Janet Cross had been found. And, for the first time in years, Amelia Johnson was crying over someone other than her son.

Chapter Seventy-seven

Annie Carr was devastated. She had held on to a tiny hope that this girl would be found alive and unharmed, that this wasn't going to be another murder, that there would be a perfectly rational reason for the girl to go on the missing list. Janet's new look might have got her invited to a party, or she might have gone to see a band with some friends. Anything would have been better than this. She was just blooming, becoming a young woman, and now she was dead.

As Annie looked at the small girl on the mortuary table, with her budding little breasts and her peeling skin, she felt the urge to cry at the waste of such a young life. She had been mutilated, like her predecessors. And no sexual contact could be ascertained, just like the other girls who had been murdered.

Megan McFee shook her head in denial. It never ceased to amaze her what people were capable of doing to each other. Only wild animals should hunt, not human beings. But she had dealt with murder enough times to know that was not the case, and it never got any easier. These recent murders were beyond anything that she had seen in a long time, and she hated that another young girl was lying on her slab bereft of her life – a life that had been stolen in the most painful way possible.

She sighed deeply, before looking at Annie and saying sadly, 'She was tortured, burned, stabbed and mutilated, just like the others. But – I am going out on a limb here, Annie, so don't quote me on it, and I can verify my findings at a later date – but I think that whoever murdered this little girl hesitated at some point. The knife marks aren't as deep as they were on Kylie and Destiny – those were done in a rage. This child's stab wounds are hesitant. By the same token he went to town on the burning, but unlike the other girls, she was already dead when he started on that. Her cause of death was asphyxiation. The fucker smothered her first. I know it's not my place to say this, but I think he felt remorse with little Janet Cross and he made it an easier death for her – a courtesy that he didn't afford to his first two victims. This girl was different somehow. It's not a scientific opinion but, in all the years I have done this job, I have a nose for what these bodies are trying to tell me.'

Annie Carr nodded, letting Megan know that she agreed with her. She respected Megan's opinion because, as Kate had *always* drummed it into her, this was a woman who knew her job backwards and sideways.

'I'm assuming there's no trace or DNA again?'

Megan sighed. 'I've swabbed but you can still smell the bleach, even though I have washed her down since she first came in. I don't hold out much hope, to be completely honest with you. Whoever is responsible has an awful lot of industrial bleach, better known as sodium hypochlorite, and I would say that she was more or less drowned in the stuff, because there is nothing left to give us a fucking inkling of who might be responsible. But I have one bright light in this constant darkness, and that is I smelt linseed oil on her hair. I've taken samples to verify that, but I know my oils.'

Annie didn't know what to say to that, so she kept her own counsel.

'One other thing I will mention, Annie, is that as clever as this fucker is, he did leave one little clue. In case you weren't listening earlier, I said that this time he had used *industrial* bleach. On the last two girls he used domestic bleach, which I have to admit does a pretty good job of neutralising any DNA or trace of any kind. That means we can narrow our search down. Also, the linseed oil tells me that, at some point after the bleach had been used, her body was in contact with something that required the use of linseed oil. My guess would be that it was used in pure form on some kind of wood. I know this doesn't say too much at the moment but I hope it does mean something down the line.'

Annie Carr looked at Megan McFee and felt, as always, the wonderment that such an articulate and intelligent woman could allow herself to be taken over by such a destructive disease. Bulimic she may be, but Megan was still the best in town, as Kate would say. Megan was stick thin, and all the layers of baggy clothing could never hide that fact.

Megan was smiling sadly as she said, 'Not a lot for you to go on, I know, Annie, but at least it's something.'

Annie Carr forced a smile then, because Megan was right; this was something different, and she hoped that whoever they were looking for had become complacent enough to make a mistake. The only downside to that thought was it meant another girl being slaughtered so they could *maybe* find another clue of some description.

'Thank you, Megan, and you are right. At some point what you have discovered could well lead us to the man we want.'

Secretly Annie wasn't going to bet on it; even she had a tin of linseed oil in her house like a whole host of other people. She used it on her beech worktops. The use of industrial bleach, though, might prove to be a better line of enquiry. There had to be some sort of documentation for that.

Megan smiled, satisfied that she had been of some help. It was frustrating when she couldn't provide the answers. 'Oh, and one other thing – unlike the first two victims, this child had a full stomach. She had eaten not that long before death. She had also recently ingested a Curly Wurly of all things!'

Annie Carr shook her head, once more thinking angrily that, of course Janet had sweets in her system! She was a fucking child, after all. Looking down at Janet's slight frame that had been so viciously assaulted and destroyed, she felt an overwhelming rush of dread.

As her Chief Super kept pointing out, they were no nearer to finding the man responsible for these atrocities and they had an ever-sensationalist media breathing down their necks. They had a better chance of winning the rollover on the EuroMillions lottery. Sarcastic fucker. It was all very well for him; he was a career man who had never been on the job.

This was the most frustrating case Annie had ever been involved with, all the more so because they just couldn't get a break. Not forensically, or through CCTV, or through good old-fashioned policing such as door-to-door. She'd had helicopters up, men and women on overtime searching everywhere they could find. So many people were volunteering to help them, yet they still had sweet FA.

She swallowed down the tears that were gathering in her eyes and walked stiffly from the mortuary. Janet Cross's body was invading her mind and she couldn't force those images away. She had a feeling that she never would.

Once she was back, settled in her car, she lit a cigarette and smoked it silently until she felt competent to drive. She had never felt so helpless in her life before, and it wasn't a good feeling.

Chapter Seventy-eight

Kate was in shock, unable to believe what she knew was true.

'Fucking hell, Kate, that mad bitch has attacked Joseph's bird! Acid, they think! Straight in the poor fucker's boatrace!' Patrick was shaking his head in disbelief.

But Kate knew it was so because Bella had called her, begging for her help, but she couldn't say that to Patrick. She knew that she had to go and try to help Bella in some way. She wasn't sure how she would even start to achieve that, but she had to try. Kate understood, after all those years in the police force, that things were very rarely how they seemed.

She knew in her heart that Bella had been pushed over the edge, and that it had been on the cards for a long time. Despite Bella's treatment of her, Kate did genuinely feel for the woman who was desperate at the thought of losing not only her husband but the opportunity to be a part of Patrick Kelly's lavish world. Kate had known from day one just how important Bella regarded money and property, had seen how she craved recognition through being seen as rich and successful. She had never taken to Bella but that didn't mean she didn't understand the woman's predicament. Her ex-husband, Dan, had made sure she knew what it was like to feel second best constantly, to know that no matter what you did you couldn't compete with the woman your husband was enamoured with.

That Bella was off her fucking tree she didn't dispute, but Kate knew that she had to see her before she went on the trot. Because on the trot she would go! And take the kids with her – at least Amanda, who was still young enough to believe what she was told.

So against her better judgement she saw Patrick off at the door, and told him she would meet up with him and Joseph later on in the day. As she watched him leave, she hoped she was making the right decision. Whatever Bella was, or wasn't, she was still the mother of those children, and as such she deserved at least a hearing. Kate hoped that if she could see Bella she might be able to talk some sense into her.

As she got into her car, she wondered if Annie had got her message, because she had a feeling she was going to need her help quick sharp. The state Bella was in, she needed to be handled carefully, especially as she had her young daughter with her. She couldn't get out of her where young Joey was, and Patrick had not enlightened her.

It was a mess. The moment Joseph had walked through their front door she had felt that a bomb had gone off in her life, and she wasn't at all sure she wanted this upset and aggravation. She also knew though that Patrick was happier than she had ever seen him, even with all this going on. It meant that she had no choice but to go along with what Patrick wanted and, until today, she had not really minded that. But these latest events had put a different complexion on things. As she drove, she wondered what the rest of the day would bring.

Chapter Seventy-nine

Patrick and Joseph were at the hospital and, even though it went against the grain, the older man hoped that the Old Bill threw the book at Bella. Her rival's face was half-destroyed, and there was a huge bald patch on the side of her head where Christine's beautiful hair had been. Even in her present state he could see what had attracted his son to her; she had been a looker, and she was well built into the bargain.

The damage looked worse than it was, according to the doctor, who had babbled on about skin grafts and plastic surgery in the future. But it was watching his son that had really opened Patrick's eyes; the man was distraught at what his wife had been capable of. It was also evident to Patrick that Joseph didn't know what to do about the situation, and was still coming to terms with what his wife had done to the woman he loved.

He had to admit he had been shocked by the attack but, unlike his son, he had guessed from his first meeting with the delectable Bella that she was a few slices short of being the full loaf. There was something about her that Patrick had seen in some of the hardest men he had ever known; the suspicion that they were capable of great violence was evident to anyone who cared to take the trouble to look. It was how controlled they were, because they needed to be. Bella had that same suppressed violence about her. Now he had been proved right – and that did not give him any satisfaction.

He stood awkwardly by as his son and his girlfriend tried to make some kind of connection. Which, after the turn of events, was not an easy thing to do. Christine was naturally in pieces and Joseph was helpless to comfort her. Patrick made his excuses and left them together, knowing that his presence was not helping the situation in any way.

Outside the hospital, he lit a cigar and drew on it for a few seconds as he pondered this new set of problems. Once Bella was found and charged, he would be having his son and his grandchildren living at his house until things were sorted out. Bella would be looking at going to the Big House or to the nuthouse. He had a feeling it would be the latter in this case, as Bella O'Loughlin was as mad as a box of the proverbial frogs! She definitely didn't have her nut screwed on tight like everyone else around her.

He was worried about his granddaughter being left with her now. Even though Joseph didn't think Bella was capable of hurting the children, Patrick wasn't so sure. Bella was vindictive, and vindictive people did outrageous things to hurt other people if they felt it was needed. He remembered, years before, an old friend of Renée's had stabbed her old man while he slept, and that had been over a bit of strange as well.

Women were unpredictable coves, especially the ones who had a high opinion of themselves. It did not do to antagonise certain people. It wasn't a good idea to antagonise *him*, if truth be told, and Bella had fucked him off big time. He would see to it that those kids were as far away from that mad bitch as possible. He wouldn't mind betting his son had known she wasn't right for a long time, but Bella could put on a good front for the short term.

He understood that finding out about his bird was not something she would be exactly thrilled about, but this reaction was over the top; it was cruel and it was calculated, and it was about doing permanent damage. It was a planned and vicious attack by a woman whose blood ran in his grandchildren's veins. He wasn't too happy about that, but all he could do now was be there for his son and his new-found family. And he intended to do whatever was needed to sort this out for everyone concerned. Anything that kept those children near him could only be a good thing in his book. He was looking forward to having them in the house. It would become a home again, he was sure of it, and he relished having his grandchildren close by. He was just sorry it had to come about in such terrible circumstances.

Chapter Eighty

Annie Carr was trying to concentrate on what DC Karim was telling her, but she wasn't sure she could believe it. 'You're joking?'

He shook his head sadly. He had not wanted to be the one to break the news, but there was no one else willing to do it.

'Acid! Dear Lord, is Kate all right?'

She had been very busy since Janet Cross's body had been discovered, and she knew that Kate had rung her a couple of times. But she had assumed it was about the case and she would get back to her when she could and bring her up to speed on the latest developments. She had never dreamt of anything like this happening.

'Kate's been trying to get you for a while. She's with Bella, but she won't tell me where. She says she wants to talk to you first.'

Annie sat down at her desk and nodded imperceptibly. Then, standing up once more, she said quickly, 'Find me a coffee and find it quick, please. I'll call her now and see what is going on. Does everyone know?'

He nodded, but said quietly, 'Obviously police had to

attend. But no one of importance knows that Kate's been trying to get you, or that she's with the suspect.'

Annie sighed heavily and thanked him. With all that was going on, this was the last thing she needed.

Chapter Eighty-one

Bella was agitated and Kate felt her heart go out to this fussy, stupid woman who, it seemed, had finally cracked. Bella was staying at a small hotel in Essex and, even though Kate knew she should not feel any sympathy for her, she couldn't help herself. Whatever she had done, she was a broken woman now; it had gone too far, and there was no going back.

Little Amanda was all big eyes and nervousness when Kate had finally reached them, and she was glad she had stopped off for colouring books and felt-tip pens. It seemed that in the hurry to leave they had not brought any chargers with them for her to watch anything on their iPad, and she was happy to see Amanda settle down to colour happily. She knew that the little girl felt safer with someone else there, and that knowledge saddened Kate.

Bella had had the presence of mind to drop Joey off with a friend, so that was something. He was old enough to understand everything that was going on if he was here and to realise there would be consequences. It was best he was out of the way for a while. She had been worried at how much the children had witnessed. But from what she could gather, they had no idea of what exactly had happened.

It was getting late and she poured more tea. Placing a cup beside Bella, she said quietly, 'Look, Bella, you and I both know that you have to face up to this, and I promise I will help you in any way I can.'

Bella was staring at her without any real expression on her face. Kate could tell that she was having difficulty in accepting what she had done. She could understand that, of course, but there was something about this woman that unsettled her, because people like Bella were not trustworthy. She was passive now, but Kate was aware that she could go off at any moment. She could only hope that Amanda's presence would keep this woman under control.

If the police turned up mob-handed, there would be far more trouble, because Bella was not in her right mind, and Kate wanted to avoid that. She also felt that she owed it to Patrick to try to give this sad state of events the best outcome she could. She might not be a serving police officer any more, but she still had enough clout to pull in a few favours.

She picked up the teacup and placed it in Bella's hand, watching as Bella sipped it automatically. The woman looked defeated, and Kate knew that the enormity of what she had done was starting to hit her.

'I did love him, you know, Kate. Not how he wanted me to love him. But the knowledge that he was with her killed me. I could feel him pulling away from me – she was giving him something I couldn't. But I believed that the children would be enough, you know? He adores his children, especially little Amanda. But it turns out I was wrong. They weren't enough.'

Kate sighed heavily. 'It happens, and I know how hard it can be. But you have to face up to what you have done. I can bring you in quietly and with the least amount of fuss. Because there is no going back from here.' Bella looked at her with those empty eyes, and Kate instinctively grabbed her hand. 'Make this easy on yourself and the children, Bella. I promise you I will do everything I can to help.'

Bella swallowed noisily and, pulling her hand away, she grabbed the front of her T-shirt and scrunched it up into a ball, and then the tears finally came. 'I will go to prison, won't I?'

Kate tried to smile reassuringly as she said, 'Maybe not. Patrick will see that you get the best representation that money can buy. He will help you and so will I, Bella. But you need to end this now. I put myself out on a limb here for you because I know that it was a moment of madness. It could happen to any of us.'

Bella smiled crookedly. 'I imagined doing it, you know? Seeing her face burn up. I wanted to hurt her so badly. If I am honest, I still do, Kate. I still want to harm that fucking cunt who destroyed my life and my children's lives. I would happily rip her fucking head off her shoulders, if I had the opportunity.'

Her words turned Kate cold but she just shrugged. 'I'm going to ring my friend Detective Annie Carr, and she will make sure that you are taken care of properly, OK? But, Bella, this has to happen. You do understand that?'

Bella looked into Kate's eyes and she nodded her head. 'I don't have any choice, do I? That is the hardest thing for me. I can't get out of it this time.'

Kate wondered what she meant but she stayed silent; she didn't know what to say.

Chapter Eighty-two

Janet Cross's mother had gone to pieces, and Annie wasn't going to get anything of value from her for a while. The doctor had sedated her and, though Annie knew it was the best thing for the poor woman, it didn't help her in any way.

Sue Border – the mum's friend and, by the sound of it, young Janet's mentor – had been as helpful as she possibly could. What Annie had gleaned, though, from the photos she shared was that Janet had recently changed her appearance, and Sue had been the brains behind that. Annie didn't have the heart to tell her that she was probably the reason that Janet was now dead. As she rubbed her eyes with tiredness, she saw PC Boyd coming over to her desk, and she smiled automatically. He was a nice lad and he would go far, she believed. Tall and good-looking, he suited the uniform, and he had a natural reticence that attracted the ladies. In short, as Annie had once remarked, he had the whole package. Annie also knew that he was gayer than a Mexican tablecloth but she kept that bit of knowledge to herself.

He handed her a file. 'Interesting reading, ma'am.'

Annie smiled her thanks and watched him walk away. She took a sip of her coffee and then opened the file. Boyd was absolutely right; this did make interesting reading, but for all the wrong reasons. She sat back in her chair and wondered at the scale of some people's lies, and the thought made her feel depressed. She saw that young Boyd had made two copies of the file and she put one into her bag for Kate's perusal later in the day.

Chapter Eighty-three

Amanda was subdued, and young Joey was trying his hardest to keep her amused. He clearly understood more than they realised about what had gone on and that he was aware that they needed to keep as much from his sister as they could. Joseph O'Loughlin was walking around like 'a tit in a trance', as Patrick had so colourfully put it, and, in between running to the hospital to see his amour and then coming back to the house and drinking with his father, he was not exactly being what Kate would term helpful. Beverley was being an absolute star, and she was relishing looking after the children, especially little Amanda.

Kate was doing her best to make everyone welcome and see that they all had what they needed but, if she was brutally honest, she resented the way her home was being taken over. Unlike Patrick, who was loving every second of having his new-found family around him. She understood that she had to allow for it. Patrick was being given a second chance at a life, at a family, and she knew how much that meant to him. But what she wouldn't give for a quiet night together, just the two of them! It looked like that wasn't going to happen any time in the near future.

She consoled herself with the fact that, when this mess finally started to be sorted out, Joseph would move back into his own home. She hoped so anyway. If it was up to Patrick, they would all move in, bag and baggage, and she knew that Joseph would be quite happy for that to be the case. He had given over all the responsibility for his children to her and Patrick, and she was determined to make sure that he understood this was only in the short term. If she heard the music to *Frozen* one more time, she would not be responsible for her actions. But then, when Amanda climbed on her lap, needing to be hugged, she couldn't deny her. She was a lovely child who had been put into an impossible situation. She missed her mother, even though she had cottoned on to the fact that her mother had done something bad. Kate really didn't know how they would ever explain the truth of the situation to her.

When she'd explained to Patrick why she'd gone to find Bella, he'd been a diamond about it. After all, he wanted to see her punished for what she'd done and this way she'd been brought in with the minimum of fuss. Annie Carr had been fantastic, and even Patrick had been singing her praises – which was unusual, to say the least. He had never really taken to her, but that was understandable; Patrick had never really taken to *anyone* in the blue uniform – except Kate, of course. She was what he said was his only exception to *that* rule.

She went out to the kitchen and poured herself a

coffee. Bev was out there making a huge dinner for everyone and Kate, as always, thanked God for this woman. Without her, she didn't know what she would do. She sat at the table and sipped her coffee, and then she lit a cigarette and drew on it deeply before letting the smoke out in one long continuous stream.

Bev smiled at her then. 'That bad, eh?'

Kate laughed gently. 'I know – I should feel ashamed, and considering what's happened . . .' She left the sentence unfinished.

Beverley smiled and, walking to Kate, she sat opposite her. Placing her hands over Kate's, she said sadly, 'It won't be for that long – just until they all digest what's happened. It's a tragedy, as we all know. Where do you go when something like this happens? You go to your own, Kate. To your own flesh and blood. Did you know my father died in the Maze prison? Patrick knows – I never asked if you knew. I suppose I assumed. But it was a terrible time for us all, and it's a terrible time now for those children. And Joseph? Well, he needs to be near someone strong, and you and Patrick are strong.'

Kate didn't know how to reply. She had believed she knew everything there was to know about Beverley, and yet she had known nothing about her father. Patrick had, but that was him all over; he would feel it was Bev's business who she told, and Kate respected that. It still rankled that she had waited this long to tell her though.

'I remember when I first came to work here, I felt like I had won the lottery, Kate. I had my lovely flat and I had peace of mind. Do you know how important that is? I had my own place in the world. That is what these children need, for a while anyway. Joseph is no good to man or beast. He has to come to terms with his wife's lunacy. And sure, Jesus, she was a fecking nutcase of the first water. I'll help you in any way I can, Kate, because I owe you and Patrick, but also because it's the good Christian thing to do. Now I think that you can trust me to babysit if you need to get out of this madhouse!'

Kate looked at this plain woman, with a heart that should have been given a family of her own, and she knew she was being given, if not a lecture, then a reminder of what was important. She also knew that Bev was right; this wasn't about her, or her home being invaded. This was about her accepting that Patrick had another family, and they were not going anywhere. Not that she wanted them to, of course, but she was honest enough to admit to herself that she did hate having her whole life and home taken over.

Amanda ran out into the kitchen and climbed on to her lap, and Kate automatically put her arms around the child and hugged her close.

'Nanny Kate, why does my granddad call me Mandy? Is it because I look like the girl in the pictures who died?'

Kate smiled gently and, kissing the top of the child's head, she said quietly, 'It's a bit about that, but also your granddad has a habit of shortening people's names. Like Joey is really a Joseph, like his dad.'

Amanda nodded at her words, and then she said, 'Is Mummy coming back soon?'

Kate sighed softly, and then she said honestly, 'I don't think so, darling. She did something naughty, I'm afraid.'

'She hurt Daddy's friend, didn't she?'

Kate didn't answer her, because she didn't have the words.

'I heard Granddad and Joey talking about it, and Daddy said she wouldn't be home for a long time. So we have to live here.' She pulled herself out of Kate's embrace and looked her in the eyes as she said, 'You will take care of me, won't you, Nanny Kate, until my mummy comes home?'

Kate smiled then and, hugging the girl tightly, she said, 'Of course I will, sweetheart. You have your own room here and we all adore having you here with us! Your poor mummy isn't well, darling, and she needs to get better. Until then, you will be here with us and we will keep you safe.' She felt the child's arms going around her waist, and she hugged her back tightly. Amanda started to cry then, and Kate held her closer to her body until she felt the child relax into her.

'Mummy had her scary face on that day.'

Kate looked over the girl's head and locked eyes with Beverley. 'Mummy is OK, darling. I promise you that when it's the right time, I will take you to see your mummy myself.'

Amanda pulled herself away and, looking up into Kate's face, she said honestly, 'I don't want to see my mummy yet. She can be very frightening sometimes.'

Kate felt all the breath leaving her body; she was

genuinely deflated. She heard the door opening and she saw Joey Junior looking at them with a look of complete horror on his handsome face. She knew he had been listening to them talking.

As he walked to her and picked his sister up in his arms, he said sadly, 'You don't have to do anything you don't want to. I promise you, and Nanny Kate promises you too.'

Amanda allowed him to carry her from the room and, as they left, Kate heard Beverley say in a whisper, 'Jesus Christ.'

Kate looked at her for a few moments, before saying, 'I think a glass of wine is in order, don't you, Bev?'

Beverley smiled ruefully as she said, 'I think a glass of Bushmills, personally.'

It was something her mother would have said, and Kate started to laugh then. 'You are absolutely right, Bev. This is what my old mum would call "a whiskey moment".'

'A wise woman! I have a bottle in my flat for emergencies like!' As she walked past Kate, she grabbed her shoulder and, squeezing it tightly, she said, 'What a fecking state of affairs! But God is good, you know. He makes the back to bear the burden.'

It was another one of her mother's sayings, and Kate smiled as she watched the woman walk out of the room. Bev was younger than she was, and yet she was like an ancient in comparison. But Kate knew that, whatever happened, these kids needed her and she had to be there for them. It was a wake-up call all right.

Chapter Eighty-four

He was looking at his pictures again; they always gave him a modicum of happiness. He loved to see the fear and the dawning comprehension on the girls' faces when they finally realised he was going to hurt them. But he didn't feel like that about Janet Cross; if he didn't know better, he would think he was going soft in his old age.

He knew, as soon as he had seen her lying there on the mattress, that she had not really changed at all. But of course, by then, it was too late. It didn't feel like a good kill, and he didn't like this sensation that he had maybe made a mistake. He reminded himself, over and over again, that he had a mission and that Janet Cross was now a part of that. He still thought that he maybe should have waited a bit longer, but there was an urge in him to carry out this work and carry it out properly.

He had felt a strange connection with little Janet that he had not felt with any of the others. Her face when she had woken up, and then the knowledge that she was still as pure as the driven snow. That was not in his remit. He wanted to show the whores that they had made themselves known to him with their fucking disgusting behaviour. They looked exactly what they were – cheap and nasty individuals. Oh, he didn't feel any remorse for what he had done to them.

Janet Cross was different. But he told himself that he had cut her off at the pass, because eventually she would have been just like the others. He knew exactly what these girls were really like. Janet Cross would have become a part of those whores' world, because she was ripe for it. There was no escaping that fact. Eventually she would have succumbed, just like that cunt Kylie and that slag Destiny.

He looked at the Polaroids once again, making sure that Janet Cross's were left in the box. He knew that he had done the right thing, because he had a purpose. He had been planning this for a while, and he was pleased with what he had accomplished. He was systematically ridding the world of tainted, disgusting individuals who should never have been within his orbit anyway. They had been placed there for a reason, and that reason was so he could dispose of them while at the same time setting an *example*.

Oh, he knew what he had to do, and he was determined to keep on doing it. That was what he had been put on this earth for. And it was what made him feel alive.

Chapter Eighty-five

Annie Carr was well aware she looked like shit. She had only slept intermittently for the last two weeks, and she was chasing what felt like a ghost. She still had no information of any import and that rankled, because she wanted to solve these girls' murders more than anything – not for her, but for the families.

As Kate poured her a glass of wine, she sat down in the large kitchen chair and sighed with relief. 'Oh, Kate, you don't know how good this feels, lady!'

Kate grinned. 'Oh yes, I do! I was you for years, remember.'

Annie took a large gulp of wine before answering her. 'I know that, darling. But it doesn't make it any easier. Honestly, Kate, it's like this fucker has some kind of divine protection going on, you know? He's like the wind. We can't get anything from the bodies because he soaks them in bleach. He's clearly done his research on how to get rid of his DNA so as to remove anything that might be of value to us. I feel we're being mocked! You know Margaret Dole – I mean, fucking hell, if she can't find anything online then it isn't there. As much as

269

she can fuck me off – and, believe me, she does at times, the arrogant mare – I know that she is the future of policing. She fucking knows it too – cybercrime is the new big thing apparently, as she tells me daily. But this bastard! He's like Margaret, I suppose, because he knows how to cover his tracks and keep under our radar. So as much as Margaret can irritate me, she is probably the most valuable officer we have right now. Did you know she was headhunted by the Met?'

Kate shook her head in disbelief. 'Bloody hell, Annie! And she refused?'

Annie laughed nastily. 'Oh yeah, she stayed. Because I think she knows she would be a small fish in a big pond, whereas here she's the dog's knob.'

Kate laughed but, filling up the glasses, she said seriously, 'She's not going to win any popularity contests, I admit, but she is good at what she does, and that is what matters in the end. She certainly proved her worth on the Miriam Salter case and I know she tried her best to fit in with the team but I think she's missing the likeability factor, as they call it. She will never be on my faves list, but I respect what she can do. If Margaret can't find this fucker online then he has no presence there. Now *that* gives you a whole new set of possibilities, doesn't it? It tells me you are dealing with Old School. Someone who might reject the new cyber generation and who doesn't have an online persona. Not everyone is online, believe it or not. I was reading about silver surfers the other week, and I realised they were talking about me, *my* generation. All these people are now online and looking for love among other things. It's a different world, so it needs a different style of policing. If Margaret Dole can't find anything then I would lay my last fiver on the fact that there isn't anything to find.'

Annie knew that Kate was right. 'But by the same token, Kate, she can't find anything on CCTV anywhere that puts anyone in the vicinity of the girls' abductions. That is practically unheard of these days. You and I know that the chance of being caught on camera somewhere is a given. But this fucker seems like he has a charmed life. Because there is fuck-all anywhere and, in fairness to Margaret Dole, she has looked. Credit where it's due, she is there morning, noon and night, trawling through hours and hours of footage, and she has not found a fucking thing.' Annie picked up her bag off the floor and, taking out a file, she threw it across the table to Kate. 'On another note, this is what I found out about Bella. And it is not pleasant reading, I am afraid.'

Kate hadn't asked if Annie had had the chance to look into Bella's past yet because she knew she had a lot on her plate. She'd been granted bail, thanks to her father-in-law's connections, on the condition that she checked into a secure facility while she awaited her first court appearance. Patrick had found a good brief to represent her, and they were hoping to avoid a custodial sentence, but, as Patrick had pointed out, that depended on Bella using her loaf and doing what she was told to do. Joseph thought she would be sensible enough to listen, but Patrick wasn't so sure – and neither was Kate. Bella was a loose cannon and, after what little Amanda had said, Kate had already guessed there was more to this story than met the eye.

'I'll pass it on to Patrick, but give me the low-down.'

Annie lit another cigarette and said tiredly, 'Bella has hurt someone before – badly, I might add. She was thirteen when she violently attacked another girl. No one seems to be able to understand why it happened. She ended up in the care system after she was released from a juvenile facility. Her parents refused to have anything to do with her and she was basically left to fend for herself by sixteen. She seemed to be doing OK, according to the social worker reports. She did well in the education programmes and she basically kept her head down, her nose clean, and made another life for herself. As you and I both know, this was in the early days of computer records and she just slipped through the cracks. She accepted all the help on offer and then she was deemed fit to rejoin society. But reading between the lines, she is a fucking psychopath. There is a lack of real information in these files, and that tells me there was trouble but the social workers played it down. We both know how that works, don't we?'

Kate sighed; this was what she had feared. 'Do you know the saddest thing, Annie? I actually feel sorry for her. I know how it feels to have the person you love treat you like shite. My ex-husband did it to me on more than one occasion.'

Annie nodded and said seriously, 'But you didn't scar his lover, did you? In all honesty, Kate, I think the best thing for this mad bitch would be *actual* prison time, with the big girls who would walk over her like a cheap carpet. She needs to understand the seriousness of what she has done. She got a swerve the first time, and that makes her think she can do what she likes. She needs to take responsibility for her actions. She needs to be punished.'

Kate could see that Annie had a point, but that wouldn't stop Patrick and Joseph trying to get Bella a good deal for the children's sakes. She wondered how they would feel when they saw this file and what Bella was capable of. She closed her eyes in distress, because she was sick and tired of it all.

She looked at her friend, and she said sadly, 'It's like the world has gone fucking mad, Annie.'

Annie Carr laughed then, a real laugh, loud and raucous. 'Fuck me, Kate, I think that ship's sailed, don't you? We are living in a nightmare of a world, where people can hide behind a computer or a phone and do their worst. We are living in a world of faceless people who we call friends on social networks. We are living in a world where anything you want to know is at the touch of a button on a Google search engine. You know what someone said to me recently? Remember Jacqui Brown who runs the canteen – not the sharpest knife in the fucking drawer – she said that she didn't understand why schools still handed out homework when her kids could find out what they wanted to know on their iPads. I think she has summed up what's wrong with the world now. No one takes responsibility. There is always an answer at the touch of a button, and anyone, no matter how weird they are, can find like-minded people online. And what really scares me is we can't find the fuckers, because they hide behind said computer screens.'

Kate knew that what Annie said was true. But she also believed that, as police, they had to fight crime, no matter what. She raised her glass and said loudly, 'To Margaret Dole.'

And Annie clinked her glass against Kate's, saying sadly, 'To Margaret Dole – a pain in the arse, and the best weapon we have to hand!' Then, after they had both taken a large gulp of wine, Annie held her glass up again and said, 'Allegedly!'

They were still laughing their heads off when Patrick came into the kitchen, saying, 'So what's the big joke, then, ladies?'

They didn't answer him – they were laughing too much.

Eventually Kate handed him the file that Annie had given her, saying soberly, 'I think you need to read this, Patrick – you and Joseph.'

He took the file from her and he had a feeling from the expression on her face that it was not going to be good news.

Kate said as much. 'You and Joseph need to think long and hard about where you are going next where Bella is concerned, Pat. This isn't going to help her in any way.'

Patrick nodded, and Kate knew that he had guessed what Annie's research would dig up. He was a lot of things but he wasn't stupid.

'I will leave you two ladies to talk while I have a look-see.'

Annie looked at him and she said honestly, 'Listen, Patrick, you and Joseph have to read that and take it in properly. I understand that Joseph feels guilty about what happened. But Bella can't be allowed to walk away from this. I won't let her. I need you to know that I *can't* let her.'

Patrick didn't say a word; he just nodded and left the room.

Annie turned to Kate, saying, 'You know I am right, Kate.'

And Kate refilled their wine glasses, before saying wearily, 'I know, Annie. I know.'

Chapter Eighty-six

Patrick and Danny Foster were in their new offices in Tilbury. Patrick had recently purchased a scrapyard from an old mate who had felt the urge to go on the trot before it all fell out of bed for him. The scrapyard was completely legitimate, unlike his old mate's other nefarious businesses, which had finally caught up with him. That was what happened these days. And Patrick Kelly knew that if you wanted to stay on the ball you had to make sure you kept up with the times. It was the only way to survive in their world.

Patrick was glad that he wasn't a young, up-and-coming Face in this new world. He felt like a fucking dinosaur at times, but he was sensible enough to realise that every generation had felt like that. There was always something new happening, and there were always people like himself, waiting to take advantage of those new opportunities. It was the law, because it was how newcomers made their mark. If you had half a brain, you used it to further your own ends. It was healthy and it was expected, because the young Faces needed someone to back their plans and utilise their ideas. They needed someone to see their vision and bankroll it, because that was how it had always worked.

It was the same in every walk of life – there was the legit, and the not-so legit. It depended on what side of the road you chose to walk on. He had read in *The Times* that civilisation had come on more in the last thirty years than ever before in the history of man. He could believe that too. He didn't envy the new generation of Faces. It was nigh on impossible to rob a fucking bank, let alone do a common-or-garden wages snatch! Money was nearly obsolete these days; it was all internet banking – not that he would trust anything like that himself. He still used cheques. But this new scrapyard was a perfect cash business – one of the few that was left, unfortunately.

Danny Foster had invested in a lot of what he called online gaming. Turned out they were serious money-spinners. Patrick was sensible enough to have someone else look at the businesses, make sure Danny wasn't having him over. He might not be a fucking contender for *Eggheads*, but it was common sense to always make sure he got a second opinion when it was deemed necessary. Patrick Kelly trusted Danny Foster, but it was second nature to him to have another set of eyes look into his interests. It was also to ensure that Danny Foster wasn't being ripped off either. There was plenty of room for all that kind of skulduggery in their line of work. Even though his Kate had pointed out on more than one occasion that he didn't need to keep such a beady eye on Danny.

She felt he should take a big step back from everything, but that was easier said than done. He was supposed to be retired but anyone who knew him didn't believe that for a second, and that included his Kate. She had even arranged for Margaret Dole to keep a clear eye on his businesses – for a fee, of course. Margaret Dole was the best of the best, and he respected her nous. He also liked that a Filth was on *his* payroll – it appealed to his sense of humour.

Even so, Patrick Kelly still preferred a real cash business, and he guessed that was why Danny had invested in this scrapyard to keep him happy. He loved him for that; the boy was thinking of him, and that was a good thing. He appreciated that Danny Foster, who he trusted implicitly, had his best interests at heart. Not just financially but also in the physical sense. This was a hands-on business, and that was what he knew the best, like the lap-dancing clubs and the other so-called social businesses, restaurants and bars. But they were heavily reliant on credit cards, and even though they could launder money and wash the proceeds, he still liked to see actual cash in his hand. Or, as he referred to it, 'cash on the hip', meaning in his pocket and tax free. That was why he liked the scrapyards.

There would always be a need for this kind of business in the world they inhabited. A body could always be disposed of in the boot of a car that was to be crushed as scrap. There were a lot of things that could be disposed of in a scrapyard. Patrick should know – he had cut his teeth on similar money-making schemes.

He walked into the Portakabin and was pleasantly surprised at how clean and tidy it was.

Danny started laughing at his surprise, and he said jovially, 'I fucking knew you would like this, Pat. I bought it off Jackie O'Toole, as you know, and I couldn't believe it myself. But from what I can gather his wife has fucking terrible OCD and spends her life cleaning! The whole place is spotless.'

Patrick laughed with him. 'Believe it or not, Jackie's wife was a real fucking looker in her day, and right on the ball and all. She could work out a fifty-horse accumulator in her head! Straight up. The days before the till could work out the bets, the people who worked in the betting shops had to be able to do their fucking sums! Right intelligent she was. She had legs that could get a man arrested, and the face of an angel. But she went a bit radio rental when her oldest boy was murdered and then her youngest son got thirty years. It is hard on the women, losing their sons to the prison system, especially when they are given a serious fucking lump. But Jackie still worships her, as I am sure you know.

'Did you know Jackie used to have a hostess club in Soho? A right high-class place – beautiful girls there and a lot of money changed hands. I never once heard even a *whisper* of him playing away from home. I always respected him for that, Danny, because in our world it is so fucking easy to forget what really matters, you know? We have it offered to us on a plate on a daily basis. I loved my Renée, she was all I ever needed. Oh, I had a flyer occasionally but nothing that could get me slaughtered, because she would have walked away without a backward glance. And knowing that was what kept me on the straight and narrow, I suppose.'

Danny smiled genuinely. He loved hearing the old stories; there was an honesty in the old days that was gradually disappearing in the criminal world. He knew that there was a new world of villainy, and he made sure that he was at the top of his game where that was concerned. But he yearned to be a part of the days when a bank robbery was still a viable option and people still had to find a phone booth to dial 999. It seemed unbelievable now to realise that was actually not that long ago.

Danny Foster envied Patrick Kelly and his counterparts because he knew that they had lived through times that were not just exciting but were also gone for ever. Now in his forties, he wasn't that young by today's standards; in many respects he was seen as getting long in the tooth. He respected that Patrick Kelly and his ilk were still seen as innovators and part of the real criminal underworld, all these years later. Patrick Kelly was the last of a dying breed – not that Danny would ever point that out, of course.

He opened one of the filing cabinets and took out a bottle of Famous Grouse and two glasses. He poured them both a hefty measure, and they toasted the new business together.

Patrick settled himself in Jackie's big leather chair and said contentedly, 'This is the fucking life, mate. I always preferred a proper cash business. I loved going out in the morning, waiting to see what the day would bring.' He was laughing at his own words, because those days were nearly gone, and he felt old. 'I loved the promise of the new day and the possibility of a new earn! That must sound like fucking ancient history to you lot now.'

Danny smiled that easy smile of his and said, 'You know that I love hearing the old stories, Pat. You're a true raconteur, mate.'

Patrick sipped his Scotch and said happily, 'I like this place. We did good, Danny.'

They were easy in each other's company, as always, and Patrick knew that he had a diamond and that he should appreciate him more. His son's arrival had been a blow to Danny, and he understood that. He also knew that he had to ensure that Danny didn't feel left out of everything. He had relied on this man for a long time and he had never found him wanting. Loyalty was important to Patrick Kelly, and Patrick knew that Danny Foster felt exactly the same.

'What is happening with Joseph's wife, Pat? It must have been fucking mental.'

Patrick scowled and waved a hand, as if batting off a nuisance fly. 'Fucking loon she is. By the way, thank you for finding that brief for me – she seems on the ball. But Kate thinks that Bella needs serious help. She has fucking previous form and all, if you please! She lost her mind before, as a young girl, and caused fucking murders. But what I don't understand is how Joseph didn't see it. I knew from the second I clapped eyes on her that she wasn't the full two bob. There was something off about her – she was really rude to my Kate, and that didn't go in her favour, as you can imagine. But I was more interested in the kids, obviously. And to be truthful, I would have put up with anything for their sakes. Bella didn't exactly endear herself to any of us, but, as Kate pointed out, Joseph *married* her. I can't argue with that, can I? He says she wasn't like that when he met her. Oh, I don't fucking know! I love having the kids there with us, of course. But I think it is hard on Kate.'

Danny Foster refilled their glasses and said gently, 'Look, Patrick, I have to be honest, I wasn't too thrilled at Joseph turning up out of the blue. I've always looked on you as the father I wished I'd had. You knew that, I think. But having met Joseph, I like him, and you know he is not the first man to be blind-sided by a woman. So don't think any less of him – it's happened to a lot of blokes. Look at Dino Renshaw! I mean, his wife seemed to be beyond reproach, and then it turned out she was putting it out for anyone who tipped her the wink. When it comes to relationships, we all make the same mistake. We see what we *choose* to see, because we are all loved up.

'I feel sorry for Joseph, because this isn't a normal situation, is it? He had to finally admit that he had picked a wrong 'un. She gave him two beautiful kids, and even you said she was a good mother. What she is guilty of is not being able to control her anger and her aggression. Fuck me, Pat – if she was a man we would have had her on the payroll. All you can do is be there to pick up the pieces. When all is said and done, he is your flesh and blood.'

Patrick Kelly listened to what Danny had to say; he was talking a lot of sense. But Patrick couldn't help feeling that his son should have seen this coming.

Danny Foster leaned forward in his chair and, looking intently into Patrick's face, he said, 'Listen, Pat, he's not you or me. He doesn't live in our world. He thought she was a nice girl. He believed her and everything she said because, unlike us, it never occurred to him to question what she was saying. You can't start allocating blame, because that is the road to nowhere. Then he got himself a bit of strange and fell in love with it. It happens but, unlike our world, he didn't know how to cope. He's a university boy, Patrick, and he worked. And he realised, like a lot of men and women before him, that he had made the mistake of his life. He had tied himself to a woman he didn't love any more. He couldn't know what she was capable of, could he? Let the courts sort her out, and be there for your son and those grandchildren.'

Patrick smiled gratefully. It had taken Danny a lot to come to terms with Joseph coming into his life, and for him to treat this new competitor for Patrick's affections so magnanimously was something to be admired.

'You are right, Danny Boy. I shouldn't be so quick to judge Joseph, because he couldn't have foreseen this. No one could. I think I'm just disappointed in the way this has played out. What I need to do now is get a grip and make sure that it is dealt with in such a way that my grandchildren are not too affected.'

Danny Foster nodded his agreement. 'You need to remember that Joseph isn't like us, Pat. He's a civilian.'

Patrick sipped at his Scotch and felt himself relaxing.

This was exactly what he needed to hear, and it was why he had come to this yard today. He craved this normality, a reminder of what he was capable of, and of what he could still achieve, if he wanted to. He needed to remember exactly who and what he was – that he was a man to be reckoned with.

Chapter Eighty-seven

Annie Carr had come to talk to Miss Betterway again, and she wasn't impressed with having to wait. It seemed the teacher had managed to hang on to her job for now even after revealing the details of the sex circle to Annie. But then, as the headmaster himself had been in on the cover-up, he didn't exactly have a leg to stand on to give her the sack. Annie wouldn't like to be in either of their shoes when it came to the next school governors' meeting though.

Annie stood up and walked around the empty corridor and breathed in the smell of a school. Disinfectant, and the heat – combined with the closed glass doors and windows – made the whole place feel muggy. She slipped her cotton jacket off and put it into her bag, not even bothering to fold it up. She caught a glimpse of her reflection in the double doors and saw that she looked very unkempt. That wasn't unusual – she often looked untidy – but she needed to up her game and at least try to keep herself on the right side of scruffy. But until this case was over, she would eat, sleep and shit her job, if that was what it took to find the man responsible. She opened her bag up again and took out the folder with the pictures of Janet Cross in, and she held the file against her chest as if she was warding off some kind of evil.

When Miss Betterway finally invited her into her office, Annie Carr was seriously pissed off. And she was also ready to take Miss Betterway down, if the occasion warranted it. She couldn't understand a woman who couldn't, or wouldn't, drop everything to try to help three of her pupils who had been murdered. It was beyond Annie's comprehension.

As she walked into the familiar office, she said brightly but with no small amount of suppressed sarcasm, 'Thank you for finding the time in your busy day to see me. It is very much appreciated, I can assure you.'

Miss Betterway had the grace to look ashamed and, as she sat down, Annie saw the pile of books on her desk, and the different files that were dotted around the room.

'I'm working on the lessons for the new term and also trying to arrange the memorials for Kylie, Destiny and Janet. It's been a difficult time, as you can imagine, Detective Carr.'

Annie felt her anger deflate, because she knew that this had to be as hard for this woman as it was for her. Probably harder, because Miss Betterway had known them all personally.

'Can I get you a coffee?'

Annie forced herself to smile as she said lightly, 'That would be lovely, thank you.'

She used the time while Miss Betterway made the coffees to look around the office. She saw that a lot of time and effort went into making sure these children had the best education that their teacher could offer, and Annie felt a sliver of shame at how she had treated the woman. She saw that there was a thank-you letter being drafted for the Carters; they had once more put much-needed money into the school. From what she could see they had come to the school's aid by paying a lot of money for what she thought said 'gym equipment'. Annie had not realised how bad the financial state of the education system was, but then she wouldn't, as she didn't have any children of her own. But it seemed that schools like this, which were state-funded, struggled to make ends meet.

When Miss Betterway came back with the coffees, Annie smiled her thanks and tried to look as friendly as possible. Miss Betterway sat down at her desk, and Annie saw the way that the woman smoothed down her skirt and checked the buttons on her blouse. She was so self-contained, and Annie wondered if that was because of her job. It couldn't be easy – Annie knew that she wouldn't want to do it.

Smiling gently, Annie sipped her coffee a few times before saying, 'I need to talk to you about Janet Cross again in more detail. This is the third girl from the same school in the same year. I think that whoever we are looking for has some kind of connection with either the school or the girls. It stands to reason. So I need you to tell me *everything* you know or can remember about Janet Cross.'

Miss Betterway licked her lips nervously. The deaths had obviously hit her hard, and that was a natural reaction. But they had investigated everyone involved with this school, and no one stood out. Every one of them had an alibi for the nights in question. It was almost impossible to believe but, after every line of enquiry, there was still nothing to tie these girls together or even give an inkling as to who was involved in their disappearances and deaths.

Miss Betterway was quiet for a few moments, thinking hard. 'Janet Cross was a good girl. She wasn't like Kylie or Destiny – and I mean that in the nicest possible way. She wasn't involved with the bracelet stuff. She was nondescript really. She tried hard to fit in, but she just didn't have what it takes. A late developer in many ways, I suppose.'

Annie took the latest photos of Janet Cross out of the file and handed them to Miss Betterway, who was stunned.

'She certainly didn't look like this at school! But I can see that she was starting to blossom, at last.' She put the photos down and dropped her head into her hands in distress. 'She never did a thing to anyone. Janet was a nice kid, and that just isn't enough once they get to the "big school", as we used to call it. There is so much pressure on young people – the girls especially – these days. But Janet *never* indulged in risky behaviour like the other girls.'

'No attention from any boys?' Annie asked.

'Not that I know of. Stephen Carter was always kind to her, and that wasn't so surprising, he is nice to everyone. I wish there were more kids like him. I asked him to help her with a history project she was struggling with as he did so well on that module last year, and they sometimes ate lunch together after that, which didn't go down too well with a lot of the girls, as you can imagine. He is the *dream* boyfriend, and all the more so because he doesn't take any interest in the so-called popular girls. But he always had time for Janet. She adored him, of course. But that wasn't unusual, because all the girls adore him. He's good-looking, well dressed, and his dad drives a Rolls Royce! He is what the Americans term "the full package".'

Annie laughed despite herself, because she knew that Miss Betterway was absolutely right. Stephen Carter did seem to be a good lad.

'Do you know he's actually friendly with a lot of the loner kids. Because he doesn't care about being trendy, like the majority of his peers here, he's a breath of fresh air.'

Annie smiled. She had to admit she had found Stephen to be charming too. He had a nice family as well. She said as much, and Miss Betterway couldn't wait to sing their praises.

'Yes, they are good people. His father is a bit of a rough diamond, as I am sure you could tell. But he's a self-made man and very successful. He puts a lot of money into this school.'

Annie nodded her agreement. 'It would probably have been cheaper for them to send him to a good private school, I should imagine.' As soon as she said the words, she wished she could have taken them back. Miss Betterway was obviously deeply offended, and Annie was at pains to explain that she didn't mean what she said. 'I really didn't mean that how it came out, Miss Betterway. I wasn't meaning that the education would necessarily be better privately. I was talking purely from a financial point of view. I know that you all do a great job here and under difficult circumstances, I am sure.'

Miss Betterway was far from happy, but Annie felt she had smoothed her ruffled feathers enough to keep the peace.

'It *is* difficult, Detective Carr, and we pride ourselves on how well our pupils do.'

Annie Carr knew that she wouldn't get anything more that would be useful now and that it would be much better to retreat on this occasion. She stood up and held her hand out.

As Miss Betterway shook her hand, the woman said seriously, 'A private education cannot guarantee anything. My kids work because they want to. Not all of them – you can't reach the ones who are brought up on a diet of apathy by parents who never wanted to achieve either. But we do our best here to make sure our children have the opportunities, should they want to explore them.'

Annie Carr was suitably chastened, so she said sincerely, 'I am sure you do. Thank you for your time.'

Chapter Eighty-eight

'It is a big no, Patrick. It is not a good idea for Christine to come here when she leaves hospital – whenever that might be. What are you thinking! These children have just lost their mother. Whatever the circumstances, you *cannot* bring that woman into their home.'

Patrick had expected as much, but he had promised Joseph that he would try. The truth was he had not wanted to be the one to say no to his son. It was cowardly, but he didn't know what else to do. Joseph felt so guilty about what had happened to Christine that he felt he was honour bound to take care of her. She was going to have a long and painful road to any sort of recovery and Patrick wasn't too sure that she actually *wanted* to become a surrogate mother overnight anyway. He wondered how the kids would have taken it – especially young Joey. He had sussed far more than was good for him about the circumstances. Patrick was relieved that Kate had put her foot down, as he had been counting on her to do.

Now he had fulfilled his half of the bargain and asked

her. And he could tell Joseph that it was Kate who had put the kibosh on it.

'I know you are right, Kate, but I had to ask, darling. Joseph feels responsible for what happened—'

Kate interrupted him then, shouting angrily, 'He *should* feel responsible, Pat, because he *is*. I know he is your new blue-eyed boy, but *he* caused all this. How either of you could even think about bringing Christine Murray here I don't know! Bella is banged up in a psychiatric facility for the moment with that expensive brief on the case to boot – which is costing *you* a bomb, I know – and we have opened our home to him and the children. I have no problem with that. But I will *not* let that woman into the same house with his children. It is not only wrong, it is fucking creepy. Whatever Bella is, or whatever she has done, she is still those children's mother.'

Patrick Kelly was now desperately trying to find the words to extricate himself from Kate's wrath. Because when she said it out loud, it sounded even worse than he had first thought. Of course they couldn't house his son's bird – it was ludicrous.

Young Joey came into the office and, looking at Kate, he said quietly, 'Thank you, Kate. And could you inform my dad that if she comes here then I will leave? My friend Peter's parents would happily put me up.'

Patrick had the grace to look ashamed and, smiling sadly, he said to his grandson, 'Look, Joey, I wasn't exactly thrilled at the prospect. But you know she's in a bad way and she needs looking after.'

Joey Junior shrugged nonchalantly. 'My mum did a really awful thing, I know that. One day in the future I am sure we will be ready to meet with Christine. But that time is not now. I know my mum has done something very wrong but, as Kate just pointed out, she is still our mother, and we love her. Dad did something wrong too, remember.'

Patrick and Kate looked at this handsome young lad who spoke such a cartload of common sense – he was honest and not afraid to speak his mind.

'You are going nowhere, Joey. I can categorically state now that Christine Murray is not going to come and live in this house.'

Joey looked at Kate and she could see the tears shining in his eyes, and she felt a huge surge of affection for this decent and sensible young man.

'Thank you, Kate.' He left the room as quietly as he had entered it.

Kate looked at Patrick and raised her eyebrows in a questioning manner.

Patrick held up his hands in defeat. 'I know! I know I should never have even asked. But Joseph feels bad – as anybody would, if this had happened to them.'

Kate sighed heavily and loudly, and Patrick knew she was really annoyed with him.

'You might want to point out to your new-found *golden* boy, Patrick Kelly, that moving his fucking bird into what is, in effect, his children's new home might be seen as a *tad* fucking selfish. These children have been uprooted from everything they knew, have lost their mother – even if she is a bit suspect, shall we say – and are now trying to settle in with the new granddad they didn't even know existed until a few days ago. Now I know you very well, Patrick Kelly, and I know that, as moronic as you can be at times, you ain't that fucking stupid. You couldn't tell your Joseph no, so you wanted me to do it for you.'

He looked like a rabbit caught in headlights.

Kate smiled triumphantly. 'I am absolutely right, aren't I?'

'Look, Kate, I wasn't too thrilled myself at what he wanted, but he's in shock. He feels guilty about what happened to her.'

'I know he does, you have mentioned that enough times tonight, trying to justify all this old fanny! Well, you can tell him it is a dirty great big *no*. Not just from me but from his own son as well.'

Patrick Kelly knew that he had, in effect, shot himself in the foot and he decided to bow out of this situation as gracefully as possible. He was saved from further animosity by Annie Carr's arrival, and he had never been so pleased to see anyone in his life.

Annie noticed it and guessed she had arrived at what Patrick Kelly would call 'the right time'. As she walked through to the kitchen with Kate, she could see and feel the difference in the house. It had a completely different dynamic; it was untidy, for a start, and where once there had been a controlled quietness, there were now the sounds of televisions and chattering.

She wasn't sure if Kate was happy with the new

arrangement or not, but one thing she had observed was that Patrick Kelly was in his element. She could understand that all right; he had lost a daughter in the worst way possible, and now he had been given a second chance at a real family, so she could see what the big attraction was. Whereas Kate had had these kids thrust on her. It was one thing hosting them for a swimming party or a lunch, or even a sleepover. It was a different thing having them living under your roof. Especially given the circumstances that had brought them here. Annie Carr was glad that she had her single life at times like this, even if it felt like the price she had to pay to get on in her chosen profession.

She accepted a glass of cold white wine and, as she settled down at the kitchen table, she said carefully, 'I am getting the distinct impression that all is not quiet on this Western Front.'

Kate started to laugh and Annie joined in, and the atmosphere was immediately lighter. Annie opened her bag and took out the files she had copied. She needed to talk this through with Kate. What she needed was a different set of eyes.

Chapter Eighty-nine

Kate was scanning the paperwork Annie had given her while listening to her as she brought her up to speed on the developments.

'So this latest girl, Janet Cross, seems to have blossomed suddenly. Beautiful child, bless her, but she seems to have completely reinvented herself.'

Annie nodded in agreement. 'Janet started babysitting for her mum's friend, and she's a bit of an airhead. She took Janet under her wing and gave her make-up lessons and, from the money Janet earned, she was amassing a new wardrobe for herself. I think the goal was to go back to school at the end of the summer as a different girl.'

Kate looked at the pictures and saw what the score was. 'I had the same thing with Lizzy. She went from my baby girl, all legs and clumsiness, to all tits and teeth in a few months. It is so hard to be a teenager, because you look like a woman and everyone still treats you like a child. I have never had boobs in my life, but my girl went into a D cup overnight. She must have inherited them from Dan's side of the family! But it was hard for me, seeing her dress differently, act differently. Overnight they stop confiding in you. You become the enemy.'

Annie was familiar with the story and knew better than to go there tonight. 'With Kylie and Destiny there was a clear link, Kate. They were friends, they hung out together, and they were sort of the "popular girls" for want of a better expression. But Janet Cross doesn't fit the profile, she wasn't like them in any way. I am sure she aspired to be like them. But I feel that her abduction was opportunistic. I mean, according to the pathologist, the knife marks were hesitant and she was dead when the real torture started. I think there was an element of regret there. I think he took her on a whim. Then I think he wished he had left her alone.'

Kate nodded her agreement. 'I think your hunch is spot on, Annie. Have you had any luck with the searches? There are plenty of abandoned places around and about that could be used by the offender. He needs privacy, obviously, and somewhere that the girls' cries and screams won't be heard.'

Annie lit a cigarette and sighed noisily as she blew out the smoke. Kate automatically got up and opened the patio doors that led on to the garden. Now she had the kids in the house she was aware that smoking inside was not an option any more.

'That's the frustrating thing, Kate. We have been over every fucking inch of Grantley and the surrounding areas. There is absolutely nowhere we haven't fucking looked. We are chasing our own arses.'

Kate could sympathise with her friend. Unlike in TV, films and books, most crimes were solved through the most mundane reasons. Someone saw something, or the person responsible fucked up. There was very rarely a big dramatic climax. It was the everyday that normally tripped them up, the mundane was often the reason for them being caught. It had been proved time and time again. The Yorkshire Ripper was caught by accident – and he had been questioned, like a lot of other lorry drivers. It was always something small, something that became crucial because the police could use it to build a case. It was all trial and error; otherwise none of these multiple murderers would ever have gone on to the second victim.

'This is just a thought, but have you got Margaret to look through the old records from the council and the land registry, see if there are any properties with basements or something? I reckon these girls are being held locally. You said yourself that there are no tyre marks. No cars seen in the vicinity, either on CCTV or by members of the public. What you need, Annie, is to find out how these girls are being transported. That's the key, I think. I am not ruling out a car or a van, which makes sense, but whoever this is *knows* how to keep off the radar. I might be putting myself out on a limb here, darling, but I think you were right when you said that it all revolves around the woodland. That is a fucking big area, and there are a lot of houses that back on to it. Plus the businesses on the industrial estates – those are all near the woods. Remember that councillor – what was her name? – she fought to keep those woods from being destroyed. It was a few years ago, and it turned out that the wood used for the *Mary Rose*, Henry the Eighth's ship that sank, if I remember rightly, had come from the oak trees that grew there. That is why the woods are still so thick and still cover such a large area. She made sure that no one could destroy the habitat to build houses, or whatever.'

Annie Carr was smiling, because Kate was like a walking encyclopaedia of trivia. Only Kate would have known all that without looking it up.

'I remember her name now! Mary Barker Smith. Do you want me to go and have a chat with her? I bet she remembers which of the older properties could have cellars et cetera. She knows everything there is to know about Grantley and the surrounding areas. She fights to stop developments that she thinks will be a blot on the landscape, to quote Tom Sharpe! She has done a lot of good, in fairness to her – stopped a lot of unnecessary buildings that would play havoc with local wildlife.

'She also writes books on local history about the houses that were here and the people who lived in them. I actually have a few of them, Patrick likes all that kind of stuff. When she argued about the *Mary Rose* she caused a big stir at the time, and she gathered a lot of followers.'

Kate topped their glasses up, and Annie toasted her silently.

'I agree that we must be looking for a resident. They live locally, otherwise we would have found tyre tracks – something that we could use. Even by the shop where Destiny was found, there was literally nothing of note. Whoever had brought the body there had used the woods. Kylie was found in the woods, and Janet was found in the graveyard that leads to the woods. But, Kate, we have been over every inch. There is nothing in those woods that we haven't searched. There are old concrete bunkers from the war – we were amazed at what was there – old houses falling down. We looked all over the industrial estates, lock-up garages. We found nothing. And the amount of blood these girls lost, wherever they were they left their fucking mark.'

Kate gulped at her wine and said seriously, 'Then you are looking for a private property, aren't you? Like I said earlier, get Margaret to have a look at the houses that are near or back on to the woodland. See if any have basements, cellars or anything underground. It can't hurt, can it?'

Annie was writing everything down so she didn't forget it. 'No, Kate, you are right. It can't hurt. Let's face it, we have fuck-all else.'

Kate hugged her friend tightly. 'Listen, Annie, we've all been there. It never gets any easier though – that's the real tragedy.'

They sipped their wine quietly, each immersed in their own thoughts.

Chapter Ninety

Joseph O'Loughlin was in a quandary. His company had given him compassionate leave while they worked out their next move. He understood why, even if it rankled. The scandal involving two of their employees had rocked the company. At least he was on full pay – that was something. But he was finished, his reputation was ruined – his career basically over. Still, he had bigger fish to fry at the moment, and he knew that he had to sort his life out.

Bella's attack on Christine had been like an explosion, and he was angry with himself, because he had been aware for a long time that she was a woman on the edge. Finding Patrick Kelly had been a big part of why he had decided he couldn't live a lie any more. His father might be a criminal – 'a Face', as he would put it – but he didn't live a lie in any way, shape or form. What you saw was exactly what you got, and that had appealed to Joseph. Unfortunately, it had all backfired on him, and now he was in an impossible situation. He felt that he was drowning in guilt for what had happened to Christine, and for pushing Bella so casually over the edge.

Kate had given him the file on his wife and her previous violent behaviour and it had been an eye-opener. Bella had not had the greatest start in life, and he had pushed her to the limit. His major guilt was because of his children, who were to all intents and purposes motherless, and who he needed to be strong for. Patrick had pointed out the folly of Christine recuperating in his house with his children. He had hoped that Kate and his father could have acted as a buffer between his kids and Christine but he saw now it wasn't viable. He realised that he was unable to think clearly, or know what he was supposed to do to make it better for everyone involved, and that included Bella.

Although Christine wouldn't be able to go home for a little while, she had already said she was frightened to be in her flat on her own, and who could blame her? She had been through a very traumatic experience, and he was the reason that it had happened to her. She was so vulnerable right now – convinced he wasn't going to want her any more when he saw the full extent of the damage his wife had caused to her beautiful face. Joseph had told her he didn't care about that – it was her – Christine, the person – who he loved and he wasn't going anywhere. They would get through this together. But deep down when he caught a glimpse of the raw, devastating injuries Bella had inflicted on his lover he wanted to weep. Things would never be the same again for them.

Joseph was torn in so many ways. His children needed him too, and he knew that they should be his priority.

But he had never looked after them for a full day since they had been brought into the world. Bella had always been the main carer. He hated himself for admitting it, but they were too much for him. He couldn't look them in the face, the guilt was overpowering him. He was so grateful that his father was happy to have the children in his home and take care of them.

He knew that his son – his Joey – was cold and distant towards him, as if he held him responsible for what had happened. And he wouldn't blame him if he did. It was all a complete shambles. Only Amanda still treated him as she always had, but that was a disaster waiting to happen because one day she would be told the full story, and he knew that he wasn't going to come out of it with flying colours.

The shame of it all was weighing him down, and he knew that he had to get a grip and 'step up to the plate', as his father so succinctly termed it, and be there for the people who needed him. It was all a fucking mess – a terrible, terrible mess.

Kate came out to the conservatory and placed a mug of coffee in his hands, and he smiled his thanks. She was a looker, even at her age; it was the bone structure, he supposed, and the fact she was slim as a wand. He envied his father his happiness with this woman. Since Patrick and Kate had come into his life, he had seen what was important – and, more to the point, what he wanted. What he wanted had not included Bella, and he had tossed her aside after a few drinks and a few dinners with his dad. Patrick and his lifestyle had made him understand what was missing in his life, and now this was the upshot.

'Look, Joseph, I put the hard word on your dad about Christine coming here. You must know it would be fucking lunacy. Your children need you now, not your girlfriend. Patrick knew I would gainsay it, and he wanted me to say no. He can't refuse you anything, because of the lost time between you. Like Patrick, you are letting guilt eat away at you. Well, take it from me, it's a fruitless occupation – guilt is an emotion that is overrated. I know that myself from personal experience.

'You need to see to it your children go back to school next week, you need to give them a routine. Kids thrive on routine, especially when everything has fallen to shit. Of course you need to make sure that Christine is looked after too, and not left alone. So I would advise getting a nurse, or a carer of some description, in place for when she comes out. But you have to face up to your responsibilities, and one of those responsibilities is Bella. You must go and see her, and make sure that she understands that you do not blame her. You read her file, so you know she was always a bit on the dark side. Only you can put this all right. I'm happy to have the kids here – they are lovely children. But they need you now, more than Christine does because, at the end of the day, they are your flesh and blood.' She smiled, to take the sting out of her words. 'Lecture over, you can relax now.'

Joseph placed the mug of coffee on to the table nearby and, putting his head in his hands, he started to cry, saying over and over, 'What have I done?' He cried silently at first, and then his whole body started to shake with the enormity of what had happened to him and his family.

Kate pulled him into her arms and she held him close to her while he cried out all his pain and his fear. Patrick saw them from where he was sitting by the pool, and he sighed with relief. He trusted that Kate would know what to do. She always knew what was right. That was one of the reasons he loved her so much.

Chapter Ninety-one

Mary Barker Smith was in her eighties, but she looked a lot younger. Kate was impressed with the tiny woman's sheer energy. When she had rung her to arrange an appointment earlier in the morning, the woman had insisted that she come for lunch. Kate guessed that was because she had told her that she had read and enjoyed her books and was interested in finding out more about the older houses in Grantley. As she pulled on to the woman's drive, she admired the house and its gardens; she thought that Patrick would have loved it. It wasn't a huge property but it was old and it was well maintained, and the garden was a riot of colour.

She saw Mary Barker Smith waiting for her by the front door. It was arch-shaped and had a huge brass ring that was the knocker. Even the hinges were fantastic, and well looked after; everything shone in the summer sun.

'Kate Burrows, I remember you from when you were on the police force here. You were an asset, I know. Good to see a woman holding her own in what was, to all intents and purposes, a man's world. Come inside. I like a gin and tonic about now, and I am sure you would like one too.'

Kate followed her into the hallway and suppressed a smile. She sensed that Mary had already had a head start on her in the G&T department.

When they were settled on the patio, Kate sipped her drink and said genially, 'Your garden is absolutely beautiful. All your own work?'

Mary nodded. 'I have a gardener, of course, but I do a lot of it myself. I so enjoy the physical labour – I believe it keeps you in shape.'

Kate smiled her agreement, knowing that she was in the company of a true eccentric. 'I think you are probably right about that. I'm not much of a gardener myself. We have a man who looks after ours.'

Mary Barker Smith grinned happily. She was like a little bird, with small hands and feet and a luxuriant head of thick chestnut hair, and her make-up was perfect. She was wearing casual trousers and a pale lemon silk shirt. She looked cool and contained, which Kate was sure she was.

'You have a beautiful property too. I remember it before Mr Kelly bought it. His first wife was a charming woman, as I am sure you've heard. It's a delightful old property, and I was thrilled to see it come back to life. It had been empty for such a long time, and of course Mr Kelly got it for a song. A wonderful investment, if I might say. My husband, God bless his soul, adored that house. The thing is, Kate – I can call you Kate? – people don't realise just how much history is actually around them.

Did you know that Grantley St Saviour's Church can be traced back to the eleventh century? Oh, it was added on to, of course, over the years, but the crypt and some of the walls are from the original building. There is history everywhere you look, but so many people can't see it. I love history, and I actively seek it.'

She laughed, a light bubbling laugh, and Kate found herself laughing with her. Patrick would love her; he was fascinated by old buildings and what stories they could tell.

'That is why I wanted to talk to you today, Mary. I was wondering about the older houses around and about, especially the ones that border the woods and the commons. I understand that some of them have quite interesting beginnings.'

Mary took a big gulp of her drink, before saying excitedly, 'Undoubtedly. There are some beautiful examples of Georgian architecture, and a few that go back to medieval times. Most are from the Victorian age but still impressive, I can tell you. A lot were built on land that once held very old properties. The Victorians were clever because they would utilise whatever was already there. Many of those properties have underground cellars et cetera. When you asked me about it earlier, it got me thinking. There are a lot of old tunnels here too. St Saviour's, for example, has a tunnel that goes right to Fernbrook House – you know, the big place out by Dutton Moat? It's a hotel now, of course. Well, it has a priest hole that leads directly to the church. It's where the priests would have been hidden during the Reformation. There are a lot of hidden places – you just have to know where to look. Take Gallows Farm, for example, out by Helmsley. The house is quite new, only a hundred or so years old, but it was built over a very old place, so they utilised the underground cellars. There was a wine cellar, you know, the usual.'

A short, heavyset lady of indeterminate age came out to them and smiled at Kate. She said in a soft Welsh lilt, 'Lunch will be served in five minutes, Mary.'

Mary thanked her and, winking at Kate, she said cheerfully, 'That's Bronwyn – I inherited her with the house! She's been with me over forty years. Wonderful cook. I could burn water, I'm afraid!'

She led them through to the dining room, and Kate sat down on an old Georgian ladder-back chair that had seen better days but was still handsome. Her view was of the rolling lawns and the rose garden, and Kate had to admit that she was enjoying herself. Mary was good company, and interesting to listen to, and also she was able to sit back and relax for a change. Bronwyn brought in an attractively presented salmon, and some new potatoes with butter and mint, and a really colourful bowl of salad.

'Everything comes from the garden, dear – except the salmon, of course. That came from Waitrose!'

Kate laughed with delight, and as they helped themselves to the food Mary kept up a constant stream of conversation.

'I remember seeing you on the TV, when that

Markham man was terrorising the place. You were very clever to catch him like you did. Do you have any children?'

Kate smiled, saying, 'Just one daughter. She lives in New Zealand with her husband and children. I do miss them. We visit, but it is a very long way to go. Do you have any children yourself?'

'Oh goodness me, no! Never happened – not for want of trying, I can tell you. I think my husband was firing blanks! Not that I ever said that to him, of course! But there were few children on his side of the family, whereas my family seemed to knock them out at the drop of a hat! But I must admit I was happy enough with my James. We travelled and we had lots of nieces and nephews – thanks to my six brothers and sisters – so we didn't really miss out. Now let's get back to what you came here for.'

Bronwyn had already replenished their glasses, and Kate was enchanted by the whole set-up. She was determined to invite this lovely lady to dinner; she knew that Patrick would love her. As Mary talked about the different houses around and about, she seemed to come to life, and Kate found herself fascinated with the different histories the houses held. She was especially interested in the houses that were built on the ruins of other properties. These were the ones that could hold the key to Annie's case. It was a long shot, but it was worth exploring.

Plus it got her out of her own home, and that was

something she wouldn't want to admit to anybody. As much as she liked those children, and as much as she was sorry for them, she would be a liar if she didn't admit that it had all been a big upheaval for everyone concerned.

Chapter Ninety-two

Stephen Carter was lying by the swimming pool when Annie Carr and DC Karim arrived at his home. Sylvie Carter welcomed them like long-lost relatives, and they both felt relaxed to be in such wonderful surroundings. As they settled down on the patio, they gratefully accepted long cold glasses of home-made lemonade. Jonny Carter wasn't there – he was at one of his sites – but Sylvie introduced them to his mother, Wanda Carter, a real old cockney with dyed-blond hair and heavy gold jewellery. She sat down with them and smiled in a friendly way as she gave them both the once-over. Annie Carr felt the urge to laugh, but she held it in.

Wanda sat back in her chair and said, in a real, deep cockney accent, 'So come on, then, what's he done this time?'

Sylvie pushed her mother-in-law's shoulder playfully, saying loudly, 'He ain't done nothing, Wanda! He knew those poor girls who were murdered, that's all. They went to his school.'

Wanda didn't say anything, she just shrugged gently. Annie and DC Karim were watching the exchange with barely concealed mirth. It was obvious that Wanda was a force to be reckoned with.

Stephen didn't get up from his sunlounger, he just smiled at them in his usual friendly way. Sitting up, he said sadly, 'Poor Janet, she was such a nice girl. I helped her on a project on the Industrial Revolution. Janet was like me – happy to trawl through the books in the library rather than Google what she wanted to know online. She understood that if you had to track knowledge down personally then you didn't forget it. She was just a really good girl.'

He looked so upset that Annie felt terrible for him. But she had to ask him if he knew anything about Janet that maybe her mother didn't. 'Miss Betterway told me that you were friendly with Janet.' Annie opened her bag and took out the pictures of her. She showed them to Stephen, and she watched as he frowned in confusion.

'That is Janet, but she looks so different to how she usually did.' The incredulity in his voice was evident. 'Mum, look at this.'

Sylvie came over and took the pictures from her son and, after she glanced at them, she said frankly, 'Oh, she looks completely different. I always said that she would blossom, a late developer like I was. She was a nice kid, and she was always polite company when she came here. After Stephen helped her with her homework, I would drop her home afterwards. But she never looked like that! She always seemed very young for her age and she didn't have a lot of confidence, but that's par for the course with some teenage girls, I suppose.'

Annie didn't answer her. Instead she looked at Stephen as she said seriously, 'I understand that she didn't have that many friends. Stephen, can you think of anyone that might have come into her orbit recently that you knew of? It could just be something she said, or someone she mentioned in passing.'

Stephen sat there for a while, and he put his hand up to his lips in consternation. 'I don't know if this is important but I did see her in a car with Justin Barber. But that was ages ago. Janet wasn't the kind of girl to attract much attention to herself, she was painfully shy.'

DC Karim asked quietly, 'When did you see her with Justin Barber?'

Stephen shrugged. 'It was a while ago, I can't really remember. I just saw them at the traffic lights in the high street. You know the ones outside Marks and Spencer's?'

'What kind of car was Justin driving?'

Stephen shook his head. 'I can't remember exactly. It was black, I know that, and it had what looked like zebra-skin covers on the front seats. I do remember thinking, what was Janet doing in the car with him? Everyone knows the Barbers deal drugs, and are in a gang.' He sighed heavily.

DC Karim pushed further, 'Didn't you ask her about it? I mean, it doesn't sound like something Janet Cross would do. As you said yourself, she was painfully shy.'

Stephen Carter just sighed again sadly. 'It was a while ago and, to be honest, I suppose I just forgot about it. It was only you two asking me to think of anything unusual that brought it into my mind. She would know Clinton from my year too – they are from the same estate. I just didn't think anything significant of it at the time.'

Annie Carr smiled at him and she watched as DC Karim wrote down everything in his notebook.

Wanda seemed to come back to life, as she said jovially, 'You from round here?'

DC Karim shook his head. 'No, I'm a London boy like you are a London lady!'

Wanda smiled at him, showing her startlingly white false teeth to their best advantage. 'I'm a Whitechapel girl myself. My old dad was an Italian immigrant, my mother was Irish. My son, Jonny, has the darker skin, you know. My father was a handsome fucker – it was how we made our money. He would sell ice cream all over the East End, and he was so good-looking that all the women would break their necks to come out and get served by him!'

They all laughed with her, even Stephen and his mother.

Sylvie agreed. 'He was a looker – I've seen the photos!'

Wanda smiled at her daughter-in-law, happy to remember her father.

Annie laughed with them. 'You are a very good-looking family, I must say.'

Wanda grinned again, enjoying the compliment, and Annie could see from her bone structure that she had been very attractive in her day.

'Oh, you should have seen my husband, now he could turn heads! Dressed like a male model, he had all his suits handmade. Didn't have a pot to piss in at times, but always well turned out. "Clothes maketh the man" he always said – the lying two-faced bastard that he was.' She was roaring with laughter again.

Sylvie joined in. 'Here, Wanda, remember our wedding? That was so funny!' She turned to face Annie and DC Karim, and she said laughingly, 'He turned up in a new suit, all done up like the dog's knob, and we were already in the church. He was late, as always! What was he like for his time-keeping, Wanda?'

Wanda was laughing her head off now. 'A nightmare! He never looked at his watch, the fucking imbecile.'

Sylvie carried on with the story through her laughter. 'He was all full of himself, as usual, and as he slipped into the church trying not to be noticed because he was late, his mate who had dropped him off started playing the bells of the ice-cream van he had brought him in. I walked down the aisle in my wedding dress and everyone in the church started singing along to "Windmill In Old Amsterdam"! Made the day, though – it was hilarious.'

Wanda grinned with happiness. 'He was about as much use as an ashtray on a canoe, but we did have some good times.'

Sylvie hugged her mother-in-law, and Annie saw genuine affection there.

'He was a real character, Wanda, no doubt about that.' Sylvie filled up everyone's glasses again and, suddenly serious, she said, 'I feel bad, having a laugh and a joke, and that poor child is dead.'

Wanda grabbed her hand in both of hers, and she said firmly, 'All the more reason to be thankful for what you have, darling. Remember that it can all be snatched away from you at any time. You have to enjoy life while you can – believe me, girl, I know.'

Sylvie smiled sadly. 'Wise words, Wanda, very wise words.'

Annie and Ali Karim felt like intruders. The two women were obviously very close. It was a pleasure to watch them together. Then Jonny Carter turned up, and Annie and DC Karim were sorry to break up the party. It was a really beautiful and happy home.

Chapter Ninety-three

Annie and DC Karim turned up at Justin and Clinton Barber's home at five o'clock in the evening. It was another beautiful day and they were both sweating as they walked up the front steps of the block of maisonettes. Annie looked around her sadly; it was a real shithole of an estate and, in the brightness of this summer's day, it looked worse than usual. There was graffiti everywhere, and the stench from the communal bins was so overpowering her eyes were actually watering. The smell of urine as they passed the lifts was strong, and the noise of different music from each individual flat was irritating in itself. A lot of the front doors were wide open where people were attempting to get a breath of air to cool them down. It was as depressing as it was filthy.

Annie hoped that the council hurried up and sorted the place, because no one should have to live like animals in this day and age. She felt bad as soon as the thought entered her head, but that was the trouble, everyone was guilty of it. This was a bona fide shithole. And, unfortunately, as a policewoman, her experience was that so were a lot of the people who lived here. Harsh but true. She came from a similar background and she had not turned out like these people. She knew that she was a snob in some of their eyes, but she couldn't help the way she felt.

Patrick Kelly always said that people make slums not houses, and she agreed to a certain extent. He argued that when you were given these kinds of places to live in, and they were already destroyed, that didn't give the people too much choice. There were a couple of maisonettes and flats that were well looked after, but they were few and far between. The people inside these boxes were fighting a losing battle. Patrick Kelly, the criminal fucker that he was, believed that people should all be treated with respect. He was very vocal about it, and most of the time Annie Carr was in agreement with him. But not on days like today.

The Barbers' front door was wide open and they could hear Desmond Dekker blaring out as they walked into the hallway. The paper was peeling off the walls, and the carpet had seen much better days, but for all that it was clean after a fashion. A blond-haired woman in a sequinned T-shirt came out of the small kitchen and, looking them up and down, she rolled her eyes and shouted up the stairs, 'Boys, you have visitors!' Then she went back into the kitchen and carried on stirring a pot on the stove.

Annie Carr raised her eyebrows and made a funny face, and then she started to walk up the stairs with DC Karim close behind her. They could smell the marijuana but they ignored it. Annie motioned to the door to her left and then she opened the door directly in front of her. Justin was lying on his bed watching a soft porn film with a young black girl who was wearing nothing but a very surprised look on her face.

Justin looked at Annie standing there and, closing his eyes in obvious annoyance, he said with feeling, 'Oh, what the fuck do you want now, lady?'

The girl pulled a sheet around her to cover her nakedness and Justin, who was in bright blue boxers, turned off the film. Standing up, he pulled on a pair of jeans from a pile of clothes lying on a chair.

Annie said sarcastically, 'Sorry to interrupt. Downstairs, *please.*'

Clinton was already on his way down, and Annie was pleased to see that he was at least alone and fully dressed. She was always grateful for small mercies. Once they were all in the tiny front room, she looked through the serving hatch and was not surprised to see that the mother had no interest in what was occurring in her home with her sons. She carried on with what she was doing as if they weren't there. This had happened before, and she knew the drill. It was soul-destroying, but Annie didn't say a word. This was the usual where this estate was concerned, and there was nothing she could do or say to make a difference.

'So, Justin, I have been informed that you knew Janet Cross? Is that right?'

He shrugged nonchalantly. 'Yeah, and? We all live around here, innit?'

Annie took a deep breath, because she wasn't in the mood for his rudeness at this moment in time. She bellowed at him, at the top of her lungs, 'You taking the fucking piss out of me? You know she is *dead*, idiot boy, just like Kylie and Destiny. And once more your name has come up! You were seen with her in a black car with zebra-striped seats. Now I don't think that car is going to be hard to find, do you? So use your fucking loaf and tell me the score.'

Clinton was frightened, but Justin wasn't – that much was evident. The mother, on the other hand, was still acting like she was completely alone in her home. It was surreal.

'That is fucking unbelievable. That was months ago, and I gave her a lift because she was on her own and waiting at a bus stop near Gains Lane. It was getting dark and I saw her and offered her a lift. No fucking law against that, is there?'

Annie Carr looked at DC Karim, and they locked eyes for a few seconds.

'Did she tell you what she was doing there?'

Justin rolled his eyes again, before saying angrily, 'Why the fuck would I even be interested? She was a kid from the estate – I was just doing my civic duty.'

DC Karim said loudly, 'There are two bus stops there. Which one was she standing at?'

Justin opened his arms wide, and sighed heavily before saying, 'The top of the lane, by the old brick works. You know, I never thought nothing of it, but there ain't nothing out there, so I don't know why she would have been there. But she was OK. She didn't say much, was just grateful for the lift. I was playing my music, you know, and smoking my spliff. I dropped her off by her flats and never thought about it again. She's just a kid, man.' He sighed once more. 'Just a nice little kid. This is all so fucked up, man, people dying like that. You should be doing something about it.'

Annie didn't even bother to dignify that with an answer. 'How about you, Clinton? When was the last time you saw her?'

Clinton shook his head in bewilderment. 'I don't know. I see her around school and on the estate. I don't really take any notice of her.'

Sandra Barber stuck her head through the serving hatch and said offhandedly, 'I seen her. I complimented her on her hair actually.'

Annie looked at the woman who suddenly seemed interested in what was going on in her sons' lives. 'When was this?'

Sandra Barber turned off the gas stove and, wiping her hands on a grubby tea towel, she walked through the hallway and into the front room.

'I work out at the petrol station by Crooks Point. We're the last place before you hit the M25. I saw her on my way to work last week . . . might have been the week before. I take a shortcut through the woods to the bus stop, and she was there. I chatted to her until the bus arrived. Beautiful hair, and all natural too. She looked lovely, bless her, so I told her.'

'Where did she get off the bus?'

Sandra sighed and shook her head. 'I have no idea. I was reading my magazine and she sat right at the front.

I sit at the back. To be honest, I wasn't taking any notice. I mean, why would I?'

Annie Carr was listening intently. She fished a card out of her pocket and placed it on the coffee table. 'If any of you can think of anything else, please give me a ring.' Then, turning to Justin, she said in a warning tone, 'Don't make me get you busted, boy. No more dealing from here, OK?'

He barely nodded.

Annie and DC Karim left the maisonette, both with food for thought.

Chapter Ninety-four

'She sounds a right card.'

Kate laughed softly as she said, 'Honestly, Annie, it's like I said to Pat, she's better than a play. Really interesting, though a bit eccentric. But she is a mine of information where Grantley and the surrounding areas are concerned. I told her that you would be in touch with her, and she was happy for you to do that.'

Annie was smiling into the phone. 'I'm still looking into what Sandra Barber had to say. It's interesting that Justin picked Janet Cross up by Gains Lane, and his mum saw her on a bus that goes out to nowhere. We are going to follow the route and see what we can come up with.'

Kate sighed over the line. 'Yes, it is odd. But then one thing I can guarantee you about young girls, there is never a rhyme to their reason! She might have just fancied a bus ride to show off her new finery. But by the same token the precinct would be a better option for her to do that. I can't think what is out that way that would interest a young girl. There are few houses out that way, and not even a decent pub. But you need to get a car out to follow the route, see what might be out there. Somewhere the kids might be meeting up to drink, take drugs, whatever. There are a few abandoned places out there.' She sighed once more. 'Kids can find a place to meet up, and they ain't fussy. All they want is privacy.'

Annie laughed sadly. 'It's a melon scratcher all right. I've had Margaret Dole searching through all the planning applications going back through the years. Bloody hell, Kate, you would be amazed at how many people have requested cellars for wine, cold storage and the like. I said to Ali Karim, it's like being in America where those nuts build bunkers in case there's a nuclear war or the Rapture starts one night!'

Kate laughed with her. 'Some nut-nuts, I grant you that one, darling!'

They were quiet for a few moments, both wondering what might be the importance of the latest information.

'Anyway, look, I have to go. I promised Patrick we would go out to dinner tonight. We need a bit of alone time, I think.'

'OK, Kate. I'll keep you posted, and thanks.'

Annie turned her phone off and looked at her desk. She wondered what the hell she was missing. And like Kate before her, she sat back in her chair and started to trawl through everything once again, in the vain hope that she might see something of importance.

DC Karim was at his desk and looking through his files too. Like Annie he felt that they were at an impasse. There was nothing new happening, and there was nothing that they had not seen and looked into. It was frustrating for them all, but there was nothing any of them could do about it.

Annie Carr actually felt a depression washing over her as she scanned the statements and the evidence; she knew that if there had been anything of value, someone would have found it by now. That stood to reason.

She glanced at her watch and saw that it was gone seven, and she yawned noisily. 'I am calling it a day, people. I suggest you all do the same. Get some sleep, and hopefully we will have fresh eyes tomorrow.'

DC Karim walked to her desk and said quietly, 'Fancy a drink, boss?'

Annie smiled, and nodded her agreement. 'Sounds good to me. Fuck-all going on here.'

As they left the station together, Annie lit a cigarette and smoked it with relish while they walked to the local pub. They were soon settled in the small garden area, drinks in front of them.

DC Karim said tiredly, 'Nice family, the Carters, but if I'm honest, Annie, I don't like that kid, Stephen. There is something about him. I can't take to him.'

Annie shrugged. 'Why? What bothers you?'

DC Ali Karim was quiet for a few moments, before he said seriously, 'I am not sure, Annie. But there is something underlying there . . . with him . . . with the way he acts. I know that it is completely without any substance, but I wouldn't trust him as far as I could throw him.'

Annie laughed at his words. 'We all feel like that about people, but there's nothing we can do about it.'

She leaned towards him and said in a whisper, 'I don't like DC Allison's wife. Now if you want off, she's the one! Strange as fuck and twice as weird! But that doesn't mean anything, Ali. All it means is that they rub us up the wrong way.'

DC Karim laughed at her words. 'You're right, but there's something about him, especially today. I felt like he was laughing at us. The fact he didn't get off the sun-lounger when we came . . . Oh, I don't know exactly what bothered me. His grandmother saying, "What's he done this time?" stuck with me because, the more I think about it, the more I think she wasn't joking.'

Annie was listening to him intently; she sympathised. Everyone got feelings like that in their job, and she was not going to shoot him down in flames. So she sipped her wine and said evenly, 'Look, mate, we have three dead girls, and fuck-all to go on. That makes us all fuck-ing irritated, and it makes us look for things to latch on to. I get that, but what we have to do is keep it in per-spective, you know?'

Ali Karim nodded his agreement, but he wasn't con-vinced. And Annie could see that.

Instead she said brightly, 'Tell you what you can do. Tomorrow have a closer look at him and see what comes up. His school records and everything else so far seem to be in order. But I'm willing to go along with you, because it will put your mind at rest. Still, he has an alibi for everything. We made sure of that with everyone concerned.'

DC Karim smiled as he sipped his gin and tonic. He

suspected his feeling was without foundation, but he was determined to find out what he could about the boy and his family.

A couple of other officers were in the pub, and Annie waved them over. Before long they were all chatting and telling old war stories. DC Ali Karim put his thoughts to the back of his mind. After a couple of gins he wasn't so sure that he was being rational about the situation after all.

Chapter Ninety-five

Todd Richards was small for his age, but with a big personality and a natural confidence. He lived in a small cul-de-sac in the nicer part of Grantley. His parents, Alice and Jim, both worked in local government and were a quiet couple who were well liked and respected. Todd had been a late child; Alice and her husband had never thought they were going to be parents, and Todd's arrival when they were in their forties had been like a miracle. He was everything to them, and they adored him.

It was now gone ten o'clock, and his parents were starting to get genuinely worried about him. He'd been unusually quiet the past couple of days but they hadn't wanted to pry. Fifteen year olds were prone to mood swings after all. But this wasn't Todd-like behaviour. They had rung his mobile but couldn't get through. Then they had rung round his friends, and no one had seen him. As they watched the news they were both on red alert to hear his key in the front door.

At ten thirty Jim went to the landline and phoned the police. He knew that his son wasn't the type to stay out or cause them any kind of worry. Even if Jim was made to look a fool, he didn't care. He had a bad feeling, and he needed to feel like he was doing something.

He poured his wife a medicinal brandy as they waited for the police to arrive.

Chapter Ninety-six

Danny Foster was so angry he had to go into the office in his house and pour himself a large Scotch. He wasn't a man who suffered fools gladly, and that was one of his strengths, one of the reasons that Patrick Kelly held him in such esteem. So to find out that a pair of absolute fuckers like the Christmas brothers could even think of aggravating him was *outrageous*. But it seemed that, even though he had given them the hard word, they still thought they could take him for a cunt.

He knew that he had to sort this before Patrick Kelly found out about it, and that is exactly what he was going to do.

He made a few phone calls and then, when he was satisfied he had done all he could, he drove himself into East London.

Chapter Ninety-seven

Annie Carr felt like shit, but she had sobered up enough to take a quick shower and make her way to the Richards' house. She had called PC Jenner to pick her up, because she wasn't sure she should drive. But she kept that to herself, obviously.

As they made their way over, she got the girl to stop off so she could get herself a strong coffee. She also bought some extra-strong mints; she knew the drill. Her brain was telling her that this could not have anything to do with the missing girls, but she was too experienced to rule anything out. The fact the boy was a pupil in the same school was a red flag in itself. But she knew that she had to look at this with completely fresh eyes.

She remembered the kid and he didn't seem like a troublemaker. But she was hoping he would turn up, half-pissed and embarrassed. She felt sick and tired, and she was wishing that she had not had the last few drinks, but there wasn't much she could do about that now.

She walked into the house and the fear in the air was palpable; her heart went out to the couple who were obviously going out of their minds with worry. It was at times like this she was glad that she wasn't a parent – she didn't envy these poor people their fear or their terror. Because they both looked absolutely terrified, and she didn't blame them. She would be the same if she was in their position. It was the price you paid when you had a child.

As she turned to the boy's parents she forced a smile on to her face, but she wasn't fooling anyone. 'So where did Todd say he was going tonight?'

His father was sitting on the sofa, his arms around his wife, who, Annie could see, was incapable of coherent conversation, and he said sadly, 'Well, that's just it. We don't know. He left the house in a hurry about five, saying he'd be back later. We didn't think anything of it. It's summer, with the long evenings, we just assumed he was off meeting his friends. But he *never* stays out late without calling us. He's a good kid. He just *wouldn't* worry us like this.'

'Did he say where he was going, or mention a friend's name today?'

Jim Richards shook his head sadly. 'He didn't say anything, we trust him to come home at a reasonable time. If he is going to be late, he *always* lets us know. This is not like him, Todd knows that we worry, especially his mother. He *wouldn't* frighten us like this.'

Annie believed the man, but she knew that teenagers could go AWOL on a whim. Not that she would say that, of course. But most missing kids turned up with their tails between their legs and the promise of a serious bollocking – even the so-called good ones. It was par for the course and part of growing up.

She sat down on a dining chair and, taking out her notebook, she started to question them in as kind a way as possible. But she had a bad feeling about this; and she felt in her heart that it was connected somehow with the girls who had been murdered. She couldn't prove anything, but the timing was too coincidental for there not to be a link. Now she had to question these two people about how well their son knew the dead girls.

Chapter Ninety-eight

Kate and Patrick were both relaxed and pleasantly enjoying being in his restaurant in Manor Park. It was a new endeavour; Patrick had financed it, and it had turned out to be a good investment. It was full of Faces, but they paid, so that was a result in itself. Patrick had put out the word that anyone who took the piss had to answer to him. The chef was a young guy whose cooking was unbelievable and who also had a good head for business. He was a diamond, and he could have a row if the situation was needed; Patrick really liked him. All in all, he was pleased with the purchase, and Patrick knew that the restaurant was already getting a lot of interest through word of mouth. What more could he want?

Tonight had been a really good night; both he and Kate had needed some time together, especially since he had just done whatever he wanted, without even asking her about any of it, where Joseph O'Loughlin was concerned. The fact that she had accepted his decisions was something he appreciated more than she realised.

'I love you, Kate – you know that, darling. I know that this isn't what we envisaged, but I can't do anything else. He is my son, and those kids are my flesh and blood.'

Kate sighed and then laughed. 'I know they are your flesh and blood – it's not like you haven't reminded me fifty times a day, Pat. For fuck's sake, I get it, OK? I understand, but you must remember that Joseph needs a fucking serious wake-up call, and that is my last word on it. Now let's change the subject, shall we? This is supposed to be about us, not anything or *anyone* else.'

Patrick laughed at her. 'Do you know what, Kate? You are the only woman who could talk to me like that.'

Kate picked up her wine glass and sipped loudly. Then she pretended to do a loud swallow. 'I'm not so sure, Mr Kelly – I think Renée might have had a few words with you over the years!'

Patrick grinned. 'Not like you do, though, Kate. She would keep me in my place, but she wouldn't jump on me as often as you do. She picked her fights, and she was shrewd enough to make sure they were fights she could win. Big difference, lady.'

Kate looked at the man she had loved for so long, and she understood that he was trying to tell her that she had finally replaced Renée. And the strange thing was she didn't care about that any more.

'All I want is you to sort Joseph out, because I think he's weak, Pat, and those children need him to be strong.'

Patrick nodded and said sadly, 'I know, Kate, he's all over the place. But he will get there, I'll make sure of that.'

Kate knew when to let things go; she had said her piece and she would leave it at that. It was useless with a man like Patrick Kelly to keep smashing the point home – that would just make him more determined to prove himself right. She smiled to herself, because she knew him better than he knew himself.

Her mobile rang and she answered it as Patrick was ordering himself a brandy and a cigar. It was the Chief Superintendent, and Kate listened to him in shock as he asked her humbly if she would be kind enough to come on board and give her valued opinion on the murders of the three local girls. He also informed her that a young man was now missing, and he would appreciate it if she would be good enough to give her invaluable insight into the cases.

Kate was so shocked she didn't know whether to laugh or cry. But she knew that the fact he had rung her – on her mobile and at this time of night, no less – meant that this was serious.

'Of course, sir, anything I can do to help.'

She didn't tell him that she already had everything pertaining to the cases and that she had been helping Annie Carr from the get-go, although she had no doubt the two-faced fucker already knew. Instead she just said nicely, 'I assume you have already talked to everyone concerned and they are aware that you have requested my help?'

She couldn't resist sticking the knife in. She knew, and he knew, that she was already on board – had been from day one. Now he was just making it official. She smiled to herself as he assured her that he would make sure that she would be welcomed with open arms.

'I know that your experience will be invaluable, Kate, and I appreciate you agreeing to come in.'

Kate couldn't resist saying innocently, 'I will do my best, sir.'

When she put the phone down, she immediately called Annie who, it was clear, had no idea that Kate had been seconded to the team. She was pleased to have Kate back on board in a professional capacity, but she was not thrilled that it had been done behind her back. But, as Kate pointed out to her, this wasn't personal; it was about the Chief Super saving his own arse.

Chapter Ninety-nine

Kate was in bed and Patrick was enjoying a solitary nightcap when he took the call about the Christmas brothers. He was not impressed at all. In fact, he was fucking fuming at the diabolical liberty they thought they could take with him. He was also not impressed with Danny Foster, who apparently didn't think that he should have even mentioned it to him. As he was driving into East London he wished that he had not had another large brandy but, as he told himself, there wasn't much he could do about that now.

He pulled up outside the garages he owned off the Caledonian Road and, getting out of his motor, he wondered at these two brothers who could be so fucking dense that they thought they could have him over. They'd been warned to keep away from the clubs and had they listened? Had they fuck! It was a complete fucking piss-take of the first water. He opened the boot of his Mercedes Sport and took out a baseball bat, and then he walked over to the garages and banged on the only door with the light showing underneath it.

He shouted loudly and very angrily, 'Open up, Danny Boy, the fucking cavalry has finally arrived.'

The door was opened slowly, and Patrick sensed immediately that he wasn't welcome. That annoyed him even more. He knew that he was being unreasonable, but he couldn't help himself. *This* was what he missed, *this* was what he craved being part of again. It was also what he paid Danny Foster for, though he chose to forget that momentarily. All he could think was he was too far out of the game these days – even though that was what he had wanted and what he was paying exorbitant amounts of money for.

Noel Christmas was tied to a chair and already looking seriously battered and his elder brother, Nick, was watching it all from his vantage point – on the floor.

Patrick looked at Danny and said loudly, 'You didn't think to tell me about this, then?'

Danny Foster looked at his boss, at the man who he revered and who he respected more than anyone else on the planet, and he said snidely, 'No, Pat. I was under the impression that *you* were *retired* and *I* was being paid to make sure that you didn't have to deal with shit like this.'

Patrick Kelly knew that Danny was absolutely right and that he should not have been within a donkey's roar of this place, but he didn't care. He was incensed that the Christmas brothers had thought they were in with a fucking chance. That told him that they didn't think he was a worthy opponent any more. He didn't care who was behind this pair of muppets, because that is exactly what they were – a pair of fucking wannabes. A pair of wankers who actually thought that they could have *him* over. It was ludicrous, and it was an insult. And Patrick Kelly had never responded well to insults of any kind, as they were all about to find out.

'You know who is bankrolling them, don't you, Danny Boy?'

Danny Foster nodded his agreement.

'Then we shall deliver them to their doorstep as a warning, won't we?'

Danny knew that he had no choice but to agree with Patrick. After all, he paid their wages. He also knew that there would be no talking to Patrick Kelly while he was like this. Pissed and with a problem that involved his son, his daughter-in-law and his grandchildren. Patrick *needed* this tonight, if for no other reason than it would take his mind off what was really bothering him. The other men in the lock-up were thrilled to be in the company of Patrick Kelly, and Danny knew that Patrick would not disappoint.

That was his secret weapon; Patrick Kelly could harm and maim, and it didn't bother him in the least. Danny Foster had watched and learned from the master. A man who had been around since the old days, when this kind of thing was expected. Danny looked around him and he knew that he had to let Patrick have his head, because this would go down in history. It would become a story that harked back to the old days, and that could only be good for them.

Patrick looked at Danny Foster, and he said jovially,

'Pour us all a drink, Danny Boy, this is going to be a long night.' Then he looked at the Christmas brothers, and he said quietly, 'You fucking pair of retards really thought you could have me over? Thought that I would swallow my knob on the say-so of a pair of fucking *degenerates*? What fucking planet are you two on, for fuck's sake?'

Then he set about Noel Christmas with the baseball bat, and everyone there knew that neither of the Christmas brothers was going to see the light of day ever again. Patrick Kelly was on a mission, and he had the fucking hump. He was not a happy bunny. They were also aware that they were in the presence of a real *Face*, a man who had been in the game since before they were born. It was a privilege to be a part of something so Old School and so fucking violent. It was a real learning curve for all those who were there.

Danny Foster stepped back and let Patrick Kelly do his worst. At the end of the day, he had no other choice.

Chapter One Hundred

The next morning, Patrick and Danny were ordering breakfast in a café Patrick owned on Bethnal Green Road. He had acquired it many years before from a Turkish guy who had owed him a serious amount of wedge – a degenerate gambler who Patrick had always liked but who had eventually queered his own pitch. In the end, even Patrick Kelly had to be seen to sort the fucker out. It was about showing strength and, because everything was common knowledge, he had to rout him for the safety of everyone concerned.

Patrick, being Patrick, had let the man stay on and run the place and still let him live in the flat above – and he took a good cut from the profits. It was another story that had helped give Patrick the persona he had sought. Hard but fair was the general consensus, and that suited Patrick. Plus he had always liked Oscan; Patrick had known his father way back when they were all kids. He could have earholed the whole family, but he hadn't done that. He had no interest in proving a point – he didn't need to. He was a mate, and that meant something to Patrick.

He had always understood that the people around you needed to see you not only fight your corner but also show that you were capable of loyalty to the people in your orbit. He had never wanted to out them from their home and business. He liked the family, for fuck's sake! But he had been put in an impossible position. He could not be seen to swallow his knob; he had to be seen to be looking after his interests, and that is what he had done. He had to prove that he would not be taken for a cunt.

It had been hard, but he'd had no choice. He had arranged though for a private poker game to be held on the premises on a regular basis. That had been for the family's benefit – not that anyone else had been privy to that, of course, but it was his way of giving a helping hand.

He was enjoying the food and the treatment that he was getting from the people around him here. And that was how it should be – he knew his worth better than anybody else. It was the secret of surviving in the world they inhabited.

He was well aware in the cold light of day that Danny had the arse with him. But Danny knew that Patrick was not a man to be fucked with, and Patrick felt that other people needed to be reminded of that occasionally too. He had needed to show his hand, especially with all this shit that was coming from the Christmas brothers; he needed to step in because it was fucking *personal*. Pair of tossers thought they could actually have him over? It was unbelievable in Patrick Kelly's world, and not something he would forgive or forget. It was a direct insult to him, and he had not been about to let that go without a fucking word.

He would show the powers-that-wished-to-be just what they were dealing with, because the Christmas brothers had royally pissed him off. Never a good idea, no matter who they might be, because he was a man who could happily hold a grudge and who could happily pay out anyone who was foolish enough to irritate him. He had had to make a serious point, and show any pretenders that he was not quite ready to give up his crown easily. But it was also about him too, and how he was feeling.

Last night, Patrick had felt for the first time in years that he was still a part of his world, that he was still capable of running his own businesses. He knew that it was childish – he had taken a step back deliberately, he had retired voluntarily. But he couldn't deny that he needed to feel that he could still fight his corner if required. Last night had proved to him that he was still someone to be reckoned with, and he had loved every second of it. He had missed the adrenaline and the act of proving that he was still capable of fighting his own end personally. Oh, he had done a wrong 'un and he was well aware that he should have kept as far away as physically possible from the garage, but the drink, the anger and the want had overridden all of that.

He had been on a mission, and now he was wondering how Kate would react to it all, should she hear about it. But he missed this life and, with everything that had happened, he had been desperate for something to take his mind off it all. Unfortunately, he had completely overlooked Danny's standing in the business and that was not something he should have done in front of others. It was a double-edged sword, as usual: what he wanted to do, and what he *should* have done. That had been the story of his life in many respects.

Now, he looked at Danny Foster and grinned sheepishly. 'I made a cunt of myself, didn't I?'

Danny laughed and said honestly, 'No, actually, you didn't. You gave a few of our younger employees a window on to the Old School, and they were genuinely fucking impressed.'

Patrick sighed heavily. 'I was completely pissed and trying to prove a point. But I miss all this, Danny Boy. I feel like I'm getting old, and I needed to prove myself, I suppose. It was good to get back into the fray, though. I had to take a step back for Kate, you know? But I miss being a real part of everything.'

Danny shook his head slowly, and he was genuinely laughing as he said with honesty, 'You, Patrick, don't need to prove *anything* to *anyone* any more – that fucking boat sailed years ago. You still have your creds. What's really wrong with you is you don't know what to do about the situation with Joseph and that mad fucker he married. You now have an impossible dilemma. You have a new family and they are suddenly all living at your house. You need to think about how you can help them and at the same time help yourself.'

Patrick sipped at his mug of tea and looked out into the street that was part of his old stomping ground. 'I know you are right, Danny. Last night, I admit, I went a bit far. But it felt so fucking good to be back in the game. I have missed it.'

'Of course you have, Pat. That's real life, mate. But you also know that you retired to be with Kate and play *golf*! Fucking hell, you have a place in Florida so you can *play* fucking golf. Why are you suddenly so determined to get back in the saddle? You are a legend, Pat, and I am so honoured to be a part of your legacy. But, Patrick, you can't put yourself out there like that. If you do, it is going against everything you wanted with Kate. You brought me up through the ranks because you knew that you had to step back, mate. Last night wasn't about the Christmas brothers – it was about *you*, Pat, and what is going on with your new family. Can I be honest with you? Without us two falling out because of what I have to say?'

Patrick sat back in his chair and said sadly, 'Of course, you can say anything to me, Danny. You are my number one. You are the only person I trusted with everything that pertains to this part of my life.'

Danny believed that Patrick was speaking the truth, and he knew that he had to say what needed to be said, whether it would please or offend. This was all getting complicated now, and he would rather walk away than fall out with the man he looked on as a father and a friend.

'Look, Patrick, if I am being totally upfront with you, I think you need to get your house in order. I get Joseph, and I get his family, and I get the importance of all that shit. Believe me, I *really* do. But you have to fucking get back in the *real* world and sort your son's shit out with that mad cunt he married, and let it all go from there. He *can't* be a part of this, Patrick, it's not in his nature. He's a coward, and you know that as well as I do. He's a great guy, and I like him, but he is not and never will be a part of our world. Tell me now – are you planning on bringing him on board? Because, honestly, if you do, Pat, then I will have to go, because I refuse to carry him. And that is what I would be doing.'

Patrick looked at the handsome fucker that he still saw as a son, and he understood that the man was not only speaking the truth, he was also giving him an ultimatum. They had been together a long time, and Danny had earned the privilege to say whatever he thought and be listened to with the utmost respect. Danny Boy had been running his businesses well, and without fault, for a long time.

Patrick Kelly knew that if the boot had been on the other foot, he would have said exactly the same and Patrick would not have been as easy-going as Danny was. *He* would have gone off like a fucking firework! Patrick had to really swallow the proverbial knob, because he couldn't argue with anything Danny Foster was saying to him.

'I know you are talking sense, Danny Boy, but he is still my son.'

Danny laughed loudly, a big rip-roarer of a laugh, and it was so infectious that Patrick laughed with him. 'Oh, for fuck's sake, Pat, buy him a business, a restaurant, *whatever*. But he can't join the firm. You know that as well as I fucking do! He wouldn't last five minutes. He isn't like us, Patrick, he is a fucking corporate lawyer. Think about it, please! You and I know that the people we deal with would distance themselves from him – we would all be hung out to dry.'

Patrick agreed that he was speaking the truth; he had already worked it out for himself. 'He needs help, and he needs me and a family, but he doesn't have the nous for what we do, and he never will. I get it, and I will bear that in mind for the future.'

Danny Foster felt a deep sorrow for Patrick and his predicament. He understood that for a man like Patrick Kelly to have a son that he found lacking was a difficult thing. Joseph might have been good at his job but he would be finished in the City after this. He didn't belong in either world now.

It was an abortion, and Danny suspected that Joseph O'Loughlin was waiting for Patrick Kelly to offer him a helping hand. Patrick had realised that much too, and it was a hard lesson for him to learn, because Patrick had assumed that any son of his would be as strong and capable as he was. That had not been the case and Joseph was not coming out of any of this looking even remotely without stain. In fact, he had shown himself so far to be as weak as a kitten in many respects. That was fine in the real world, but it wouldn't fly in the world that they lived and worked in. At the end of the day, Patrick Kelly was a businessman and that would always come first and foremost for him. It was what had made him into the man that he was – the man who had the knack of earning a living, and earning it against all the odds. A man who had worked his way up from the bottom to the very top of his chosen profession.

Patrick Kelly shrugged his trademark shrug that, even in this day, could instil fear into his enemies, because they knew that when he shrugged there would be no more talking to him. 'Danny Boy, I bow down to you and your wisdom. I can only apologise, mate, because I was put into an impossible position. I had hoped that Joseph would be like me, and he's not. I have to help him in any way I can, but I think deep inside that he is a fucking pussy. I can't change the fact that he's my son and I'm thrilled I have grandchildren now – I had basically accepted that was something I would never have.

'But you are my heir in every way, Danny Boy. I have given you everything that I could, because you are worthy and Joseph isn't. He's a nice guy, and I'm sure he is clever in his own way, but not in our league. He would be a liability, because he can't defend himself.'

Danny Foster smiled gently. 'He is still your son, though, and that is something you need in your life, Pat. You need blood family, for fuck's sake. You are even making me feel the need to reproduce!'

They sat back in their chairs as their full English breakfasts arrived and they toasted each other with mugs of tea.

'Do you know what, Danny Boy? I might have needed last night, but I hope that my Kate never finds out about it! She would have my nuts on a plate.'

Danny stabbed his fork into a large slice of black pudding, and he said with all seriousness, 'Not a chance, mate. Those pricks have already disappeared. Ain't anyone going to ever see that pair of fucking romancers again, I can guarantee you that much.'

Patrick Kelly tucked into his breakfast with a renewed vigour, because that is exactly what he had wanted to hear.

Danny grinned mischievously as he said in a whisper, 'Good to know that there is someone you are still afraid of!'

They laughed together then as the enormity of the situation hit both of them.

'Danny, she is a woman to be in fear of, take it from me!'

'I never doubted that for a second, Pat. She has given me one, on occasion.'

They both laughed, but they knew that they would never discuss this situation again; it was over with, finished, done. That suited Patrick Kelly right down to the ground.

Chapter One Hundred and One

Kate was down at the station and she was enjoying being back there. She missed this, and she knew that feeling was never going to leave her; she relished being back with a team and working on a case. It was what had been her life for so long, and she had felt the want of a reason to get up in the morning, more than ever since all the aggravation with Patrick and his new-found family – that's when it had truly hit home. For all that, though, she was not going to take over Annie's job. She was going to make sure that she was seen as no more than someone who had experience with other cases that dealt with multiple deaths.

Kate had never been comfortable with the term 'serial killer'. She had always felt that it gave the person concerned too much kudos with the people who were obsessed with them. It was too much like some kind of badge of honour that was given to people who were not worthy of being admired. They were scum. They killed indiscriminately, and they did it for their own enjoyment and, she believed, so they would be remembered after they were dead. If it was left to her, she would not let anyone write books about these fuckers, and certainly not treat them like they were special, because they weren't.

No, she was going to make sure that she was regarded by the team as someone who was only there to advise. The fact that she had been the lead investigator on three different serial killer cases was already in the public domain. She didn't feel the need to remind anyone of that. Annie Carr had to be seen as the boss, and Kate would do everything she could to make sure that no one was unaware of that fact. She was here to give the benefit of her experience, and that was what she was going to do. She just hoped that experience would be of use.

She would happily help Annie, as she had already, only now she would be a real part of the investigation and she would have access to everything that pertained to these cases. You had a different overview when you were a part of it all, because you had access to everything that the people around you saw or felt or even wondered about. It was a great help to be around the people involved and to listen to their different takes on everything.

Kate sat down with the others and waited patiently for Annie Carr to give them what she knew about the latest murder. Kate looked around her and saw with dismay the youth of so many of the officers concerned. It had been so different in her day, when longevity had been respected and had been rewarded, even if it wasn't warranted. Now they all looked like children. But that was her issue, as she knew, and she hated herself for it. As she scanned the room, she couldn't help wondering how these people could find their own front doors let alone a fucking murderer. It was like a youth club and Kate knew that a lot of these officers were here because they had scored well at university. It was a different world all right. None of these people looked like they had any real experience of *life*, let alone anything else.

She knew that she was seen as interesting, and that she was also seen as old and a has-been by the people around her. But her creds were something that none of these youngsters could deny. She had broken some of the biggest cases in history without the benefit of computers, mobile phones or any of the things that were so important in this day and age. She was from a different time.

The truth was, though, that she did feel completely out of her depth in this new era, and she knew that she would be reliant on the Margaret Doles of this world – something she wasn't relishing. She just hoped that she could cast a different eye over the evidence and hopefully give them all some kind of take on it that they had not seen or even thought about. She didn't feel comfortable yet and that really bothered her. She had actually never felt so nervous in her life. She was only there because the investigation was going nowhere, and the newspapers would be tripping over themselves to put her name on the page and bring up her association with Patrick Kelly all over again. From his daughter's murder to Patrick being shot because of his nefarious businesses. She had known that risk from the off, but she had still agreed, so that told her that she wanted this no matter what.

Annie stood in front of the team with a coffee from Starbucks and a vape cigarette that she pulled on deeply before blowing the so-called smoke out noisily. Kate looked at her friend and felt a deep urge to laugh, because she was from the days when everyone smoked, ate bacon sandwiches at their desks and drank like fishes.

'OK, everyone, I want to bring you up to speed on last night. As you know, another child has gone missing, from the same school that Janet, Kylie and Destiny attended. This young man, Todd Richards, went out yesterday afternoon and hasn't returned. He is in the year above the three murdered girls, and he is, to all intents and purposes, a nice kid. He has never been a worry to his parents, and he has never gone on the missing list before. You each have a file with all the information about him and what we need to do now is expand on what we already know. I do not think this is a coincidence. I think that his disappearance could be related to the girls. I hope to Christ that I am wrong. We need to be looking at what ties these kids together, other than the school they attend. There is nothing that we can find on CCTV, there is nothing that we can find that puts *any* of them together on the nights they were murdered.'

She held up her arm as if stopping traffic. 'Not that we know, of course, that Todd Richards is dead. Please God, he wanders home and we can all breathe a sigh of relief. But until he does, we can only assume the worst.

This is Grantley, not fucking Soho. We have been looking for this boy since last night, and there is no trace of him. He is not a child who has ever come on to our radar. He has never been in trouble at school, and he has never been late home either. That tells me he is in some kind of trouble now.'

She took a deep drink of her coffee once more, and then she looked at Kate and she smiled gently. 'We have been very lucky in that the Chief Super has *finally* asked Kate Burrows to come on board as a "consultant", for want of a better word. But, as you all know, Kate is one of the best when it comes to serial murders. She's willing to give us the benefit of her experience. And that, I know personally, is something that you will *all* find invaluable. I admit that I have asked the brass for her input from basically day one, and now that they have finally acquiesced I am over the fucking moon. We have the opportunity to use her experience, which is absolutely fucking immense. I have worked with Kate before, as you are all aware, and I know that she will bring a new dimension to this case. She is here for you all to go to her and offer up anything that you think might be relevant.'

Annie walked to Kate and, taking her hand, she pulled her from her seat. Kate just stood there as everyone in the room clapped and smiled, as if she was the answer to their prayers.

When they were finally alone together, Kate said, 'Really, Annie? I am so out of the loop that when I walked in here today I wondered what the hell I was doing.'

Annie Carr ran her hands through her hair in annoyance. Looking at Kate, she said briskly, 'Oh, please stop it, will you? You are the best thing that ever happened to this station, to this fucking whole place. You have got to stop this talk of feeling old and out of it. Most of those fuckers out there couldn't find a fucking full stop at the end of a sentence. They look up to you, Kate. *I* look up to you, I want to fucking *be* you. They see you as the person that caught not just Markham but the others. You single-handedly did more than anyone here will ever do if they live a hundred lifetimes. You are a fucking legend! Look, Kate, everyone here can say that they actually worked with you – that alone will help with morale. Do you know how much you are admired and venerated? I know that you are what we need here.

'It's all gone a bit Pete Tong. This boy who is missing is a part of this fucking lunacy, but I don't know how he fits into all this. He is at the same school, it's all too incestuous. There is nothing that we can find that links all of these kids together outside their lives at school. You know, as well as I do, that if Margaret Dole can't find anything then there is nothing to find online. You are still a valuable asset, and you need to remember that. Because you coming on board has given my team a new lease of life.'

Kate looked at her friend and remembered when she had first met her, and she sighed as she said, 'Annie, darling, I feel like I'm past all this.'

Annie Carr laughed again now in irritation and she said, 'Oh Kate, fuck off, will you, and do us all a favour? Get with the programme!'

357

Even Kate had to laugh at that.

'You wanted out of Patrick's fucking drama, and you also wanted to be back in the fray. So do us all a favour, will you? *Relax* and do what you are good at.'

Kate knew that Annie was right; she had to do what was asked of her. 'OK, then, let's go through everything from day one. I need to see it all for myself.'

Annie smirked. 'Well, I could have told you that!'

Deep down, Kate knew Annie wasn't as pleased with her coming on board as she pretended, because it signified that Annie and her team had basically got nowhere. Three girls were dead – tortured and murdered – and now a young man, who was a part of their world, was also missing. It was a fuck-up of fuck-ups, and they were all more than aware of that fact.

Chapter One Hundred and Two

Margaret Dole was pleased to see Kate back in the station again; they had never been bosom buddies, but they had respected each other and Kate had valued her input on the Miriam Salter case they worked together. Still, Margaret wasn't someone who you warmed to easily and, if truth be told, she wasn't someone who tried to make friends.

Margaret knew that if the person they were after was clever enough to keep away from anything that would put them online, they were far more savvy than anyone was giving them credit for. It was almost an impossibility to move around the local area without a record of it turning up somewhere. The only way she might find the killer was through CCTV, so she was once more trawling through everything that she could access, public and private.

Margaret Dole could not believe that anyone could sneak under her radar. She prided herself on her ability to access anything that she wanted to. She was distraught that she couldn't find anything that was relevant to the deaths of the girls or the disappearance of Todd Richards.

When she saw Kate and Annie coming towards her work station, she said loudly, 'Oh, Kate! So good to see you back.' She really did sound pleased to see her former colleague.

Kate smiled, and she said in a friendly manner, 'Anything new that you can tell us, Margaret?' Then she turned to Annie and said, 'Margaret is the best at what she does. If there is something to be found, Margaret will find it!' She knew the value of talking up Margaret to keep her onside.

But Margaret Dole was at her wits' end, because this was the first time in her life – let alone in her job – that she could not find anything that mattered, anything at all that might help them to find whoever was responsible. She knew that it was nigh on impossible to swerve the cameras that documented everybody's daily lives. People were on camera, and they didn't even realise that fact, and that was something that Margaret relied on – it was what she *did*. It was so unusual to have nothing that was of worth, because everywhere a person went there was a seeing eye, watching their every move. That was just a fact of life. And yet whoever they were searching for was not on film anywhere. It was not pleasant for her to have to admit this to Kate.

'I cannot find anyone anywhere that could even be seen as a *suspect*. It is like whoever we are looking for is really invisible. There is nothing anywhere that I can use to our advantage. It's just not possible these days. Everything is fucking documented somewhere. There are a staggering five point six million CCTV cameras in this country and most people in towns and cities are caught on camera at least seventy times a day. That is a fact of life. But whoever we are looking for has to be aware of that. Or at least they know to keep as far away from cameras as possible. I have even hacked into private equipment, and still *nothing*.

'The woods that surround Grantley have to be where he hunts. But how does he get the girls there without anyone seeing them? It just doesn't make sense. It's not luck either – believe me, no one is *that* lucky. If you walk through any town centre you will be on camera every eighteen seconds. But this fucker knows how to avoid being seen on camera. More to the point, he knows how to get these girls to a place where there are no cameras and nothing that can be brought back to him. I am telling you that he is hunting in those woods, but this guy has a real knowledge of cameras and he knows exactly how to avoid them.'

'So what's your take on it, Margaret? I would be very interested to know, mate. I'd like your take on everything.'

Margaret Dole was over the moon that Kate had asked for her opinion. She felt that she had a lot to offer, yet no one truly listened to her. She knew that she wasn't on anyone's best-friend list, but she also knew that she was the best at what she did, and no one could ever take that away from her.

She looked straight into Kate's eyes as she said with passion, 'We all know that he uses the woods to hunt. So the girls that he met up with, or who he deliberately targeted, were all in his orbit – they were all where he wanted them to be. The woods are really huge. There are acres and acres of woodland, and there are so many paths that are used by everyone around and about because they know them so well. They use those paths like they do the pavements where they live. This man hunts there, and he doesn't go out of his comfort zone. The woods are where he feels comfortable, where he can look for his victims.'

Kate nodded in agreement and Margaret sighed deeply, because she had been saying this since the second girl's murder. But no one had been listening to what she was saying to them, they just saw her as the computer whizz-kid. But she had hoped that Kate would listen to her and take what she said on board, and that was important to her.

Kate was interested in what Margaret had to say; as awkward as she could be, Margaret was a mine of infor-mation. She stored minutiae like other people stored the words to records that they loved.

She was a loner, and that was not unusual in the police force. Kate had come across more than a few over the years. That was par for the course in many ways; the police force, like the armed forces, sometimes attracted people who had trouble fitting in with society. People who were attracted by the uniform and the know-ledge that they would be told what to do, and who would be more than happy to let that happen. It suited them to be seen as authority figures by strangers, by the general public.

Margaret Dole might not be someone who you would choose to be with, but she was good at her job. And at the end of the day, that was what really mattered. The police force was not about a popularity contest, though that seemed to be the case these days. There was a lot that had gone since her day, and Kate wasn't sure that she was comfortable with it – especially now, given that it was only her appearance on the case that had allowed Margaret to finally be able to voice her opinion. It was not good for Margaret, or the people that she had to work with, that they didn't respect her.

She was annoyed because it was evident that Annie Carr didn't see what Margaret had to say as relevant. Annie had no real respect for Margaret and that was obvious in her body language and in her demeanour. She saw Margaret Dole as no more than a computer person, and that was wrong. There was every reason to listen to anyone who was close to a case. There were times when people heard or were told things that seemed to have no bearing on what they were working on, and then that one little word could change the whole outlook for everyone. Kate knew the relevance of that, because she had seen it for herself.

She smiled at Margaret, and said encouragingly, 'Margaret, are there any properties that are near the woods that you *couldn't* see online? I know that you are looking through all the old house plans and through the council records to see who has cellars, or who might have applied for planning permission to build a cellar. But what I'm interested to know, Margaret, is if you have seen anything that *you* think might be of interest to us? You know, an old place that is abandoned. Or a place that you've found that might fit the criteria of what we are looking for. I know that you are the best at what you do. After all, me and Patrick have used you in the past – as a friend, of course.' She smiled then at Annie and raised her eyebrows, as if questioning her.

Annie Carr knew when to keep her mouth shut but it didn't mean she was happy about it. She didn't like where this was going at all, and she didn't think that Kate should have been all over Margaret Dole like a cheap suit when she could have been talking to the real police.

'What I am interested in particularly are the places that are maybe off the grid a bit? That are not on the maps or the council plans and not there for everybody to find. I mean, whoever this is, he obviously has somewhere that no one knows about. He feels confident about that, so he must have somewhere that is local and that is accessible. He must be laughing up his sleeve at us, Margaret. But you and I know that eventually we will find the fucker.'

Margaret was listening avidly. She held Kate Burrows in high esteem – who wouldn't? This was a woman who had not only been behind the capture of three different mass killers; she had also tamed one of the most dangerous criminals to boot. Kate Burrows was everything that any policewoman would want to be. She also had a knack of finding the person she was looking for, and that was something that appealed to Margaret Dole.

'I'm on it, Kate.'

Kate smiled at her and squeezed her hand tightly as she said, 'I knew that I could count on you, Margaret.'

And then she walked out of the room with Annie, who she knew was about as happy as a pimp on remand. She was really dismissive as she turned and spoke to Annie.

'Listen, Margaret Dole will look through everything that she can, and also what she *shouldn't*. She is really good at what she does, and you lot need to remember that. You also need to keep in mind that you are all focusing solely on the children who have died – I think your next step should be looking at the children who are *left*. If this boy is a part of what is happening then we need to start looking at him. If he has been murdered by the same person then we need to find out why. What did he know? And more to the point, what might he have found out? There has been no body so far, and the others – the girls – were all left where they could be seen and admired. They were the murderer's way of saying: "Look at me, look what I have done." But this lad is a different kettle of fish altogether. If he's part of this, I would lay money that he either knew about what was going on, or he found out. I don't think his body is going to turn up any time soon.'

Annie knew that Kate had a point; she should not feel so annoyed with her and what she was doing. But she couldn't help it. Kate had been in the building less than three hours and she was already taking everything over. But that was what Kate did; she was larger than life, and she had her creds. Annie herself had brought Kate into all this from day one, and she had given her everything that she needed to help her with this case. She had wanted Kate's input and she had hoped that Kate would help her make some sense of everything. Now she was feeling the resentment that she knew was wrong, and she hated it, but Kate *was* a hard act to follow. A very hard act to follow. Yet she was also a good friend, and Annie knew that she had to concentrate on that.

Kate was a real, live legend, and that was something that Annie couldn't do anything about. She loved Kate and she knew that she was lucky to have been given the opportunity to work with her and learn from her. She had to content herself with that. Nevertheless it burned, all the same, knowing that Kate had been asked by the powers-that-be to come in and take over what had been her case. But there was nothing she could do or say that would not offend Kate, the Chief Super and everyone else within the vicinity, so she did what she had to do. She smiled and swallowed down her natural antagonism.

Kate grabbed her hand and said quietly, 'I know how you feel. It has happened to us all, darling. This is par for the course in our line of work, believe me. I've been there and I have been *you*, darling. It's not personal, even if it feels like it.'

Chapter One Hundred and Three

Patrick was sitting with his son, and they were drinking a particularly nice malt that Patrick had acquired from an old friend in return for a favour he had done him. It had been a particularly violent favour, and the malt whisky had been accompanied by a large fiscal payment. But that was neither here nor there. They both savoured the whisky, and Patrick smiled in contentment as he looked at this big handsome son he had acquired.

'That is a good Scotch.'

Patrick laughed in agreement. 'Indeed it is. There's a story behind it, which I will tell you one day. What I want to talk to you about tonight is completely different.'

Joseph O'Loughlin had been expecting this, but he didn't say anything. He was waiting for his father to say his piece.

'Look, Joseph, you know that you wanting Christine here just isn't feasible. Not just because you have your two children here, but because Kate would nail my balls to the wall – and yours too, probably.'

Joseph laughed gently. 'I get it, I really do. I was

clutching at straws because I feel so guilty about what happened to Christine. I also feel guilty about Bella, about my kids . . .' He sighed heavily. 'I caused all this upset, but I couldn't have foreseen any of this shit. I mean, who could have?'

Patrick didn't answer that because, personally, he thought that anyone with half a brain could have seen the stupidity of Joseph's little plan to ditch Bella. But he kept his own counsel, and instead changed the subject completely.

'I have a lot of properties, as you know, and I have one not too far from here, so you could be with Christine and also near the children. They will stay here for the time being, and you can see them whenever you want, mate, but you can spend your nights with Christine. I have a couple of fellas on my payroll who will be outside, day and night, so that Christine feels safe until such time as Bella has been dealt with – for want of a better expression.'

Joseph didn't say anything for a while. He just looked at Patrick as he took in what was being said to him. It was the answer to all his problems. This man would clearly move heaven and earth to help him, should he need it. He felt such a failure, and so bad about everything that had happened, but his father was right. He had to start making some kind of life for them all, and his biggest fear had been what he would do with the children. Because, as much as he loved his children, he had not envisaged being their sole carer, and the thought frightened him. The reality of looking after them all day, every day was so far different to what he had thought. They were both such great kids, but they were also damaged by what had happened, and he didn't know how he was supposed to make everything better for them. With what had happened to Christine he had so many responsibilities he didn't know where to start.

Patrick watched his son as he digested everything that he had said to him, and he was sad to see that the man wasn't as strong as he had first believed. Joseph was more interested in his girlfriend than his children, and that was something that Patrick Kelly could not even imagine. Like Kate had said, not everyone was the same as him, but he knew that Ruby would have agreed and would have thought in exactly the same way. Joseph was weak – and that wasn't a criticism, it was a fact of life. Kate had said the main thing they had to look out for was the children, and he knew she was also looking out for that mad cunt Bella. He wasn't so sure about that, but Kate was usually right about certain things. After all, she had far more experience with people than he did.

'Look, Joseph, we have Beverley and she is a diamond. And she loves having the kids, as I do. Obviously, I don't want them to leave – I'm still getting to know them. But they will be safe as houses here, and you can look after Christine and still be a part of the kids' lives. They are back at school, and we can make sure that they are in a safe and loving environment, and that's the most important thing at the end of the day.'

Joseph O'Loughlin couldn't look his father in the

eye. He was ashamed that Patrick Kelly was looking at him and finding him lacking. He couldn't blame him; he wasn't strong enough to cope with everything that was going on. It was all so far out of his normal life, and he honestly didn't know how to deal with it all. He was so glad that he had Patrick and Kate to pick up the slack. He had never thought that he would be like this, until he had been put into such an impossible position. It was amazing what real life could throw at you. And he was even more amazed at how he couldn't do what he had assumed should have come naturally. He didn't know how to look after his children any more; he loved them, but he also loved Christine. He couldn't choose, because he owed them all. And that was the problem; everything that had happened had been because of him.

'I know that I am taking the coward's way out, Pat, but I just don't know what I am supposed to *do*.'

Patrick Kelly didn't answer him how he wanted to answer him. He wanted to punch him out of his chair and demand to know why he wasn't putting his children *first*, why he was dithering and even had to be asked to make a decision. But he didn't, because this way he got unlimited access to the grandchildren that he had never even known existed.

So he kept his peace and he said gently, 'It will all work out. Don't worry about it.'

Chapter One Hundred and Four

Kate took everything home with her and was thanking the Good Lord for having given her a reason to get out of her own home. She was a realist and she knew that Patrick was going to put the hard word on his new-found son – and that meant they would be left with the children. It wasn't an ideal situation, but there wasn't much she could do about it.

She had been asked to do seminars over the years, and she decided that she might revisit that option. It would be good for her, and it would get her out of the house. She suspected that she would need something in the future that was *hers* and that it would give her a much-needed boost, as well as a few nights away now and again.

It wasn't that she didn't care about those kids. She did – and they were wonderful children, considering what had happened to them. But at her age and her time of life she wasn't relishing becoming a surrogate mother. Not that she wouldn't do whatever was needed for them, but, unlike Patrick, she wasn't as emotionally involved. At least not yet anyway.

She let herself into the house and went to the kitchen as quietly as possible, even though that wasn't really necessary. This was a big house and the kids were not going to hear her unless she went on screech mode, and that wasn't going to happen. It was just her natural reaction to having them there. After pouring herself a large glass of cold wine, she sipped it and then, placing the glass against her forehead, she savoured the coolness and the peace.

She had forgotten just how noisy and dirty police stations were. But for all that, she had still loved every second of being there. Now she was getting involved in the investigation on a deeper level, she wanted to look over everything again in her own time. That was what she had always done, and it felt good to be back in the saddle.

She laid all the files over the large kitchen table and then placed them in order of time and dates for the interviews. And as she started to read them, she felt herself finally relaxing. *This* was what she was good at, *this* was what she missed. As she read through the mountain of statements, she was hit by the same thought every time – that whoever this was had the knack of never being seen.

She read back through all the girls' text messages and looked at the copies of their social media accounts, and there was nothing untoward there. In fact, even knowing what she did about the bracelets and the sex circle, she would never have dreamt that these girls were capable of such underhandedness. The man responsible had used horrific torture on these girls, and that meant that they had made him very angry. This was a punishment, and he was meting it out with as much violence as physically possible. But he had held back on little Janet Cross, which told her that he had regretted taking her. He had not tortured her like the other two girls; she was already dead when he started to burn her. That meant that he had known her, that he knew a lot about her, and that he had taken her on a whim. She couldn't prove it, but she would lay money that he was close to her in some way, and that somehow no one had put the pieces together.

Like Annie said, these girls were all from the same school, the same year, and were known to each other. Every teacher had been questioned and every person who had worked at the school, or had an affiliation to the school, had been ruled out. But Kate felt sure that this man, whoever he was, knew these girls very well. She finished the glass of wine and poured herself another and then, settling back down, she began reading once again.

The real red herring here was Todd Richards, because he was male and in a different school year. His body had not been recovered as yet, whereas all the girls had been left out in the open. The man concerned had wanted them to be found, so why not Todd? She looked at all the children who were in the murdered girls' orbit, and there were a lot of them. She knew that these children and their parents had been ruled out. There had been a lot of legwork on this case, and she knew from experience just how much time and effort that took on a big case like this – especially with the media breathing down everyone's neck.

Part of the reason she was now back was because she had the creds needed to satisfy the public that everything possible was being done. That was a compliment to her – even though she knew that the papers would drag up her association with a man who had not only been shot but who was *allegedly* in the criminal underworld. She knew what to expect – she wasn't a fool – but she had been here before and survived, and she was sure that she would again. She also was aware that while the papers were wasting inches of print on her personal life, they would not be asking why no one had been arrested yet. Oh, she knew the score better than anyone where the media were concerned.

She also knew it wouldn't be long before they dug up her link to Bella and the acid attack. That was a given and, once more, there wasn't anything any of them could do about it. As Patrick had once informed her, in that way he had of going straight to the crux of a problem, she would have to swallow her knob and get over the public attention. Wise words, even if they were a little crude. But that was all by the by now. She was interested in what she was doing, and that was all she was interested in.

She began reading once again. She wanted to know everything that there was to know about these girls' deaths and, if possible, try to find the common denominator. There was nothing on the girls' social media, and nothing from anyone in their lives who might be capable of shedding some light on whoever they had been in contact with. Even Kate knew that, in this climate, it was not feasible. This generation lived their whole lives in the public eye. It was about looking like you had the perfect life, the perfect looks, the perfect photos; it was sad, but it was what the youth of today had been reduced to. Not that they would see it like that, of course. She had read through the dead girls' social accounts and it had broken her heart to think that they really believed that they were only worth how many likes their latest picture had garnered. It was a very sad indictment of the times they were living in.

Kate carried on reading and making notes, even though what she was reading made her feel depressed. After all the years of feminism, these girls still thought they were judged by how they looked. They thought that other people's opinions were far more important than having a real life. They lived in cyberspace and they needed validation from people they didn't even know. It didn't matter how much money social media magnates and their ilk poured into charity research or whatever, playing the big philanthropists, they were still guilty of creating a generation of young people who would never understand real life. Because they didn't know how to live in the real world, let alone understand the importance of it.

She was still reading when the sun came up.

Chapter One Hundred and Five

Liam Leary was not a big lad for his age, but what he lacked in stature he made up for in loudness. He was also a pretty good fighter if he needed to be, and that was because of his older brothers, who were all bigger and harder than him, and who also had a different father. He knew that they loved him and that he was seen as the baby of the family, and he didn't have any qualms about using that to his advantage.

He had been working on this paper round for eight months, and he wasn't particularly enamoured of it, but he liked the money that he was paid. He wanted to earn his own wages, because that was how he had been brought up – unlike his so-called father, who couldn't hold a job down if his life depended on it. He was more like his older brothers, who were all out on the earn and who were very vocal about that fact. But he knew that they were right about what they said; it was important to make sure that you earned your own living. Liam took notice of what his older brothers said, and he appreciated that they were so good to him. He was the runt of the litter but his personality and his humour went a long way towards endearing him to them.

As he rode his bike from the shop, he thought about the headlines in the papers that all seemed to be about Grantley. He understood that it was a really fucked-up situation, because his older brother had talked a lot about it; he was avidly following every social media update he could find. His older brother Jake was the designated intellectual in his house, and Liam hung on every word he said.

As he cycled through the woods that would let him cut ten minutes off his journey, he was a happy bunny. He had this round off pat. He knew who ordered what paper and who liked certain other papers, such as the *Sun* and the *Daily Mirror*, as well. He wrapped those papers inside whatever other newspaper they ordered. He was enjoying the early morning, because it was such a nice day and, as he cycled through the woods, he was feeling good about himself and about his life in general. He had a lot to look forward to over the summer months.

He stopped his bike by a huge oak tree, for a cigarette; he loved smoking, and he always stopped in the same place to have 'a quick drag', as his mum had always referred to it. He didn't remember too much about his father, but what he did remember was that he always had the aroma of tobacco. His brothers had verified that for him, so he knew that it wasn't something he had dreamt up. His father had been a smoker, as well as a complete piece of shit and an unreliable tosser, which was how his brothers had described him. He could only assume they were right as they were older and they had known him better, so he couldn't disagree with them even if he wanted to.

As he lit his Marlboro Light, Liam felt himself relax. He enjoyed the whole ritual of smoking, from lighting the cigarette and taking the first pull on it to the eventual stamping it out. It made him feel good about himself, made him feel like a real adult, as if he was finally growing up. And, unlike his brothers, he didn't mind being like his dad in this respect. He thought that maybe his dad had got a bad press, because his mum didn't like him at all. She had made that quite clear to anyone who would listen to her – especially his brothers. They all seemed to agree with his mum, and that hurt him. Because unlike all of them, he had never known the man whose name he had and who had left them all when he was so young. He pushed the thoughts from his mind, because he knew that it would just upset him. He loved his mum and his brothers very much, but his dream was to one day meet the man who had sired him, and hopefully hear his side of the story.

As he crushed the cigarette underfoot, he sighed. And, as he looked around him at the thick undergrowth, he stopped in his tracks. Getting off his bike, he laid it gently on the ground and, taking a deep breath, he walked over to where there was a lot of greenery and also where he thought he could see a bare leg. He was sweating, because he feared he knew exactly what he was going to find and, even though he knew that he didn't really want to see anything so shocking, he still made his way over there.

When he saw that the leg was real and not an optical illusion but was attached to an actual body, he knew that he had to scroll through the numbers on his phone until he found his oldest brother's number. He rang it three times before it was answered, and when his brother Damien finally answered, he broke down and through his tears he told him what he had found. Then he lit another cigarette with shaking hands and waited for the police and his brothers, in that order.

Chapter One Hundred and Six

'We searched these woods again yesterday, Kate. There was *nothing* to be found. If there was anything, don't you think we would have seen it?' Annie Carr was completely outraged; she really couldn't understand how this could have happened.

Kate had her own thoughts about that. But she didn't air them, as this was not the time or the place. She was angry though, and when she had Annie Carr alone she would give her both barrels. This was a complete abortion, and that was obvious to everyone who was involved in this investigation. It was a fucking joke, and everyone needed to be reminded that they had fucked up, and fucked up big time. Kate was tired, and she wasn't in the mood for any of this, because this was a spectacular fuck-up. No matter how you looked at it, this was just *bollocks*. It was an embarrassment that no one would be living down any time soon.

'I know that this looks bad, Kate, but we have been all over these woods and there was nothing of value to be found.'

Kate didn't say a word, but she was fit to be tied. At least this was the first body that she could look at, and that was important to her. Everything she had on this case was second-hand. And now Annie Carr – who she had brought through the ranks and who she had always respected – was going to be questioned about how this boy had been left here without anyone even fucking noticing. It should never have been allowed to happen. Even before she had been brought on board these woods had been a big part of the investigation. Annie had assured her that they were being watched and that there was a constant police presence. What Annie had not made clear until now was that the police presence was not actually *in* the woods. The so-called police presence was no more than squad cars keeping an eye out on the periphery.

Kate knew that Annie Carr's explanation would be that there wasn't the money to do as much as they wanted. Well, Kate would tell her that she had been there and done that. Annie's job was to fight for that extra money and fight to get what she thought was needed, and then to get it done. That was how it had always worked, and that was never going to change. There would *never* be enough money to do what was needed. It was simply about making that money available in whatever way possible.

Kate looked down now at the body of Todd Richards and then, turning to Annie, she said sadly, 'Tell that to him, Annie, and to his parents. Because do you know what? I couldn't give a flying *fuck* at the moment.'

Annie didn't answer, because she didn't know what she was supposed to say. She had dropped the ball, and that was not good for any of them.

Chapter One Hundred and Seven

Megan McFee was her usual self, and she didn't hide her pleasure at seeing Kate; the two women had been friends for a long time. Annie was still feeling like she was an outsider, even though rationally she knew that it was ridiculous. But Kate being back had been like a kick in the teeth for her. Everyone was treating Kate like she was special – and of course she was, because she had her creds, and she deserved her renown. It still rankled, though.

'So what have you got for us, Megan?'

Megan McFee sighed and stifled a yawn. 'Not a lot, to be honest. I am sure you can all smell the bleach – industrial again, so it's strong – and it's destroyed anything that might have been of relevance. He wasn't tortured anyway. He died from blunt force trauma – eleven blows to the head. Probably a hammer, but I will be able to tell you more later after I have confirmed everything. He was well nourished and small for his age. Other than that, nothing of interest – at least nothing that will be of any help. Unless you find his clothes, of course. But I think whoever we are dealing with is too fucking shrewd.'

Kate nodded in agreement, Megan knew what she was talking about. Burning was the best way to get rid of evidence. They were all subdued as they left the hospital building.

She looked at Annie and said tiredly, 'Let's go back to mine. It's nearest, and I'll get Bev to knock us up some lunch.' She handed her car keys to DC Karim and said, on a laugh, 'I am assuming you know the address! If not, you are the only Filth this side of the water who doesn't!'

They were all laughing as they climbed into the car.

Then Kate said seriously to them both, 'So this kid was a friend of this Stephen Carter, yeah? What do we know about him and his family? I'm assuming that someone has been looking into them?'

Annie Carr nodded. 'Margaret Dole is on it as we speak. She will ring if there is anything important.'

Kate nodded at her as she said, 'Good.'

Chapter One Hundred and Eight

Danny Foster and Patrick were in his office at Kate and Patrick's house. Patrick Kelly was well pleased – Danny had played a blinder for them all, and he said as much.

'You thought this through, and I can't disagree with you. It's the answer to all our problems. I take my hat off to you, son.'

Danny laughed, because he knew that he had given them all a swerve – especially Joseph O'Loughlin. It was now common knowledge that Joseph O'Loughlin was Patrick's son, and many of the older Faces and their wives remembered Ruby. It had started a nine-day wonder, and Patrick was pleased that it was out in the open. After all, he wasn't bothered about the past and neither was Kate, and that was all that mattered to him. Patrick Kelly knew that it would just add to his cachet, and that could only be a good thing. And Kate accepting Joseph was basically the icing on the cake.

'The restaurant is a goer in every way, Patrick. A good earner, and in the middle of Soho, so it is already established. All Joseph has to do is keep it running as it has been, and that will give him a nice living. I think he'll enjoy it as well. He just has to run the place because I have put in a fuck-off manager who will make sure it doesn't go tits up.'

Patrick nodded, satisfied. This was exactly what he wanted to hear. He loved his new-found son, but he still didn't know him well enough to trust him with anything important. Joseph was a civilian, but he wanted to give the boy a decent earn, and that was what he was concentrating on. It wasn't like Joseph was going to be welcomed back with open arms to his old job; they had made it quite clear that it was all over for him. Patrick was making sure that his lawyers were thrashing out a decent pay-off for the boy. After all, his bosses were the ones who wanted him gone. If it was left to fucking Joseph, he would be forced out with fuck-all, and that was not going to happen on Patrick's watch.

'What's the latest on Bella?'

Danny grinned. 'The brief I got her is shit-hot, and I have a handle on the judge she appears in front of.'

Patrick was pleased. 'I know it isn't fucking cheap but it looks like this will all work in our favour then, and that is the main thing. Whatever Annie Carr says, any kind of custodial sentence will not be beneficial to anyone involved, especially the kids. I know a top private place for the long-term where she will get the best that money can buy. If she sorts her head out then all to the good. If she don't, then it ain't a bad space to be locked up in.'

Patrick wanted to do what was best for his family. He knew that what happened to Bella would be decided by the best doctors, and he was quite happy to leave it at that. Mental illness terrified him, even though he was more than aware that a lot of the men he had dealt with over the years were more than a bit radio rental. But they were a different breed altogether, and their nuttiness could be used if need be. He wasn't comfortable thinking about it all too closely. He had solved some problems, and that was more than enough for him.

'Fancy a beer?'

Danny laughed. He could tell when Patrick Kelly wanted a conversation over. 'Sounds good to me, Pat.'

He knew when to let things go; it was one of the first things he had learned when he had come to work for Patrick Kelly. When to let things go and just move on to the next problem as quickly as possible. Because, as Patrick had taught him, there would always be another problem to solve. It was the nature of their particular beast.

Chapter One Hundred and Nine

Annie Carr could see how impressed DC Karim was with Kate's home, and she hated herself for feeling irritated. It was a beautiful property, there was no denying that. Annie also knew that it wasn't Kate's home that she was aggravated about; it was the fact that, even though she was the SIO on the case, everyone around her was treating Kate as if *she* was. She was annoyed with herself for her petty-mindedness.

As they walked into the kitchen, Beverley had already made them a gorgeous lunch. She poured the coffee while Kate motioned for them both to sit down.

Beverley smiled at them all as she said, 'You have a guest. She is in the garden. A wonderful lady, Kate – very interesting.'

Kate smiled and, picking up a slice of quiche, she said happily, 'I am assuming it is Mary Barker Smith?' Bev nodded, and Kate said seriously, 'I told her to come if she had anything of interest. I'll go and get her. Is Pat in?'

Bev nodded again. 'Pat and Danny have been holed up in the office all morning.'

Kate went out through the double doors, waved at Mary and invited her in for lunch. She introduced her to Annie Carr and Ali Karim, and they all sat together amiably and tucked into the lunch that Beverley had provided.

'Can I get you a nice gin and tonic, Mary?'

Mary laughed heartily, saying, 'What do you think?'

It was a very genial gathering and when Mary was settled in with a large drink, she said to Kate, 'I have been going through all my old notes, because you really did give me something to think about when you visited. I remembered that there were a few places that were knocked down in the eighties. It was awful – beautiful houses that should never have been allowed to be demolished – but it was when the housing boom was at its height. And these were properties that had the land required for the more well-heeled, I suppose you would say.

'Anyway, a few of these properties had cellars and cold stores already in situ, so to speak. So I have made a list for you of these places, in the hope that it might be of help to you.' She opened her handbag and, taking out a file, she placed it on the table. 'It's all there for your perusal. There are so many hidden places in the old properties – some go right back to the Tudors, and even before. They built to last, in the old days. You only have to look at the Tower of London!'

She laughed with delight, and they all laughed with her. Kate picked up the file and started to flip through it while Mary continued talking.

'Look at the Carters' house. Now that has a lot of

land, and it also has a wealth of secrets hidden there. Jonny Carter built his new house, and it is beautiful, but there was a wonderful old house there originally, dating back to the fifteenth century, but it was eventually destroyed by fire unfortunately. I suspect it was an insurance job. Not that I am accusing anyone of anything! It was in terrible disrepair. But it had an amazing network of tunnels that had been built during the years of the Reformation. My husband believed that there was a smuggling ring in Grantley at some time, and the people who owned the house were involved. It was a very lucrative business, and of course it would have been the perfect hiding place outside London. It was near the sea, and they would have been camouflaged by the woodland.'

Everyone was listening to her avidly.

'So these Carters, they have built a new property on the same plot of land, I assume?'

Mary Barker Smith nodded. 'Oh yes, it is a wonderful house. They are a lovely family actually. The grandfather was an Italian who sold his ice cream all over the East End of London. He had a wooden bike with a cold store on the back! It is a marvellous piece of history, and it is still in beautiful condition. I was thrilled to see it, because so much gets destroyed and forgotten, you know? But they have kept it and oiled it perfectly so it still works.'

Kate looked at Annie, who had the grace to look away. Kate smiled and said to Mary Barker Smith quietly, 'Where do they keep this piece of history? It must have been fascinating to see it, Mary.'

Mary laughed delightedly. 'Oh, it was! And that son of theirs, he really looks after it. But as he said to me, it is a part of his heritage. And of course that is exactly what it is.'

Kate excused herself and, going out into the hallway, she rang Margaret Dole and told her to search for anything she could find about the land that the Carters' house was built on. Kate knew that Stephen Carter had been acquainted with all the children who had been murdered. She also knew from DC Karim that he had a bad feeling about the kid – that the last time Ali had been there he had felt that this Stephen Carter was off. He couldn't describe it; all he could say was that there was something different about the boy. He was polite, but he had felt that there was an underlying sense that the boy was laughing at them. He had no basis for that, it was just how he had felt. Kate was a great believer in hunches, and she was a great believer in following those hunches, no matter what.

She went into Patrick's office and, smiling, she said, 'Come on, you two, we have company, and I want to introduce you.' Patrick sighed, and she ruffled his hair as if he was a kid. 'Come on, you know you are a big part of my creds!'

He laughed and, getting up, he said to Danny Foster jovially, 'See what I mean? The old ball and chain!'

Kate smiled and slapped him gently around the face. 'Not so much of the old, Pat, OK?'

'Do I have to?'

Kate shrugged and said seriously, 'Yes, Patrick, you

do! Because I need this room, and I need you to talk to a lovely lady who knows everything that is relevant to Grantley.'

Sighing, he followed her out the door, with Danny Foster close behind him.

Chapter One Hundred and Ten

Kate, Annie and DC Karim were in Patrick's office, digesting more than Bev's magnificent lunch. Mary Barker Smith had given them plenty to think about.

Kate looked at Annie Carr as she said to Karim, 'Tell me what you think is relevant about Stephen Carter?'

DC Karim felt that he was really on the spot. He looked at Annie, before saying truthfully, 'Well, he seems to be a part of the lives of all the kids that have been murdered – even in a small way – and he was particularly close to Janet and Todd. We have looked into all the children and staff at the school, as you already know, Kate. There was something not right when we went to his house the last time. I can't explain it, but I felt that he was laughing at us, as I said to you before. I have no foundation whatsoever for my thinking, but I still feel that he has something to do with what has happened.'

Annie sighed heavily. 'I think he might have a point, Kate.'

'Well, we can't just storm in there, can we? We need a reason to get a search warrant. And if what Mary says is true, there are so many fucking different tunnels, or whatever, that we would need a blanket warrant. I have been in touch with Margaret and she is doing searches as we speak. And isn't his father in construction? He's probably got access to industrial bleach, right? But what I am most interested in is the antique ice-cream bike. Could you transport a body in it? Because there are no tyre tracks, nothing to say that a motorised vehicle was used, are there? Jesus fucking Christ, if you have been looking at a kid right under your noses this whole time, that will not go down too fucking well with the powers-that-be. Am I right that I read that he was helping to arrange the dead girls' memorials? How the fuck did you not look closer at him, Annie?'

Annie Carr didn't answer. She just opened her arms in a gesture of forgiveness, and she said honestly, 'Look, they are a nice family, and we could find nothing in his background or his family's background that raised any flags. Listening to the school, he's the perfect pupil, for fuck's sake. We were looking for a man, Kate, and you know that no one could have thought it was a kid.'

Kate shook her head slowly, saying angrily, 'I know exactly what kids are capable of, Annie. I saw it for myself, remember? I dealt with young girls who were happily involved in paedophilia. Who were more inter-ested in the people who were abusing them than their own families! How many fucking times have I got to remind you that in cases like this *everyone* is a fucking suspect?' She pointed at DC Karim and shouted, 'He felt there was something off, and you should have fucking listened to him. It might have gone somewhere, for crying out loud! Chances are, this won't go anywhere. We just don't know, do we? But it is our job to look at *everyone* that comes into our orbit. It is our job to follow a lead, a hunch, or a fucking trail of bread if necessary. If that is what it takes then we have to do it. You fucked up, Annie, and you fucked up big time.'

Annie Carr didn't say anything, she just looked at Kate and shook her head in denial. 'He comes across as a good kid, and I didn't feel anything bad from him.'

DC Karim said supportively, 'I have to say, Kate, that he does come across as completely plausible.'

Kate sighed. All the anger had left her, but she wasn't happy, and that was obvious. 'Oh, *really*? They all do! That is the fucking problem, Annie. No one looks like a fucking murderer. This isn't a film or a book – this is real life, love. The scary people walk among us, as you should know better than anyone, lady!'

Annie Carr didn't answer her. But she knew that Kate wasn't expecting an answer. Kate was making a point.

Chapter One Hundred and Eleven

Patrick and Danny knew that there was something going down, but they didn't mention it. They just sat in the kitchen and listened for hours as Mary Barker Smith regaled them with stories about the history around and about. Patrick Kelly was actually fascinated at the woman's knowledge of where they all lived. She was like a walking encyclopaedia on Grantley, Essex and the importance of those places in the history of England. Even Danny was intrigued, because she had a real knack for telling a story and making it interesting.

Patrick knew that Kate liked Mary and that she would become a regular visitor, and he didn't mind that. He liked her too; she was a real character, and she didn't even realise it. He heard the children coming in from school with Bev, and he smiled contentedly. This was what he enjoyed, these days – the good life – and he knew that he should have kept as far away from the Christmas brothers as possible. He had another life now, and that was all that mattered. He had no right to fuck it up because he had lost his temper, and that was the truth of the matter.

'Hello, kids, did you have a good day? Your dad will be back soon. Let's get you sorted out with some tea, shall we? Want a quick swim first, though?'

They walked off with him happily, and Danny was quite content to sit with Mary Barker Smith and listen to her stories. He felt that Patrick Kelly was finally finished with their world, and he was pleased about that. He was looking forward to the future now that it was all mapped out.

He smiled at Mary and he said to her nicely, 'Can I get you another drink?'

She gave him her empty glass as she said coquettishly, 'A gin and tonic, please, young man.'

Danny smiled at her and, taking her empty glass, he said jovially, 'Of course!'

One thing that he loved about spending time with Kate Burrows and Patrick Kelly – it was never predictable.

Chapter One Hundred and Twelve

Kate and Annie pressed the button for the gate that would give them access to the Carters' house. As they pulled on to the drive, Kate looked around her and was impressed. It wasn't anything like her home with Patrick, it was too new for that. But it was still a stunning property. The brickwork was perfect, and they had spared no expense when it came to the picture windows and landscaping the gardens. It was a really well-thought-out and well-executed home. Kate knew, from all the years with Patrick, about property and what it was worth and could tell that this place was worth a small fortune.

She saw a woman at the door smiling as she welcomed them into her home, and she looked at Annie and sighed sadly. They both got out of the car, smiling in a friendly fashion, and they followed the woman into her beautiful home, fearing that the chances were that their presence would be the worst thing that could ever have happened to her. It was just gone nine in the evening, and the sun was setting, as they walked into the large, well-equipped and ultra-modern kitchen. Kate had waited until she had what she felt she needed from Margaret Dole before she came to the Carters' property.

Kate saw an older woman sitting in the kitchen, and she assumed that this was Wanda – the famous grandmother that she had heard about. As they were introduced, she smiled at the older woman and shook her hand firmly.

They were all sitting in the kitchen and waiting for the coffee to brew when Kate broke the silence, saying, 'This is a beautiful property, Mrs Carter. How much land do you have here? We have nearly three acres at mine and I love that we have that privacy.'

Sylvie Carter laughed, saying, 'I know who you are, and I know that you have that wonderful house. My husband never fails to remark on it when we drive by.'

Kate grinned. 'Where is your husband tonight?'

Sylvie Carter looked at her for long moments before saying uneasily, 'He is at his yard – he puts in a lot of hours.'

Kate smiled once again. 'I can imagine. He has a big company, and an even bigger workforce to look after.'

Sylvie Carter shrugged nonchalantly as she poured the drinks. 'He won't be long now – he's due home any minute.'

Annie sipped her coffee before she said carefully, 'We are here to talk to Stephen, as I'm sure you must have guessed. Is he around?'

Sylvie Carter looked at them once more. 'He's doing his homework. Why do you need to talk to him again?'

Kate sat at the big expensive glass table that looked like something from a science fiction film, and she said gently, 'Well, we need to talk to him because his friend Todd Richards was found murdered last night, as I am sure you've heard. From what I gather, they were good friends. We wondered if Stephen might be able to help us with our investigation.'

Sylvie Carter was not happy, and it showed. She was frowning, and she looked at Annie Carr as she said in bewilderment, 'I don't understand what my Stephen could tell you that is so important. He was here last night – he's here most nights. Todd was a lovely boy – and we're devastated by the news – but we haven't seen him for a few days, have we, Wanda?'

The older woman didn't say anything, she just shrugged.

Kate smiled once again and then, looking at Sylvie Carter, she said honestly, 'Stephen has known all the children who have died in some way. He is what we call a common denominator.' She smiled once more. 'That's why we need to talk to him again, Mrs Carter. We need to ask your son if he could help us with our enquiries.'

Sylvie Carter looked at Kate and Annie as if they were from another planet. 'He is doing his homework, like I told you. He rarely goes out of an evening. He is a good lad, he sticks close to home.'

Kate smiled once more and, taking Sylvie Carter's hand, she said smoothly, 'Where does he do his homework? Is he upstairs? Could you call him down for us?'

Sylvie Carter pulled her hand from Kate's, as if she had been burned. 'He goes for a walk sometimes, to think. There is a lot of land here. I really think you should wait for my husband to come home.'

Annie Carr and Kate exchanged glances.

'Do you actually know where your son is, Mrs Carter?' Kate asked.

Sylvie Carter didn't answer the question, she just sat there looking at the two policewomen. Kate saw her bite her bottom lip in consternation, and she knew everything that she needed to.

'He isn't in the house, is he, Mrs Carter?'

Wanda Carter banged her fists on to the table heavily, and she looked at her daughter-in-law as she cried loudly, 'For fuck's sake, Sylvie, you know as well as I do that he is not all the fucking ticket! Never has been, from when he was a little child. He is my flesh and blood, but I can't fucking stand him. I know as well as you do that he has something missing up top. You can't protect him any more, Sylvie – it's all gone too far. Tell them you saw him arguing with Todd the night he disappeared.'

Wanda looked at Kate, and it seemed as if her whole body had collapsed in on her. 'I knew that he had something to do with all this, but I couldn't prove it. I didn't *want* to believe it but I *know* that he is capable of real evil. Todd must have finally seen it too. Stephen is not right in the head. And it doesn't matter how much these two try and buy him out of trouble, they can't make him better. There are some things that you can't fucking repair, and that boy is one of them.'

She slumped back into her chair, and she was nearly in tears as she said, 'His baby brother, for a start – that wasn't a cot death. He hated that child from the day he was born. I know my son knew the score as well as I did. Stephen is wrong in the head, and that is the truth of it. He is out there in one of his underground passages, and this pair pretend that it is all fucking *normal*. He can spend two days out there and this pair still act like that is completely normal behaviour.'

Kate and Annie Carr sat and listened to the woman, and they both knew that she was finally unburdening herself.

'He killed my dog, and they both knew that, and they acted like it wasn't that big a deal. He always walks away from everything that he does, because this pair seem to think that he can do no wrong! That he can be helped by psychiatrists, but he can't.' Wanda was on the verge of weeping.

Kate turned to Sylvie Carter and, motioning for her to get up from her chair, she said quietly, 'I think it's time for you to show us where he is.'

Sylvie Carter shook her head slowly and she refused to get out of her chair. 'You are all wrong. My Stephen is a good boy. He knows that he has done wrong, but he is making up for all that.'

Kate and Annie walked from the kitchen and made their way through the gardens – the beautiful land-scaped gardens that were lit up like Battersea Power Station – and they followed the paths to where the uni-forms were waiting for them patiently. Kate was impressed with how hidden these tunnels were; if you didn't know about them, you would walk right by them without a thought. Margaret Dole had really come up trumps when she had unearthed the plans of the original buildings, there was no denying that.

Kate took the lead, pushing through the thick undergrowth and carefully making her way down the ancient steps. The doorway was smaller than she had expected and she was amazed to find that it wasn't locked from the inside. But why would it be? Stephen Carter didn't think that anyone would find it.

She walked inside slowly and the smell of bleach was overpowering. There was a large room that had been carved out of the earth so many years ago. The ceiling was like a work of art; the wood that was shoring it up had been carved beautifully by a real craftsman. She walked into the room and she looked about her in wonderment. There was a lot of light from candles, and she knew that Stephen was here somewhere. She saw another small doorway and she approached it slowly.

When she got to the doorway she said loudly, 'Stephen? My name is Kate and I would like to talk to you, if you wouldn't mind.'

She pushed the door open gently and she looked into a tiny room that was dark and dank and covered in blood. There was only one candle burning, and that didn't give out much light. She shone her torch around and then she saw the young boy they were all looking for, and she closed her eyes tightly.

She heard DC Karim asking her quietly, 'Is there anything there, ma'am?'

Kate turned around quickly, saying, 'Bring Megan down, for fuck's sake! The little fucker has hung himself!'

Chapter One Hundred and Thirteen

Patrick Kelly knew that Kate was not thrilled at the way everything had turned out. But, if retribution was not to be had, he personally believed that it was a perfect solution; he just wished that more fucking nutters topped themselves. The piece of shit had killed other kids! What the fuck was that all about? Kate was, once again, the woman of the hour, though she wasn't taking any credit. He wasn't going to piss all over her firework by giving his personal opinion; he knew better, these days. But he was sorry that she didn't see that, whatever the outcome, *she* had been the one to find that mad bastard. That should be something that she was proud of. He knew that he would be, if he was her. But he wasn't her, as Kate would point out forcibly should he try and give his opinion.

He was waiting patiently for her to join him so they could go to the dinner being held in her honour. He was already suited and booted and drinking a rather good Scotch when Kate came down the stairs.

She smiled at the two children who were already a big part of the household. She was genuinely developing a great fondness for Patrick's grandchildren, and she was also pleased that they both returned her affection. She was becoming closer to them both, and Joseph was settling into his new life as a restaurateur. He was happy helping Christine recover and seeing his children daily, even though they were still living with Patrick and Kate. They couldn't fault his devotion to his lover – that was one thing in his favour. Like Patrick, Kate wasn't sure she wanted the children to leave now, because they were nice kids and after everything that had gone on they gave them both something to concentrate on.

Kate smiled at Patrick, and he looked at her in her expensive outfit and he raised his eyebrows and made a leering face. 'Cor, girl, you still ring my fucking bells!'

Kate put her head back and laughed. 'And you still ring mine, Kelly.'

He went to her and kissed her gently on the lips. 'Enjoy tonight, Kate. You deserve it, darling.'

Kate shrugged but she smiled at him. 'I love you, Patrick Kelly, and don't you ever forget that.'

He smiled that crooked smile of his back at her. 'Come on, girl, get your arse in gear. We have a dinner to attend in your honour.'

Kate grinned. 'You will never change, will you, Kelly?'

'No, Kate, I won't. And neither will you.'

Kate kissed him on his lips. 'Then let's get this fucking show on the road!'

Epilogue

Of all animals, the boy is the most unmanageable

Plato (*c*.428–*c*.348 BC)

How sharper than a serpent's tooth it is to have a thankless child

William Shakespeare (1564–1616), *King Lear*

'Oh Kate, what would we have done without you? Fuck me, I knew you were in the right!'

Annie Carr was sitting by the pool with Kate. She was drinking a very expensive wine and offering her apologies.

Kate laughed sadly. 'Look, Annie, I love you dearly, and you know that. But you have to start listening to the people around you. That is the secret of our job, darling. We feed off other people – not just the ones we are trying to catch, but also the people that we are working with. You were not in a good place, I don't think. You weren't seeing the big picture, were you? You know that as well as I do, but I am not going to labour that point. You need to get your act together.'

Annie sighed heavily. 'I know that, Kate. If I am honest, I was too fucking close to it all. I should have listened to Ali. He had alerted me to something being off with Stephen Carter in the beginning, and I didn't see it. I didn't *want* to see it. I was convinced that we were looking for a grown man. Honestly, Kate, it never even occurred to me that it might be a young boy.'

Kate laughed again, a deep and soulful laugh. 'Look, Annie, we are all guilty of it. Until you experience a case like that, no one wants to believe that these kinds of things are even possible. That there are actually people in this world who are capable of such evil. Once you realise that there are, it changes your whole perspective. I know what I am talking about, believe me.'

Annie Carr sipped her drink and then she lit a cigarette. 'Well, I have learned a lesson. And thank you so much, Kate, for what you did for me. I know I didn't deserve it.'

Kate snatched her cigarette from her friend's hand and drew on it deeply. 'Oh, Annie, will you fuck off! You were there with me, and so was DC Karim. I gave you both a big shout, especially Ali – he has the makings of a fucking good detective, as you know. But believe me, Annie, it can only really come from experience. Though I think young Ali has a good shit detector – make sure you listen to him in the future.'

They laughed together, and Kate knew that they were back on track. But Kate also was under no illusions that she would be looking over Annie's cases until Annie finally learned to trust her own judgement. Not that Kate minded. If she was to be totally honest, she was looking forward to it. Kate changed the subject, and they were soon laughing and joking, as usual.

Annie Carr knew that she was lucky to have Kate on her side, and she valued her and her experience. She also knew that Kate would happily give her all the help she needed, and she would do that without a second thought.

Wanda Carter knew exactly what she was going to do. She had planned it all perfectly. She had driven herself to the rubbish tip, and she had made her way over the tons of rubbish until she had reached what she felt was a good place. She stopped for a few seconds to catch her breath; it wasn't just the walk across such a difficult terrain, it was also the stench of the place. It was disgusting, but that was *exactly* what she wanted.

She opened the container that held her grandson's ashes and she scattered them all over the filthy nappies and the maggot-ridden meat that was lying everywhere. She watched as the ashes settled and then, satisfied, she threw away the container and made her way slowly back to where she had parked the car. She was happy knowing that her grandson was exactly where he deserved to be. She was smiling for the first time in months.

She hadn't told anyone that she had helped her grandson on his way. She honestly hadn't felt that she needed to unburden herself when her confession wouldn't have helped anyone. The pathologist had found the drugs in Stephen's system and the coroner assumed that he had intentionally taken them before he had hanged himself. 'Sweeten the pot' was how her husband would have described it. She had known that that fucker had to go, and sooner rather than later. She wondered how she could have done what she did so easily and without any guilt whatsoever. But that was something she would never understand, she supposed – at least not until she passed herself. And then, of course, everything would be made clear. What she did truly think, though, was that she had done the right thing.

Her daughter-in-law would never have believed what Stephen was capable of. The boy would have been in her son's life like a cancer, and like a tumour Stephen needed to be cut out, because if he wasn't he would have infected the rest of their lives. She couldn't let that happen. She *refused* to let that happen.

She was happy now that she had done everything that was needed to ensure that Stephen couldn't damage anyone's life ever again.

Even his ashes were gone now. He was where she knew he was meant to be.

'I think anyone who grew up on or near a council estate like I did understands my books, the background'

Read on for more about Martina Cole

MARTINA COLE was just 18 when she got pregnant with her son. Living in a council flat with no TV and no money to go out, she started writing to entertain herself.

It would be ten years before she did anything with what she wrote.

She chose her agent for his name – Darley Anderson – and sent him the manuscript, thinking he was a woman. That was on a Friday. Monday night, she was doing the vacuuming when she took the call: a man's voice said 'Martina Cole, you are going to be a big star'.

The rest is history: *Dangerous Lady* caused a sensation when it was published, and launched one of the bestselling fiction writers of her generation. Martina has gone on to have more No. 1 original fiction bestsellers than any other author.

She won the British Book Award for Crime Thriller of the Year with *The Take*, which then went on to be a hit TV series for Sky 1. Four of her novels have made it to the screen, with more in production, and three have been adapted as stage plays.

She is proud to be an Ambassador for charities including Reading Ahead and Gingerbread, the council for one-parent families. In 2013, she was inducted to the Crime Writer's Association Hall of Fame, and in 2014 received a *Variety* Legends of Industry Award.

Her son is a grown man now, and she lives in Kent with her daughter – except when she chases the sun to Cyprus, where she has two bookshops.

Her unique, powerful storytelling is acclaimed for its hard-hitting, true-to-life style – there is no one else who writes like Martina Cole.

'I've always been a book fanatic from when I was a little kid...'

- Martina is the youngest of five children.

- Her nan taught her to read and write before she went to school.

- She secretly signed her mum and dad up to the library and borrowed books in their names.

- Her dad was a merchant seaman, away on the boats for long stretches. He'd come back for Christmas and bring the books that were big in America at the time.

- She used to bunk off school to go and read in the park.

- She was expelled from school – twice – and left school for good at 15: 'They said, don't come back.'

- She was expelled from a convent school for reading *The Carpetbaggers* by Harold Robbins ('They were nuns, how did they know what was in it?!')

- Her first boyfriend was a bank robber. He was really handsome, he had a Jag. 'We're still really really great friends.'

- The first book she remembers reading is Catherine Cookson's *The Round Tower* – she borrowed it from her nan.

- She reads on average two or three books a week.

- Martina wrote her first book when she was 14. It was about a girl who was at a convent but secretly worked for the CIA.

- Her first paid job as a writer was for her neighbour – a Mills & Boon fanatic who paid Martina in cigarettes to write her beautiful stories where they kissed on the swings at the end. Her neighbour's son used to steal the exercise books from school for her to write in!

- Her books are the most requested in prison – and the most stolen from bookshops.

- She sells hugely in Russia, and sometimes thinks it's because the Russians think it's a handbook to the London underworld.

- She has her own Film/TV production company with Lavinia Warner, the woman who produced *Tenko* – the first TV series with really great female characters.

- Alan Cumming did his own hair and make-up as well as singing for his part as Desrae in the TV adaptation of *The Runaway*.

- *The Faithless* made her the first British female adult-audience novelist to break the 50 million sales mark since Nielsen Bookscan records began.

- *The Take* won the British Book Award for Crime Thriller of the Year in 2006.

- Her fans include Rio Ferdinand – he was snapped with a copy of *Revenge*.

'I'm a great believer in anything that gets anyone reading...'

Martina on Kate

Martina Cole's first police procedural novel, *The Ladykiller*, was published in 1993. Before this, Martina had chosen to write very much from the perspective of the criminal, but in *The Ladykiller* Martina tells the story from the side of the law through her female detective Kate Burrows. Since *The Ladykiller*, Martina has written three more Kate Burrows novels, *Broken*, *Hard Girls* and *Damaged*. Here she tells us a little more about her hard-but-fair detective.

You usually write from the perspective of the criminal rather than the police. What made you decide to create Kate Burrows? And what was it like writing from the perspective of the other side, the law?

I do love writing my criminal characters. But I wanted to try something different with Kate. When I created her, I knew she had to be a strong woman in this predominantly male world, the world of the police. I also found it interesting that such a straight-laced woman could fall in love with a notorious hard man like Patrick Kelly. I still got to have one of my beloved criminals in this story with Kelly!

What is it about Kate's character that draws you to her?

I really enjoyed exploring the relationship between Kate and Patrick Kelly. Kate is a tough policewoman who has risen through the ranks the right way, not through corruption or fear. She's followed the rules and worked hard, and she's brilliant at her job. But then she does the unexpected and starts a relationship with one of the most powerful gangsters in town. It was that relationship and how Kate handles it in terms of her career that meant I had to continue to write about her.

Why did you bring her back in *Damaged*?

Well, I created Kate in 1993, so over two decades on she is quite a bit older now! It would be tricky to keep following her story as a policewoman indefinitely, but I did think she should have an end to her story after spending three books with her. That's why I wrote a fourth and final Kate Burrows novel. I wanted to see what happened between her and Patrick too, and how their story ended.

Would you ever write from the perspective of the police again in the future?

I think now that Kate Burrows' story is complete. But I might create a new detective in the future. You never know. I do love my bad boys and bad girls though, so we'll see.

> ## 'I write because I love it and won't ever stop'

Keep your eye on Facebook
f/OfficialMartinaCole to be the first to
hear when the next Martina Cole
is coming out.

And if you don't want to wait, treat
yourself to a nice bit of vintage Cole.
Here's a reminder of those blinding bestsellers
that have made Martina Cole the undisputed
matriarch of crime drama – and some quotes
from the lady herself to help you choose
which one you fancy reading next...

'Your family is either the best thing that ever happened to you or it's the worst thing that ever happened to you.'

Family life is always at the heart of Martina's storytelling: loyalty, protection and how the ties that bind us can also sometimes choke the very thing we want to protect...

FACES

THE FAMILY

THE FAITHLESS

BETRAYAL

'I deal with the mums, the wives, the girlfriends, the sisters, the grandmothers whose children or family are caught up in this life.'

Anyone who's ever read Martina Cole knows her women are the best: strong, resilient, vengeful – nothing will get in the way of these ladies when they know what they want

GOODNIGHT LADY

THE KNOW

CLOSE

GET EVEN

'My books are very anti-violence. I say this is what happens to you if you get caught up in the violent life.'

With her unflinching talent, Martina's stories reveal a world that many would rather ignore

THE GRAFT

THE BUSINESS

THE LIFE

REVENGE

'I wrote what I'd like to read and as luck would have it other people liked to read them too – they either love them or they can't read them, they find them too shocking to read'

The brand new novel from
Martina Cole

Publishing October 2018

Pre-order your copy of *No Mercy* at:
http://smarturl.it/PreorderMartina2018

LUTHER

JOHN OSBORNE

faber and faber

LONDON · BOSTON

First published in 1961
by Faber and Faber Limited
3 Queen Square London WC1N 3AU
First published in this edition 1965
Reprinted 1966, 1967, 1968, 1974, 1979, 1984, 1986 and 1988

Printed in Great Britain by
Cox & Wyman Ltd, Reading
All rights reserved

ISBN 0 571 06239 3

The first performance of LUTHER was given at the Theatre Royal, Nottingham, on June 26th, 1961, by the English Stage Company. It was directed by Tony Richardson and the décor was by Jocelyn Herbert. The part of Luther was played by Albert Finney.

CAST

KNIGHT

PRIOR

MARTIN

HANS

LUCAS

WEINAND

TETZEL

STAUPITZ

CAJETAN

MILTITZ

LEO

ECK

KATHERINE

HANS, THE YOUNGER

AUGUSTINIANS, DOMINICANS,

HERALD, EMPEROR, PEASANTS, ETC.

ACT ONE

ACT TWO

ACT THREE

NOTE

At the opening of each act, the Knight appears. He grasps a banner and briefly barks the time and place of the scene following at the audience, and then retires.

11

ACT ONE

SCENE ONE

The Cloister Chapel of the Eremites of St. Augustine. Erfurt, Thuringia, 1506. MARTIN *is being received into the Order. He is kneeling in front of the* PRIOR *in the presence of the assembled convent.*

PRIOR: Now you must choose one of two ways: either to leave us now, or give up this world, and consecrate and devote yourself entirely to God and our Order. But I must add this: once you have committed yourself, you are not free, for whatever reason, to throw off the yoke of obedience, for you will have accepted it freely, while you were still able to discard it.
(*The habit and hood of the Order are brought in and blessed by the* PRIOR.)

PRIOR: He whom it was your will to dress in the garb of the Order, oh Lord, invest him also with eternal life.
(*He undresses* MARTIN.)

PRIOR: The Lord divest you of the former man and of all his works. The Lord invest you with the new man.
(*The* CHOIR *sings as* MARTIN *is robed in the habit and hood. The long white scapular is thrown over his head and hung down, before and behind; then he kneels again before the* PRIOR, *and, with his hand on the statutes of the Order, swears the oath.*)

MARTIN: I, brother Martin, do make profession and promise obedience to Almighty God, to Mary

13

the Sacred Virgin, and to you, my brother Prior
of this cloister, in the name of the Vicar General
of the order of Eremites of the holy Bishop of
St. Augustine and his successors, to live without
property and in chastity according to the Rule
of our Venerable Father Augustine until death.
(*The* PRIOR *wishes a prayer over him, and* MARTIN
*prostrates himself with arms extended in the form
of a cross.*)

PRIOR: Lord Jesus Christ, our leader and our strength,
by the fire of humility you have set aside this
servant, Martin, from the rest of Mankind. We
humbly pray that this fire will also cut him off
from carnal intercourse and from the community
of those things done on earth by men, through
the sanctity shed from heaven upon him, and
that you will bestow on him grace to remain
yours, and merit eternal life. For it is not he who
begins, but he who endures will be saved. Amen.
(*The* CHOIR *sings Veni Creator Spiritus (or perhaps
Great Father Augustine). A newly lighted taper is
put into* MARTIN'S *hands, and he is led up the
altar steps to be welcomed by the monks with the
kiss of peace. Then, in their midst, he marches
slowly with them behind the screen and is lost to
sight.*
*The procession disappears, and, as the sound of
voices dies away, two men are left alone in the
congregation. One of them,* HANS, *gets up
impatiently and moves down-stage. It is* MARTIN'S
FATHER, *a stocky man wired throughout with a
miner's muscle, lower-middle class, on his way to
become a small, primitive capitalist; bewildered,
full of pride and resentment. His companion,*
LUCAS, *finishes a respectful prayer and joins him.*)

HANS: Well?

LUCAS: Well?

HANS: Don't 'well' me you feeble old ninny, what do

you think?

LUCAS: Think? Of what?

HANS: Yes, think man, think, what do you think, pen and ink, think of all that?

LUCAS: Oh—

HANS: Oh! Of all these monks, of Martin and all the rest of it, what do you think? You've been sitting in this arse-aching congregation all this time, you've been watching, haven't you? What about it?

LUCAS: Yes, well, I must say it's all very impressive.

HANS: Oh, yes?

LUCAS: No getting away from it.

HANS: Impressive?

LUCAS: Deeply. It was moving and oh——

HANS: What?

LUCAS: You must have felt it, surely. You couldn't fail to.

HANS: Impressive! I don't know what impresses me any longer.

LUCAS: Oh, come on——

HANS: Impressive!

LUCAS: Of course it is, and you know it.

HANS: Oh, you—you can afford to be impressed.

LUCAS: It's surely too late for any regrets, or bitterness, Hans. It obviously must be God's will, and there's an end of it.

HANS: That's exactly what it is—an end of it! Very fine for you, my old friend, very fine indeed. You're just losing a son-in-law, and you can take your pick of plenty more of those where he comes from. But what am I losing? I'm losing a son; mark: a son.

LUCAS: How can you say that?

HANS: How can I say it? I do say it, that's how. Two sons to the plague, and now another. God's eyes! Did you see that haircut? Brother Martin!

15

LUCAS: There isn't a finer order than these people, not the Dominicans or Franciscans——

HANS: Like an egg with a beard.

LUCAS: You said that yourself.

HANS: Oh, I suppose they're Christians under their damned cowls.

LUCAS: There are good, distinguished men in this place, and well you know it.

HANS: Yes—good, distinguished men——

LUCAS: Pious, learned men, men from the University like Martin.

HANS: Learned men! Some of them can't read their own names.

LUCAS: So?

HANS: So! I—I'm a miner. I don't need books. You can't see to read books under the ground. But Martin's a scholar.

LUCAS: He most certainly is.

HANS: A Master of Arts! What's he master of now? Eh? Tell me.

LUCAS: Well, there it is. God's gain is your loss.

HANS: Half these monks do nothing but wash dishes and beg in the streets.

LUCAS: We should be going, I suppose.

HANS: He could have been a man of stature.

LUCAS: And he will, with God's help.

HANS: Don't tell me. He could have been a lawyer.

LUCAS: Well, he won't now.

HANS: No, you're damn right he won't. Of stature. To the Archbishop, or the Duke, or——

LUCAS: Yes.

HANS: Anyone.

LUCAS: Come on.

HANS: Anyone you can think of.

LUCAS: Well, I'm going.

HANS: Brother Martin!

LUCAS: Hans.

HANS: Do you know why? Lucas: Why? What made

him do it?

He has ceased to play a role by this time and he asks the question simply as if he expected a short, direct answer.

HANS: What made him do it?

LUCAS *grasps his forearm.*

LUCAS: Let's go home.

HANS: Why? That's what I can't understand. Why? Why?

LUCAS: Home. Let's go home.

They go off. The convent bell rings. Some monks are standing at a refectory table. After their prayers, they sit down, and, as they eat in silence, one of the Brothers reads from a lectern. During this short scene, MARTIN, *wearing a rough apron over his habit, waits on the others.*

READER: What are the tools of Good Works?

First, to love Lord God with all one's heart, all one's soul, and all one's strength. Then, one's neighbour as oneself. Then, not to kill.

Not to commit adultery
Not to steal
Not to covet
Not to bear false witness
To honour all men
To deny yourself, in order to follow Christ
To chastise the body
Not to seek soft living
To love fasting
To clothe the naked
To visit the sick
To bury the dead
To help the afflicted
To console the sorrowing
To prefer nothing to the love of Christ

Not to yield to anger
Not to nurse a grudge

17

Not to hold guile in your heart
Not to make a feigned peace
To fear the Day of Judgment
To dread Hell
To desire eternal life with all your spiritual
longing
To keep death daily before your eyes
To keep constant vigilance over the actions of
your life
To know for certain that God sees you
everywhere
When evil thoughts come into your heart, to
dash them
at once on the love of Christ and to manifest
them to your spiritual father
To keep your mouth from evil and depraved
talk
Not to love much speaking
Not to speak vain words or such as produce
laughter
To listen gladly to holy readings
To apply yourself frequently to prayer
Daily in your prayer, with tears and sighs to
confess your past sins to God
Not to fulfil the desires of the flesh
To hate your own will

Behold, these are the tools of the spiritual craft.
If we employ these unceasingly day and night,
and render account of them on the Day of
Judgment, then we shall receive from the Lord
in return that reward that He Himself has
promised: Eye hath not seen nor ear heard
what God hath prepared for those that love
him. Now this is the workshop in which we
shall diligently execute all these tasks. May God
grant that you observe all these rules cheerfully
as lovers of spiritual beauty, spreading around

you by the piety of your deportment the sweet
odour of Christ.

The convent bell rings. The MONKS *rise, bow their
heads in prayer, and then move upstage to the
steps where they kneel.* MARTIN, *assisted by
another brother, stacks the table and clears it.
Presently, they all prostrate themselves, and,
beneath flaming candles, a communal confession
begins.* MARTIN *returns and prostrates himself
downstage behind the rest. This scene throughout
is urgent, muted, almost whispered, confidential,
secret, like a prayer.*

BROTHER: I confess to God, to Blessed Mary and our holy
Father Augustine, to all the saints, and to all
present that I have sinned exceedingly in
thought, word and deed by my own fault.
Wherefore I pray Holy Mary, all the saints of
God and you all assembled here to pray for me.
I confess I did leave my cell for the Night
Office without the Scapular and had to return
for it. Which is a deadly infringement of the
first degree of humility, that of obedience
without delay. For this failure to Christ I
abjectly seek forgiveness and whatever
punishment the Prior and community is
pleased to impose on me.

MARTIN: I am a worm and no man, a byword and a
laughing stock. Crush out the worminess
in me, stamp on me.

BROTHER: I confess I have three times made mistakes in
the Oratory, in psalm singing and Antiphon.

MARTIN: I was fighting a bear in a garden without flowers,
leading into a desert. His claws kept making my
arms bleed as I tried to open a gate which
would take me out. But the gate was no gate
at all. It was simply an open frame, and I
could have walked through it, but I was covered
in my own blood, and I saw a naked woman

19

riding on a goat, and the goat began to drink
my blood, and I thought I should faint with the
pain and I awoke in my cell, all soaking in the
devil's bath.

BROTHER: Let Brother Norbert remember also his breakage
while working in the kitchen.

BROTHER: I remember it, and confess humbly.

BROTHER: Let him remember also his greater transgression
in not coming at once to the Prior and
community to do penance for it, and so
increasing his offence.

MARTIN: I am alone. I am alone, and against myself.

BROTHER: I confess it. I confess it, and beg your prayers
that I may undergo the greater punishment for
it.

MARTIN: How can I justify myself?

BROTHER: Take heart, you shall be punished, and severely.

MARTIN: How can I be justified?

BROTHER: I confess I have failed to rise from my bed
speedily enough. I arrived at the Night Office
after the Gloria of the 94th Psalm, and though
I seemed to amend the shame by not standing
in my proper place in the choir, and standing in
the place appointed by the Prior for such
careless sinners so that they may be seen by all,
my fault is too great and I seek punishment.

MARTIN: I was among a group of people, men and women,
fully clothed. We lay on top of each other in
neat rows about seven or eight across.
Eventually, the pile was many people deep.
Suddenly, I panicked—although I was on top
of the pile—and I cried: what about those
underneath? Those at the very bottom, and
those in between? We all got up in an orderly
way, without haste, and when we looked, those
at the bottom were not simply flattened by the
weight, they were just their clothes, they were
just their clothes, neatly pressed and folded on

the ground. They were their clothes, neatly
pressed and folded on the ground.

BROTHER: I did omit to have a candle ready at the Mass.

BROTHER: Twice in my sloth, I have omitted to shave, and
even excused myself, pretending to believe my skin
to be fairer than that of my Brothers, and my
beard lighter and my burden also. I have been
vain and slothful, and I beg forgiveness and ask
penance.

MARTIN: If my flesh would leak and dissolve, and I could
live as bone, if I were forged bone, plucked bone
and brain, warm hair and a bony heart, if I
were all bone, I could brandish myself without
terror, without any terror at all—I could be
indestructible.

BROTHER: I did ask for a bath, pretending to myself that
it was necessary for my health, but as I lowered
my body into the tub, it came to me that it was
inordinate desire and that it was my soul that
was soiled.

MARTIN: My bones fail. My bones fail, my bones are
shattered and fall away, my bones fail and all
that's left of me is a scraped marrow and a
dying jelly.

BROTHER: Let Brother Paulinus remember our visit to our
near sister house, and lifting his eyes repeatedly
at a woman in the town who dropped alms into
his bag.

BROTHER: I remember, and I beg forgiveness.

BROTHER: Then let him remember also that though our
dear Father Augustine does not forbid us to see
women, he blames us if we should desire them
or wish to be the object of their desire. For it is
not only by touch and by being affectionate that a
man excites disorderly affection in a woman.
This can be done also even by looks. You
cannot maintain that your mind is pure if you
have *wanton* eyes. For a wanton eye is a wanton

21

heart. When people with impure hearts manifest
their inclination towards each other through the
medium of looks, even though no word is
spoken, and when they take pleasure in their
desire for each other, the purity of their
character has gone even though they may be
undefiled by any unchaste act. He who fixes his
eyes on a woman and takes pleasure in her
glance, must not think that he goes unobserved
by his brothers.

MARTIN: I confess that I have offended grievously against
humility, being sometimes discontented with the
meanest and worst of everything, I have not
only failed to declare myself to myself lower and
lower and of less account than all other men,
but I have failed in my most inmost heart to
believe it. For many weeks, many weeks it
seemed to me, I was put to cleaning the latrines.
I did it, and I did it vigorously, not tepidly,
with all my poor strength, without whispering
or objections to anyone. But although I
fulfilled my task, and I did it well, sometimes
there were murmurings in my heart. I prayed
that it would cease, knowing that God, seeing
my murmuring heart, must reject my work, and
it was as good as not done. I sought out my
master, and he punished me, telling me to fast
for two days. I have fasted for three, but, even
so, I can't tell if the murmurings are really gone,
and I ask for your prayers, and I ask for your
prayers that I may be able to go on fulfilling
the same task.

BROTHER: Let Brother Martin remember all the degrees of
humility; and let him go on cleaning the
latrines.

*The convent bell rings. After lying prostrate for a
few moments, all the* BROTHERS, *including*
MARTIN, *rise and move to the* CHOIR. *The office*

begins, versicle, antiphon and psalm, and MARTIN
is lost to sight in the ranks of his fellow MONKS.
*Presently, there is a quiet, violent moaning, just
distinguishable amongst the voices. It becomes
louder and wilder, the cries more violent, and
there is some confusion in* MARTIN'S *section of the*
CHOIR. *The singing goes on with only a few heads
turned. It seems as though the disturbance has
subsided.* MARTIN *appears, and staggers between
the stalls. Outstretched hands fail to restrain him,
and he is visible to all, muscles rigid, breath
suspended, then jerking uncontrollably as he is
seized in a raging fit. Two* BROTHERS *go to him,
but* MARTIN *writhes with such ferocity, that they
can scarcely hold him down. He tries to speak,
the effort is frantic, and eventually, he is able to
roar out a word at a time.*

MARTIN: Not! Me! I am *not!*

*The attack reaches its height, and he recoils as if
he had bitten his tongue and his mouth were full
of blood and saliva. Two more* MONKS *come to
help, and he almost breaks away from them, but
the effort collapses, and they are able to drag him
away, as he is about to vomit. The Office
continues as if nothing had taken place.*

(*End of Act One—Scene One*)

ACT ONE

Scene Two

A knife, like a butcher's, hanging aloft, the size of a garden fence. The cutting edge of the blade points upwards. Across it hangs the torso of a naked man, his head hanging down. Below it, an enormous round cone, like the inside of a vast barrel, surrounded by darkness. From the upstage entrance, seemingly far, far away, a dark figure appears against the blinding light inside, as it grows brighter. The figure approaches slowly along the floor of the vast cone, and stops as it reaches the downstage opening. It is MARTIN, *haggard and streaming with sweat.*

MARTIN: I lost the body of a child, a child's body, the eyes of a child; and at the first sound of my own childish voice. I lost the body of a child; and I was afraid, and I went back to find it. But I'm still afraid. I'm afraid, and there's an end of it! But *I* mean . . . (*shouts*) . . . Continually! For instance of the noise the Prior's dog makes on a still evening when he rolls over on his side and licks his teeth. I'm afraid of the darkness, and the hole in it; and I see it sometime of every day! And some days more than once even, and there's no bottom to it, no bottom to my breath, and I can't reach it. Why? Why do you think? There's a bare fist clenched to my bowels and they can't move, and I have to sit sweating in my little monk's house to open them. The lost body of a child, hanging on a mother's tit, and close to the warm, big body of a man, and I can't find it.

(*He steps down, out of the blazing light within the*

24

cone, and goes to his cell down L. *Kneeling by his
bed, he starts to try and pray but he soon
collapses, From down* R *appear a procession of*
MONKS, *carrying various priest's vestments,
candles and articles for the altar, for* MARTIN *is
about to perform his very first Mass. Heading
them is* BROTHER WEINAND. *They pass* MARTIN'S
cell, and, after a few words, they go on, leaving
BROTHER WEINAND *with* MARTIN, *and disappear
into what is almost like a small house on the
upstage left of the stage: a bagpipe of the period,
fat, soft, foolish and obscene looking.*)

BRO. WEINAND: Brother Martin! Brother Martin!

MARTIN: Yes.

BRO. WEINAND: Your father's here.

MARTIN: My father?

BRO. WEINAND: He asked to see you, but I told him it'd be
better to wait until afterwards.

MARTIN: Where is he?

BRO. WEINAND: He's having breakfast with the Prior.

MARTIN: Is he alone?

BRO. WEINAND: No, he's got a couple of dozen friends at least,
I should say.

MARTIN: Is my mother with him?

BRO. WEINAND: No.

MARTIN: What did he have to come for? I should have
told him not to come.

BRO. WEINAND: It'd be a strange father who didn't want to be
present when his son celebrated his first Mass.

MARTIN: I never thought he'd come. Why didn't he tell
me?

BRO. WEINAND: Well, he's here now, anyway. He's also given
twenty guilden to the chapter as a present, so he
can't be too displeased with you.

MARTIN: Twenty guilden.

BRO. WEINAND: Well, are you all prepared?

MARTIN: That's three times what it cost him to send me
to the University for a year.

BRO. WEINAND: You don't look it. Why, you're running all over with sweat again. Are you sick? Are you?

MARTIN: No.

BRO. WEINAND: Here, let me wipe your face. You haven't much time. You're sure you're not sick?

MARTIN: My bowels won't move, that's all. But that's nothing out of the way.

BRO. WEINAND: Have you shaved?

MARTIN: Yes. Before I went to confession. Why, do you think I should shave again?

BRO. WEINAND: No. I don't. A few overlooked little bristles couldn't make much difference, any more than a few imaginary sins. There, that's better.

MARTIN: What do you mean?

BRO. WEINAND: You were sweating like a pig in a butcher's shop. You know what they say, don't you? Wherever you find a melancholy person, there you'll find a bath running for the devil.

MARTIN: No, no, what did you mean about leaving a few imaginary sins?

BRO. WEINAND: I mean there are plenty of priests with dirty ears administering the sacraments, but this isn't the time to talk about that. Come on, Martin, you've got nothing to be afraid of.

MARTIN: How do you know?

BRO. WEINAND: You always talk as if lightning were just about to strike behind you.

MARTIN: Tell me what you meant.

BRO. WEINAND: I only meant the whole convent knows you're always making up sins you've never committed. That's right—well, isn't it? No sensible confessor will have anything to do with you.

MARTIN: What's the use of all this talk of penitence if I can't feel it.

BRO. WEINAND: Father Nathin told me he had to punish you only the day before yesterday because you were in some ridiculous state of hysteria, all over some verse in Proverbs or something.

26

MARTIN: "Know thou the state of thy flocks."

BRO. WEINAND: And all over the interpretation of one word
apparently. When will you ever learn? You
must know what you're doing. Some of the
brothers laugh quite openly at you, you and
your over-stimulated conscience. Which is
wrong of them, I know, but you must be able
to see why.

MARTIN: It's the single words that trouble me.

BRO. WEINAND: The moment you've confessed and turned to the
altar, you're beckoning for a priest again. Why,
every time you break wind they say you rush
to a confessor.

MARTIN: Do they say that?

BRO. WEINAND: It's their favourite joke.

MARTIN: They say that, do they?

BRO. WEINAND: Martin! You're protected from many of the
world's evils in here. You're expected to master
them, not be obsessed by them. God bids us
hope in His everlasting mercy. Try to remember
that.

MARTIN: And you tell me this! What have I gained from
coming into this sacred Order? Aren't I still the
same? I'm still envious, I'm still impatient, I'm
still passionate?

BRO. WEINAND: How can you ask a question like that?

MARTIN: I do ask it. I'm asking you! What have I
gained?

BRO. WEINAND: In any of this, all we can ever learn is how to
die.

MARTIN: That's no answer.

BRO. WEINAND: It's the only one I can think of at this moment.
Come on.

MARTIN: All you teach me in this sacred place is how to
doubt——

BRO. WEINAND: Give you a little praise, and you're pleased for a
while, but let a little trial of sin and death come
into your day and you crumble, don't you?

27

MARTIN: But that's all you've taught me, that's really all you've taught me, and all the while I'm living in the Devil's worm-bag.

BRO. WEINAND: It hurts me to watch you like this, sucking up cares like a leech.

MARTIN: You *will* be there beside me, won't you?

BRO. WEINAND: Of course, and, if anything at all goes wrong, or if you forget anything, we'll see to it. You'll be all right. But nothing will—you won't make any mistakes.

MARTIN: But what if I do, just one mistake. Just a word, one word—one sin.

BRO. WEINAND: Martin, kneel down.

MARTIN: Forgive me, Brother Weinand, but the truth is this——

BRO. WEINAND: Kneel.

(MARTIN *kneels.*)

MARTIN: It's this, just this. All I can feel, all I can feel is God's hatred.

BRO. WEINAND: Repeat the Apostles' Creed.

MARTIN: He's like a glutton, the way he gorges me, he's a glutton. He gorges me, and then spits me out in lumps.

BRO. WEINAND: After me. "I believe in God the Father Almighty, maker of Heaven and Earth . . .

MARTIN: I'm a trough, I tell you, and he's swilling about in me. All the time.

BRO. WEINAND: "And in Jesus Christ, His only Son Our Lord . . .

MARTIN: "And in Jesus Christ, His only Son Our Lord . . .

BRO. WEINAND: "Who was conceived by the Holy Ghost, born of the Virgin Mary, suffered under Pontius Pilate . . .

MARTIN: (*almost unintelligibly*). "Was crucified, dead and buried; He descended into Hell; the third day He rose from the dead, He ascended into Heaven, and sitteth on the right hand of God

28

the Father Almighty; from thence He shall come to judge the quick and the dead." And every sunrise sings a song for death.

BRO. WEINAND: "I believe——

MARTIN: "I believe——

BRO. WEINAND: Go on.

MARTIN: "I believe in the Holy Ghost; the holy Catholic Church; the Communion of Saints; the forgiveness of sins;

BRO. WEINAND: Again!

MARTIN: "The forgiveness of sins.

BRO. WEINAND: What was that again?

MARTIN: "I believe in the forgiveness of sins.

BRO. WEINAND: Do you? Then remember this: St. Bernard says that when we say in the Apostles' Creed "I believe in the forgiveness of sins" each one must believe that *his* sins are forgiven. Well?——

MARTIN: I wish my bowels would open. I'm blocked up like an old crypt.

BRO. WEINAND: Try to remember, Martin?

MARTIN: Yes, I'll try.

BRO. WEINAND: Good. Now, you must get yourself ready. Come on, we'd better help you.

(*Some* BROTHERS *appear from out of the bagpipe with the vestments, etc. and help* MARTIN *put them on.*)

MARTIN: How much did you say my father gave to the chapter?

BRO. WEINAND: Twenty guilden.

MARTIN: That's a lot of money to my father. He's a miner, you know.

BRO. WEINAND: Yes, he told me.

MARTIN: As tough as you can think of. Where's he sitting?

BRO. WEINAND: Near the front, I should think. Are you nearly ready?

(*The Convent bell rings. A procession leads out from the bagpipe.*)

MARTIN: Thank you, Brother Weinand.

29

BRO. WEINAND: For what? Today would be an ordeal for any
kind of man. In a short while, you will be
handling, for the first time, the body and blood
of Christ. God bless you, my son.
(*He makes the sign of the cross, and the other*
BROTHERS *leave.*)

MARTIN: Somewhere, in the body of a child, Satan
foresaw in me what I'm suffering now. That's
why he prepares open pits for me, and all kinds
of tricks to bring me down, so that I keep
wondering if I'm the only man living who's
baited, and surrounded by dreams, and afraid
to move.

BRO. WEINAND: (*really angry by now*). You're a fool. You're
really a fool. God isn't angry with you. It's you
who are angry with Him.
(*He goes out. The* BROTHERS *wait for* MARTIN,
who kneels.)

MARTIN: Oh, Mary, dear Mary, all I see of Christ is a
flame and raging on a rainbow. Pray to your
Son, and ask Him to still His anger, for I can't
raise my eyes to look at Him. Am I the only
one to see all this, and suffer?
(*He rises, joins the procession and disappears off*
with it.
As the Mass is heard to begin offstage, the stage
is empty. Then the light within the cone grows
increasingly brilliant, and, presently MARTIN
appears again. He enters through the far entrance
of the cone, and advances towards the audience.
He is carrying a naked child. Presently, he steps
down from the cone, comes downstage, and
stands still.)

MARTIN: And so, the praising ended—and the blasphemy
began.
(*He returns, back into the cone, the light fades*
as the Mass comes to its end.)
(*End of Act One—Scene Two*)

ACT ONE

Scene Three

The Convent refectory. Some monks are sitting at table with HANS *and* LUCAS. LUCAS *is chatting with the* BROTHERS *eagerly, but* HANS *is brooding. He has drunk a lot of wine in a short time, and his brain is beginning to heat.*

HANS: What about some more of this, eh? Don't think you can get away with it, you know, you old cockchafer. I'm getting me twenty guilden's worth before the day's out. After all, it's a proud day for all of us. That's right, isn't it?

LUCAS: It certainly is.

BRO. WEINAND: Forgive me, I wasn't looking. Here—— (*He fills* HANS'S *glass.*)

HANS: (*trying to be friendly*). Don't give me that. You monks don't miss much. Got eyes like gimlets and ears like open drains. Tell me—Come on, then, what's your opinion of Brother Martin?

BRO. WEINAND: He's a good, devout monk.

HANS: Yes. Yes, well, I suppose you can't say much about each other, can you? You're more like a team, in a way. Tell me, Brother—would you say that in this monastery—or, any monastery you like—you were as strong as the weakest member of the team?

BRO. WEINAND: No, I don't think that's so.

HANS: But wouldn't you say then—I'm not saying this in any criticism, mind, but because I'm just interested, naturally, in the circumstances—but wouldn't you say that one bad monk, say for instance, one really monster sized, roaring great

31

bitch of a monk, if he really got going, really
going, couldn't he get his order such a
reputation that eventually, it might even have
to go into—what do they call it now—
liquidation. That's it. Liquidation. Now, you're
an educated man, you understand Latin and
Greek and Hebrew——

BRO. WEINAND: Only Latin, I'm afraid, and a very little Greek.

HANS: (*having planted his cue for a quick, innocent
boast*). Oh, really. Martin knows Latin and
Greek, and now he's half-way through Hebrew
too, they tell me.

BRO. WEINAND: Martin is a brilliant man. We are not all as gifted
as he is.

HANS: No, well, anyway what would be your opinion
about this?

BRO. WEINAND: I think my opinion would be that the Church
is bigger than those who are in her.

HANS: Yes, yes, but don't you think it could be dis-
credited by, say, just a few men?

BRO. WEINAND: Plenty of people have tried, but the Church is
still there. Besides, a human voice is small and
the world's very large. But the Church reaches
out and is heard everywhere.

HANS: Well, what about this chap Erasmus, for
instance?

BRO. WEINAND: (*politely. He knows* HANS *knows nothing about
him*). Yes?

HANS: Erasmus. (*Trying to pass the ball*). Well, what
about *him*, for instance? What do you think
about him?

BRO WEINAND: Erasmus is apparently a great scholar, and
respected throughout Europe.

HANS: (*resenting being lectured*). Yes, of course, *I*
know who he is, I don't need you to tell me
that, what I said was: what do you think about
him?

BRO. WEINAND: Think about him?

32

HANS: Good God, you won't stand still a minute and let yourself be saddled, will you? Doesn't he criticize the Church or something?

BRO. WEINAND: He's a scholar, and, I should say, his criticisms could only be profitably argued about by other scholars.

LUCAS: Don't let him get you into an argument. He'll argue about anything, especially if he doesn't know what he's talking about.

HANS: I know what I'm talking about, I was merely asking a question——

LUCAS: Well, you shouldn't be asking questions on a day like today. Just think of it, for a minute, Hans——

HANS: What do you think I'm doing? You soppy old woman!

LUCAS: It's a really 'once only' occasion, like a wedding, if you like.

HANS: Or a funeral. By the way, what's happened to the corpse? Eh? Where's Brother Martin?

BRO. WEINAND: I expect he's still in his cell.

HANS: Well, what's he doing in there?

BRO. WEINAND: He's perfectly all right, he's a little—disturbed.

HANS: (*pouncing delightedly*). Disturbed! Disturbed! What's he disturbed about?

BRO. WEINAND: Celebrating one's first Mass can be a great ordeal for a sensitive spirit.

HANS: Oh, the bread and the wine and all that?

BRO. WEINAND: Of course; there are a great many things to memorize as well.

LUCAS: Heavens, yes. I don't know how they think of it all.

HANS: I didn't think he made it up as he went along! But doesn't he know we're still here? Hasn't anybody told him we're all waiting for him?

BRO. WEINAND: He won't be much longer—you see. Here, have some more of our wine. He simply wanted to be on his own for a little while before he saw

33

anyone.

HANS: I should have thought he had enough of being on his own by now.

LUCAS: The boy's probably a bit—well, you know, anxious about seeing you again too.

HANS: What's he got to be anxious about?

LUCAS: Well, apart from anything else, it's nearly three years since he last saw you.

HANS: I saw *him*. He didn't see me.

(*Enter* MARTIN.)

LUCAS: There you are, my boy. We were wondering what had happened to you. Come and sit down, there's a good lad. Your father and I have been punishing the convent wine cellar, I'm afraid. Bit early in the day for me, too.

HANS: Speak for yourself, you swirly-eyed old gander. We're not *started* yet, are we?

LUCAS: My dear boy, are you all right? You're so pale.

HANS: He's right though. Brother Martin! Brother Lazarus they ought to call you!

(*He laughs and* MARTIN *smiles at the joke with him.* MARTIN *is cautious,* HANS *too, but manœuvring for position.*)

MARTIN: I'm all right, thank you. Lucas.

HANS: Been sick, have you?

MARTIN: I'm much better now, thank you, father.

HANS: (*relentless*). Upset tummy, is it? That what it is? Too much fasting I expect. (*Concealing concern*). You look like death warmed up, all right.

LUCAS: Come and have a little wine. You're allowed that, aren't you? It'll make you feel better.

HANS: I know that milky look. I've seen it too many times. Been sick have you?

LUCAS: Oh, he's looking better already. Drop of wine'll put the colour back in there. You're all right, aren't you, lad?

MARTIN: Yes, what about you——

LUCAS: That's right. Of course he is. He's all right.

34

HANS: Vomit all over your cell, I expect. (*To* BROTHER WEINAND). But he'll have to clear that up himself, won't he?

LUCAS: (*to* MARTIN). Oh, you weren't were you? Poor old lad, well, never mind, no wonder you kept us waiting.

HANS: Can't have his mother coming in and getting down on her knees to mop it all up.

MARTIN: I managed to clean it up all right. How are *you*, father?

HANS: (*feeling an attack, but determined not to lose the initiative*). Me? Oh, I'm all right. I'm all right, aren't I, Lucas? Nothing ever wrong with me. Your old man's strong enough. But then that's because we've got to be, people like Lucas and me. Because if *we* aren't strong, it won't take any time at all before we're knocked flat on our backs, or flat on our knees, or flat on something or other. Flat on our backs and finished, and we can't afford to be finished because if we're finished, that's it, that's the end, so we just have to stand up to it as best we can. But that's life, isn't it?

MARTIN: I'm never sure what people mean when they say that.

LUCAS: Your father's doing very well indeed, Martin. He's got his own investment in the mine now, so he's beginning to work for himself if you see what I mean. That's the way things are going everywhere now.

MARTIN: (*to* HANS). You must be pleased.

HANS: I'm pleased to make money. I'm not pleased to break my back doing it.

MARTIN: How's mother?

HANS: Nothing wrong there either. Too much work and too many kids for too long, that's all. (*Hiding embarrassment*). I'm sorry she couldn't come, but it's a rotten journey as you know,

35

and all that, so she sent her love to you. Oh, yes, and there was a pie too. But I was told (*at* BROTHER WEINAND) I couldn't give it to you, but I'd have to give it to the Prior.

MARTIN: That's the rule about gifts, father. You must have forgotten?

HANS: Well, I hope you get a piece of it anyway. She took a lot of care over it. Oh yes, and then there was Lucas's girl, she asked to be remembered to you.

MARTIN: Oh, good. How is she?

HANS: Didn't she, Lucas? She asked specially to be remembered to Martin, didn't she?

LUCAS: Oh she often talks about you, Martin. Even now. She's married you know.

MARTIN: No, I didn't know.

LUCAS: Oh, yes, got two children, one boy and a girl.

HANS: That's it—two on show on the stall, and now another one coming out from under the counter again—right, Lucas?

LUCAS: Yes, oh, she makes a fine mother.

HANS: And what's better than that? There's only one way of going 'up you' to Old Nick when he does come for you and that's when you show him your kids. It's the one thing—that is, if you've been lucky, and the plagues kept away from you—you can spring it out from under the counter at him. *That* to you! Then you've done something for yourself forever—forever and ever. Amen. (*Pause*). Come along, Brother Martin, don't let your guests go without. Poor old Lucas is sitting there with a glass as empty as a nun's womb, aren't you, you thirsty little goosey?

MARTIN: Oh, please, I'm sorry.

HANS: That's right, and don't forget your old dad. (*Pause*). Yes, well, as I say, I'm sorry your mother couldn't come, but I don't suppose

36

she'd have enjoyed it much, although I dare say
she'd like to have watched her son perform the
Holy Office. Isn't a mother supposed to dance
with her son after the ceremony? Like Christ
danced with *his* mother? Well, I can't see her
doing that. I suppose you think *I'm* going to
dance with you instead.

MARTIN: You're not obliged to, father.

HANS: It's like giving a bride away, isn't it?

MARTIN: Not unlike.

(*They have been avoiding any direct contact until
now, but now they look at each other, and both
relax a little.*)

HANS: (*encouraged*). God's eyes! Come to think of it,
you look like a woman, in all that!

MARTIN: (*with affection*). Not any woman you'd want,
father.

HANS: What do *you* know about it, eh? Eh? What do
you know about it? (*He laughs but not long*).
Well, Brother Martin.

MARTIN: Well? (*Pause*). Have you had some fish? Or a
roast, how about that, that's what you'd like,
isn't it?

HANS: Brother Martin, old Brother Martin. Well,
Brother Martin, you had a right old time up
there by that altar for a bit, didn't you? I
wouldn't have been in your shoes, I'll tell you.
All those people listening to you, every word
you're saying, watching every little tiny
movement, watching for one little lousy
mistake. I couldn't keep my eyes off it. We all
thought you were going to flunk it for one
minute there, didn't we, Lucas?

LUCAS: Well, we had a couple of anxious moments——

HANS: Anxious moments! I'll say there were. I thought
to myself, "he's going to flunk it, he can't get
through it, he's going to flunk it". What was
that bit, you know, the worst bit where you

37

stopped and Brother——

MARTIN: Weinand.

HANS: Weinand, yes, and he very kindly helped you up. He was actually holding you up at one point, wasn't he?

MARTIN: Yes.

BRO. WEINAND: It happens often enough when a young priest celebrates Mass for the first time.

HANS: Looked as though he didn't know if it was Christmas or Wednesday. We thought the whole thing had come to a standstill for a bit, didn't we? Everyone waiting and nothing happening. What was that bit, Martin, what was it?

MARTIN: I don't remember.

HANS: Yes, you know, the bit you really flunked.

MARTIN: (*rattling it off*). Receive, oh Holy Father, almighty and eternal God, this spotless host, which I, thine unworthy servant, offer unto thee for my own innumerable sins of commission and omission, and for all here present and all faithful Christians, living and dead, so that it may avail for their salvation and everlasting life. When I entered the monastery, I wanted to speak to God directly, you see. Without any embarrassment, I wanted to speak to him myself, but when it came to it, I dried up—as I always have.

LUCAS: No, you didn't, Martin, it was only for a few moments, besides——

MARTIN: Thanks to Brother Weinand. Father, why do you hate me being here?

(HANS *is outraged at a direct question*.)

HANS: Eh? What do you mean? I don't hate you being here.

MARTIN: Try to give me a straight answer if you can, father. I should like you to tell me.

HANS: What are you talking about, Brother Martin,

38

you don't know what you're talking about.
You've not had enough wine, that's your
trouble.

MARTIN: And don't say I could have been a lawyer.

HANS: Well, so you could have been. You could have
been better than that. You could have been a
burgomaster, you could have been a magistrate
you could have been a chancellor, you could
have been anything! So what! I don't want to
talk about it. What's the matter with you!
Anyway, I certainly don't want to talk about it
in front of complete strangers.

MARTIN: You make me sick.

HANS: Oh, do I? Well, thank you for that, Brother
Martin! Thank you for the truth, anyway.

MARTIN: No, it isn't the truth. It isn't the truth at all.
You're drinking too much wine—and I'm . . .

HANS: Drinking too much wine! I could drink this
convent piss from here till Gabriel's horn—and
from all accounts, that'll blow about next
Thursday—so what's the difference? (*Pause.*
HANS *drinks.*) Is this the wine you use? Is it?
Well? I'm asking a straight question myself
now. Is this the wine you use? (*To* MARTIN).
Here, have some.
(MARTIN *takes it and drinks.*)
You know what they say?

MARTIN: No, what do they say?

HANS: I'll tell you:
Bread thou art and wine thou art
And always shall remain so.
(*Pause*)

MARTIN: My father didn't mean that. He's a very devout
man, I know.
(*Some of the* BROTHERS *have got up to leave.*)

MARTIN: (*to* LUCAS). Brother Weinand will show you over
the convent. If you've finished, that is.

LUCAS: Yes, oh yes, I'd like that. Yes, I've had more

39

than enough, thank you. Right, well, let's go, shall we, Brother Weinand? I'll come back for you, shall I. Hans, you'll stay here?

HANS: Just as you like.

LUCAS: (*to* MARTIN). You're looking a bit better now, lad. Good-bye, my boy, but I'll see you before I go, won't I?

MARTIN: Yes, of course.

(*They all go, leaving* MARTIN *and* HANS *alone together. Pause.*)

HANS: Martin, I didn't mean to embarrass you.

MARTIN: No, it was my fault.

HANS: Not in front of everyone.

MARTIN: I shouldn't have asked you a question like that. It was a shock to see you suddenly, after such a long time. Most of my day's spent in silence you see, except for the Offices; and I enjoy the singing, as you know, but there's not much speaking, except to one's confessor. I'd almost forgotten what your voice sounded like.

HANS: Tell me, son—what made you get all snarled up like that in the Mass?

MARTIN: You're disappointed, aren't you?

HANS: I want to know, that's all. I'm a simple man, Martin, I'm no scholar, but I can understand all right. But you're a learned man, you speak Latin and Greek and Hebrew. You've been trained to remember ever since you were a tiny boy. Men like you don't just forget their words!

MARTIN: I don't understand what happened. I lifted up my head at the host, and, as I was speaking the words, I heard them as if it were the first time, and suddenly—(*pause*) they struck at my life.

HANS: I don't know, I really don't. Perhaps your father and mother are wrong, and God's right, after all. Perhaps. Whatever it is you've got to find, you could only find out by becoming a

40

monk; maybe that's the answer.

MARTIN: But you don't believe that. Do you?

HANS: No; no I don't.

MARTIN: Then say what you mean.

HANS: All right, if that's what you want, I'll say just what I mean. I think a man murders himself in these places.

MARTIN: (*retreating at once*). I am holy. I kill no one but myself.

HANS: I don't care. I tell you it gives me the creeps. And that's why I couldn't bring your mother, if you want to know.

MARTIN: The Gospels are the only mother I've ever had.

HANS: (*triumphantly*). And haven't you ever read in the Gospels, don't you know what's written in there? "Thou shalt honour thy father and thy mother."

MARTIN: You're not understanding me, because you don't want to.

HANS: That's fine talk, oh yes, fine, holy talk, but it won't wash, Martin. It won't wash because you can't ever, however you try, you can't ever get away from your body because that's what you live in, and it's all you've got to die in, and you can't get away from the body of your father and your mother! We're bodies, Martin, and so are you, and we're bound together for always. But you're like every man who was ever born into this world, Martin. You'd like to pretend that you made yourself, that it was *you* who made you—and not the body of a woman and another man.

MARTIN: Churches, kings, and fathers—why do they ask so much, and why do they all of them get so much more than they deserve?

HANS: You think so. Well, I think I deserve a little more than you've given me——

MARTIN: I've given you! I don't have to give you! I *am*

41

—that's all I need to give to you. That's your
big reward, and that's all you're ever going to
get, and it's more than any father's got a right
to. You wanted me to learn Latin, to be a
Master of Arts, be a lawyer. All you want is
me to justify *you*! Well, I can't, and, what's
more, I won't. I can't even justify myself. So
just stop asking me what have I accomplished,
and what have I done for you. I've done all for
you I'll ever do, and that's live and wait to die.

HANS: Why do you blame *me* for everything?

MARTIN: I don't blame you. I'm just not grateful, that's
all.

HANS: Listen, I'm not a specially good man, I know,
but I believe in God and in Jesus Christ, His
Son, and the Church will look after me, and I
can make some sort of life for myself that has
a little joy in it somewhere. But where is your
joy? You wrote to me once, when you were at
the University that only Christ could light up
the place you live in, but what's the point?
What's the point if it turns out the place you're
living in is just a hovel? Don't you think it
mightn't be better not to see at all?

MARTIN: I'd rather be able to see.

HANS: You'd rather see!

MARTIN: You really are disappointed, aren't you? Go on.

HANS: And why? I see a young man, learned and full
of life, my son, abusing his youth with fear and
humiliation. You think you're facing up to it in
here, but you're not; you're running away,
you're running away and you can't help it.

MARTIN: If it's so easy in here, why do you think the
rest of the world isn't knocking the gates down
to get in?

HANS: Because they haven't given up, that's why.

MARTIN: Well, there it is: you think I've given up.

HANS: Yes, there it is. That damned monk's piss has

42

given me a headache.

MARTIN: I'm sorry.

HANS: Yes, we're all sorry, and a lot of good it does any of us.

MARTIN: I suppose fathers and sons always disappoint each other.

HANS: I worked for you, I went without for you.

MARTIN: Well?

HANS: Well! (*Almost anxiously*). And if I beat you fairly often, and pretty hard sometimes I suppose, it wasn't any more than any other boy, was it?

MARTIN: No.

HANS: What do you think it is makes you different? Other men are all right, aren't they? You were stubborn, you were always stubborn, you've always had to resist, haven't you?

MARTIN: You disappointed me too, and not just a few times, but at some time of every day I ever remember hearing or seeing you, but, as you say, maybe that was also no different from any any other boy. But I loved you the best. It was always *you* I wanted. I wanted your love more than anyone's, and if anyone was to hold me, I wanted it to be you. Funnily enough, my mother disappointed me the most, and I loved her less, much less. She made a gap which no one else could have filled, but all she could do was make it bigger, bigger and more unbearable.

HANS: I don't know what any of that means; I really don't. I'd better be going, Martin. I think it's best; and I dare say you've got your various duties to perform.

MARTIN: She beat me once for stealing a nut, your wife. I remember it so well, she beat me until the blood came, I was so surprised to see it on my finger-tips; yes, stealing a nut, that's right. But

43

that's not the point. I had corns on my
backside already. Always before, when I was
beaten for something, the pain seemed outside
of me in some way, as if it belonged to the rest
of the world, and not only me. But, on that
day, for the first time, the pain belonged to me
and no one else, it went no further than *my*
body, bent between *my* knees and *my* chin.

HANS: You know what, Martin, I think you've always
been scared—ever since you could get up off
your knees and walk. You've been scared for
the good reason that that's what you most like
to be. Yes, I'll tell you. I'll tell you what! Like
that day, that day when you were coming home
from Erfurt, and the thunderstorm broke, and
you were so piss-scared, you lay on the ground
and cried out to St. Anne because you saw a
bit of lightning and thought you'd seen a vision.

MARTIN: I saw it all right.

HANS: And you went and asked her to save you—on
condition that you became a monk.

MARTIN: I saw it.

HANS: Did you? So it's still St. Anne is it? I thought
you were blaming your mother and me for your
damned monkery!

MARTIN: Perhaps I should.

HANS: And perhaps sometime you should have
another little think about that heavenly vision
that wangled you away into the cloister.

MARTIN: What's that?

HANS: I mean: I hope it really was a vision. I hope it
wasn't a delusion and some trick of the devil's.
I really hope so, because I can't bear to think
of it otherwise. (*Pause*) Good-bye, son. I'm
sorry we had to quarrel. It shouldn't have
turned out like this at all today.
(*Pause*)

MARTIN: Father—why did you give your consent?

44

HANS: What, to your monkery, you mean?

MARTIN: Yes. You could have refused, but why didn't you?

HANS: Well, when your two brothers died with the plague . . .

MARTIN: You gave me up for dead, didn't you?

HANS: Good-bye, son. Here—have a glass of holy wine.

(He goes out. MARTIN *stands, with the glass in his hand and looks into it. Then he drinks from it slowly, as if for the first time. He sits down at the table and sets the glass before him.)*

MARTIN: But—but what if it isn't true?

CURTAIN

(End of Act One)

DÉCOR NOTE

After the intense private interior of Act One, with its outer darkness and rich, personal objects, the physical effect from now on should be more intricate, general, less personal; sweeping, concerned with men in time rather than particular man in the unconscious; caricature not portraiture, like the popular woodcuts of the period, like DÜRER. Down by the apron in one corner there is now a heavily carved pulpit.

ACT TWO

Scene One

The market place, Juterbög, 1517. The sound of loud music, bells as a procession approaches the centre of the market place, which is covered in the banners of welcoming trade guilds. At the head of the slow-moving procession, with its lighted tapers and to the accompaniment of singing, prayers and the smoke of incense, is carried the Pontiff's bull of grace on a cushion and cloth of gold. Behind this the arms of the Pope and the Medici. After this, carrying a large red wooden cross, comes the focus of the procession, JOHN TETZEL, *Dominican, inquisitor and most famed and successful indulgence vendor of his day. He is splendidly equipped to be an ecclesiastical huckster, with alive, silver hair, the powerfully calculating voice, range and technique of a trained orator, the terrible, riveting charm of a dedicated professional able to winkle coppers out of the pockets of the poor and desperate.*

The red cross is taken from TETZEL *and established prominently behind him, and, from it are suspended the arms of the Pope.*

TETZEL: Are you wondering who I am, or what I am? Is there anyone here among you, any small child, any cripple, or any sick idiot who hasn't heard of me, and doesn't know why I am here? No? No? Well, speak up then if there is? What, no one? Do you all know me then? Do you all know who I am? If it's true, it's very good, and just as it should be. Just as it should be, and no more than that! However, however—just in case—just in case, mind, there is one blind, maimed midget among you today who can't hear, I will open his ears and wash them out with sacred soap for him! And, as for the rest of you. I know I can rely on you all to listen patiently

47

while I instruct him. Is that right? Can I go on? I'm
asking you, is that right, can I go on? I say "can I
go on"?
(*Pause*)
Thank you. And what is there to tell this blind,
maimed midget who's down there somewhere
among you? No, don't look round for him, you'll
only scare him and then he'll lose his one great
chance, and it's not likely to come again, or if it
does come, maybe it'll be too late. Well, what's the
good news on this bright day? What's the information
you want? It's this! Who is this friar with his red
cross? Who sent him, and what's he here for?
Don't try to work it out for yourself because I'm
going to tell you now, this very minute. I am John
Tetzel, Dominican, inquisitor, sub-commissioner to
the Archbishop of Mainz, and what I bring you is
indulgences. Indulgences made possible by the red
blood of Jesus Christ, and the red cross you see
standing up here behind me is the standard of those
who carry them. Look at it! Go on, look at it!
What else do you see hanging from the red cross?
Well, what do they look like? Why, it's the arms of
his holiness, because why? Because it's him who sent
me here. Yes, my friend, the Pope himself has sent
me with indulgences for you! Fine, you say, but
what are indulgences? And what are they to me?
What are indulgences? They're only the most
precious and noble of God's gifts to men, that's all
they are! Before God, I tell you I wouldn't swap my
privilege at this moment with that of St. Peter in
Heaven because I've already saved more souls with
my indulgences than he could ever have done with
all his sermons. You think that's bragging, do you?
Well, listen a little more carefully, my friend,
because this concerns *you*! Just look at it this way.
For every mortal sin you commit, the Church says
that after confession and contrition, you've got to do

48

penance—either in this life or in purgatory—for seven years. Seven years! Right? Are you with me? Good. Now then, how many mortal sins are committed by you—by you—in a single day? Just think for one moment: in one single day of your life. Do you know the answer? Oh, not so much as one a day. Very well then, how many in a month? How many in six months? How many in a year? And how many in a whole lifetime? Yes, you needn't shuffle your feet—it doesn't bear thinking about, does it? You couldn't even add up all those years without a merchant's clerk to do it for you! Try and add up all the years of torment piling up! What about it? And isn't there anything you can do about this terrible situation you're in? Do you really want to know? Yes! There is something, and that something I have here with me now up here, letters, letters of indulgence. Hold up the letters so that everyone can see them. Is there anyone so small he can't see? Look at them, all properly sealed, an indulgence in every envelope, and one of them can be yours today, now, before it's too late! Come on, come up as close as you like, you won't squash me so easily. Take a good look. There isn't any one sin so big that one of these letters can't remit it. I challenge any one here, any member of this audience, to present me with a sin, anything, any kind of a sin, I don't care what it is, that I can't settle for him with one of these precious little envelopes. Why, if any one had ever offered violence to the blessed Virgin Mary, Mother of God, if he'd only pay up—as long as he paid up all he could—he'd find himself forgiven. You think I'm exaggerating? You do, do you? Well, I'm authorized to go even further than that. Not only am I empowered to give you these letters of pardon for the sins you've already committed, I can give you pardon for those sins you haven't even committed (*pause . . . then slowly*) but,

which, however you *intend* to commit! But, you ask
—and it's a fair question—but, you ask, why is our
Holy Lord prepared to distribute such a rich grace
to me? The answer, my friends, is all too simple.
It's so that we can restore the ruined church of St.
Peter and St. Paul in Rome! So that it won't have
its equal anywhere in the world. This great church
contains the bodies not only of the holy apostles
Peter and Paul, but of a hundred thousand martyrs
and no less than forty-six popes! To say nothing of
the relics like St. Veronica's handkerchief, the
burning bush of Moses and the very rope with
which Judas Iscariot hanged himself! But, alas, this
fine old building is threatened with destruction, and
all these things with it, if a sufficient restoration fund
isn't raised, and raised soon. (*With passionate irony*)
. . . Will anyone dare to say that the cause is not a
good one? (*Pause.*) . . . Very well, and won't you,
for as little as one quarter of a florin, my friend,
buy yourself one of these letters, so that in the hour
of death, the gate through which sinners enter the
world of torment shall be closed against you, and
the gate leading to the joy of paradise be flung open
for you? And, remember this, these letters aren't
just for the living but for the dead too. There can't
be one amongst you who hasn't at least one dear
one who has departed—and to who knows what?
Why, these letters are for them too. It isn't even
necessary to repent. So don't hold back, come
forward, think of your dear ones, think of
yourselves! For twelve groats, or whatever it is we
think you can afford, you can rescue your father
from agony and yourself from certain disaster. And
if you only have the coat on your back to call your
own, then strip it off, strip it off now so that you
too can obtain grace. For remember: As soon as
your money rattles in the box and the cash bell
rings, the soul flies out of purgatory and sings! So,

50

come on then. Get your money out! What is it then, have your wits flown away with your faith? Listen then, soon, I shall take down the cross, shut the gates of heaven, and put out the brightness of this sun of grace that shines on you here today.

(*He flings a large coin into the open strong box, where it rattles furiously.*)

The Lord our God reigns no longer. He has resigned all power to the Pope. In the name of the Father, and of the Son and of the Holy Ghost. Amen.

(*The sound of coins clattering like rain into a great coffer as the light fades.*)

(*End of Act Two—Scene One*)

ACT TWO

Scene Two

The Eremite Cloister, Wittenberg. 1517. Seated beneath a single pear tree is JOHANN VON STAUPITZ, *Vicar General of the Augustinian Order. He is a quiet, gentle-voiced man in late middle age, almost stolidly contemplative. He has profound respect for Martin, recognizing in him the powerful potential of insight, sensitivity, courage and, also heroics that is quite outside the range of his own endeavour. However, he also understands that a man of his own limitations can offer a great deal to such a young man at this point in his development, and his treatment of Martin is a successful astringent mixture of sympathy and ridicule. Birds sing as he reads in the shade, and* MARTIN *approaches, prostrating himself.* STAUPITZ *motions him to his feet.*

MARTIN: (*looking up*). The birds always seem to fly away the moment I come out here.

STAUPITZ: Birds, unfortunately, have no faith.

MARTIN: Perhaps it's simply that they don't like me.

STAUPITZ: They haven't learned yet that you mean them no harm, that's all.

MARTIN: Are you treating me to one of your allegories?

STAUPITZ: Well, you recognized it, anyway.

MARTIN: I ought to. Ever since I came into the cloister, I've become a craftsman allegory maker myself. Only last week I was lecturing on Galatians Three, verse three, and I allegorized going to the lavatory.

STAUPITZ: (*quoting the verse*). "Are ye so foolish, that ye have begun in the spirit, you would now end in the flesh."

MARTIN: That's right. But allegories aren't much help in theology—except to decorate a house that's been

52

already built by argument.

STAUPITZ: Well, it's a house you've been able to unlock for a great many of us. I never dreamed when I first came here that the University's reputation would ever become what it has, and in such a short time, and it's mostly due to you.

MARTIN: (*very deliberately turning the compliment*). If ever a man could get to heaven through monkery, that man would be me.

STAUPITZ: I don't mean that. You know quite well what I mean. I'm talking about your scholarship, and what you manage to do with it, not your monkishness as you call it. I've never had any patience with all your mortifications. The only wonder is that you haven't killed yourself with your prayers, and watchings, yes and even your reading too. All these trials and temptations you go through, they're meat and drink to you.

MARTIN: (*patient*). Will you ever stop lecturing me about this?

STAUPITZ: Of course not, why do you think you come here— to see me in the garden when you could be inside working?

MARTIN: Well, if it'll please you, I've so little time, what with my lectures and study, I'm scarcely able to carry out even the basic requirements of the Rule.

STAUPITZ: I'm delighted to hear it. Why do you think you've always been obsessed with the Rule? No, I don't want to hear all your troubles again. I'll tell you why: you're obsessed with the Rule because it serves very nicely as a protection for you.

MARTIN: What protection?

STAUPITZ: You know perfectly well what I mean, Brother Martin, so don't pretend to look innocent. Protection against the demands of your own instincts, that's what. You see, you think you admire authority, and so you do, but unfortunately, you can't submit to it. So, what you do, by your exaggerated attention to the Rule, you make the authority ridiculous. And

the reason you do that is because you're determined
to substitute that authority with something else—
yourself. Oh, come along, Martin, I've been Vicar
General too long not to have made that little
discovery. Anyway, you shouldn't be too concerned
with a failing like that. It also provides the
strongest kind of security.

MARTIN: Security? I don't feel *that*.

STAUPITZ: I dare say, but you've got it all the same, which is
more than most of us have.

MARTIN: And how have I managed to come by this strange
security?

STAUPITZ: Quite simply: by demanding an impossible
standard of perfection.

MARTIN: I don't see what work or merit can come from a
heart like mine.

STAUPITZ: Oh, my dear, dear friend, I've sworn a thousand
times to our holy God to live piously, and have I
been able to keep my vows? No, of course I haven't.
Now I've given up making solemn promises because
I know I'm not able to keep them. If God won't be
merciful to me for the love of Christ when I leave
this world, then I shan't stand before Him on
account of all my vows and good works, I shall
perish, that's all.

MARTIN: You think I lavish too much attention on my own
pain, don't you?

STAUPITZ: Well, that's difficult for me to say, Martin. We're
very different kinds of men, you and I. Yes, you do
lavish attention on yourself, but then a large man is
worth the pains he takes. Like St. Paul, some men
must say "I die daily".

MARTIN: Tell me, Father, have you never felt humiliated to
find that you belong to a world that's dying?

STAUPITZ: No, I don't think I have.

MARTIN: Surely, this must be the last age of time we're living
in. There can't be any more left but the black
bottom of the bucket.

STAUPITZ: Do you mean the Last Judgment?

MARTIN: No. I don't mean that. The Last Judgment isn't to come. It's here and now.

STAUPITZ: Good. That's a little better, anyway.

MARTIN: I'm like a ripe stool in the world's straining anus, and at any moment we're about to let each other go.

STAUPITZ: There's nothing new in the world being damned, dying or without hope. It's always been like that, and it'll stay like it. What's the matter with you? What are you making funny faces for?

MARTIN: It's nothing, Father, just a—a slight discomfort.

STAUPITZ: Slight discomfort? What are you holding your stomach for? Are you in pain?

MARTIN: It's all right. It's gone now.

STAUPITZ: I don't understand you. What's gone now? I've seen you grabbing at yourself like that before. What is it?

MARTIN: I'm—constipated.

STAUPITZ: Constipated? There's always something the matter with you, Brother Martin. If it's not the gripes, insomnia, or faith and works, it's boils or indigestion or some kind of belly-ache you've got. All these severe fasts——

MARTIN: That's what my father says.

STAUPITZ: Your father sounds pretty sensible to me.

MARTIN: He is, and you know, he's a theologian too. I've discovered lately.

STAUPITZ: I thought he was a miner.

MARTIN: So he is, but he made a discovery years and years ago that took me sweat and labour to dig out of the earth for myself.

STAUPITZ: Well, that's no surprise. There's always some chunk of truth buried down away somewhere which lesser men will always reach with less effort.

MARTIN: Anyway, he always knew that works alone don't save any man. Mind you, he never said anything about faith coming first.

STAUPITZ: (*quoting*). "Oh, well, that's life, and nothing you can

55

do's going to change it."

MARTIN: The same speech.

STAUPITZ: You can't change human nature.

MARTIN: Nor can you.

STAUPITZ: That's right, Martin, and you've demonstrated it only too well in your commentaries on the Gospels and St. Paul. But don't overlook the fact that your father's taken a vow of poverty too, even though it's very different from your own. And he took it the day he told himself, and told *you*, that he was a complete man, or at least, a contented man.

MARTIN: A hog waffling in its own crap is contented.

STAUPITZ: Exactly.

MARTIN: My father, faced with an unfamiliar notion is like a cow staring at a new barn door. Like those who look on the cross and see nothing. All they hear is the priest's forgiveness.

STAUPITZ: One thing I promise you, Martin. You'll never be a spectator. You'll always take part.

MARTIN: How is it you always manage somehow to comfort me?

STAUPITZ: I think some of us are not much more than pretty modest sponges, but were probably best at quenching big thirsts. How's your tummy?

MARTIN: Better.

STAUPITZ: One mustn't be truly penitent because one anticipates God's forgiveness, but because one already possesses it. You have to sink to the bottom of your black bucket because that's where God judges you, and then look to the wounds of Jesus Christ. You told me once that when you entered the cloister, your father said it was like giving away a bride, and again your father was right. You are a bride and you should hold yourself ready like a woman at conception. And when grace comes and your soul is penetrated by the spirit, you shouldn't pray or exert yourself, but remain passive.

MARTIN: (*smiles*). That's a hard role.

56

STAUPITZ: (*smiles too*). Too hard for you, I dare say. Did you know the Duke's been complaining to me about you?

MARTIN: Why, what have I done?

STAUPITZ: Preaching against indulgences again.

MARTIN: Oh, that—I was very mild.

STAUPITZ: Yes, well I've heard your mildness in the pulpit. When I think sometimes of the terror it used to be for you, you used to fall up the steps with fright. Sheer fright! You were too frightened to become a Doctor of Theology, and you wouldn't be now if I hadn't forced you. "I'm too weak, I'm not strong enough. I shan't live long enough!" Do you remember what I said to you?

MARTIN: "Never mind, the Lord still has work in heaven, and there are always vacancies."

STAUPITZ: Yes, and the Duke paid all the expenses of your promotion for you. He was very cross when he spoke to me, I may say. He said you even made some reference to the collection of holy relics in the Castle Church, and most of those were paid for by the sale of indulgences, as you know. Did you say anything about them?

MARTIN: Well, yes, but not about those in the Castle Church. I did make some point in passing about someone who claimed to have a feather from the wing of the angel Gabriel.

STAUPITZ: Oh yes, I heard about him.

MARTIN: And the Archbishop of Mainz, who is supposed to have a flame from Moses' burning bush.

STAUPITZ: Oh dear, you shouldn't have mentioned that.

MARTIN: And I just finished off by saying how does it happen that Christ had twelve apostles and eighteen of them are buried in Germany?

STAUPITZ: Well, the Duke says he's coming to your next sermon to hear for himself, so try to keep off the subject, if you possibly can. It's All Saints' Day soon, remember, and all those relics will be out on

57

show for everyone to gawp at. The Duke's a good chap, and he's very proud of his collection, and it doesn't help to be rude about it.

MARTIN: I've tried to keep off the subject because I haven't been by any means sure about it. Then I did make a few mild protests in a couple of sermons, as I say.

STAUPITZ: Yes, yes, but what did you actually say?

MARTIN: That you can't strike bargains with God. There's a Jewish, Turkish, Pelagian heresy if you like.

STAUPITZ: Yes, more mildness. Go on.

MARTIN: I said, oh it was an evil sanction because only *you* could live *your* life, and only you can die your death. It can't be taken over for you. Am I right?

STAUPITZ: (*doubtfully*). Yes, what's difficult to understand is why your sermons are so popular.

MARTIN: Well, there are plenty who sit out there stiff with hatred, I can tell you. I can see their faces, and there's no mistaking them. But I wanted to tell you something——

STAUPITZ: Yes?

MARTIN: About all this. The other day a man was brought to me, a shoemaker. His wife had just died, and I said to him, "What've you done for her?" so he said, "I've buried her and commended her soul to God." "But haven't you had a Mass said for the repose of her soul?" "No," he said, "what's the point? She entered heaven the moment she died." So I asked him, "How do you know that?" And he said, "Well, I've got proof, that's why." And out of his pocket he took a letter of indulgence.

STAUPITZ: Ah.

MARTIN: He threw it at me, and said, "And if you still maintain that a Mass is necessary, then my wife's been swindled by our most holy father the Pope. Or, if not by him, then by the priest who sold it to me."

STAUPITZ: Tetzel.

MARTIN: Who else?

STAUPITZ: That old tout!

58

MARTIN: There's another story going around about him
which is obviously true because I've checked it at
several sources. It seems that a certain Saxon
nobleman had heard Tetzel in Jötebog. After Tetzel
had finished his usual performance, he asked him if
he'd repeat what he'd said at one stage, that he—
Tetzel I mean—had the power of pardoning sins
that men intended to commit. Tetzel was very high
and mighty, you know what he's like, and said,
"What's the matter, weren't you listening? Of course
I can give pardon not only for sins already
committed but for sins that men *intend* to commit."
"Well, then, that's fine," says this nobleman,
"because I'd like to take revenge on one of my
enemies. You know, nothing much, I don't want to
kill him or anything like that. Just a little slight
revenge. Now, if I give you ten guilden, will you
give me a letter of indulgence that will justify me—
justify me freely and completely?" Well, it seems
Tetzel made a few stock objections, but eventually
agreed on thirty guilden, and they made a deal. The
man went away with his letter of indulgence, and
Tetzel set out for the next job, which was Leipzig.
Well, half-way between Leipzig and Treblen, in the
middle of a wood, he was set on by a band of thugs,
and beaten up. While he's lying there on the grass
in a pool of his own blood, he looks up and sees
that one of them is the Saxon nobleman and that
they're making off with his great trunk full of
money. So, the moment he's recovered enough, he
rushes back to Jöteborg, and takes the nobleman to
court. And what does the nobleman do? Takes out
the letter of indulgence and shows it to Duke
George himself—case dismissed!

STAUPITZ: (*laughing*). Well, I leave you to handle it. But try
and be careful. Remember, *I* agree with all you say,
but the moment someone disagrees or objects to
what you're saying, *that* will be the moment when

you'll suddenly recognize the strength of your belief!

MARTIN: Father, I'm never sure of the words till I hear them out loud.

STAUPITZ: Well, that's probably the meaning of the Word. The Word is me, and I am the Word. Anyway, try and be a little prudent. Look at Erasmus: he never really gets into any serious trouble, but he still manages to make his point.

MARTIN: People like Erasmus get upset because I talk of pigs and Christ in the same breath. I must go. (*Clutches himself unobtrusively.*)

STAUPITZ: Well, you might be right. Erasmus is a fine scholar, but there are too many scholars who think they're better simply because they insinuate in Latin what you'll say in plain German. What's the matter, are you having that trouble again? Good heavens! Martin—just before you go: a man with a strong sword will draw it at some time, even if it's only to turn it on himself. But whatever happens, he can't just let it dangle from his belt. And, another thing, don't forget—you began this affair in the name of Our Lord Jesus Christ. You must do as God commands you, of course, but remember, St. Jerome once wrote about a philosopher who destroyed his own eyes so that it would give him more freedom to study. Take care of your eyes, my son, and do something about those damned bowels!

MARTIN: I will. Who knows? If I break wind in Wittenberg, they might smell it in Rome.

(*Exit. Church bells.*)

(*End of Act Two—Scene Two*)

ACT TWO

SCENE THREE

The steps of the Castle Church, Wittenberg, October 31st, 1517. From inside the Church comes the sound of Matins being sung. Sitting on the steps is a child, dirty, half-naked and playing intently by himself. MARTIN *enters with a long roll of paper. It is his ninety-five theses for disputation against indulgences. As he goes up the steps, he stops and watches the child, absorbed in his private fantasy. He is absorbed by the child, who doesn't notice him at first, but, presently, as soon as the boy becomes aware of an intruder, he immediately stops playing and looks away distractedly in an attempt to exclude outside attention.* MARTIN *hesitates briefly, then puts out his hand to the child, who looks at it gravely and deliberately, then slowly, not rudely, but naturally, gets up and skips away sadly out of sight.* MARTIN *watches him, then walks swiftly back down the steps to the pulpit and ascends it.*

MARTIN: My text is from the Epistle of Paul the Apostle to the Romans, chapter one, verse seventeen: "For therein is the righteousness of God revealed from faith to faith."

(*Pause*)

We are living in a dangerous time. You may not think so, but it could be that this is the most dangerous time since the light first broke upon the earth. It may not be true, but it's very probably true—but, what's most important is that it's an assumption we are obliged to make. We Christians seem to be wise outwardly and mad inwardly, and in this Jerusalem we have built there are blasphemies flourishing that make the Jews no worse than giggling children. A man is not a good Christian because he understands Greek and Hebrew. Jerome knew five languages, but

61

he's inferior to Augustine, who knew only one. Of course, Erasmus wouldn't agree with me, but perhaps one day the Lord will open his eyes for him. But listen! A man without Christ becomes his own shell. We are content with shells. Some shells are whole men and some are small trinkets. And, what are the trinkets? Today is the eve of All Saints, and the holy relics will be on show to you all; to the hungry ones whose lives are made satisfied by trinkets, by an imposing procession and the dressings up of all kinds of dismal things. You'll mumble for magic with lighted candles to St. Anthony for your erysipelas; to St. Valentine for your epilepsy; to St. Sebastian for the pestilence; to St. Laurentis to protect you from fire, to St. Appolonia if you've got the toothache, and to St. Louis to stop your beer from going sour. And tomorrow you'll queue for hours outside the Castle Church so that you can get a cheap-rate glimpse of St. Jerome's tooth, or four pieces each of St. Chrysostom and St. Augustine, and six of St. Bernard. The deacons will have to link hands to hold you back while you struggle to gawp at four hairs from Our Lady's head, at the pieces of her girdle and her veil stained with her Son's blood. You'll sleep outside with the garbage in the streets all night so that you can stuff your eyes like roasting birds on a scrap of swaddling clothes, eleven pieces from the original crib, one wisp of straw from the manger and a gold piece specially minted by three wise men for the occasion. Your emptiness will be frothing over at the sight of a strand of Jesus' beard, at one of the nails driven into His hands, and at the remains of the loaf at the Last Supper. Shells for shells, empty things for empty men. There are some who complain of these things, but they write in Latin for scholars. Who'll speak out in rough German? Someone's got to bell the cat! For you must be made to know that there's no security, there's no security at all, either in

indulgences, holy busywork or anywhere in this
world. It came to me while I was in my tower, what
they call the monk's sweathouse, the jakes, the john
or whatever you're pleased to call it. I was struggling
with the text I've given you: "For therein is the
righteousness of God revealed, from faith to faith; as
it is written, the just shall live by faith." And seated
there, my head down, on that privy just as when I
was a little boy, I couldn't reach down to my breath for
the sickness in my bowels, as I seemed to sense
beneath me a large rat, a heavy, wet, plague rat,
slashing at my privates with its death's teeth.
(*He kneads his knuckles into his abdomen, as if he
were suppressing pain. His face runs with sweat.*)
I thought of the righteousness of God, and wished his
gospel had never been put to paper for men to read;
who demanded my love and made it impossible to
return it. And I sat in my heap of pain until the
words emerged and opened out. "The just shall live
by faith." My pain vanished, my bowels flushed and
I could get up. I could see the life I'd lost. No man is
just because he does just works. The works are just
if the man is just. If a man doesn't believe in Christ,
not only are his sins mortal, but his good works.
This I know; reason is the devil's whore, born of one
stinking goat called Aristotle, which believes that
good works make a good man. But the truth is that
the just shall live by faith alone. I need no more than
my sweet redeemer and mediator, Jesus Christ, and I
shall praise Him as long as I have voice to sing; and
if anyone doesn't care to sing with me, then he can
howl on his own. If we are going to be deserted, let's
follow the deserted Christ.
(*He murmurs a prayer, descends from the pulpit, then
walks up the steps to the Church door, and nails his
theses to it. The singing from within grows louder as he
walks away.*)
(*End of Act Two—Scene Three*)

ACT TWO

Scene Four

The Fugger Palace, Augsburg. October 1518. As a backcloth a satirical contemporary woodcut, showing, for example, the Pope portrayed as an ass playing the bagpipes, or a cardinal dressed up as a court fool. Or perhaps Holbein's cartoon of Luther with the Pope suspended from his nose. However, there is a large area for the director and designer to choose from.

Seated at a table is THOMAS DE VIO, *known as Cajetan, Cardinal of San Sisto, General of the Dominican Order, as well as its most distinguished theologian, papal legate, Rome's highest representative in Germany. He is about fifty, but youthful, with a shrewd broad, outlook, quite the opposite of the vulgar bigotry of* TETZEL, *who enters.*

TETZEL: He's here.

CAJETAN: So I see.

TETZEL: What do you mean?

CAJETAN: You look so cross. Is Staupitz with him?

TETZEL: Yes. At least *he's* polite.

CAJETAN: I know Staupitz. He's a straightforward, four-square kind of a man, and probably very unhappy at this moment. From all accounts, he has a deep regard for this monk—which is all to the good from our point of view.

TETZEL: He's worried all right, you can see that. These Augustinians, they don't have much fibre.

CAJETAN: What about Dr. Luther? What's he got to say for himself?

TETZEL: Too much. I said to him if our Lord the Pope were to offer you a good Bishopric and a plenary indulgence for repairing your church, you'd soon start

singing a different song.

CAJETAN: Dear, oh, dear, and what did he say to that?

TETZEL: He asked me——

CAJETAN: Well?

TETZEL: He asked me how was my mother's syphilis.

CAJETAN: It's a fair question in the circumstances. You Germans, you're a crude lot.

TETZEL: He's a pig.

CAJETAN: I've no doubt. After all, it's what your country's most famous for.

TETZEL: That's what I said to him—you're not on your own ground here, you know. These Italians they're different. They're not just learned, they're subtle, experienced antagonists. You'll get slung in the fire after five minutes.

CAJETAN: And?

TETZEL: He said, "I've only been to Italy once, and they didn't look very subtle to me. They were lifting their legs on street corners like dogs."

CAJETAN: I hope he didn't see any cardinals at it. Knowing some of them as I do, it's not impossible. Well, let's have a look at this foul-mouthed monk of yours.

TETZEL: What about Staupitz?

CAJETAN: Let him wait in the corridor. It'll help him to worry.

TETZEL: Very well, your eminence. I hope he behaves properly. I've spoken to him.

(TETZEL *goes out and returns presently with* MARTIN, *who advances, prostrates himself, his face to the ground before* CAJETAN. CAJETAN *makes a motion and* MARTIN *rises to a kneeling position, where* CAJETAN *studies him.*)

CAJETAN: (*courteous*). Please stand up, Dr. Luther. So you're the one they call the excessive doctor. You don't look excessive to me. Do you feel very excessive?

MARTIN: (*conscious of being patronized*). It's one of those words which can be used like a harness on a man.

CAJETAN: How do you mean?

MARTIN: I mean it has very little meaning beyond traducing

65

him.

CAJETAN: Quite. There's never been any doubt in my mind that you've been misinterpreted all round, and, as you say, traduced. Well, what a surprise you are! Here was I expecting to see some doddering old theologian with dust in his ears who could be bullied into a heart attack by Tetzel here in half an hour. And here you are, as gay and sprightly as a young bull. How old are you, my son?

MARTIN: Thirty-four, most worthy father.

CAJETAN: Tetzel, he's a boy—you didn't tell me! And how long have you been wearing your doctor's ring?

MARTIN: Five years——

CAJETAN: So you were only twenty-nine! Well, obviously, everything I've heard about you is true—you must be a very remarkable young man. I wouldn't have believed there was one doctor in the whole of Germany under fifty. Would you, Brother John?

TETZEL: Not as far as I know.

CAJETAN: I'm certain there isn't. What is surprising, frankly, is that they allowed such an honour to be conferred on anyone so young and inexperienced as a man must inevitably be at twenty-nine.

(*He smiles to let his point get home.*)

Your father must be a proud man.

MARTIN: (*irritated*). Not at all, I should say he was disappointed and constantly apprehensive.

CAJETAN: Really? Well, that's surely one of the legacies of parenthood to offset the incidental pleasures. Now then, to business. I was saying to Tetzel, I don't think this matter need take up very much of our time. But, before we do start, there's just one thing I would like to say, and that is I was sorry you should have decided to ask the Emperor for safe conduct. That was hardly necessary, my son, and it's a little—well, distressing to feel you have such an opinion of us, such a lack of trust in your mother church, and in those who have, I can assure you, your dearest

66

interests at heart.

MARTIN: (*out-manœuvred*). I——

CAJETAN: (*kindly*). But never mind all that now, that's behind us, and, in the long run, it's unimportant, after all, isn't it? Your Vicar General has come with you, hasn't he?

MARTIN: He's outside.

CAJETAN: I've known Staupitz for years. You have a wonderful friend there.

MARTIN: I know. I—have great love for him.

CAJETAN: And he certainly has for you, I know. Oh my dear, dear son, this is such a ridiculous, unnecessary business for us all to be mixed up in. It's such a tedious, upsetting affair, and what purpose is there in it? Your entire order in Germany has been brought into disgrace. Staupitz is an old man, and he can't honestly be expected to cope. Not now. I have my job to do, and, make no mistake, it isn't all honey for an Italian legate in your country. You know how it is, people are inclined to resent you. Nationalist feeling and all that—which I respect—but it does complicate one's task to the point where this kind of issue thrown in for good measure simply makes the whole operation impossible. You know what I mean? I mean, there's your Duke Frederick, an absolutely fair, honest man, if ever there was one, and one his holiness values and esteems particularly. Well, he instructed me to present him with the Golden Rose of Virtue, so you can see . . . As well as even more indulgences for his Castle Church. But what happens now? Because of all this unpleasantness and the uproar it's caused throughout Germany, the Duke's put in an extremely difficult position about accepting it. Naturally, he wants to do the right thing by everyone. But he's not going to betray you or anything like that, however much he's set his heart on that Golden Rose, even after all these years. And, of course he's perfectly right. I know he has the greatest

67

regard for you and for some of your ideas—even though, as he's told me—he doesn't agree with a lot of them. No, I can only respect him for all that. So, you see, my dear son, what a mess we are in. Now, what are we going to do? Um? The Duke is unhappy. I am unhappy, his holiness is unhappy, and, you, my son, you are unhappy.

MARTIN: (*formal, as if it were a prepared speech*). Most worthy father, in obebience to the summons of his papal holiness, and in obedience to the orders of my gracious lord, the Elector of Saxony, I have come before you as a submissive and dutiful son of the holy Christian church, and acknowledge that I have published the proposition and theses ascribed to me. I am ready now to listen most obediently to my indictment, and if I have been wrong, to submit to your instruction in the truth.

CAJETAN: (*impatient*). My son, you have upset all Germany with your dispute about indulgences. I know you're a very learned doctor of the Holy Scriptures, and that you've already aroused some supporters. However, if you wish to remain a member of the Church, and to find a gracious father in the Pope, you'd better listen. I have here, in front of me, three propositions which, by the command of our holy father, Pope Leo the Tenth, I shall put to you now. First, you must admit your faults, and retract all your errors and sermons. Secondly, you must promise to abstain from propagating your opinions at any time in the future. And, thirdly, you must behave generally with greater moderation, and avoid anything which might cause offence or grieve and disturb the Church.

MARTIN: May I be allowed to see the Pope's instruction?

CAJETAN: No, my dear son, you may not. All you are required to do is confess your errors, keep a strict watch on your words, and not go back like a dog to his vomit. Then, once you have done that, I have been authorized by our most holy father to put everything

	to rights again.
MARTIN:	I understand all that. But I'm asking you to tell me where I have erred.
CAJETAN:	If you insist. (*Rattling off, very fast.*) Just to begin with, here are two propositions you have advanced, and which you will have to retract before anything else. First, the treasure of indulgences does not consist of the sufferings and torments of our Lord Jesus Christ. Second, the man who received the holy sacrament must have faith in the grace that is presented to him. Enough?
MARTIN:	I rest my case entirely on Holy Scriptures.
CAJETAN:	The Pope alone has power and authority over all those things.
MARTIN:	Except Scripture.
CAJETAN:	Including Scripture. What do you mean?
TETZEL:	Only the Pope has the right of deciding in matters of Christian faith. He alone and no one else has the power to interpret the meaning of Scripture, and to approve or condemn the views of other men, whoever they are—scholars, councils or the ancient fathers. The Pope's judgement cannot err, whether it concerns the Christian faith or anything that has to do with the salvation of the human race.
MARTIN:	That sounds like your theses.
TETZEL:	Burned in the market place by your students in Wittenberg—thank you very much——
MARTIN:	I assure you, I had nothing to do with that.
CAJETAN:	Of course. Brother John wasn't suggesting you had.
MARTIN:	I can't stop the mouth of the whole world.
TETZEL:	Why, your heresy isn't even original. It's no different from Wyclif or Hus.
CAJETAN:	True enough, but we mustn't try to deprive the learned doctor of his originality. An original heresy may have been thought of by someone else before you. In fact, I shouldn't think such a thing as an original heresy exists. But it is original so long as it originated in *you*, the virgin heretic.

69

TETZEL: The time'll come when you'll have to defend yourself before the world, and then every man can judge for himself who's the heretic and schismatic. It'll be clear to everyone, even those drowsy snoring Christians who've never smelled a Bible. They'll find out for themselves that those who scribble books and waste so much paper just for their own pleasure, and are contemptuous and shameless, end up by condemning themselves. People like you always go too far, thank heaven. You play into our hands. I give you a month, Brother Martin, to roast yourself.

MARTIN: You've had your thirty pieces of silver. For the sake of Christ, why don't you betray someone?

CAJETAN: (*to* TETZEL). Perhaps you should join Staupitz.

TETZEL: Very well, your eminence.
(*He bows and goes out.*)

CAJETAN: In point of fact, he gets eighty guilden a month plus expenses.

MARTIN: What about his vow of poverty?

CAJETAN: Like most brilliant men, my son, you have an innocent spirit. I've also just discovered that he has managed to father two children. So there goes another vow. Bang! But it'll do him no good, I promise you. You've made a hole in that drum for him. I may say there's a lot of bad feelings among the Dominicans about you. I should know—because I'm their General. It's only natural, they're accustomed to having everything their own way. The Franciscans are a grubby, sentimental lot, on the whole, and mercifully ignorant as well. But your people seem to be running alive with scholars and would-be politicians.

MARTIN: I'd no idea that my theses would ever get such publicity.

CAJETAN: Really now!

MARTIN: But it seems they've been printed over and over again, and circulated well, to an extent I'd never dreamed of.

70

CAJETAN: Oh yes, they've been circulated and talked about wherever men kneel to Christ.

MARTIN: Most holy father, I honour the Holy Roman Church, and I shall go on doing so. I have sought after the truth, and everything I have said I still believe to be right and true and Christian. But I am a man, and I may be deceived, so I am willing to receive instruction where I have been mistaken——

CAJETAN: (*angrily*). Save your arrogance, my son, there'll be a better place to use it. I can have you sent to Rome and let any of your German princes try to stop me! He'll find himself standing outside the gates of heaven like a leper.

MARTIN: (*stung*). I repeat, I am here to reply to all the charges you may bring against me——

CAJETAN: No, you're not——

MARTIN: I am ready to submit my theses to the universities of Basle, Freibourg, Louvain or Paris——

CAJETAN: I'm afraid you've not grasped the position. I'm not here to enter into a disputation with you, now or at any other time. The Roman Church is the apex of the world, secular and temporal, and it may constrain with its secular arm any who have once received the faith and gone astray. Surely I don't have to remind you that it is not bound to use reason to fight and destroy rebels. (*He sighs.*) My son, it's getting late. You must retract. Believe me, I simply want to see this business ended as quickly as possible.

MARTIN: Some interests are furthered by finding truth, others by destroying it. I don't care—what pleases or displeases the Pope. He is a man.

CAJETAN: (*wearily*). Is that all?

MARTIN: He seems a good man, as Popes go. But it's not much for a world that sings out for reformation. I'd say that's a hymn for everyone.

CAJETAN: My dear friend, think, think carefully, and see if you can't see some way out of all this. I am more than prepared to reconcile you with the Church, and the

sovereign bishop. Retract, my son, the holy father prays for it——

MARTIN: But won't you discuss——

CAJETAN: Discuss! I've not *discussed* with you, and I don't intend to. If you want a disputation, I dare say Eck will take care of you——

MARTIN: John Eck? The Chancellor of Ingolstadt?

CAJETAN: I suppose you don't think much of him?

MARTIN: He knows theology.

CAJETAN: He has a universal reputation in debate.

MARTIN: It's understandable. He has a pedestrian style and a judicial restraint and that'll always pass off as wisdom to most men.

CAJETAN: You mean he's not original, like you——

MARTIN: I'm not an original man, why I'm not even a teacher, and I'm scarcely even a priest. I know Jesus Christ doesn't need my labour or my services.

CAJETAN: All right, Martin, I *will* argue with you if you want me to, or, at least, I'll put something to you, because there is something more than your safety or your life involved, something bigger than you and I talking together in this room at this time. Oh, it's fine for someone like you to criticize and start tearing down Christendom, but tell me this, just tell me this: what will you build in its place?

MARTIN: A withered arm is best amputated, an infected place is best scoured out, and so you pray for healthy tissue and something sturdy and clean that was crumbling and full of filth.

CAJETAN: Can't you see? My son, you'll destroy the perfect unity of the world.

MARTIN: Someone always prefers what's withered and infected. But it should be cauterized as honestly as one knows how.

CAJETAN: And how honest is that? There's something I'd like to know: suppose you *did* destroy the Pope. What do you think would become of you?

MARTIN: I don't know.

72

CAJETAN: Exactly, you wouldn't know what to do because you
need him, Martin, you need to hunt him more than
he needs his silly wild boar. Well? There have always
been Popes, and there always will be, even if they're
called something else. They'll have them for people
like *you*. You're not a good old revolutionary, my
son, you're just a common rebel, a very different
animal. You don't fight the Pope because he's too
big, but because for your needs he's not big enough.

MARTIN: My General's been gossiping——

CAJETAN: (*contemptuous*). I don't need Staupitz to explain you
to me. Why, some deluded creature might even come
to you as a leader of their revolution, but you don't
want to break rules, you want to make them. You'd
be a master breaker and maker and no one would be
able to stand up to you, you'd hope, or ever
sufficiently repair the damage you did. I've read some
of your sermons on faith. Do you know all they say
to me?

MARTIN: No.

CAJETAN: They say: I am a man struggling for certainty,
struggling insanely like a man in a fit, an animal
trapped to the bone with doubt.
(MARTIN *seems about to have a physical struggle with
himself.*)

CAJETAN: Don't you see what could happen out of all this?
Men could be cast out and left to themselves for ever,
helpless and frightened!

MARTIN: Your eminence, forgive me. I'm tired after my
journey—I think I might faint soon——

CAJETAN: That's what would become of them without their
Mother Church—with all its imperfections, Peter's
rock, without it they'd be helpless and unprotected.
Allow them their sins, their petty indulgences, my son,
they're unimportant to the comfort we receive——

MARTIN: (*somewhat hysterical*). Comfort! It—doesn't concern
me!

CAJETAN: We live in thick darkness, and it grows thicker. How

73

will men find God if they are left to themselves each man abandoned and only known to himself?

MARTIN: They'll have to try.

CAJETAN: I beg of you, my son, I beg of you. Retract. (*Pause*)

MARTIN: Most holy father, I cannot. (*Pause*)

CAJETAN: You look ill. You had better go and rest. (*Pause*) Naturally, you will be released from your order.

MARTIN: I——

CAJETAN: Yes?

MARTIN: As you say, your eminence. Will you refer this matter to the Pope for his decision?

CAJETAN: Assuredly. Send in Tetzel.

(MARTIN *prostrates himself, and then kneels.* CAJETAN *is distressed but in control.*)

You know, a time will come when a man will no longer be able to say, "I speak Latin and am a Christian" and go his way in peace. There will come frontiers, frontiers of all kinds—between men—and there'll be no end to them.

(MARTIN *rises and goes out.* TETZEL *returns.*)

TETZEL: Yes?

CAJETAN: No, of course he didn't—that man hates himself. And if he goes to the stake, Tetzel, you can have the pleasure of inscribing it: he could only love others.

(*End of Act Two—Scene Four*)

ACT TWO

Scene Five

A hunting lodge at Magliana in Northern Italy, 1519. Suspended the arms, the brass balls, of the Medici. KARL VON MILTITZ, *a young Chamberlain of the Pope's household is waiting. There are cries off, and sounds of excitement.* POPE LEO THE TENTH *enters with a* HUNTSMAN, *dogs and* DOMINICANS. *He is richly dressed in hunting clothes and long boots. He is indolent, cultured, intelligent, extremely restless, and well able to assimilate the essence of anything before anyone else. While he is listening, he is able to play with a live bird with apparent distraction. Or shoot at a board with a crossbow. Or generally fidget.* MILTITZ *kneels to kiss his toe.*

LEO: I should forget it. I've got my boots on. Well? get on with it. We're missing the good weather.
(*He sits and becomes immediately absorbed in his own play, as it seems.* MILTITZ *has a letter, which he reads.*)
MILTITZ: "To the most blessed father Leo the tenth, sovereign bishop, Martin Luther, Augustine friar, wishes eternal salvation. I am told that there are vicious reports circulating about me, and that my name is in bad odour with your holiness. I am called a heretic, apostate, traitor and many other insulting names. I cannot understand all this hostility, and I am alarmed by it. But the only basis of my tranquillity remains, as always, a pure and peaceful conscience. Deign to listen to me, most holy father, to me who is like a child.
(LEO *snorts abstractedly.*)
"There have always been, as long as I can remember, complaints and grumbling in the taverns about the avarice of the priests and attacks on the power of the

75

keys. And this has been happening throughout
Germany. When I listened to these things my zeal was
aroused for the glory of Christ, so I warned not one,
but several princes of the Church. But, either they
laughed in my face or ignored me. The terror of your
name was too much for everyone. It was then I
published my disputation, nailing it on the door of the
Castle Church here in Wittenberg. And now, most
holy father, the whole world has gone up in flames.
Tell me what I should do? I cannot retract; but this
thing has drawn down hatred on me from all sides,
and I don't know where to turn to but to you. I am
far too insignificant to appear before the world in a
matter as great as this.

(LEO *snaps his fingers to glance at this passage in the
letter. He does so and returns it to* MILTITZ *who
continues reading.*)

"But in order to quieten my enemies and satisfy my
friends I am now addressing myself to you most holy
father and speak my mind in the greater safety of the
shadow of your wings. All this respect I show to the
power of the keys. If I had not behaved properly. it
would have been impossible for the most serene Lord
Frederick, Duke and Elector of Saxony, who shines in
your apostolic favour, to have endured me in his
University of Wittenberg. Not if I am as dangerous as
is made out by my enemies. For this reason, most holy
father, I fall at the feet of your holiness, and submit
myself to you, with all I have and all that I am.
Declare me right or wrong. Take my life, or give it
back to me, as you please. I shall acknowledge your
voice as the voice of Jesus Christ. If I deserve death,
I shall not refuse to die. The earth is God's and all
within it. May He be praised through all eternity, and
may He uphold you for ever. Amen. Written the day
of the Holy Trinity in the year 1518, Martin Luther,
Augustine Friar."

(*They wait for* LEO *to finish his playing and give them*
76

his full attention. Presently, he gets up and takes the
letter from MILTITZ. *He thinks.*)

LEO: Double faced German bastard! Why can't he say what
he means? What else?

MILTITZ: He's said he's willing to be judged by any of the
universities of Germany, with the exception of Leipzig,
Erfurt and Frankfurt, which he says are not impartial.
He says it's impossible for him to appear in Rome in
person.

LEO: I'm sure.

MILTITZ: Because his health wouldn't stand up to the rigours of
the journey.

LEO: Cunning! Cunning German bastard! What does
Staupitz say for him?

MILTITZ: (*reading hastily from another letter*). "The reverend
father, Martin Luther, is the noblest and most
distinguished member of our university. For many
years, we have watched his talents——"

LEO: Yes, well we know all about that. Write to Cajetan.
Take this down. We charge you to summon before
you Martin Luther. Invoke for this purpose, the aid of
our very dear son in Christ, Maximilian, and all the
other princes in Germany, together with all
communities, universities, potentates ecclesiastic and
secular. And, once you get possession of him, keep
him in safe custody, so that he can be brought before
us. If, however, he should return to his duty of his own
accord and begs forgiveness, we give you the power to
receive him into the perfect unity of our Holy Mother
the Church. But, should he persist in his obstinacy and
you cannot secure him, we authorize you to outlaw
him in every part of Germany. To banish and
excommunicate him. As well as all prelates, religious
orders, universities, counts, and dukes who do not
assist in apprehending him. As for the laymen, if they
do not immediately obey your orders, declare them
infamous, deprived of Christian burial and stripped of
anything they may hold either from the apostolic see

or from any lord whatsoever. There's a wild pig in our vineyard, and it must be hunted down and shot. Given under the seal of the Fisherman's Ring, etcetera. That's all.

(*He turns quickly and goes out.*)

(*End of Act Two—Scene Five*)

ACT TWO

SCENE SIX

The Elster Gate, Wittenberg. 1520. Evening. A single bell. As a backcloth the bull issued against Luther. Above it a fish-head and bones. The bull is slashed with the reflection of the flames rising round the Elster Gate where the books of canon law, the papal decretals, are burning furiously. MONKS *come to and fro with more books and documents, and hurl them on the fire.* MARTIN *enters and ascends the pulpit.*

MARTIN: I have been served with a piece of paper. Let me tell you about it. It has come to me from a latrine called Rome, that capital of the devil's own sweet empire. It is called the papal bull and it claims to excommunicate me, Dr. Martin Luther. These lies they rise up from paper like fumes from the bog of Europe; because papal decretals are the devil's excretals. I'll hold it up for you to see properly. You see the signature? Signed beneath the seal of the Fisherman's Ring by one certain midden cock called Leo, an over-indulged jakes' attendant to Satan himself, a glittering worm in excrement, known to you as his holiness the Pope. You may know him as the head of the Church. Which he may still be: like a fish is the head of a cat's dinner; eyes without sight clutched to a stick of sucked bones. God has told me: there can be no dealings between this cat's dinner and me. And, as for this bull, it's going to roast, it's going to roast and so are the balls of the Medici!

(He descends and casts the bull into the flames. He begins to shake, as if he were unable to breathe; as if he were about to have another fit. Shaking, he kneels.)

Oh, God! Oh, God! Oh, thou my God, my God, help
me against the reason and wisdom of the world. You
must—there's only you—to do it. Breathe into me.
Breathe into me, like a lion into the mouth of a
stillborn cub. This cause is not mine but yours. For
myself, I've no business to be dealing with the great
lords of this world. I want to be still, in peace, and
alone. Breathe into me, Jesus. I rely on no man, only
on you. My God, my God do you hear me? Are you
dead? Are you dead? No, you can't die, you can only
hide yourself, can't you? Lord, I'm afraid. I am a
child, the lost body of a child. I am stillborn. Breathe
into me, in the name of Thy Son, Jesus Christ, who
shall be my protector and defender, yes, my mighty
fortress, breathe into me. Give me life, oh Lord. Give
me life.

(MARTIN *prays as the deep red light of the flames flood*
the darkness around him.)

(*End of Act Two*)

ACT THREE

Scene One

The Diet of Worms, April 18th, 1521. A gold front-cloth, and on it, in the brightest sunshine of colour, a bold, joyful representation of this unique gathering of princes, electors, dukes, ambassadors, bishops, counts, barons, etc. Perhaps Luther's two-wheeled wagon which brought him to Worms. The mediaeval world dressed up for the Renaissance.

Devoid of depth, such scenes are stamped on a brilliant ground of gold. Movement is frozen, recession in space ignored and perspective served by the arrangement of figures, or scenes, one above the other. In this way, landscape is dramatically substituted by objects in layers. The alternative is to do the opposite, in the manner of, say, Altdorfer. Well in front of the cloth is a small rostrum with brass rails sufficient to support one man. If possible, it would be preferable to have this part of the apron projected a little into the audience. Anyway, the aim is to achieve the maximum in physical enlargement of the action, in the sense of physical participation in the theatre, as if everyone watching had their chins resting on the sides of a boxing-ring. Also on the apron, well to the front are several chairs. On one side is a table with about twenty books on it. The table and books may also be represented on the gold cloth. The rostrum has a small crescent of chairs round it. From all corners of the auditorium comes a fanfare of massed trumpets, and, approaching preferably from the auditorium up steps to the apron, come a few members of the Diet audience (who may also be represented on the gold cloth). Preceded by a HERALD, *and seating themselves on the chairs, they should include* THE EMPEROR CHARLES THE FIFTH (*in front of the rostrum*), ALEANDER, THE PAPAL NUNCIO; ULRICH VON HUTTEN, KNIGHT; THE ARCHBISHOP OF TRIER *and* HIS SECRETARY, JOHAN VON ECK, *who sit at the table with the books. The trumpets cease, and they wait.* MARTIN *appears from the stage, and ascends the rostrum centre.*

81

ECK: (*rising*). Martin Luther, you have been brought here by His Imperial Majesty so that you may answer two questions, Do you publicly acknowledge being the author of the books you see here? When I asked you this question yesterday, you agreed immediately that the books were indeed your own. Is that right?

(MARTIN *nods in agreement*.)

When I asked you the second question, you asked if if you might be allowed time in which to consider it. Although such time should have been quite unnecessary for an experienced debater and distinguished doctor of theology like yourself, His Imperial Majesty was graciously pleased to grant your request. Well, you have had your time now, a whole day and a night, and so I will repeat the question to you. You have admitted being the author of these books. Do you mean to defend all these books, or will you retract any of them?

(ECK *sits*. MARTIN *speaks quietly, conversationally, hardly raising his voice throughout, and with simplicity*.)

MARTIN: Your serene highness, most illustrious princes and gracious lords, I appear before you by God's mercy, and I beg that you will listen patiently. If, through my ignorance, I have not given anyone his proper title or offended in any way against the etiquette of such a place as this, I ask your pardon in advance for a man who finds it hard to know his way outside the few steps from wall to wall of a monk's cell. We have agreed these books are all mine, and they have all been published rightly in my name. I will reply to your second question. I ask your serene majesty and your gracious lordships to take note that not all my books are of the same kind. For instance, in the first group, I have dealt quite simply with the values of faith and morality, and even my enemies have agreed that all this is quite harmless, and can be read without damaging the most fragile Christian. Even the bull against me, harsh and cruel as it is, admits that some

82

of my books are offensive to no one. Perhaps it's the
strange nature of such a questionable compliment,
that the bull goes on to condemn these with the rest,
which it considers offensive. If I'm to begin
withdrawing these books, what should I be doing? I
should be condemning those very things my friends
and enemies are agreed on. There is a second group of
books I have written, and these all attack the power of
the keys, which has ravaged Christendom. No one can
deny this, the evidence is everywhere and everyone
complains of it. And no one has suffered more from
this tyranny than the Germans. They have been
plundered without mercy. If I were to retract those
books now, I should be issuing a licence for more
tyranny, and it is too much to ask of me.

I have also written a third kind of book against
certain, private, distinguished, and, apparently—highly
established—individuals. They are all defenders of
Rome and enemies of my religion. In these books, it's
possible that I have been more violent than may seem
necessary, or, shall I say, tasteful in one who is, after
all, a monk. But then, I have never set out to be a saint
and I've not been defending my own life, but the
teaching of Christ. So you see, again I'm not free to
retract, for if I did, the present situation would
certainly go on just as before. However, because I am
a man and not God, the only way for me to defend
what I have written is to employ the same method
used by my Saviour. When He was being questioned
by Annas, the high priest, about His teaching, and He
had been struck in the face by one of the servants, He
replied: "If I have spoken lies tell me what the lie is."
If the Lord Jesus Himself, who could not err, was
willing to listen to the arguments of a servant, how can
I refuse to do the same? Therefore, what I ask, by the
Mercy of God, is let someone expose my errors in the
light of the Gospels. The moment you have done this,
I shall ask you to let me be the first to pick up my

books and hurl them in the fire.

I think this is a clear answer to your question. I think I understand the danger of my position well enough. You have made it very clear to me. But I can still think of nothing better than the Word of God being the cause of all the dissension among us. For Christ said, "I have not come to bring peace, but a sword. I have come to set a man against his father." We also have to be sure that the reign of this noble, young Prince Charles, so full of promise, should not end in the misery of Europe. We must fear God alone. I commend myself to your most serene majesty and to your lordships, and humbly pray that you will not condemn me as your enemy. That is all.

ECK: (*rising*). Martin, you have not answered the question put to you. Even if it were true that some of your books are innocuous—a point which, incidentally, we don't concede—we still ask that you cut out these passages which are blasphemous; that you cut out the heresies or whatever could be construed as heresy, and, in fact, that you delete any passage which might be considered hurtful to the Catholic faith. His sacred and imperial majesty is more than prepared to be lenient, and, if you will do these things, he will use his influence with the supreme pontiff to see that the good things in your work are not thrown out with the bad. If, however, you persist in your attitude, there can be no question that all memory of you will be blotted out, and everything you have written, right or wrong, will be forgotten.

You see, Martin, you return to the same place as all other heretics—to Holy Scripture. You demand to be contradicted from Scripture. We can only believe that you must be ill or mad. Do reasons have to be given to anyone who cares to ask a question? Any question? Why, if anyone who questioned the common understanding of the Church on any matter he liked to raise, and had to be answered irrefutably from the

84

Scriptures, there would be nothing certain or decided in Christendom. What would the Jews and Turks and Saracens say if they heard us *debating* whether what we have always believed is true or not? I beg you, Martin, not to believe that you, and you alone, understand the meaning of the Gospels. Don't rate your own opinion so highly, so far beyond that of many other sincere and eminent men. I ask you: don't throw doubt on the most holy, orthodox faith, the faith founded by the most perfect legislator known to us, and spread by His apostles throughout the world, with their blood and miracles. This faith has been defined by sacred councils, and confirmed by the Church. It is your heritage, and we are forbidden to dispute it by the laws of the emperor and the pontiff. Since no amount of argument can lead to a final conclusion, they can only condemn those who refuse to submit to them. The penalties are provided and will be executed. I must, therefore, ask again, I must demand that you answer sincerely, frankly and unambiguously, yes or no: will you or will you not retract your books and the errors contained in them.

MARTIN: Since your serene majesty and your lordships demand a simple answer, you shall have it, without horns and without teeth. Unless I am shown by the testimony of the Scriptures—for I don't believe in popes or councils —unless I am refuted by Scripture and my conscience is captured by God's own word, I cannot and will not recant, since to act against one's conscience is neither safe nor honest. Here I stand; God help me; I can do no more. Amen.

(End of Act Three—Scene One)

ACT THREE

Scene Two

Wittenberg. 1525. A marching hymn, the sound of cannon and shouts of mutilated men. Smoke, a shattered banner bearing the cross and wooden shoe of the Bundschuh, emblem of the Peasants' Movement. A small chapel altar at one side of the stage opposite the pulpit. Centre is a small handcart, and beside it lies the bloody bulk of a peasant's corpse. Downstage stands the KNIGHT, fatigued, despondent, stained and dirty.

KNIGHT: There was excitement that day. In Worms—that day I mean. Oh, I don't mean now, not now. A lot's happened since then. There's no excitement like that any more. Not unless murder's your idea of excitement. I tell you, you can't have ever known the kind of thrill that monk set off amongst that collection of all kinds of men gathered together there—those few years ago. We all felt it, every one of us, just without any exception, you couldn't help it, even if you didn't want to, and, believe me, most of those people didn't want to. His scalp looked blotchy and itchy, and you felt sure, just looking at him, his body must be permanently sour and white all over, even whiter than his face and like a millstone to touch. He'd sweated so much by the time he'd finished, I could smell every inch of him even from where I was. But he fizzed like a hot spark in a trail of gunpowder going off in us, that dowdy monk, he went off in us, and nothing could stop it, and it blew up and there was nothing we could do, any of us, that was it. I just felt quite sure, quite certain in my own mind nothing could ever be the same again, just simply that. Something

86

had taken place, something had changed and become something else, an event had occurred in the flesh, in the flesh and the breath—like, even like when the weight of that body slumped on its wooden crotch-piece and the earth grew dark. That's the kind of thing I mean by happen, and this also happened in very likely the same manner to all those of us who stood there, friends and enemies alike. I don't think, no I don't think even if I could speak and write like him, I could begin to give you an idea of what we thought, or what some of us thought, of what we might come to. Obviously, we couldn't have all felt quite the same way, but I wanted to burst my ears with shouting and draw my sword, no, not draw it, I wanted to pluck it as if it were a flower in my blood and plunge it into whatever he would have told me to. (THE KNIGHT *is lost in his own thoughts, then his eyes catch the body of the peasant. He takes a swipe at the cart.*)

If one could only understand him. He baffles me, I just can't make him out. Anyway, it never worked out. (*To corpse*) Did it, my friend? Not the way we expected anyway, certainly not the way *you* expected, but who'd have ever thought we might end up on different sides, him on one and us on the other. That when the war came between you and them, he'd be there beating the drum for *them* outside the slaughter house, and beating it louder and better than anyone, hollering for *your* blood, cutting you up in your thousands, and hanging you up to drip away into the fire for good. Oh well, I suppose all those various groups were out for their different things, or the same thing really, all out for what we could get, and more than any of us had the right to expect. They were all the same, all those big princes and archbishops, the cut rate nobility and rich layabouts, honourable this and thats scrabbling like boars round a swill bucket for every penny those poor peasants

87

never had. All those great abbots with their dewlaps
dropped and hanging on their necks like goose's eggs,
and then those left-over knights, like me for instance,
I suppose, left-over men, impoverished, who'd seen
better days and were scared and'b stick at nothing to
try and make sure they couldn't get any worse.
Yes. . . . Not one of them could read the words WAY
OUT when it was written up for them, marked out
clearly and unmistakably in the pain of too many
men. Yes. They say, you know, that the profit motive
—and I'm sure you know all about that one—they
say that the profit motive was born with the invention
of double entry book-keeping in the monasteries.
Book-keeping! In the monasteries, and ages before any
of us had ever got round to burning them down. But,
you know, for men with such a motive, there is only
really one entry. The profit is theirs, the loss is
someone else's, and usually they don't even bother to
write it up.
(*He nudges the corpse with his toe.*)
Well, it was your old loss wasn't it, dead loss, in fact,
my friend, you could say his life was more or less a
write-off right from the day he was born. Wasn't it?
Um? And all the others like him, everywhere, now
and after him.
(THE KNIGHT *starts rather weakly to load the body on
to the cart.* MARTIN *enters, a book in his hands. They
look at each other then* MARTIN *at the* PEASANT. THE
KNIGHT *takes his book and glances at it, but he doesn't
miss* MARTIN *shrink slightly from the peasant.*
Another of yours?
(*He hands it back.*)
Do you think it'll sell as well as the others? (*Pause*)
I dare say it will. Someone's always going to listen to
you. No?
(MARTIN *moves to go, but* THE KNIGHT *stops him.*)
Martin. Just a minute.
(*He turns and places his hand carefully, ritually, on the*
88

body in the cart. He smears the blood from it over
MARTIN.)
There we are. That's better.
(MARTIN *makes to move again, but again* THE KNIGHT
stops him.)
You're all ready now. You even look like a
butcher——

MARTIN: God is the butcher——

KNIGHT: Don't you?

MARTIN: Why don't you address your abuse to Him?

KNIGHT: Never mind—you're wearing His apron.
(MARTIN *moves to the stairs of the pulpit.*)
It suits you. (*Pause*) Doesn't it? (*Pause*) That day in
Worms (*pause*) you were like a pig under glass
weren't you? Do you remember it? I could smell
every inch of you even where I was standing. All
you've ever managed to do is convert everything into
stench and dying and peril, but you could have done
it, Martin, and you were the only one who could have
ever done it. You could even have brought freedom
and order in at one and the same time.

MARTIN: There's no such thing as an orderly revolution.
Anyway, Christians are called to suffer, not fight.

KNIGHT: But weren't we all of us, all of us, without any
exceptions to please any old interested parties,
weren't we all redeemed by Christ's blood? (*Pointing
to the peasant*) Wasn't he included when the scriptures were being dictated? Or was it just you who
was made free, you and the princes you've taken up
with, and the rich burghers and——

MARTIN: Free? (*Ascends the pulpit steps.*) The princes blame
me, you blame me and the peasants blame me——

KNIGHT: (*following up the steps*). *You* put the water in the wine
didn't you?

MARTIN: When I see chaos, then I see the devil's organ and
then I'm afraid. Now, that's enough——

KNIGHT: You're breaking out again——

MARTIN: Go away——

KNIGHT: Aren't you?

(MARTIN *makes a sudden effort to push him back down the steps, but* THE KNIGHT *hangs on firmly.*)

MARTIN: Get back!

KNIGHT: Aren't you, you're breaking out again, you canting pig, I can smell you from here!

MARTIN: He heard the children of Israel, didn't He?

KNIGHT: Up to the ears in revelation, aren't you?

MARTIN: And didn't He deliver them out of the Land of Pharaoh?

KNIGHT: You canting pig, aren't you?

MARTIN: Well? Didn't He?

KNIGHT: Cock's wounds! Don't hold your Bible to my head, piggy, there's enough revelation of my own in there for me, in what I see for myself from here! (*Taps his forehead.*) Hold your gospel against that!

(THE KNIGHT *grabs* MARTIN'S *hand and clamps it to his head.*)

KNIGHT: You're killing the spirit, and you're killing it with the letter. You've been swilling about in the wrong place, Martin, in your own stink and ordure. Go on! You've got your hand on it, that's all the holy spirit there is, and it's all you'll ever get so feel it!

(*They struggle, but* THE KNIGHT *is very weak by now, and* MARTIN *is able to wrench himself away and up into the pulpit.*)

MARTIN: The world was conquered by the Word, the Church is maintained by the Word——

KNIGHT: Word? What Word? Word? That word, whatever that means, is probably just another old relic or indulgence, and you know what you did to those! Why, none of it might be any more than poetry, have you thought of that, Martin. Poetry! Martin, you're a poet, there's no doubt about that in anybody's mind, you're a poet, but do you know what most men believe in, in their hearts—because they don't see in images like you do—they believe in their hearts that Christ was a man as we are, and that He was a

90

prophet and a teacher, and they also believe in their hearts that His supper is a plain meal like their own—if they're lucky enough to get it—a plain meal of bread and wine! A plain meal with no garnish and no word. And *you* helped them to begin to believe it!

MARTIN: (*pause*). Leave me.

KNIGHT: Yes. What's there to stay for? I've been close enough to you for too long. I even smell like you.

MARTIN: (*roaring with pain*). I smell because of my own argument, I smell because I never stop disputing with Him, and because I expect Him to keep His Word. Now then! If your peasant rebelled against that Word, that was worse than murder because it laid the whole country waste, and who knows now what God will make of us Germans!

KNIGHT: Don't blame God for the Germans, Martin! (*Laughs*) Don't do that! You thrashed about more than anyone on the night they were conceived!

MARTIN: Christ! Hear me! My words pour from Your Body! They deserved their death, these swarming peasants! They kicked against authority, they plundered and bargained and all in Your name! Christ, believe me! (*To* THE KNIGHT) I demanded it, I prayed for it, and I got it! Take that lump away! Now, drag it away with you!

(THE KNIGHT *prepares to trundle off the cart and corpse.*)

KNIGHT: All right, my friend. Stay with your nun then. Marry and stew with your nun. Most of the others have. Stew with her, like a shuddering infant in *her* bed. You think you'll manage?

MARTIN: (*lightly*). At least my father'll praise me for *that*.

KNIGHT: Your father?

(THE KNIGHT *shrugs, pushes the cart wearily, and goes off.* MARTIN'S *head hangs over the edge of the pulpit.*)

MARTIN: I (*whispering*) trust you. . . . I trust you. . . . You've overcome the world. . . . I trust you. . . . You're all I wish to have . . . ever. . . .

(*Slumped over the pulpit, he seems to be unconscious.*

Then he makes an effort to recover, as if he had
collapsed in the middle of a sermon.)

I expect you must . . . I'm sure you must remember—
Abraham. Abraham was—he was an old man . . . a . . .
very old man indeed, in fact, he was a hundred years
old, when what was surely, what must have been a
miracle happened, to a man of his years—a son was
born to him. A son. Isaac he called him. And he
loved Isaac. Well, he loved him with such intensity,
one can only diminish it by description. But to
Abraham his little son was a miraculous thing, a
small, incessant . . . animal . . . astonishment. And in
the child he sought the father. But, one day, God
said to Abraham: Take your little son whom you love
so much, kill him, and make a sacrifice of him. And
in that moment everything inside Abraham seemed to
shrivel once and for all. Because it had seemed to him
that God had promised him life through his son. So
then he took the boy and prepared to kill him,
strapping him down to the wood of the burnt offering
just as he had been told to do. And he spoke softly
to the boy, and raised the knife over his little naked
body, the boy struggling not to flinch or blink his
eyes. Never, save in Christ, was there such obedience
as in that moment, and, if God had blinked, the boy
would have died then, but the Angel intervened, and
the boy was released, and Abraham took him up in
his arms again. In the teeth of life we seem to die, but
God says no—in the teeth of death we live. If He
butchers us, He makes us live.

(*Enter* THE KNIGHT, *who stands watching him, the*
Bundschuh banner in his hands.)

Heart of my Jesus save me; Heart of my Saviour
deliver me; Heart of my Shepherd guard me; Heart
of my Master teach me; Heart of my King govern
me; Heart of my Friend stay with me.

(*Enter* KATHERINE VON BORA, *his bride, accompanied by*
two MONKS. MARTIN *rises from the pulpit and goes*

92

towards her. A simple tune is played on a simple instrument. She takes his hand, and they kneel together centre. THE KNIGHT *watches. Then he smashes the banner he has been holding, and tosses the remains on to the altar.)*

(End of Act Three—Scene Two)

ACT THREE

Scene Three

A hymn. The Eremite Cloister. Wittenberg. 1530. The refectory table, and on it two places set, and the remains of two meals. MARTIN *is seated alone. The vigour of a man in his late thirties, and at the height of his powers, has settled into the tired pain of a middle age struggling to rediscover strength.*

KATHERINE *enters with a jug of wine. She is a big, pleasant-looking girl, almost thirty.*

MARTIN: How is he?

KATHERINE: He's all right. He's just coming. Wouldn't let me help him. I think he's been sick.

MARTIN: Poor old chap. After living all your life in a monastery, one's stomach doesn't take too easily to your kind of cooking.

KATHERINE: Wasn't it all right?

MARTIN: Oh, it was fine, just too much for an old monk's shrivelled digestion to chew on, that's all.

KATHERINE: Oh, I see. *You're* all right, aren't you?

MARTIN: Yes, I'm all right, thank you, my dear. (*Smile*) I expect I'll suffer later though.

KATHERINE: You like your food, so don't make out you don't.

MARTIN: Well, I prefer it to fasting. Did you never hear the story of the soldier who was fighting in the Holy Crusades? No? Well, he was told by his officer that if he died in battle, he would dine in Paradise with Christ; and the soldier ran away. When he came back after the battle, they asked him why he'd run away. "Didn't you want to dine with Christ?" they said. And he replied, "No, I'm fasting today."

KATHERINE: I've brought you some more wine.

MARTIN: Thank you.

KATHERINE: Should help you to sleep.

(STAUPITZ *enters, supporting himself with a stick.*)

MARTIN: There you are! I thought you'd fallen down the jakes—right into the devil's loving arms,

STAUPITZ: I'm so sorry. I was—I was wandering about a bit.

MARTIN: Well, come and sit down. Katie's brought us some more wine.

STAUPITZ: I can't get over being here again. It's so odd. This place was full of men. And now, now there's only you, you and Katie. It's very, very strange.

KATHERINE: I shouldn't stay up too long, Martin. You didn't sleep well again last night. I could hear you— hardly breathing all night.

MARTIN: (*amused*). You could hear me hardly breathing?

KATHERINE: You know what I mean. When you don't sleep, it keeps me awake too. Good night, Dr. Staupitz.

STAUPITZ: Good night, my dear. Thank you for the dinner. It was excellent. I'm so sorry I wasn't able to do justice to it.

KATHERINE: That's all right. Martin's always having the same kind of trouble.

STAUPITZ: Yes? Well, he's not changed much then.

MARTIN: Not a bit. Even Katie hasn't managed to shift my bowels for me, have you?

KATHERINE: And if it's not that, he can't sleep.

MARTIN: Yes, Katie, you've said that already. I've also got gout, piles and bells in my ears. Dr. Staupitz has had to put up with all my complaints for longer than you have, isn't that right?

KATHERINE: Well, try not to forget what I said. (*She kisses* MARTIN'S *cheeks.*)

MARTIN: Good night, Katie.

(*She goes out.*)

STAUPITZ: Well, *you've* never been so well looked after.

MARTIN: It's a shame everyone can't marry a nun. They're fine cooks, thrifty housekeepers, and splendid mothers. Seems to me there are three ways out of

despair. One is faith in Christ, the second is to become enraged by the world and make its nose bleed for it, and the third is the love of a woman. Mind you, they don't all necessarily work—at least, only part of the time. Sometimes, I'm lying awake in the devil's own sweat, and I turn to Katie and touch her. And I say: get me out, Katie, please, Katie, please try and get me out. And sometimes, sometimes she actually drags me out. Poor old Katie, fishing about there in bed with her great, hefty arms, trying to haul me out.

STAUPITZ: She's good.

MARTIN: Wine?

STAUPITZ: Not much. I must go to bed myself.

MARTIN: Help you sleep. You're looking tired.

STAUPITZ: Old. Our old pear tree's in blossom, I see. You've looked after it.

MARTIN: I like to get in a bit in the garden, if I can. I like to think it heals my bones somehow. Anyway, I always feel a bit more pleased with myself afterwards.

STAUPITZ: We'd a few talks under that tree.

MARTIN: Yes.

STAUPITZ: Martin, it's so still. I don't think I'd ever realized how eloquent a monk's silence really was. It was a voice. (*Pause*) It's gone. (*He shakes his head, pause.*) How's your father these days?

MARTIN: Getting old too, but he's well enough.

STAUPITZ: Is he—is he pleased with you?

MARTIN: He was never pleased about anything I ever did. Not when I took my master's degree or when I got to be Dr. Luther. Only when Katie and I were married and she got pregnant. Then he was pleased.

STAUPITZ: Do you remember Brother Weinand?

MARTIN: I ought to. He used to hold my head between my knees when I felt faint in the choir.

STAUPITZ: I wonder what happened to him. (*Pause*) He had

96

the most beautiful singing voice.

MARTIN: My old friend, you're unhappy. I'm sorry. (*Pause*)
We monks were really no good to anyone, least of
all to ourselves, every one of us rolled up like a
louse in the Almighty's overcoat.

STAUPITZ: Yes. Well, you always have a way of putting it. I
was always having to give you little lectures about
the fanatic way you'd observe the Rule all the
time.

MARTIN: Yes, and you talked me out of it, remember?
(*Pause*) Father, are *you* pleased with me?

STAUPITZ: Pleased with you? My dear son, I'm not anyone
or anything to be pleased with you any more. When
we used to talk together underneath that tree you
were like a child.

MARTIN: A child.

STAUPITZ: Manhood was something you had to be flung into,
my son. You dangled your toe in it longer than
most of us could ever bear. But you're not a
frightened little monk any more who's come to his
prior for praise or blame. Every time you belch
now, the world stops what it's doing and listens.
Do you know, when I first came to take over this
convent, there weren't thirty books published every
year. And now, last year it was more like six or
seven hundred, and most of those published in
Wittenberg too.

MARTIN: The best turn God ever did Himself was giving us
a printing press. Sometimes I wonder what He'd
have done without it.

STAUPITZ: I heard the other day they're saying the world's
going to end in 1532.

MARTIN: It sounds as good a date as any other. Yes—1532.
That could easily be the end of the world. You
could write a book about it, and just call it that—
1532.

STAUPITZ: I'm sorry, Martin. I didn't mean to come and see
you after all this time and start criticizing. Forgive

97

me, I'm getting old and a bit silly and frightened, that meal was just too much for me. It wasn't that I didn't——

MARTIN: Please—I'm sorry too. Don't upset yourself. I'm used to critics, John. They just help you to keep your muscles from getting slack. All those hollow cavillers, that subtle clown Erasmus, for instance. He ought to know better, but all he wants to do is to be able to walk on eggs without breaking any. As for that mandrill-arsed English baboon Henry, that leprous son of a bitch never had an idea of his own to jangle on a tombstone, let alone call himself Defender of the Faith.

(*Pause.* STAUPITZ *hasn't responded to his attempt at lightness.*)

Still, one thing for Erasmus, he didn't fool about with all the usual cant and rubbish about indulgences and the Pope and Purgatory. No, he went right to the core of it. He's still up to his ears with stuff about morality, and men being able to save themselves. No one does good, not anyone. God is true and one. But, and this is what he can't grasp, He's utterly incomprehensible and beyond the reach of minds. A man's will is like a horse standing between two riders. If God jumps on its back, it'll go where God wants it to. But if Satan gets up there, it'll go where he leads it. And not only that, the horse can't choose its rider. That's left up to them, to those two. (*Pause*) Why are you accusing me? What have I done?

STAUPITZ: I'm not accusing you, Martin. You know that. A just man is his own accuser. Because a just man judges as he is.

MARTIN: What's that mean? I'm not just?

STAUPITZ: You try. What else can you do?

MARTIN: You mean those damned peasants, don't you? You think I should have encouraged them!

STAUPITZ: I don't say that.

MARTIN: Well, what do you say?

STAUPITZ: You needn't have encouraged the princes. They were butchered and *you* got them to do it. And they had just cause, Martin. They did, didn't they?

MARTIN: I didn't say they hadn't.

STAUPITZ: Well, then?

MARTIN: Do you remember saying to me, "Remember, brother, you started this in the name of the Lord Jesus Christ"?

STAUPITZ: Well?

MARTIN: Father, the world can't be ruled with a rosary. They were a mob, a mob, and if they hadn't been held down and slaughtered, there'd have been a thousand more tyrants instead of half a dozen. It was a mob, and because it was a mob it was against Christ. No man can die for another, or believe for another or answer for another. The moment they try they become a mob. If we're lucky we can be persuaded in our own mind, and the most we can hope for is to die each one for himself. Do I have to tell you what Paul says? You read! "Let every soul be subject unto the highest powers. For there is no power but of God: the powers that be are ordained of God. Whosoever therefore resisteth that power, resisteth the ordinance of God": that's Paul, Father, and that's Scripture! "And they that resist shall receive to themselves damnation."

STAUPITZ: Yes, you're probably right.

MARTIN: "Love worketh no ill to his neighbour: therefore love is the fulfilling of the law."

STAUPITZ: Yes, well it seems to be all worked out. I must be tired.

MARTIN: It was worked out for me.

STAUPITZ: I'd better get off to bed.

MARTIN: They're trying to turn me into a fixed star, Father, but I'm a shifting planet. You're leaving me.

STAUPITZ: I'm not leaving you, Martin. I love you. I love you

as much as any man has ever loved most women.
But we're not two protected monks chattering
under a pear tree in a garden any longer. The
world's changed. For one thing, you've made a
thing called Germany; you've unlaced a language
and taught it to the Germans, and the rest of the
world will just have to get used to the sound of it.
As we once made the body of Christ from bread,
you've made the body of Europe, and whatever our
pains turn out to be, they'll attack the rest of the
world too. You've taken Christ away from the low
mumblings and soft voices and jewelled gowns and
the tiaras and put Him back where He belongs. In
each man's soul. We owe so much to you. All I beg
of you is not to be too violent. In spite of
everything, of everything you've said and shown us,
there *were* men, *some* men who did live holy lives
here once.Don't—don't believe you, only you are
right.

(STAUPITZ *is close to tears, and* MARTIN *doesn't know
what to do.*)

MARTIN: What else can I do? What can I do?
(*He clutches at his abdomen.*)

STAUPITZ: What is it?

MARTIN: Oh, the old trouble, that's all. That's all.

STAUPITZ: Something that's puzzled me, and I've always
meant to ask you.

MARTIN: Well?

STAUPITZ: When you were before the Diet in Worms, and they
asked you those two questions—why did you ask
for that extra day to think over your reply?

MARTIN: Why?

STAUPITZ: You'd known what your answer was going to be
for months. Heaven knows, you told me enough
times. Why did you wait?
(*Pause*)

MARTIN: I wasn't certain.

STAUPITZ: And were you? Afterwards?

MARTIN: I listened for God's voice, but all I could hear was my own.

STAUPITZ: *Were* you sure?

(*Pause*)

MARTIN: No.

(STAUPITZ *kisses him.*)

STAUPITZ: Thank you, my son. May God bless you. I hope you sleep better. Goodnight.

MARTIN: Goodnight, Father.

(STAUPITZ *goes out, and* MARTIN *is left alone. He drinks his wine.*)

MARTIN: Oh, Lord, I believe. I believe. I do believe. Only help my unbelief.

(*He sits slumped in his chair.* KATHERINE *enters. She is wearing a nightdress, and carries in her arms* HANS, *their young son.*)

KATHERINE: He was crying out in his sleep. Must have been dreaming again. Aren't you coming to bed?

MARTIN: Shan't be long, Katie. Shan't be long.

KATHERINE: All right, but try not to be too long. You look— well, you don't look as well as you should.

(*She turns to go.*)

MARTIN: Give him to me.

KATHERINE: What?

MARTIN: Give him to me.

KATHERINE: What do you mean, what for? He'll get cold down here.

MARTIN: No, he won't. Please, Katie. Let me have him.

KATHERINE: You're a funny man. All right, but only for five minutes. Don't just sit there all night. He's gone back to sleep now. He'll be having another dream if you keep him down here.

MARTIN: Thank you, Katie.

KATHERINE: There! Keep him warm now! He's *your* son.

MARTIN: I will. Don't worry.

KATHERINE: Well, make sure you do. (*Pausing on way out*) Don't be long now, Martin.

MARTIN: Good night, Kate.

(*She goes out, leaving* MARTIN *with the sleeping child in his arms.*)

MARTIN: (*softly*). What was the matter? Was it the devil bothering you? Um? Was he? Old nick? Up you, old nick. Well, don't worry. One day you might even be glad of him. So long as you can show him your little backside. That's right, show him your backside and let him have it. So try not to be afraid. The dark isn't quite as thick as all that. You know, my father had a son, and he'd to learn a hard lesson, which is a human being is a helpless little animal, but he's not created by his father, but by God. It's hard to accept you're anyone's son, and you're not the father of yourself. So, don't have dreams so soon, my son. *They'll* be having *you* soon enough.

(*He gets up.*)

You should have seen me at Worms. I was almost like you that day, as if I'd learned to play again, to play, to play out in the world, like a naked child. "I have come to set a man against his father," I said, and they listened to me. Just like a child. Sh! We must go to bed, mustn't we? A little while, and you *shall* see me. Christ said that, my son. I hope that'll be the way of it again. I hope so. Let's just hope so, eh? Eh? Let's just hope so.

(MARTIN *holds the child in his arms, and then walks off slowly*).

The End.

ff

faber and faber

'Luther in Christendom, like Mr Osborne in the microcosm of the theatre, was a stubborn iconoclast of lowly birth, resentful of authority and blind to compromise...To his surprise and alarm, Luther caused an international tumult with his attacks on indulgences, and was hailed as a popular hero by people of whose causes he thoroughly disapproved: is there not something here that might speak to the author of <u>Look Back in Anger</u>...?

'The language [of <u>Luther</u>] is urgent and sinewy, packed with images that derive from bone, blood and marrow; the prose, especially in Luther's sermons, throbs with a rhetorical zeal that has not often been heard in English historical drama since the seventeenth century.' Kenneth Tynan

Cover design by Pentagram

UK £2.95 net
CANADA $7.95

ISBN 0-571-06239-3

9 780571 062393

LUTHER

Foreword

As we approach the centenary celebrations of the Edinburgh 1910 Missionary Conference, often described as the beginning of the modern ecumenical movement, we are having to fundamentally reassess what mission means in the UK. This research is crucial in helping us consider where and what those issues are. Just as the whole modern ecumenical movement is having to reconsider what its vocation is in the 21st century, so also the church is having to consider what mission means and how we can best live out our calling today.

This research helps us to move beyond glib answers and challenges us to think deeply about the relationship between what we say mission is, and how we live out God's mission in our own context. It is not enough for us to say then 'how should the church live out its mission,' suggesting some unified understanding and approach. Rather we need to acknowledge the huge diversity and complexity that exists within the Christian community and society at large. That is why a study such as this, which digs into the foundations of mission and then looks at language, theology and praxis, helps us to uncover the assumptions and mismatches that exist. It is vitally important that we read, mark, learn and inwardly digest the outcomes of this work.

What is new, exciting and helpful in all of this is the way in which the authors have delved into new methods of communication to assess what is happening at both the theoretical and local levels. The interrogation of websites is instructive. As we move into a world of increasing diversity with various methods of social networking, how is the church to communicate its mission effectively and coherently? The use of research techniques to understand HOW we are expressing and then LIVING out our mission points to the need for greater engagement with theological principles. With the growth of programmes such as Fresh Expressions and emerging forms of 'church' we need to understand how these relate to any shared sense of ecclesiology and identity. Our mission theology must be given greater place so that we have the resources to continue working into the issues raised in this study.

The study itself is an example for the future. The close working bonds that have brought together the Mission Theology Advisory Group's work within CTBI together with Global Connections and BIAMS shows the richness of ecumenical working and the continued need for collaborative working across the churches and mission agencies.

This research is a significant step forward. We owe a great deal of thanks to the writers. There is still much to be taken on as we move into the next stage of our journey and ministry together. When it comes to the planning of the 200th anniversary of the Edinburgh Missionary Conference, I believe that this research will be viewed as a significant point of reorientation on that journey.

Bob Fyffe

Mission language

Christians respond positively to the word 'mission' and have difficulty disagreeing with statements containing the word mission. However, naming priorities within mission is much more difficult. Some kinds of mission-related words such as 'hospitality' or 'reconciliation' attract strong positive reactions from all constituencies, while 'justice' is a problematic concept. Christians respond strongly to language which implies generous, mutually giving relationships between human beings and this reflects Trinitarian relationship even where Trinity is not explicitly mentioned. However, mission theological issues about how God works through human beings and who is best equipped to undertake mission prove more difficult to deal with.

Websites are a necessary tool of communication. However, public language about mission and theological statements about mission may be less important than other website content. Pictures and stories may be underestimated as indicators of what mission is about. Websites themselves may be underestimated as actual instruments of mission.

Mission theology

A tension emerges between a vision of, or theological perspective on what mission 'ought' to look like and what in fact the world of mission activity really 'is'. The gap between what mission is and what it ought to be is nonetheless bridged by the *missio Dei* and allows the diverse forms of mission thought and action to illuminate theological principles.

A Trinitarian understanding of mission is present within mission activity in the UK and Ireland, but it is not particularly overt. The *missio Dei* itself is a weak driver for mission. At local level there is more emphasis on biblical drivers such as Matthew 28:19. Theological drivers and an understanding of *missio Dei* only emerge more clearly when embedded in mission experience. Stories and contexts prove more helpful than theological 'position' or starting points. Reflection through engagement with a missiologically experienced person is particularly helpful in exploring both implicit drivers for mission and new ideas.

Mission praxis

Leadership and representation make talking about the foundations for mission more complex especially when there is a gap between: a leader's personal vision and agency 'position'; between team members; and between the mission understanding of clergy leaders and that of their congregations. Such tensions can be both creative and frustrating and are sometimes solved by talking about 'holistic' mission which covers both sophisticated and unsophisticated views. Reflection on mission issues through a statement survey is extremely challenging but helpful in discovering such gaps and in provoking growth in self-understanding. It is clear however, that there has been a positive shift towards greater mission awareness among local clergy.

Recommendations

- Churches and agencies at national and local level should pay more attention to their websites as missiological tools. A reflective tool to help this process has been developed as a result of this research.
- Churches and agencies at national and local level should undertake mission audit as a means to understanding their own missiological drivers and understanding of mission. A range of tools based on the research survey will be developed to enable this process.
- Churches and agencies at national and local level can benefit from extended reflection and engagement with mission theological issues. A tool to enable this reflection has been developed as a result of this research.

Introduction

There has been much written about the theory and practice of mission since the Edinburgh World Missionary Conference in 1910. A hundred years later, a number of theological ideas and missionary practices have come and gone; some missiological perspectives have been discarded as inappropriate while others are still seen as experimental. One hundred years after the first Edinburgh conference questions about the theory and practice of mission in the UK and Ireland still need to be asked, particularly in a world of new technologies and news ways of reaching people. This study uses a combination of website analysis, survey research and in-depth interviews among national churches and agencies across the denominations in the UK and Ireland to show that confidently stated foundations for mission and the theological understanding of mission do not necessarily match mission practice or the rationale for mission owned by people working 'on the ground'. This means that there is often a mismatch between the theology and rationale for mission practice set out in academic study by mission theologians, offered in mission training and formation, and adopted by churches and agencies, and the complex and 'messy' nature of mission at the grass roots, especially in relation to contemporary situations such as a multicultural and religiously plural society.

We suggest that it cannot be simply assumed by church leaders that 'mission is everything' or 'we all know what mission is' since our study shows that in practice there is considerable disparity about the source of mission, how it relates to God, who is it for, and what its outcomes should actually be. Mission is therefore not something which has had its day, but is *still* waiting for a clearer understanding of its function in our present evolving contexts. We also suggest that much more attention needs to be paid to the complexity of mission theology and praxis as it is lived in local contexts across the denominations and promulgated from the UK and Ireland across the world and that there are dangers in simply subscribing to programmatic forms of mission action without careful attention to local needs and situations. [1]

---

1 A point made clearly in *Mission-Shaped Church* (London: Church House Publishing) 2004.

Edinburgh 1910

The World Missionary Conference, held in Edinburgh 1910, was considered a defining moment for the churches in the history of mission. Eight 'commissions' produced reports on what the future of mission work would look like under the headings 'Carrying the Gospel to all the Non-Christian World', 'The Church in the Mission Field', 'Education in Relation to the Christianization of National Life', 'Missionary Message in Relation to the Non-Christian World', 'The Preparation of Missionaries', 'The Home Base of Missions', 'Missions and Governments' and 'Co-Operation and the Promotion of Unity'. Because of the significance of this event and because of the changing face of mission theology and praxis in the century following, it was considered right to celebrate the centenary of the 1910 conference by holding another conference in Edinburgh in 2010. Beginning in 2005, an international group was set up to produce an inter-continental and multi-denominational project. The project, based at New College and the Church of Scotland offices in Edinburgh was headed by Dr Daryl Balia as its international director and governed by a 20 member General Council.[1] An account of the 1910 World Missionary Conference and the proposals for celebrating its centenary was given by Dr Kirsteen Kim at the BIAMS conference in July 2009.[2]

Edinburgh 2010

Building on the 'commissions' of the 1910 conference, the 2010 project included a series of nine study themes on: Foundations for mission, Christian mission among other faiths, Mission and post-modernity, Mission and power, Forms of missionary engagement, Theological education and formation, Christian communities in contemporary contexts, Mission and unity – ecclesiology and mission, and Mission spirituality and authentic discipleship. In addition, there would be seven 'transversal' themes cutting through all the other study themes, including: Women and mission, Youth and mission, Healing and reconciliation, Bible and mission, Contextualization, inculturation and dialogue of worldviews, Subaltern voices, and Ecological perspectives on mission.[3]

---

1 www.edinburgh2010.org/en/about-edinburgh-2010.html.

2 A revised version is available in pdf or audio versions at www.martynmission.cam.ac.uk/pages/hmc-seminar-papers.php.

3 See www.edinburgh2010.org/en/study-themes.html.

Foundations for Mission study theme

The first theme, that of 'Foundations for Mission', was offered to the churches for research and study with the following aims and objectives:

> **The task of this study group is to explore how a Trinitarian understanding of God as Father, Son and Holy Spirit relates to the theory and practice of mission; how the confession that God has a missionary identity impacts Christian witness; how a discernment of the Trinitarian God´s inner relationships and love impacts ecclesiology, community life and society.**
>
> **The meaning of salvation is being considered in its biblical witness and in relation to freedom from every form of slavery in every context and culture. The study group is considering the interfaces between the Trinity, mission, salvation, ecclesiology and scripture.**

In addition, the Study Process offered the following key issues and questions which a research group might address:

1. The relation of the Trinitarian nature of God to our understanding of Christian mission.
2. The relation of Christology to mission theology and practice.
3. The relation of the work of the Holy Spirit to mission theology and practice.
4. How does our understanding of the mission of the Triune God affect our ecclesiology and church practice?
5. What do we mean by salvation, present and future? What is its link to conversion, baptism and participation in the sacramental life of the church?
6. How does our understanding of salvation affect the way we do mission?
7. How does mission engagement affect our biblical hermeneutics and vice-versa?[1]

It was intended that a number of groups around the world might undertake study and research in each of the study themes and produce material which would then be contrasted and compared. Two such groups were convened to look at the 'Foundations for Mission' topic, a group from the World Council of Churches in Switzerland convened by Revd Dr Deenabandhu Manchala looking particularly at the experience of the Indian Dalits, and a group from Churches Together in Britain and Ireland (CTBI), convened by Canon Janice Price. The latter is the subject of this report.

Convening of the research group and membership

Canon Janice Price, as Secretary of the Global Mission Network (GMN) of CTBI[2] convened a group incorporating two other umbrella bodies interested in mission: Global Connections (GC), a network of evangelical churches, agencies, colleges and

---

1 See www.edinburgh2010.org/en/study-themes/1-foundations-for-mission.html.
2 Canon Price is now World Mission Policy Adviser for the Church of England (from 2009).

support services dedicated to developing churches in mission,[1] and the British and Irish Association of Mission Studies (BIAMS), a consortium of churches and agencies interested in mission theology and practice, current issues in missiology, and holding a biannual meeting to promote collaboration and exchange.[2] Martin Lee was appointed to represent GC and the Revd Dr Philip Knights was appointed to represent BIAMS. The group also then was extended to include Mr John Clark, former Director of the Mission and Public Affairs Division of the Church of England, Dr Anne Richards, National Adviser for Mission Theology for the Mission and Public Affairs Division of the Church of England and Convener of the Mission Theology Advisory Group, Dr Paul Rolph, former Head of In-service Teacher Education, University College of St Mark and St John and Tutor/Supervisor on MA in Faith and Education, University of Bangor and Revd Canon Dr Nigel Rooms, Director of Mission and Ministry, Southwell and Nottingham Diocese. The group began its preliminary work in 2007 and was in place by 2008.

Parameters of the Project

CTBI is an umbrella organisation covering the major denominations of the UK and Ireland. The constituencies with which the group was familiar therefore covered the major UK and Ireland churches, agencies, theological institutions and mission networks. It was therefore necessary to confine the research project to the UK and Ireland on the understanding that within the Edinburgh 2010 international process, the UK and Ireland material could be contrasted and compared with material emerging through the study process from other parts of the world. Given the small number of persons on the group and the limited time and resources available, it was also considered necessary to limit the scope of the study and use technological resources such as NVIVO (a qualitative research and data analysis software) and SurveyMonkey (an online tool for survey collection and analysis)[3] as much as possible. Outside resources would include the Mission Theology Advisory Group, which commented on reports from the group and acted as a focus group for part of the research and the BIAMS conference 'Sinking Foundations: Why Mission Today?' July 1st–3rd 2009 where participants took part in the research process and commented on the preliminary findings.[4] The Church of England's head of research and statistics, the Revd Lynda Barley, also assisted the group with their analysis of statistical evidence.

Paul Rolph and Janice Price also took preliminary findings from the project to a meeting in Geneva from 1st–4th May 2009 to compare results with Deenabandhu Manchala's 2010 parallel project on Foundations for Mission. It was clear from this meeting that the two approaches were extremely different particularly in terms of the subjective *experience* of mission. Dr Manchala was invited to be part of the BIAMS conference in July 2009 in order to feed this perspective into the conference but unfortunately he was unable to attend.

---

1 See www.globalconnections.co.uk.
2 See www.biams.org.uk/page.php?2.
3 See www.surveymonkey.com.
4 Papers from the BIAMS consultation are included as Phase 2.2, pp. 51-92 in this book.

Foundations for mission: a brief background

The 1910 World Missionary Conference had focused a number of questions on mission as a theological imperative and these questions had been honed by theological enquiry and practical experience of churches and missionaries in the ensuing hundred years, changing and challenging the theological understanding of mission over time in the light of historical and cultural factors, such as the loss of empire and new respect for the faith of indigenous peoples. What exactly *was* mission? Did mission originate with God (the *missio Dei*)? Was there a specific mission of, or for, the Church? Was mission only to be found in, or commissioned by, Jesus Christ? Did mission mean evangelism, leading to conversion and commitment to Christ, or evangelization, the changing of cultures and structures to reflect God's will? Should there be a robust mission to people of other faiths and should people from other nations and traditions who became Christian be left alone to spread the gospel by themselves?

These questions of theology became more complex as the fruits of mission multiplied. What about *reverse* mission, as those evangelized began to travel back to the sending nations with energy and renewed fervour? How does mission relate to justice? Is mission about preparing for the imminent arrival of Christ or is it about establishing God's Kingdom on earth? In 1991 David Bosch's monumental *Transforming Mission* was published, tracing a series of 'paradigm shifts' in the theology of mission understanding and practice and with a call to find a new paradigm for postmodern mission expression.

One of the by-products of the interest in mission theology and the work done on it was the idea by the end of the twentieth century that 'mission' activity in the UK and Ireland was the mark of churches that were *doing* something. Lesslie Newbigin had argued in *The Gospel in a Pluralist Society* that the congregation was 'the hermeneutic of the gospel' and a suitably motivated congregation was at the heart of local mission activity. His work on gospel and culture issues and that of others, such as John Finney's *Finding Faith Today* in the 1990s, changed the focus of evangelism from large events such as Billy Graham rallies to the ability of the local church to make disciples. This focus led to attention being focused again on the potential of Christians at the grass roots and so led to audit tools such as *The Measure of Mission*, the development of the 'five marks of mission' by the Anglican Consultative Council and adopted at the 1998 Lambeth conference, church planting manuals and documents, and the development of mission oriented Christian basics courses, such as *Alpha*. In line with this practical focus on local tools for mission was a developing mission theology which saw mission as *God's* mission, the *missio Dei*. As the Mission Theological Advisory Group's *Presence and Prophecy* puts it:

> Mission theology speaks of the *missio Dei* – the mission of God's love to the world. It assumes that God, having created all that is, both allows the creation freely to unfold in its own way, and at the same time retains a purpose of love towards it. This purpose is made known to us through God's revelation and we are offered a share in the process of achieving it.[1]

---

1 MTAG (2002) *Presence and Prophecy*, (London: Church House Publishing) p. 25..

MTAG went on to suggest that mission is not a theological category to be juggled alongside other forms of theological interest, but a 'function of God's own being' and 'the heart of God' overflowing continuously into the world.[1]

One problem with the concept of *missio Dei* however, highlighted by Bosch, was that if all mission emanated from God then all kinds of things could be called mission and blamed on God. This led to Bishop John V Taylor speculating in 1998 that there were dangers in the all-embracing idea of mission. The concept of the '*missio Dei*' could be used as an excuse for almost any kind of activity and labelling something as mission was a feel-good action that did not necessarily relate to God's intention for the creation.[2] These cautions focused back on the relationship between mission theology and praxis, so that for example Robert Warren in *Building Missionary Congregations* argued for mission practice that was grounded in the prayer and spirituality of the congregation. A report on church planting, *Breaking New Ground* was followed up by the best-selling *Mission-Shaped Church* and its companion books, leading to an emphasis on reflexive listening, grounding in locality and decision making based on the needs of local communities. Programmes emerging from the Mission-shaped initiative, such as Fresh Expressions, and movements such as Emerging Church, continue to encourage mission as a reflection of local need and opportunity. A number of churches and dioceses have also subscribed to 'the five marks of mission' as a template or programme for mission activity. These are:[3]

- To proclaim the Good News of the Kingdom;

- To teach, baptise and nurture new believers;

- To respond to human need by loving service;

- To seek to transform unjust structures of society;

- To strive to safeguard the integrity of creation and sustain and renew the life of earth.

In addition it was suggested in 2009 that a 'sixth' mark should be added referring to the need for peace and reconciliation.

All of these developments showed that mission is not a clear cut practice or issue and is complex, diverse, and sometimes driven by factors or needs other than a pure gospel imperative. How then do Christians, churches, agencies and institutions *decide* how mission is to be promulgated and what resources to give to it?

The Project Hypothesis

These developments, evolution and changes in the theology and practice of mission helped us formulate the hypothesis on which our research would be founded:

> **Public statements about mission by UK and Ireland churches, agencies and institutions do not necessarily match up with the mission practice, understanding and outworking of those same bodies.**

---

1 p. 26.

2 John V Taylor, (1998) *The Uncancelled Mandate*, (Loondon: Church House Publishing).

3 See, for example: www.anglicancommunion.org/ministry/mission/fivemarks.cfm.

We expected to find that statements of purpose, including any foundational theological statements, often summed up in sound bites or straplines on websites and church notice boards and which implied a particular focus or direction, would unravel when those implications were examined and their outworkings interrogated. For example, a word like 'change' or 'transform' in a statement of purpose gives an impression of doing good things for God, but can break down when we start to ask questions about what is really meant. Who or what is transformed? Who should do the transforming? What does transformation look like? When does it come to an end?

We expected to find that the missiological expression of national bodies is tested by working in a culture of web communication, advertising and marketing, and sometimes competing for funds and access while also being driven by faith, vision and vocation. We expected to find a dislocation between the technical and theological language of mission, and the understanding and activities of those using it and we designed the study to show if that dislocation existed, and if so what was its range and extent among both the national bodies and a sample of churches working at local level. The study theme asked for an emphasis on theological foundations and we included these within a wide ranging area of mission enquiry, since we felt that the wider theological rationale and theological drivers for mission would only become apparent in the context of other kinds of questions about mission praxis.

We used Bevans and Schroeder's work in *Constants in Context* (Maryknoll: Orbis, 2005) as the theoretical basis for the evaluation of theological foundations for mission. They claim, following González and Sölle, that there are essentially three types of theology discernible throughout Christian history and they call them simply, A, B and C types. Mission according to these theologies then varies so that in type A it is 'Saving souls and extending the Church', in type B 'Discovery of the truth' and in type C it is 'Commitment to liberation and transformation'. More crudely in today's terms it would be possible to describe them as conservative, liberal and radical types of theology. However Bevans and Schroeder do not believe they correspond exactly to *current* understandings of mission. Rather they discern three further positions on mission that have been taken during the twentieth century. These three positions are:

a) Mission as proclamation of Jesus Christ as Universal Saviour or 'Proclamation';

b) Mission as participation in the Triune God or *missio Dei*;

c) Mission as Liberating Service of the Reign of God or 'Kingdom' mission.

The first corresponds to type A theology, the second to a mixture of type B and C, while the third corresponds to type C.

Scope and design of the project

The project was divided into three interlocking parts which would contrast, reinforce and interrogate each other. The first part of the project entailed an examination of websites of selected national denominations, agencies and institutions, looking at the composition of the site and in particular at straplines about mission, mission language, vision statements and whether or not the site contained theological statements or descriptions about its mission purpose. This was the only phase of the project which concentrated solely on information from the national bodies. Phases two and three included a local study for comparison. It was not felt, however, that local church websites would contain enough useful information about mission theology and praxis to provide helpful comparisons about the issue of public language.

In phase one, information on language use and phrasing was collected from forty-six sites (Appendix A). The information was then subjected to an NVIVO search by Janice Price. NVIVO is a piece of software which allows qualitative data to be searched, classified or otherwise modelled and allows a large amount of data to be sorted and examined. In this case we were looking for repeated or common phrases, for popular mission statements as well as unusual statements. Following a broad search of these websites belonging to members of GMN, BIAMS and GC, looking for particular key words and concepts, the group then looked at seven specific websites more closely for information about their approach to and promotion of, their mission interests and concerns. The information from these two processes was carried over and factored into the design of the second phase of the project.

In the second phase of the project, we developed a survey as a mission audit tool. The survey was designed by composing a number of statements about mission, focusing on theological issues, but also issues of mission praxis. There were three statements in each category (only two in the category Mission and Salvation) focused on 15 particular areas of mission enquiry. The 44 statements were developed in the following categories:

- Origin and Purpose of God's Mission
- Kingdom, Mission and Church
- Who best does mission?
- Evangelism and Mission
- Mission and Development
- Mission and Improving Lives
- Mission and Other Faiths
- God at work through....
- Mission and Proclamation
- Mission and Sin
- Mission and Salvation (two statements)
- Mission and Church (essence of the Church)
- Mission and Church (function of the Church)
- Mission and Partnership
- Mission Outcomes

The purpose of providing three statements in each category was to enable different wording, and to state the same idea in different ways to see if this had an effect on the response. For example:

- † Christians have much to learn from other faith traditions (S2)
- † All faiths need to learn from one another as we share much in common (S22)

† **Christians have little to learn from those of other faiths (S24)**

In addition, similar wording was used in *different* category statements. For example:

† **Mission without social action is not mission (Mission and Development)**

† **Mission without proclamation is not mission (Mission and Proclamation)**

One of the issues of interest was whether completing a linear survey would show different responses as the participants made their way through it, meeting similar statements at different points in the survey. To enable this, the statements were randomly distributed throughout the survey (Appendix E). Respondents were asked to consider each statement in turn and to select an answer from the following categories: strongly agree; agree; neither agree nor disagree; disagree; strongly disagree. Participants were able to leave comments about the statements in a box on each of the three pages of the survey. At the end of the survey, participants were invited to tick up to five from twenty-two suggested areas of church interest which would represent the priorities for the respondents' agency, church or group. It was also possible to comment on this section via another box. Participants were then asked to identify themselves by denomination or other (eg independent evangelical) affiliation. Finally, the survey promised confidentiality but respondents were asked to supply their details for the eyes of the group only together with an indication of willingness to be approached for in-depth interview.

The group composed and sent a letter to the head person in a range of churches, agencies, and institutions drawn from those members of CTBI and from GMN, GC and BIAMS (Appendix B). Thirty-seven letters were sent to CTBI members, sixteen to members of GMN, thirty-seven to members of GC and thirty-five to members of BIAMS (numbers adjusted for overlap between the bodies). That person was asked to fill in the survey on behalf of the church, agency or institution they represented, not from personal conviction or interest. The Survey was made available online via SurveyMonkey, an online tool at www.surveymonkey.com which allowed us to compare and filter the results in a number of different ways in order to analyse the results. This constituted a national survey across the four nations of the UK, and Ireland.

In addition, Nigel Rooms sent paper surveys by post to 292 churches across the main denominations within the Anglican diocese of Southwell and Nottingham and also to independent charismatic and Pentecostal churches. There were some differences between the national survey and the local survey layout in that the 'mission priorities' page and the final page were adjusted for the local environment, – for example including activities such as 'Parent and Toddler groups' as a possible priority. Dr Rooms then collated the ninety-eight paper replies he received (33.6%). This constituted a local survey for comparison with the national survey. One difference between the completion of the national survey and the local survey was that the online survey does not allow respondents to skip responses, whereas the completion of a paper survey meant that responses could be left blank if the respondent chose not to answer.

The national survey was also critiqued and considered by the Mission Theology Advisory Group acting as a focus group. In addition, the BIAMS conference members in July 2009 also filled in and returned the survey. This constituted a third, smaller group of data.

There were seventy respondents in the national survey, ninety-eight in the local survey and twenty-seven in the BIAMS survey. The results were analysed as quantitative data with help from Lynda Barley at the Church of England's statistics department who suggested using a ranking system for the aggregated results in addition to the various filters possible with SurveyMonkey. Those results are collated in Appendix H.

The final part of the project was a follow up of the national survey by eleven in-depth interviews with a range of heads of organisations, agencies and churches undertaken by Janice Price, Martin Lee and Philip Knights. Nigel Rooms conducted in-depth interviews with 16 participants from the local survey (Appendix C). The purpose of the interviews was to collect qualitative data, opening up why participants had responded to the statements in the survey in the way that they did, and asking for further elaboration of their understanding of mission theology and praxis. The interviews were based on a template of questions prepared by Dr Rooms, then recorded and transcribed (see Appendix F and G).

Search of websites: national churches and agencies

In the first stage of the web search, texts were collected from forty-six websites of the national churches, agencies and organisations included within the three sponsoring bodies (GMN, GC, BIAMS) and these were then subjected to searches using NVIVO. Of particular interest to the triangulated national study were the mission and vision statements (where these were available) setting out the mission focus of the church or agency. The main type of search used was 'word' search and 'word frequency' search. The purpose of these searches was to ascertain the most frequent uses of terms used to express mission theologically. NVIVO analysis produced an emphasis on a number of concepts and actions:

'Transformation'

'Sharing'

'Equipping'

'Community'

'Fellowship'

'Supporting'

'Creation'

This method of analysis produced a number of variations between sites. Based purely on a word frequency search the Baptist Mission Society (BMS) emphasised 'God', while the Church Mission Society emphasised 'Jesus'. 'The Church' or 'churches' was a large focus of much of the language across the websites.

It was found that in a search of both Protestant and Roman Catholic agency sites there were frequent references to 'God' and 'mission' but rarely references to 'God's mission'. References to 'Jesus Christ' were more frequent (84) but these were not to 'Christ's mission' but to Christ as God and these two terms could have been used interchangeably. References to 'Kingdom' were infrequent (13) and the NVIVO search *only* returned these references from Roman Catholic sources. There was one reference to mission being expressed in the language of 'Trinity' and eight references to the agency of the Holy Spirit. The initial evidence of the theological foundations for mission was therefore that agencies tend to express their theological understanding of mission in the public genre of a website in terms of 'God' and 'Jesus' rather than in terms of Spirit, Kingdom or Trinity.

One interesting result was that there was a different use of the word 'community' in the texts of the Protestant agencies and the Roman Catholic New Communities. 'Community' was a frequently used word (77 references in 57 agencies and communities surveyed). However the way it was used had different nuances divided between Protestant and Roman Catholic sources. In the Protestant sources the tendency was to use the word 'community' to express the *object* of mission whereas in Roman Catholic sources 'community' was expressed as a means of evangelization. This was not entirely surprising considering the importance of ecclesiology to Roman Catholic identity and being. In the Protestant churches there has historically been a greater emphasis on the action of the individual in response to Christ. However, this finding served as a reminder that similar language ascribed to mission can be differently nuanced in ways that are easy to overlook. Therefore, this was an issue that had to be carried over to further stages of the project. This initial study of what the churches and agencies said about themselves on their public websites, even in their straplines, opened up some key terms and concepts which were instrumental in the formulation of the survey, particularly about who does mission and who receives it.

Sharing Jesus, Changing Lives **Christian Care for Families** A Community Centred on Christ for the New Evangelisation For People and Community Informing, promoting and inviting all Christians to respond to today's mission Where a little goes a long way Growing leaders, growing churches

Typical straplines.

Analysis of selected websites: national churches and agencies

Anne Richards and Janice Price then undertook a more detailed semiotic analysis[1] of the websites of the Church Mission Society, USPG, Baptist Mission Society, St Joseph's Missionary Society, the Methodist Church, the United Reformed Church and the Church of England. We expected to find that the mission agencies would have a clearer and more immediate mission focus, while the national church websites would have a wider range of initial materials. However, we still expected to find some theological or other explicated rationale for mission which would enable us to discover what churches' public statements about mission would be and what mission messages they would expect website viewers to obtain.

Some comments on the nature of websites

Some important questions have to be asked about websites as a new technology which is now considered *essential* for any organization or institution seeking to reach out to others. If a church, agency or organization is involved in mission, then surely a website in itself is a missiological tool? This led us to ask: what sort of a text is a website and what is its purpose? For Christian organizations which communicate through worship, prayer, scripture, oral faith sharing and Christian actions, how does this traditional communication affect notions of exchangeable text?

One of the key aspects of assessing a website is that it is multi-semiotic. Websites by nature can combine a variety of styles or means of communication with written text, still pictures, video, podcast, social networking and purchasing capacities among others. A website as text most often combines written and/or visual material in electronic form which also allows for an immediate exchange between users and/or viewer and originator. It also has clear boundaries between it and other texts delineated by ownership of the text and style of the message but which expresses something of a wider and bigger discourse, including textual poaching.[2] It is this combination of styles of communication through electronic means that characterize the genre of the website. This opens a key relationship between form and content. Content has to be appropriate to the form and a website that only contains written text is not judged to be as successful as those sites which combine different modes of discourse in this particular genre. The development of interactivity characterized by immediacy of

---

1 Semiotic analysis involves looking at the interplay of text, visuals, messages and signs on (for example) a website and analysing what meanings are derived from the entire system.

2 Michel de Certeau, a Jesuit, first suggested this term in relation to the way readers actively take what they read and realign its content to their own interests and purpose. See *The Practice of Everyday Life* (English trans. 1984) (Berkeley:University of California Press). An example would be reading a mission story on a website and using it in a sermon.

encounter enabled by electronic means is one of the important ways in which websites have changed communication. Early websites were focused to a greater extent on the provision of information. Today, websites have multiple uses and have become an important part of social exchange and practice for many people. The development of webinars as a form of interactivity for a group combines the ability to give, receive and discuss information. This is in contrast with webcasts which only allow data transmission is one way and do not allow interaction between presenter and the audience.[1] We were therefore looking for multi-semiotic materials about mission as well as the purely text based themes uncovered by the NVIVO search.

Results

What was immediately clear in studying the websites for their sign systems and coding is that in each case the website front page was a multi-semiotic experience in which colour, design, text, layout and images combined to promote messages to the viewer, and which could be taken away and used by the viewer. It was interesting to see what the viewer might glean about the church or agency's view of the foundations for mission and how far these were obtainable from the website. It was noticeable, sampling the websites on a number of occasions how the syntagmatic (surface) structure of many sites changed (for example to reflect the seasons of the Church's year) while paradigmatic (self-contained) structures, such as vision and mission statements remained embedded in the site. It could therefore be argued that such websites seek to combine both syntagmatic and paradigmatic structures in relaying message about mission. Paradigms of mission would be encoded by mission statements or statements of purpose and practice while syntagmatic indications of what is happening in mission *now* would be encoded in changing pictures and text perhaps pointing to specific events, fundraising initiatives, news items, quotes, links to the wider church or photo items. One important question was therefore whether these two aspects of the design and layout of the site reinforced each other or whether the linear surface of the site, especially on the front page, was actually continually dominant.

A particular focus of this analysis was the use of language about mission and about other kinds of messages about mission that might be conveyed by the layout and design; bearing in mind the concepts and ideas about language which had been generated by NVIVO analysis in the first part of this phase. Another matter was whether the primary driver for messages about mission might be conditioned by the need to raise funds and support. To that end, we concentrated mainly on the front page, 'about us' page and 'support us' page before searching the rest of the site. It was necessary to bear in mind that website design and upkeep is expensive and variations in quality would not say anything about drivers for mission, but more about available financial resources. Notwithstanding, in view of the funds available for websites, it was interesting to see what churches and agencies prioritised. The websites were also sampled at intervals to compare any changes in appearance and content.

The screenshots below are included for illustrative purposes, not to compare their relative merits in terms of layout, design or messages about mission.

---

1   What is a Webinar? Webopedia Computer Dictionary, www.webopedia.com/TERM/W/Webinar.html, accessed 9 October 2009.

Church Mission Society

Our observations about the CMS (Church Mission Society) website first led us to the permanent strapline 'sharing Jesus, changing lives' which offers an explicit vision of the agency's purpose and intention described as current ongoing action. The word 'mission' was all over the front page on each occasion it was sampled; we also noted an explicit mention of 'God's mission' and a summary of the theological drivers. All this was explicated one click away from the homepage as: 'CMS is committed to evangelistic mission, working to see our world transformed by the love of Jesus. We dream of the day when the whole of creation is restored to a living, loving relationship with God. We believe that by living a mission lifestyle, equipping people for mission work and sharing resources for mission we make our unique contribution to God's mission. We do this as a community that shares a longing to see all peoples being drawn into fellowship with the Lord Jesus Christ'. A key document setting out a commitment to 'Trinitarian faith' has to be downloaded as a pdf and says that it encourages mission service in 'those who have experienced conversion to Christ, are being renewed by the work of the Holy Spirit, are committed to the local as well as the worldwide mission of the church'. Trinitarian values were also affirmed in another downloadable 'Ethos Statement'.[1]

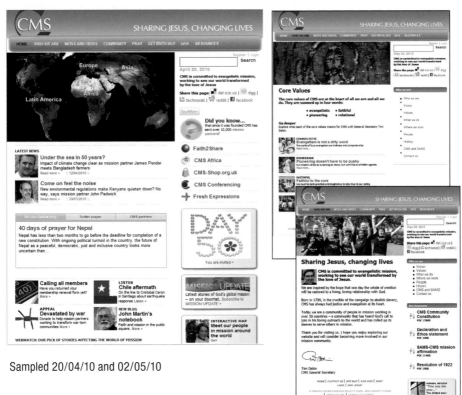

Sampled 20/04/10 and 02/05/10

The front page was laid out magazine style, with three dimensional button boxes, was seasonally directed and changing with a large amount of focus on interaction and sharing, including icons for Del.ici.ous, dig, technorati, reddit, an RSS and Facebook.

1 www.cms-uk.org/Whoweare/Vision/tabid/167/language/en-GB/Default.aspx.

There were strong incentives to explore 'mission' directed objects, to join a community. There was a personal message to the user from the General Secretary one click away highlighting both justice and evangelism. The site often included symbolic images (such as candles in November, bare feet) and a prominent tab for donation.

USPG: Anglicans in World Mission

The USPG: Anglicans in World Mission front page had a series of differently coloured boxes outlining text in similar fonts. There was no RSS or sharing icons, although Twitter was available. There were more people and faces on the front page indicating strongly the relational nature of what USPG is about but the theological rationale, like that of CMS, had to be downloaded as a pdf. This document also set out a commitment to Trinity and also explicitly to the *missio Dei*.[1] There was no evidence on the front page of the agency's view of the foundations for mission and was rather identified with 'supporting churches'. 'Doing things' was also an important mission theme but this theme was transmitted by images of people, especially women, engaged in activities, rather than text descriptions. One question arising from examination of the website through its images was whether the agency advocated doing things *to* and *for* people or whether it helped people to help themselves, so there were issues of power and helplessness in trying to ascertain the agency's drivers for mission. Donation was also prominent together with a strong impression of multi-culture and a worldwide agency, strongly supporting the agency's self description as 'Anglicans in world mission'.

Sampled 20/04/10

---

1 www.uspg.org.uk/images_cms/Pages%20from%20theological_basis-page1.pdf.

The Baptist Mission Society

The Baptist Mission Society front page was designed with two dimensional flat boxes and a left hand menu set out in strong orange and purple colours. Its foundations for mission were clearly stated in a central position on the 'about us' section, a click away from the home page: 'BMS believes in holistic mission, an approach that stays true to the Christian call to evangelisation without neglecting the duty to take care of the physical needs of the poor.' Baptism and male images, including ministers, were important signifiers on the 'about us' page. Images of women tended to show them as receivers. The front page was topical with focused news, prayer and updates and directed and used similar language to CMS about 'changing lives' and 'being transformed' by God through the work of BMS. Sharing was offered through an RSS feed and Facebook. Later, Twitter was added. The 'support us' tab gave a large amount of 'churchy' donations information with many options. The site also offered different 'channels' of information and experience which could be chosen by the user. The general impression given by the website as a whole is that it is focused at the committed person who needed to be challenged and inspired.

Sampled 20/04/10 and 02/05/10

At 25/02/10 the site offered its vision and strategy document 'For God…' for download listing its foundational driver as John 3:16 and basing its principles on words such as 'relationship', 'commitment', 'transformation', 'witnessing', 'responding', 'listening', 'engaging' and 'resourcing'. These words were strongly supported by significant images, such as a cross among minarets.[1]

St Joseph's Missionary Society (Mill Hill Missionaries)

The St Joseph's Missionary Society (Mill Hill Missionaries) offered a repeated strapline 'to love and to serve' across the top of the front page together with emblematic signifiers of the Holy Family for 'St Joseph' and of a ship crossing the ocean (for

---

1 www.bmsworldmission.org/standard.aspx?id=434374.

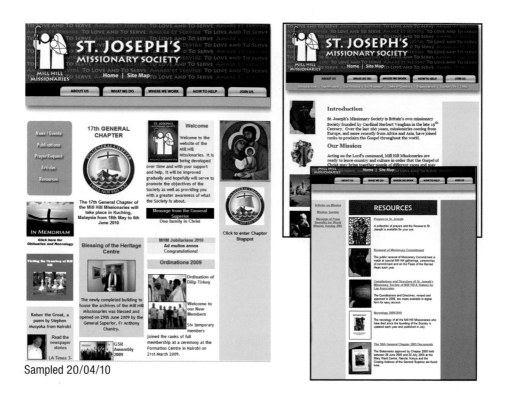

Sampled 20/04/10

mission). The front page directly addressed the viewer with a welcome message and a message and picture from the General Superior. Pictures on the front page tended to be of static, formal groups and the 'what we do' section offered only text without images. However, the front page offered a number of images of the cross in various guises as well as the 'Joseph' motif. There was a mixture of quite formal and traditional church elements (eg ordinations, blessing) with more modern images. The mission statement was quickly accessible and was set out as:

> **Acting on the Lord's command, Mill Hill Missionaries are ready to leave country and culture in order that the Gospel of Christ may bring together people of different races and may become incarnate in every culture and nation.**

The introduction traced the scriptural drivers for mission to John 1:39 and Matthew 28:19. This contrasted with another Roman Catholic mission site such as SEDOS, based in Rome which set out its driver on the front page from Luke 4:

> **The Spirit of the Lord is upon me – he has appointed me to bring good news to the poor – to proclaim liberty to the captives and new sight to the blind – to free the oppressed and announce the Lord's year of mercy.**

The Methodist Church

We then contrasted mission society websites with the front pages of a number of denominations to see how mission messages were handled and disseminated.

The Methodist Church front page also offered scripture: 'neither height not depth, nor anything else in all creation will be able to separate us from the love of God that

Sampled 20/04/10

is in Christ Jesus our Lord' (Romans 8:39). Its message is one of openness and inclusiveness. However a search was needed to find the Priorities,[1] and it was more difficult to find out what Methodism says about mission. A search for the word 'mission' led to a number of results for events and issues rather than about a Methodist view of mission. The priorities offered the closest thing to a mission statement:

> **To proclaim and affirm its conviction of God's love in Christ, for us and for all the world; and renew confidence in God's presence and action in the world and in the Church.**

The front page was laid out as columnised two dimensional boxes with small images, heavy on brown text. On the day the image above was sampled it did, however, figure the cross, arguably the most powerful signifier of what Christianity is about. There was an emphasis on prayer on the front page, but the foundations and theological drivers for mission were more difficult to ascertain. Social networking was not offered, but there was an ability to connect with the President and Vice-President's blog, featuring text and pictures, but mostly of static groups.

United Reformed Church

The URC front page featured white text on brightly coloured sections in a non-standard shape. This website offered a login for membership. The front page offered resources such as booklets and manuals. The networking possibilities included not only an RSS feed and Facebook link, but links also to Flickr and YouTube. On 25.02.10 the front page offered the URC's first webinar.

The 'about' section offered as its self description: 'Called to be God's people, transformed by the Gospel, making a difference in today's world', though this section was all text based. The 'what we do page' has a series of links under the heading Mission[2] and offers:

---

1 www.methodist.org.uk/index.cfm?fuseaction=opentogod.content&cmid=559.
2 www.urc.org.uk/what_we_do/mission/mission.

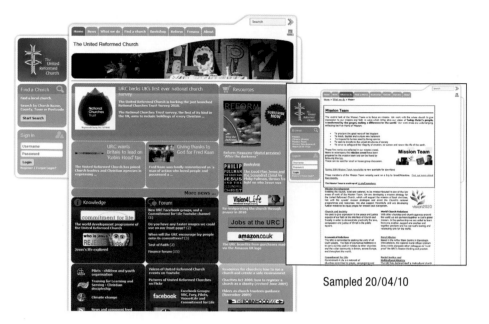

Sampled 20/04/10

We work with the whole church to give expression to our mission and faith in ways which bring alive our vision of 'being Christ's people, transformed by the gospel, making a difference to the world' Our work areas are wide-ranging, reflecting the Five Marks of Mission.

In addition to a basis for mission in the five marks, this section of the website enables the user to discover the people in the mission team and more about their interests and activities, although when it was sampled some of the links were repeated and some were missing.

The Church of England

The front page of the Church of England website was defined by its purple colour and had a two dimensional columnised layout with small pictures and colour coding for significant words such as 'faith', 'worship' and' life'. It carried no scripture on the front page and no foundations or drivers for mission, though the face of Jesus figured next to the welcome message (this image changes at intervals). Mission matters require entry through the 'faith' portal[1] and are described as:

> **The Church of England is called, as are all Churches, to carry forward the work that Jesus Christ began in all aspects of the life of people in society. Jesus said to those who followed him 'As the Father has sent me, so do I send you'. (John 20:21)**

This page was text-based with an image of an open Bible, so offering an image of yet more text. A search from the front page for the word 'mission' brought up a number of results, including the Archbishops' Council's mission statement which was the five marks of mission.[2]

---

1 www.cofe.anglican.org/faith/mission.
2 www.cofe.anglican.org/about/archbishopscouncil/missionstatement.html.

The front page was therefore clearly a portal requiring the enquirer to search for what is wanted. The front page carries an RSS feed but no icons for Facebook or Twitter. The site offered podcasts but no direct interaction with user and no message from the Archbishops (who have their own websites). The Church of England's website message was much more that it is topical and this site does carry a strapline: 'a Christian presence in every community'.

Sampled 20/04/10

Summary and Transition

An examination of these websites showed that the elucidation and explication of mission is not in general a high priority. Only CMS made a conscious effort to high-light and prioritise the idea of mission *per se*. Some other agency sites prioritised action in the world. Denominational websites covered far more ground and offered a range of options, often with portal style features. The Methodist Church featured openness and inclusiveness. Church of England promoted its ubiquity and inclusiveness.

The web-search yielded a number of interesting points.

- Websites in general are designed for the public and not necessarily for people with an in-depth or specialised knowledge of mission. We were looking for evidence of the foundations for mission and for the theological drivers and these were present within websites but usually in designated sections embedded in the site, only used as justification for action or outlook for those willing to work to find and study the relevant material.

- Many of the websites, particularly those constructed by mission agencies, were looking for support and are built with the intention of attracting interest and hopefully involvement and donation. Consequently many sites combined not only words about mission, but pictures, colours, logos, designs, interactive and social networking features. Portal designs were also present in some sites to draw searchers into the site. Denominational websites also tended to assume searchers are looking for something specific, like a local church, and sought to meet that need first.

- Theological language, especially about the Trinitarian foundations for mission, where present, was often relegated to a page or downloadable document a number of clicks away, so perhaps mission theology as a foundation for mission simply does not translate into web friendly language. Consequently, front pages offered 'snapshot' theological ideas such as CMS' *Sharing Jesus, Changing Lives*, or MHM's 'To love and to serve', a short snippet of scripture, or a picture of something related to Jesus.

- Rendle and Mann argue that: 'There are two components to all mission and vision statements: the axiomatic and the unique. The axiomatic states what is self-evident for all congregations...The unique states what is important to the particular congregation because of who it is, where it is located and the historical moment it is in.....we consistently encourage planning teams...to shape their future by giving particular attention to unique statements about themselves.. that expresses as sharply as possible the unique gifts, call, and challenge that this congregation claims'.[1] Similarly, websites have to offer what is axiomatic: Christian, missionary, inclusive, worldwide, and set this against the unique identities of the church or agency. So we can expect to see the language and pictures of God and Jesus, displayed against unique identifiers such as biblical straplines, or theological statements or purpose and intention. There was a tension between the axiomatic and the unique in all the sites, felt strongly in the CMS site and the MHM site, less strongly in the USPG site and hardly at all in the current Church of England website.

This initial phase of the project created some issues to be carried over into the design of the survey. How far did leaders of churches and agencies feel that the foundations for mission set out in their public language about mission on their websites reflected their understanding of what their church or agency was really about and how it operated in the real world? How far was such language an accurate descriptor of the behaviour and activity of the church or agency and what effect did their vision or mission statements have on complex issues of practice? For example, how far did stated foundations for mission drive attitudes to people from other faiths, or social justice? How far did views about mission condition ideas about who is best placed to act or work in mission? What about those who receive mission? Were they just receptors as some website images seemed to suggest, or participants? These questions then enabled us to create a tool for churches and agencies to discuss with web designers and writers when producing web materials related to mission (Appendix D)

These questions informed work which was then undertaken on the design of survey for church and agency leaders from the GC/GMN/BIAMS constituencies.

---

1 G. Rendle and A. Mann, (2003) *Holy Conversations: strategic planning as a spiritual practice for congregations* (Herndon, VA: Alban Institute) pp. 85-6.

Survey of national churches and agencies, local churches in Nottinghamshire, England, and BIAMS conference attendees

The website search had provided a number of key words around the issue of mission which we decided to incorporate as far as possible into the survey statements to see if these elicited a particularly positive response. Other elements of the survey would try to determine whether there were both axiomatic and unique identifiers (for example church tradition or theological position) which would carry over into the mission praxis and understanding of the people in the church or agency.

The survey was designed and tested in stages in order to make sure that the required topic areas were covered. We decided to have categories of enquiry that would be researched by using statements rather than questions. Statements were checked to make sure they were not ambiguous, loaded or leading. We also tried to cover Bevans and Shroeder's lenses of mission in the triplet statements in order to see if one lens or perspective of mission was more prominent than another. One issue that preoccupied us was the use of the word 'primarily' in a number of statements. When the ecumenical Mission Theology Advisory Group (a partnership of the Church of England and CTBI) was used as a focus group to trial the statements (09.12.08), one member commented that there was a 'but' with responding to all the statements and another felt it had stopped him from saying what he wanted to say. On reflection, however, the word 'primarily' was included in some of the statements in order to provoke a more considered response. Other comments about the design of the survey concerned whether there was a bias against proclamation and evangelism, and the statements were checked again to make sure different emphases were properly covered. It was also noted that 'Kingdom' is an outdated word for post-Christians and might not be helpful in all applications of the survey, although not likely to cause a problem for the immediate constituency. Another very pertinent question from MTAG was whether the statements were about how things are now or about how they *ought* to be. This was also noted by respondents in both the national and local survey. This was a very interesting idea and one which it was felt could be teased out helpfully in the follow-up in-depth interviews in the third stage of the project to see if people interpreted the statements as a way of describing the world as it is or the world as it ought to be in an ideal working out of the missiological process.

Comments on the survey made by respondents showed that people in general find it difficult to react to statements about mission even though the websites often offer precise statements and straplines. Respondents wrote comments such as 'needs defining…', 'it needs to be debated…' 'It depends what you mean by…'. Some were frustrated by being asked to react to the statements in a way which translated into a precise response, and commented that they were forced to be 'fence sitters' or wanted to add 'sometimes' into the statements. This showed that there was a difficulty with even the most commonplace Christian concepts, including theological concepts, all of which proved more slippery and complex than might be normally imagined. Respondents commented on the difficulty of defining, for example, 'justice', 'mission', 'partnership' and 'Church'. The comments made by the participants in the process of completing the national survey were gathered up and carried over into the design of the local survey, where changes were made in the mission priorities section to reflect more accurately the interests of churches engaging in mission 'on the ground'. There was also an added question about what kinds of advocacy and campaigning a church might be involved in in order to elicit more detail about the 'justice' question that had proved so difficult in the national survey (see Appendix E). The comments from the national survey were also taken forward into the design of the third section of the project.

Paper copies of the national survey template were given to the BIAMS conference attendees to fill in at All Nations Christian College in July 2009 and this exercise was the first item at the conference. Those results were entered into SurveyMonkey immediately by Dr Knights and provided new data for the whole research team who were reporting preliminary findings from the national and local surveys to the conference. This was extremely helpful, because those who had just filled in the survey were able to comment on the preliminary findings from their own experience. Reflections from Dr Knights and Dr Rolph about the conference, as well as papers from the conference are included in Phase 2.2 below.

The results of the survey can be understood in two ways, as quantitative data on individual questions about the foundations for mission, and qualitative data on the way Christians *deal with* questions about their understanding of mission. The data was analysed using a number of filters: by aggregating the response from the three sets of data, including ranking the scores, and by individual survey results. The national survey was filtered for response by denomination. Data is illustrated in this book by means of pie charts, but pie charts only show positive results, so where a zero result was returned, that is indicated in the legend. Complete sets of data for the survey will be available on the CTBI website.

We began with a number of assumptions about the sample. In particular, the BIAMS sample from the conference was made up of mission practitioners and theologians, most with direct overseas experience. We expected their results, in the conference setting, to be driven by theology and their personal experience rather than by theories about mission praxis. The national survey included churches, agencies, and organisations with *responsibility* for mission activity by others, so we expected this sample to show a tension between theological concerns and issues of responsible praxis. The local sample included church leaders of different Christian denominations working at local level on understandings of mission. We assumed these might be mostly praxis driven where they were dealing with mission issues together with their congregations.

Because the sample was small, we looked for emerging themes rather than definitive results. We were aware that the survey forced answers where there might be shades of meaning or different answers according to context and we expected to be able to use the in-depth interviews to address this. Some particular issues caught our attention:

- It can be hard to disagree with the word 'mission'
- Respondents had difficulty with negative words like 'condemnation' but endorsed words like 'repentance'
- 'Transforms', 'Hospitality', 'reconciliation' and 'God's love to all' were regarded most positively
- Respondents wanted to embed the statements in contexts and stories
- Ranking or prioritisation of mission perspective was extremely difficult
- Respondents had difficulty with the word 'justice'
- Engaging with the statements caused a slight shift in attitude in some respondents
- Strong assent for a missionary 'Church' but not for planting churches or bringing back people to church.
- Stronger assent for partnership at national level and BIAMS than in the local survey

These issues are discussed as emerging themes. It is possible that if the survey is taken up in other quarters and contexts and the results fed back to CTBI in the future, it will be possible to get a clearer picture of these themes and others may yet emerge.

Emerging Themes

Agreeing and Disagreeing

One significant result across the data was that respondents did not like to use the 'strongly disagree' option (coloured cyan in the pie chart) which was ranked with the lowest response in 33 out of 44 statements and next to lowest in 9 other statements.[1] Of the two remaining statements, both were expressed negatively: asserting that there is no separation between Kingdom and church and that we have little to learn from other faiths. By contrast the (blue) 'strongly agree' option was not used consistently. It appeared that there is a general tendency to want to respond positively to mission-related language even if the concepts were complex and the respondent unsure. We thought it was possible that people found it difficult to disagree with statements with the word 'mission' in them when voluntarily undertaking a survey that had to do with mission and noted this for development in interviews.

It also appeared that where the statements required a great deal of thought, respondents used (green) 'neither agree nor disagree' when they were unsure or wanted to register 'don't know'. In some cases, respondents commented that they wanted *both* to agree *and* disagree with the statements simultaneously because they

---

1 Data is recorded in Appendix H.

were aware of complexities that made a simple straightforward answer impossible. Indeed some of the comments on the statements suggested that respondents spent time agonising over some of the issues, perhaps consulting with others, before committing themselves to a response. One respondent commented that s/he wanted to strongly agree with one statement before thinking of a number of other issues which moderated the response to 'agree'. Comments also showed that some statements proved especially difficult to deal with when the person filling in the survey was trying to apply theological concepts to the church's or agency's actual outworking and this was another issue we wanted to explore further.

Another point we became aware of was that respondents treated the statements *as if* they were questions and so looked at all sides of the implicit question before deciding on a response. Consequently, some respondents had difficulty and frustration with the survey, even though the statements used common words about mission, because they were not in a position to expand on their answer and this resulted in some long explicatory comments. Another particular difficulty with decision making in response to the statements were ranking words like 'best' or 'primarily' as discussed below. One respondent also noted the difficulty of responding to statements without a context and some others who commented on the experience of taking the survey sought to provide contexts for their answers by reference to scripture or indicating the theological position they wanted to take. This was interesting because it suggested that the foundations for mission can (must?) be context-dependent rather than theological givens. Respondents tried to picture who would be involved in the statement – for example, what kind of 'poor'? These issues and difficulties were noted for address by the third part of the project in which questions would be asked and issues of this kind explored. In particular, would people want to ground their answers in stories or illustrations rather than vision statements? If that was true then it would have implications for website design and whether pictures of people engaged in activity and set in particular (especially worldwide) contexts would more accurately explicate the church or agency's foundations for mission.

Mission language

Certain words drew very high levels of positive (blue and red) agreement, especially 'transforms' 'hospitality and openness' and 'reconciliation': S05, S10, S33.

Other statements in the statement-triplets (Kingdom, mission and church; mission and evangelism; mission and improving lives)in which these three statements were found did not draw this level of positive response, so it is possible that this kind of language contains key or 'trigger' words which do constitute foundations or impetus for mission and which people want to respond to positively. Interestingly, these are principles for human *relationships*, bringing people together and working for good outcome; they create pictures of human behaviour. 'Transformation' was noted in the NVIVO search of websites and it is interesting that 'reconciliation' has now recently been added as a 'mark' of mission.

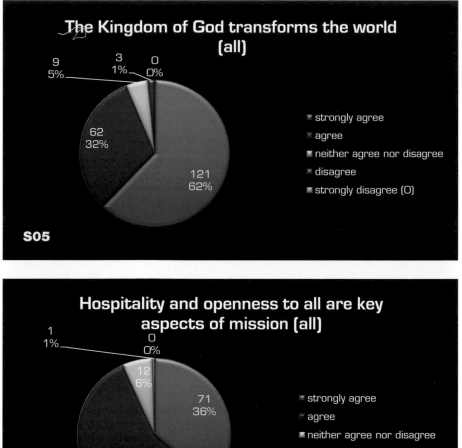

The Kingdom of God transforms the world (all)

9
5%
3
1%
0
0%

62
32%

121
62%

- strongly agree
- agree
- neither agree nor disagree
- disagree
- strongly disagree (O)

S05

Hospitality and openness to all are key aspects of mission (all)

1
1%
0
0%

12
6%

71
36%

111
57%

- strongly agree
- agree
- neither agree nor disagree
- disagree (O)
- strongly disagree

S10

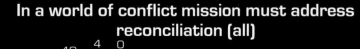
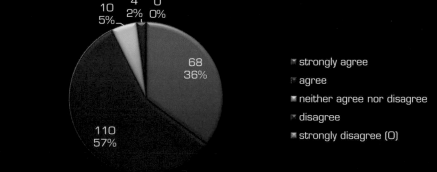

In a world of conflict mission must address reconciliation (all)

10
5%
4
2%
0
0%

68
36%

110
57%

- strongly agree
- agree
- neither agree nor disagree
- disagree
- strongly disagree (O)

S33

Difficult language

As noted, people found judgement statements using words like 'primarily' or 'best' to be difficult to deal with and it was particularly noticeable that statements including these words attracted a high degree of response in the (green) 'neither agree nor disagree' category across a range of topics. For example, one respondent commented:

> Answers which have put 'neither agree nor disagree' come with much thought. Our reason for choosing these is that we affirm the statements as part of mission, but reject the language of 'priority', or 'primarily', we see these elements as important but do not see these elements as more important than others.

This is particularly seen in a complex statement about who best carries out mission:

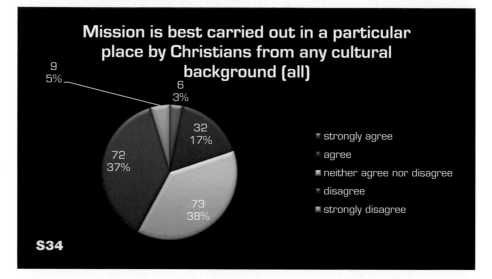

In looking at the results it was helpful to look at the rankings for the 'neither agree or disagree' option to lead us to statements with which people had had difficulty. The word 'primarily' also appeared to drive down positive responses to statements which would be expected to carry a high positive response. For example, a statement about 'welcome' which might have been expected to score as highly as 'openness' returned a much less positive result.

People found most difficulty with language about 'justice' and its relation to mission. This might be because of confusion about human justice or God's justice, the theological place of justice and a world 'under judgement' as opposed to 'social justice'. The BIAMS respondents were much clearer about their response to justice as might be expected from that constituency (see S01).

There was similar ambiguity about the triad of statements relating to mission and development, with a high degree of neutrality especially in the local survey to the statement 'mission and development are inseparable' (see S04), but there was a greater positive response to the statement mentioning 'social action' (see S15), perhaps simply because 'social action' creates clearer pictures for people than 'development' and because

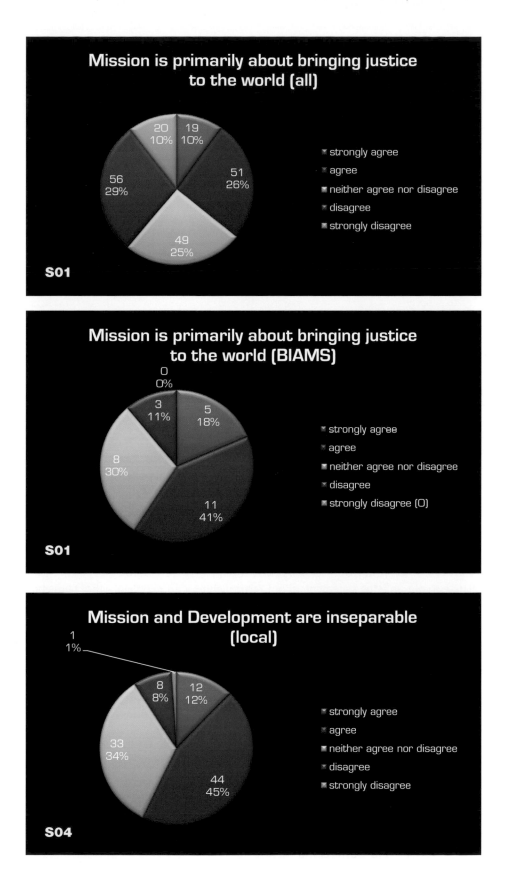

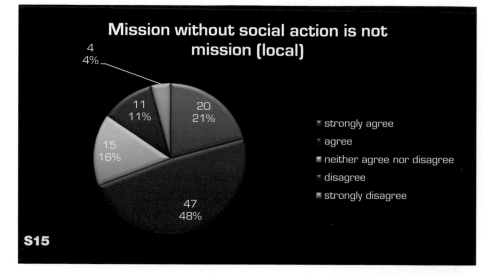

Mission without social action is not mission (local)

- strongly agree
- agree
- neither agree nor disagree
- disagree
- strongly disagree

20 21%
11 11%
4 4%
15 16%
47 48%

S15

at local level, social action, such as commitment to Fairtrade products, was easier to understand than 'development' which is passively supported but actively undertaken by others.

The final statement in the survey, about concern for the poorest, by contrast drew a high number of neutral responses.

Distributed Concepts: other faiths, how God works and who best carries out mission

Statements which were essentially the same but repeated in different formats in different parts of the survey showed that the theme was being thought about and this thought process changed the results in a few of the respondents. This was particularly true in statements about relations with people of other faiths (see S02, S22 and S24).

The triplet questions, distributed across the survey showed a small shift in response across the more complex statements particularly those which needed to be context related, so not only the statements about relationships with people of other faiths but statements about who is best equipped to carry out missionary tasks, showed such a shift in response. Further, different categories which had related issues, principally relations with other faiths, who should best carry out mission and how God works through people, all showed a spread of response and shifts to high neutrality, with particular problems about whether God works primarily through Christians (see S17).

Theology as Foundations for mission

A comparison between the three sets of data showed as expected that the BIAMS theological constituency had a stronger understanding of the origin and purpose of mission as being founded in Trinitarian theology than those in the other surveys.

Two comments in the national survey referred explicitly to the *missio Dei*. However, other theologically oriented statements, particularly concerning whether proclamation should include particular theological positions *vis a vis* sin drew a spread of response, generating higher 'disagree' responses (purple and cyan).

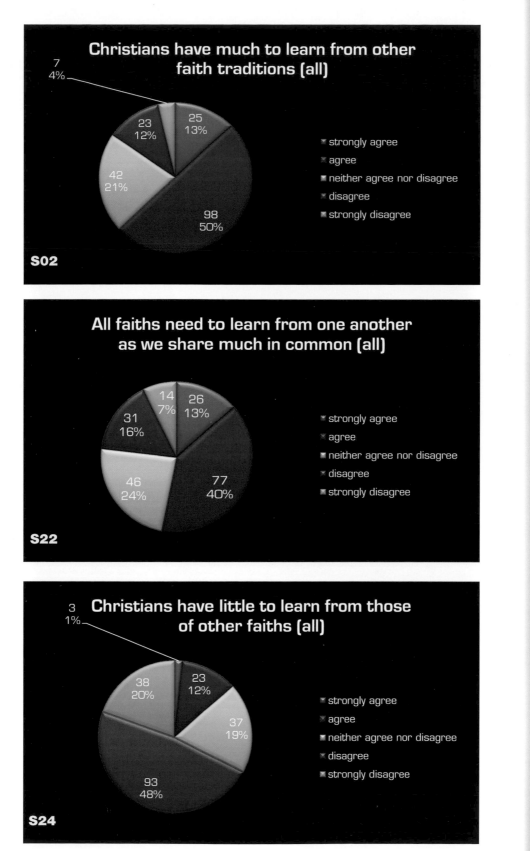

Christians have much to learn from other faith traditions (all)

7
4%

23
12%

25
13%

42
21%

98
50%

- strongly agree
- agree
- neither agree nor disagree
- disagree
- strongly disagree

S02

All faiths need to learn from one another as we share much in common (all)

14
7%

26
13%

31
16%

46
24%

77
40%

- strongly agree
- agree
- neither agree nor disagree
- disagree
- strongly disagree

S22

Christians have little to learn from those of other faiths (all)

3
1%

38
20%

23
12%

37
19%

93
48%

- strongly agree
- agree
- neither agree nor disagree
- disagree
- strongly disagree

S24

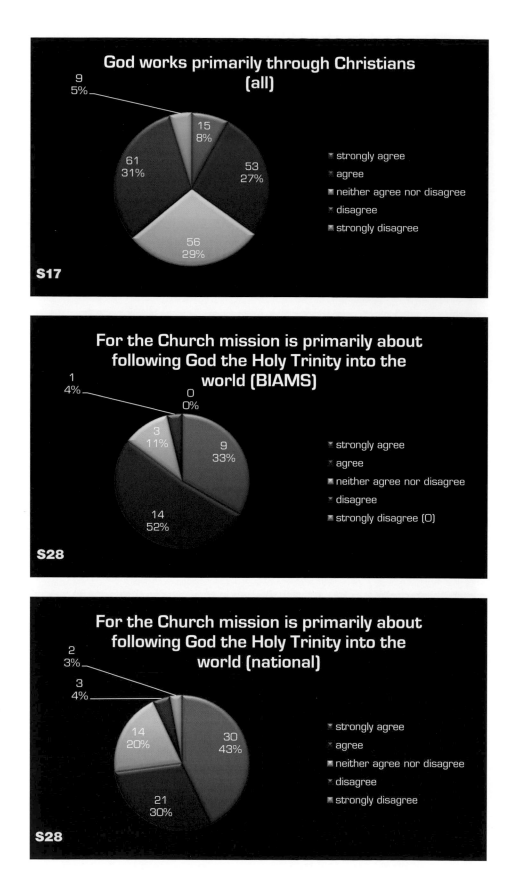

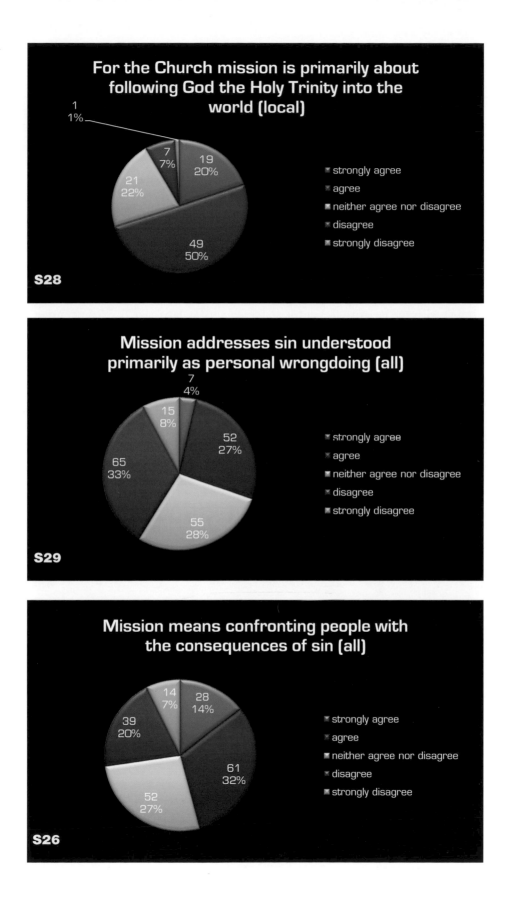

For the Church mission is primarily about following God the Holy Trinity into the world (local)

1
1%

7
7%

19
20%

21
22%

49
50%

■ strongly agree
■ agree
■ neither agree nor disagree
■ disagree
■ strongly disagree

S28

Mission addresses sin understood primarily as personal wrongdoing (all)

7
4%

15
8%

52
27%

65
33%

55
28%

■ strongly agree
■ agree
■ neither agree nor disagree
■ disagree
■ strongly disagree

S29

Mission means confronting people with the consequences of sin (all)

14
7%

28
14%

39
20%

61
32%

52
27%

■ strongly agree
■ agree
■ neither agree nor disagree
■ disagree
■ strongly disagree

S26

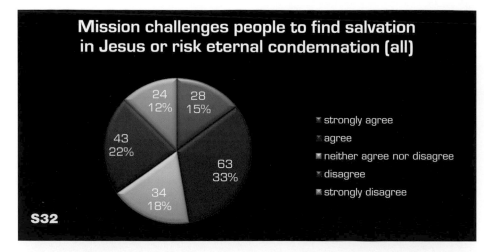

What was interesting about these responses was a high neutrality and a problem dealing with the negative feel of the statements using language like 'confronting', 'challenges' 'condemnation' and 'wrongdoing' whereas a statement about a call to 'repentance' (S13) drew high agreement. The statement about 'eternal condemnation' in the Mission and Salvation pairing had a positive twin about the 'hope of heaven' (S35) and this generated a far more positive response.

Church

The National and local surveys were committed to idea of *church* as vehicle for mission. There was strong assent around the word 'church' and about the idea that the Church is missionary of its nature.

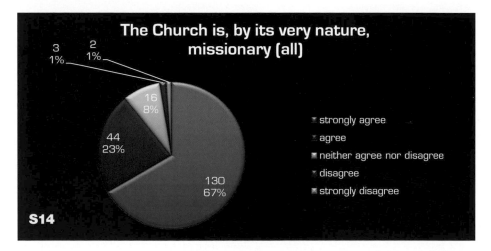

There was less certainty about the relation of the Church to Kingdom. Nearly all respondents agreed that the Kingdom of God transforms the world (see p. 37). However, they disagreed (profoundly disagreed in BIAMS) that the Kingdom and the Church are one (S16) but agreed that the Kingdom includes the Church but is wider than the Church (S07). This finding was interesting when it interrogated statements about who should be involved in mission. Respondents were equivocal about whether mission is just a task for Christians (S17) but agreed that indigenous people should be assisted by Christians from 'other contexts' (S21). But when the statement included Christians from 'any cultural background' (S34) this caused difficulties:

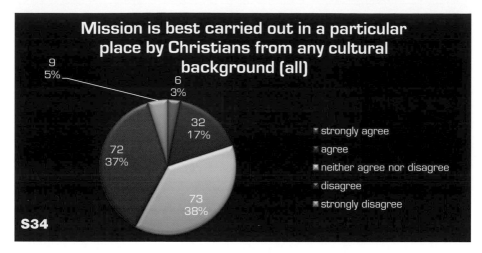

This result was returned despite a positive result for cross-cultural mission (S39, S41). So is mission still imagined as being 'us' doing to 'them'? What about reverse mission? How, exactly are people admitted to God's Kingdom? This issue of what people engaged in mission look like, how they relate to conceptions of 'Church' and the place of other Christians in the transformation of the world was again a matter we wanted to explore at interview.

Further, the issue of the 'church' seemed a difficult word to vote against, although interestingly there was high neutrality around a question about planting *more* churches (S43), and high neutrality (though general assent) to statements about recovering drifting Christians (S11), or bringing people into the worshipping community (S19): outcomes for mission which would see augmentation or even 'success' of the ecclesial community. There was a difference between the statements on 'essence of Church' and 'function of Church', where respondents agreed much more with theoretical statements about what the Church was (or should be) and what that really meant in practical mission terms.

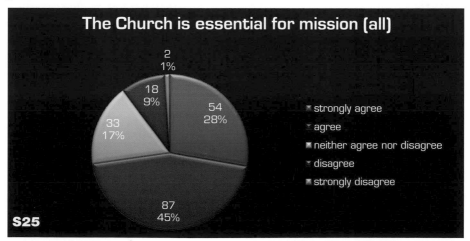

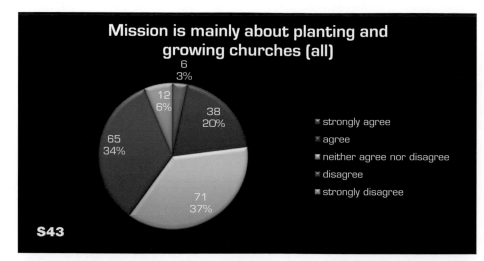

Mission is mainly about planting and growing churches (all)

- 6 — 3% strongly agree
- 12 — 6%
- 38 — 20% agree
- 65 — 34% neither agree nor disagree
- 71 — 37% disagree
- strongly disagree

S43

This seemed to suggest a relationship between mission and ecclesiology that is centred on the concept of Church as sending authority acting on the world and transforming it but not necessarily as the beneficiary of the mission process. From this we wanted to find out if there was (especially at local level) a continuing view of mission as sending missionaries and what the role and function of church or 'home mission' was expected to be. It seemed possible that there was an ecclesiological pressure in the foundations for mission which could eclipse mission theological principles. We saw this in differences between the responses from the national and local surveys and the BIAMS results. The BIAMS constituency was less positive about the word 'church'. We were also interested in seeing whether differences were generated along denominational fault lines, or more present in the Catholic new communities. For example, the Catholic respondents returned a higher 'strongly agree' level for the statement 'The Church is essential for mission' (S25) than either the Anglican or Independent Evangelical constituencies – although the numbers were too small to see definitive stratifications.

The Purpose and Outworking of Mission

A statement in the triad on 'Proclamation' that 'the Gospel is about proclaiming God's love to all' (S40) drew a very high level of assent and was the most heavily endorsed statement across all three data sets. The three dissenters were all from the national survey. Yet, as noticed, the statement about mission as primarily *welcoming* all people (S03) carried much less enthusiasm and carried more disagreement.

Further, the other two 'Proclamation' statements, concerning the relationship of proclamation to mission (S27) and proclamation as action towards others *first* (S20), further down the survey, drew a spread of response.

Partnership

Unsurprisingly, there was much stronger agreement in the national and BIAMS survey than in the local survey on the issue of the benefits of cross-cultural training, perspectives and partnership.

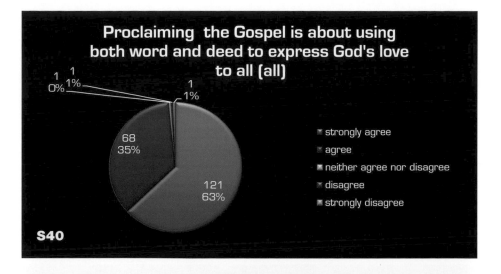

Proclaiming the Gospel is about using both word and deed to express God's love to all (all)

- 1 0%
- 1 1%
- 1 1%
- 68 35%
- 121 63%

Legend:
- strongly agree
- agree
- neither agree nor disagree
- disagree
- strongly disagree

S40

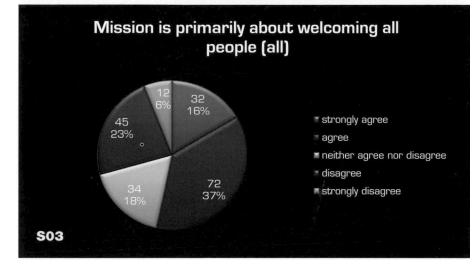

Mission is primarily about welcoming all people (all)

- 12 6%
- 32 16%
- 45 23%
- 34 18%
- 72 37%

Legend:
- strongly agree
- agree
- neither agree nor disagree
- disagree
- strongly disagree

S03

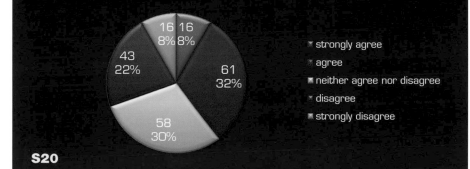

Proclaiming the Gospel is primarily about acting justly and loving neighbours, only using words if necessary (all)

- 16 8%
- 16 8%
- 43 22%
- 61 32%
- 58 30%

Legend:
- strongly agree
- agree
- neither agree nor disagree
- disagree
- strongly disagree

S20

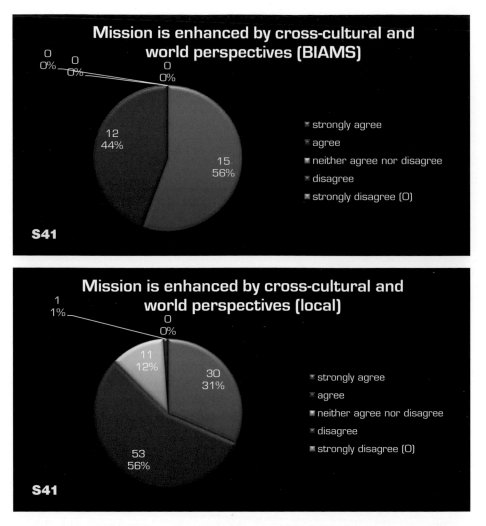

However, it might be the case that the benefits, clearly borne out by cross-cultural training and experience and brought back into mission agencies take much longer to trickle down into the understanding of local churches. If this is the case, then at local level, there might be a much greater struggle to understand both world mission insights and reverse mission insights and this in turn might affect the foundations for mission as understood at local level.

Priorities

We also had to read the data against the results from the 'priorities' page where respondents ticked up to five possibilities concerning what they saw as priorities for their church or agency. The local survey particularly came to attention here where home mission in form of 'community building' far outweighed mission giving, though mission giving outweighed mission and exchange visits. Where people ticked the 'advocacy' box this overwhelmingly meant a commitment to Fair Trade. This was interesting in terms of the local survey responses (especially neutral responses) given to statements about development, partnership and views of who carries out and receives mission. These priorities also have implications for how mission agencies interact with their constituencies and the profiles they maintain of those people who would be most likely to support them. There is therefore another tension between treating Christians at local level as passive *supporters* of overseas mission whose chief purpose is to give badly needed financial aid, and who do so because they don't do anything else, and potential *doers* who might actively become involved in mission and need support themselves.

Taking issues forward

In considering the emerging themes, it was clear that the data were complicated and difficult in many cases to interpret. Perhaps we need to ask: what pictures do these statements conjure up? Some issues are clearly much more complex than the statements allow and made it more difficult for respondents to give clear answers, especially as they started to think about them. Is it that taking the gospel into the world is *clearly* identified as missionary, with attendant images (thus relating back to the language of, for example, Matthew 28:19) or is it simply that the idea of 'justice' in the world is more difficult to picture without further context? It might be necessary to 'unpack' such a concept in order to get a picture of how it might relate to mission. From a process point of view, this might further suggest that it is only through interviews and reflection that it is possible in essence to get at the 'foundations for mission'.

Summary and Transition

The analysis and results from the three sets of data suggested some areas which were then included in the follow up in-depth interviews including:

- Whether respondents wanted to respond positively to all statements carrying the word mission and if so, why?
- What respondents felt about the relationship between mission and justice.
- Whether some of the questions made respondents think more deeply about the issues in such a way as to affect some of the later questions.
- Whether respondents chose 'neither agree nor disagree' when they meant 'don't know'.
- Whether respondents could talk more widely about their choice of response to particular questions.

Theories of Mission: the BIAMS perspective

Preliminary results from the project (national and local survey results and a preliminary website analysis) were taken to the BIAMS conference 'Sinking Foundations: Why Mission Today?' at All Nations Christian College in July 2009. The programme for the conference was planned and executed by the 2010 research group under the leadership of John Clark in consultation with the BIAMS executive. Participants were invited to complete the survey first of all for themselves and then to comment on the interim results and the process of the project. At this point, it was felt that it would be helpful to balance the interim results against some current perspectives in mission theology.

Three speakers were specially invited to give mission theological perspectives broadly following Bevans and Schroeder's three 'lenses' for mission orientation: mission as proclamation of Jesus Christ as Universal Saviour or simply 'proclamation'; mission as participation in the Triune God or *missio Dei*; and mission as liberating service of the Reign of God or 'Kingdom' mission. These lenses were also applied in the in-depth interviews in the third part of the project.

The speakers were: Michael Doe on '*Missio Dei*', Ann Morisy on 'Mission as Transformation' and Wonsuk Ma on 'Mission as Proclamation'. In addition Philip Knights gave a paper on the Roman Catholic perspective and Paul Rolph was invited to produce a paper as conference reflector. Kirsteen Kim also gave a paper on the historical perspectives for Edinburgh 2010 as noted above on page 11.

The papers on mission theological perspectives, together with the conference reflection are reproduced here, as they provided a context for further work on the project and in particular the dirrction of the in-depth analysis in phase three of the project. Dr Rolph's observations were particularly important in shaping the tasks and processes of the remainder of the project.

Mission as *missio Dei*

I have been asked to address the topic, *Sinking Foundations: Why Mission Today?*, in preparation for the centenary of Edinburgh 1910 next year, from the particular perspective of the *missio Dei*. I do this as a convinced Anglican, yet someone whose ministry and thinking has been very much within an ecumenical context. And I do it as the General Secretary of *USPG: Anglicans in World Mission*, with SPG going back more than 300 years, and an UMCA history which began with David Livingstone. A hundred years ago SPG was part of Edinburgh, but UMCA formally boycotted it: supporters of both were fearful of being seen with 'dissenters' and even 'heretics'!

Today, in a very different world, we seek to be part of the movement from Colonialism to Communion, yet aware that the impacts of globalisation, also reflected in much that is happening in the Church, are resulting in the creation of new and equally damaging colonialisms. In all of this, what we believe about the *missio Dei* could not be more important. My paper has three main sections: the *missio Dei* itself, the Five Marks of Mission, and the role of Mission and other agencies.

1. The theology of *missio Dei*

First, some theological background. One definition goes like this: 'the *missio Dei* is God's self-revelation as the One who loves the world and is actively involved in and with the world, it embraces both church and world, and the church is privileged to be called to participate in God s mission.'[1] Or in the words of David Bosch: 'To participate in mission is to participate in the movement of God's love toward people, since God is a fountain of sending love.'[2] Twentieth-century theology, reacting against the kind of theology which resulted from the Enlightenment, put the emphasis back on the initiative of God, rather than seeing mission as primarily a human activity. This found particular expression in the work of Karl Barth, to whom the concept of *missio Dei*, if not the exact words, is often attributed.

So the Willingen Statement from the 1952 meeting of the International Missionary Council said that Mission must be first and foremost God's mission. It went on to say that we can only understand this mission of God in terms of the Triune character of God. It is in the very nature of God to give and receive, to send and return, fundamentally to love the other, and where this overflows in the world, in creation, in Christ, and ultimately in the consummation of all things in Christ, we see the mission of God, the work of God, and the self-revelation of God himself (herself/themselves).

---

1 Euntes Asian Centre, Mindanao, Philippines.
2 David Bosch (1991) *Transforming Mission* (Maryknoll: Orbis Books).

And we are called to join in, to discover what God is doing and to reflect who God is. This raises the question of where the Church fits into the *missio Dei*. The Willingen Statement was clear that 'the Missionary Calling of the Church is derived from the mission of God': the Church has a missionary calling rather than a mission, and that calling is to engage in God's mission. Our mission therefore has no life of its own, only in the hands of the sending God can it truly be called mission, because the missionary initiative comes from God alone. The Church is both part of what God is doing, as a particular expression or embodiment of the work of God flowing from the very nature of God, and the Church has a particular vocation to engage with God in this work, in and for the world. In the words of Jurgen Moltmann, 'It is not the church that has a mission of salvation to fulfil in the world; it is the mission of the Son and the Spirit through the Father that includes the church.'[1]

In USPG's own theological statement we have focussed on the concept of 'Communion' ('*koinonia*') as a way of speaking about such things. We say:

1) **Communion is at the heart of God, the very life of the Trinity.**
   God yearns to draw each one of us into this communion with him.
   It is in communion with God that we know and are known, we love
   and are loved.
2) **Communion is God's gift to the Church.**
   We respond in worship, most of all when this communion is made
   real in the Eucharist.
   The Church is called to be the sign, foretaste and anticipation of
   God's mission.
   We are called to support each other as we engage in this mission
   wherever God has set us.
3) **Communion is God's will and desire for all humanity and the whole
   of creation.**
   Mission is therefore 'holistic', responding to all of God's liberating
   activity so that people may 'grow spiritually, thrive physically, and
   have a voice in an unjust world.[2]

One consequence of all this is the need to exercise care when we use the word 'Mission' and especially when we talk about the 'Mission of the Church'. Last year I was invited to the Missions Conference of The Episcopal Church in the U.S.A., and asked to make a contribution on 'The Overseas Mission of the Episcopal Church'. My short response was that it shouldn't have one! Partly because, as we've just said, it is God who has a mission not the church, but also because a proper understanding of this *missio Dei* means that Mission can no longer be seen as the activity of one Church overseas or in another culture.

Similarly, when people ask: 'How many countries does USPG work in?' I answer 'None, or at least none outside Britain and Ireland'. God works in every country,

---

1 Jurgen Moltmann (1977) *The Church in the Power of the Spirit: A Contribution to Messianic Ecclesiology* (London: SCM Press).
2 USPG: Anglicans in World Mission (2008) *Our Theological Basis and Ways of Working.*

Anglican churches are found in most countries, and USPG supports their work in between sixty and seventy countries. We should watch our language and stop talking about 'going on mission', 'short-term missions', 'mission teams', and so on.

The frontier of mission is no longer primarily a geographical one. Indeed, what we have been saying about the *missio Dei* raises fundamental questions about the kind of imperialism which shaped mission in the colonial age, where mission was about moving from the world that immediately surrounded the church to beyond the frontiers of the empire(s) of Christendom. It also raises questions about new and more contemporary imperialism – geo-political, economic, and intellectual – which can be seen as shaping mission in our own day.

This mission shift away from such Christendom thinking was described by the 1963 meeting of the Commission on World Mission and Evangelism, in Mexico, in this way: the missionary frontier now runs around the world, it is the line which separates belief from unbelief, the unseen frontier which cuts across other frontiers and presents the universal Church with its primary missionary challenge.

So the *missio Dei* both challenges each one of us with the need to do mission in our own situation, and also causes us to rethink how we relate to the rest of the world.

In *Transforming Mission*, David Bosch summarised how people had seen mission in the past.

> During preceding centuries mission was understood in a variety of ways. Sometimes it was interpreted primarily in soteriological terms: as saving individuals from eternal damnation. Or it was understood in cultural terms: as introducing people from East and the South to the blessings and privileges of the Christian West. Often it was perceived in ecclesiastical categories: as the expansion of the church (or of a specific denomination). Sometimes it was defined salvation-historically: as the process by which the world—evolutionary or by means of a cataclysmic event—would be transformed into the Kingdom of God.

He went on to describe the new emphases within *missio Dei*.

> Mission was understood as being derived from the very nature of God. It was thus put in the context of the doctrine of the Trinity, not of ecclesiology or soteriology. The classical doctrine on the missio Dei as God the Father sending the Son, and God the Father and the Son sending the Spirit was expanded to include yet another 'movement': The Father, Son and the Holy Spirit sending the church into the world. As far as missionary thinking was concerned, this linking with the doctrine of the Trinity constituted an important innovation ... Our mission has no life of its own: only in the hands of the sending God can it truly be called mission. Not least since the missionary initiative comes from God alone ... Mission is thereby seen as a movement from God to the world; the church is viewed as an instrument for that mission. There is church because there is mission, not vice versa.[1]

---

1 Bosch, *op. cit.*, p. 390.

Let me end this more theological introduction to *missio Dei* by noting two opposing directions in which it has been interpreted or misinterpreted, so leading us away from where some of us might think it should be taking us, and giving one word of warning.

The first direction, and in many ways in reaction to its Barthian origins, has been to emphasise the worldly context of the *missio Dei* and to see God's engagement in the world as primarily humanistic. This rather modalist God, stripped of any real Trinitarian character or relationship, creates the world, identifies with it in Jesus, and remains active through the Spirit who blows wherever he (or she) wills. The Law is not so much transformed by grace as replaced by a new kind of good works. Programmes like the World Council of Churches' 'The World sets the Agenda' – which I have to say profoundly influenced my own training and early ministry – are often accused of having reinforced this trend. It is found in the critique which liberation theology makes of even the global and holistic agenda of someone like David Bosch. It is seen today in many Christian charities, and in Development Agencies who have much to say about 'life before death' but without any larger context of life beyond it. It assesses the Church not as part of the activity of God but in terms of whether it can deliver certain goods.

In the opposing corner is the second direction in which *missio Dei* may be seen by some of us to have been misinterpreted, where the emphasis on God's initiative and agency is taken to mean that only those who are in conscious relationship with Christ or his Church can be caught up in it.

For some, this leads to the more Evangelical/Charismatic belief that God only works, or at least works most effectively, through those who have in some way been 'born again' or who are filled with the Spirit.

For others, the role of the Church is so understood within the *missio Dei* as to see little or none of God's activity beyond its confines. This may be being particularly evident where a more Catholic or Orthodox ecclesiology regards the church as the ark of salvation.

Finally, the danger that needs noting is John Taylor's warning about what he called this 'gloriously inclusive term'. He said 'There is an inherent, if not deliberate vagueness in the term "Mission of God" which lays it open to abuse. It can be made to include anything under the sun that anyone considers a Good Thing.' [1]

2. The Five Marks of Mission

As one way of putting some of this into practical form, and to avoid what I have suggested could be distorting directions, let me turn to the Five Marks of Mission.

I'm aware that these began as an Anglican formulation – although one of the things which interests me is the relationship between Anglicanism, with its incarnational and sacramental emphases, and Mission in both its historical and contemporary expressions, and I was asked to write an introductory paper on this for last year's Lambeth Conference. [2] But although the Five Marks of Mission originated within

---

1 John V Taylor (1998) *The Uncancelled Mandate* (London: Church House Publishing) pp 1–2.

2 TEAC Signposts No 2 (2008) *Towards an Anglican Understanding of Mission and Evangelism*, Anglican Communion Office.

the Anglican Communion, they have been adopted far more widely, perhaps more in Protestant than Catholic circles, and for many people they provide a template for how the Church is engaging with the *missio Dei.*

The first thing to say about the Five Marks of Mission is that they begin with the statement: 'the mission of the Church is the mission of Christ.'[1] If we see the *missio Dei* as the overflowing of God into the world, nowhere is that more evident and more effectual than in the life, death and resurrection of Jesus.

Many see the Five Marks holding together the various aspects of mission:

1) To proclaim the Good News of the Kingdom;

2) To teach, baptise and nurture new believers;

3) To respond to human need by loving service;

4) To seek to transform unjust structures of society.

And, added a little later;

5) To strive to safeguard the integrity of creation and sustain and renew the life of the earth

Many churches find these five marks a useful check list for their engagement in mission. But they are not without their dangers. The Anglican Communion's own Commission in Mission (Missio), meeting in Ely in 1996, raised some of these.[2] First, as we've already noted, they must not obscure the fact that it's God's mission not ours. Then, do they sufficiently take into account the different contexts in which churches find themselves? Next, do they take seriously enough the life of the churches themselves? For we are called to be not just doers of mission but a people of mission: that is, says the report, 'we are learning to allow every dimension of church life to be shaped and directed by our identity as a sign, foretaste and instrument of God's reign in Christ.'

Within this comes that central activity in the life of the church – our Worship. To quote the report again, 'worship is not just something we do alongside our witness to the good news: worship is itself a witness to the world. It is a sign that all of life is holy, that hope and meaning can be found in offering ourselves to God (cf. Romans 12:1). And each time we celebrate the Eucharist, we proclaim Christ's death until he comes (1 Cor. 11:26). Our liturgical life is a vital dimension of our mission calling; and although it is not included in the Five Marks, it undergirds the forms of public witness listed there.'

On these more ecclesiological questions, I found Tim Yates' article on David Bosch and 'Ecclesiology in the Emerging Missionary Paradigm' very useful.[3] Yates says that 'Ecclesiology provided the essential antidote to a world of post-Enlightenment individualism which had spawned the voluntarist missionary societies as its missionary expression.' He also reminds us that Bosch believed in 'theory' – unapologetically 'from above', living as he did before the time of postmodern suspicion – and also

1 Report of the Sixth meeting of the Anglican Consultative Council, Anglican Communion Office, 1984. *Bonds of Affection.*

2 Report of the Inter-Anglican Commission on Mission and Evangelism (2006) *Communion in Mission,* Anglican Communion Office: www.anglicancommunion.org/ministry/mission/fivemarks.cfm.

3 Timothy Yates (2009) 'David Bosch: South African Context, Universal Missiology – Ecclesiology in the Emerging Missionary Paradigm', *International Bulletin of Missionary Research* (April) pp. 72–8.

– contrary to the criticism from liberation theologians – 'praxis', but he added a third element, 'poiesis': the need for beauty and for worship.

So, returning to the Five Marks of Mission, some have wanted to add more marks acknowledging the life, and the worship, of the Church. From another direction the Anglican Consultative Council meeting in Jamaica in May 2009 sought a different sixth Mark, on Reconciliation: it endorsed a request from the Anglican Church of Canada to add one relating to peace, conflict transformation and reconciliation. We will have to wait and see how this develops.

But there is something still more fundamental to say about the Five Marks, which takes us back to the nature of the *missio Dei*: how do we interpret the first Mark, and is it just one amongst five or do the rest follow from it and depend upon it? That 1996 report from the Anglican Communion commission[1] said that the first mark of mission, which was 'identified at [the sixth meeting of the Anglican Consultative Council] with personal evangelism, is really a summary of what *all* mission is about, because it is based on Jesus' own summary of his mission (Matthew 4:17, Mark 1:14–15, Luke 4:18, Luke 7:22; cf. John 3:14–17). Instead of being just one (albeit the first) of five distinct activities, this should be the key statement about *everything* we do in mission.' Is that right? More particularly, is the *Missio* Report right to identify the first Mark so explicitly with Personal Evangelism?

So we are back at the questions: what is God doing in the world and where does it connect with the response of the individual and the life of the Church? The answer to these questions will determine how we engage in mission – including how we relate to people of other faiths, yet another issue which there is no time to address here – and therefore what kind of mission activities we set up. It's that, in terms of mission and other agencies, to which I turn in my final section.

3. Mission and other Agencies

I have been asked to directly address how USPG seeks to engage in the *missio Dei*, perhaps in contrast to other agencies. I've already said that USPG's theological state- ment roots our work in the mission of the Triune God. Recent Anglican theology of church and mission has majored on the Trinity,[2] and although aware of the danger of over-structuralising what we believe here[3] it does root our identity as part of God's drawing-in and sending-out activity. That leads us to four central emphases.

The first is holistic mission. So all the issues raised here about the priority, inter- pretation and inter-relationship of the Five Marks of Mission, and what may need adding to them, come into play. I want to affirm our belief that the witness of Scrip- ture to the activity of God – in creation, through the saving acts of Christ, and looking to the coming together of all things in Christ – gives us an agenda far wider and deeper than either a crusading evangelism or what might unkindly be called a social gospel. Those who fail to preach Christ (but, remember, Christ crucified), *and* those who fail to see Christ in the poor, have minimised the *missio Dei*.

1 *Communion in Mission,* op. cit., www.anglicancommunion.org/ministry/mission/fivemarks.
2 *The Virginia Report,* Report of the Lambeth Conference 1998 – www.lambethconference.org/1998/documents/report-1.pdf.
3 Bruce Kaye (2008), *An Introduction to World Anglicanism* (Cambridge: Cambridge University Press).

The second is our commitment to the Church. When we extended our name to "Anglicans in World Mission" we were aware how counter-cultural this could be. Who, in this day and age, wants to identify with an inherited, institutional church? Fundamentalists who (although they pretend the opposite) are the products of Modernism, and charismatic evangelicals who (although they cannot see it) are the children of post-Modernism, prefer to choose their own loyalties. But USPG – and maybe it will be our undoing – works with the Church because we believe that it is an integral part of the *missio Dei* and, for us, the Anglican Communion is a 'given', literally our communion is a gift from God.

The third emphasis arises from the challenges of being post-colonial and coping with the plurality of contexts. We try, in this post-Christendom era, to play our part in the worldwide Church in the spirit of 'inter-dependence and mutual responsibility', and to recognise and respect the different and sometimes conflicting contexts in which our partners are seeking to engage in God's mission. That determines how we understand the Anglican Communion with its current tensions, and how as a Society we decide about priorities and budgets: we start from the basis that relationships come before resource-sharing, we do our decision-making together with partners, and they largely nominate how their allocation of money, personnel and scholarships will be used. Our Advocacy agenda also arises directly out of their concerns. Again, all this may be our undoing, because it flies in the face of the kind of sponsorship, even ownership, which now dominates our donor culture.

The final emphasis guiding the future of USPG needs to be a dynamic spirituality, although I admit that all the pressures of fund-raising for the more attractive kind of Development projects has sometimes threatened to unbalance us here. Again we return to the Holy Trinity, for in the end our assurance and the energy for our activity does not depend upon an institution or a book, but from the love of the Father, incorporating us in the Son, through the power of the Spirit.

I believe that the *missio Dei* can help us avoid the pitfalls into which other agencies may have fallen. Mission must be about real and costly engagement with the world, embracing all that is meant by prophetic dialogue, but not to the extent where some Christian Development agencies and many Christian charities play down the first and second Marks of Mission, concentrating on humanitarian work and justice issues, and ignoring both personal evangelism and the life of the church. That seems very like the Pelagian heresy.

Equally, for USPG mission must be about acknowledging and proclaiming the centrality of Jesus Christ, but not to the extent of those who interpret the first Mark of Mission in such a way that the *missio Dei* becomes a marketing and recruitment exercise where success will only be measured by individual conversion and church membership. That seems to me where the Gnostic heretics were heading.

God's activity in the world is larger and more challenging than all of these. And that's why we like to say in USPG that 'Mission is an adventure', God's adventure, which he calls us to join in.

Ann Morisy [1]

Mission as transformation

Faith? A positive link with wellbeing...

- 'Doing business with God' – American researchers suggest that going to church once a week improves people's wellbeing equivalent to their salary being doubled (cited in 'Life Satisfaction: The State of Knowledge and Implications for Government' published by The Prime Minister's Strategy Unit, Dec. 2002).

- Also the work of Dan Blazer and Erdman Palmore 'Religion and Aging in a Longitudinal Panel' *The Gerontologist*, Vol 16 (1) 1976 – and this work has been regularly repeated by other researchers and on each occasion a positive experience of growing old is strongly linked with 'doing business with God'.

- *Religious experience* has survival value i.e. when people feel they are at rock bottom or in a sudden crisis from which they have no way out, the experience of God's 'alongsideness' enable people to 'dig deeper and hang in. And particularly significantly, having once had a religious experience the person is invariably more open to the needs and fragility of others; Religious experience lessens the likelihood of 'authoritarianism' (i.e. assuming one is right and everyone else is wrong) and reassures that 'all will be well and all manner of things will be well'. (See David Hay, 2006 *Something There* [London: DLT])

Faith is good for *young people*...Who says?

- John J Dilulio [2] ... regularly!
- Leslie Francis and Mandy Robbins [3] regarding urban 13–15 year-olds in England.

In the report *Spiritual Health and the Well-Being of Urban Young People* by Leslie Francis and Mandy Robbins [4] the following findings were noted:

- – Confirmation of lots of other research that having a sense of purpose is important to the flourishing of young people.

---

1 This paper © Ann Morisy 2010.
2 Google 'John J Dilulio' 'Faith Factor' for more, also visit www.religionandsocialpolicy.org. Also of interest may be Ronald J Sider and Heidi Rolland (2005) *Saving Souls, Serving Society* (Oxford: OUP).
3 Leslie J Francis and Mandy Robbins (2006), *Urban Hope and Spiritual Health: The Adolescent Voice* (London: Epworth Press).
4 *Spiritual Health and the Well-Being of Urban Young People* by Gwyther Rees, Leslie J. Francis and Mandy Robbins, published by the Commission on Urban Life and Faith, University of Wales, Bangor, The Children's Society. Copies of this report (two versions are available – 8 page or the fuller 32 page version) can be downloaded from www.childrenssociety.org.uk/resources/documents/Research/Spiritual_Health_and_the_Well_Being_of_Urban_Young_People_3194.html. This reseach has been written up in more detail in Leslie J Francis and Mandy Robbins (2006), *op. cit.*

- Young people were more likely to have a sense of purpose if they:
  - had a religious affiliation;
  - prayed regularly;
  - believed in eternal life.

Detailed analysis suggested that each of these 3 factors were independently related to 'sense of purpose' (i.e. these 3 religious factors were not attributable to economic differences etc). Young people who were identified as having a religious affiliation and / or were regularly involved in prayer fared better than other young people on a number of different measures of wellbeing:

- they will more likely to have a 'sense of purpose';
- they will be more likely to have an active and constructive relationship with the community and the environment;
- they will be more likely to have positive views towards ethnic diversity.

The independent significance of religious affiliation and prayer in relation to sense of purpose and overall wellbeing suggests that a strong spiritual dimension to young people's lives might act as a protective factor, promoting well-being and mitigating the impact of other factors such as poverty and family change.[1]

Why focus on positive psychology?

I focus on positive psychology because positive psychologists are not theologians or Christian missioners! And because of this they pass what John Rawls terms 'the test of public reason' unlike perceived self-interested recommendations or commendations made by the theologian or the clergy, or the committed lay person for that matter. Let me re-code – or decode Rawls' term 'the test of public reason'…. 'Self-praise is no recommendation!' In our secular world, all faiths have to submit themselves to the test of public reason if they are to have a right to a public platform.

A fraudulent narrative of transformation: that money makes us happy

Richard Layard, the economist who has pioneered work on wellbeing and wealth,[2] makes a case that is almost shocking in its simplicity: *Even for those who are only moderately financially secure, more money brings disappointment.*

Layard's analysis highlights 'habituation' (which means we quickly get used to our circumstances), as one of the reasons why the anticipated delight associated with high earnings or a windfall dulls quite quickly. Basically we get used to what we have and the lifestyle associated with wealth becomes routine.

The second factor that Layard identifies is that of status anxiety. We cannot resist comparing our circumstances with others: rivalry is hard to resist. So, rather than relax in financial security, we find ourselves having to negotiate a new batch of worries about losing out on the advantages that others have secured. In other words, we rarely assess our circumstances objectively, but rather we assess them in comparison with others.

---

1 The report *Spiritual Health and the Well-Being of Urban Young People* from which this evidence was drawn was produced in 2005 and was based on the analysis of surveys returned by 23,418 young people living in urban areas.

2 Richard Layard, (2005) *Happiness: Lessons from a new science* (London: Allen Lane).

One of the most fraudulent narratives that has infused our world, is that money and happiness go together. Get money; spend money; get possessions (or 'Get Stuff'); become secure; relax and enjoy. This has been the implicit life plan that has dominated our lives for more than a century; it is a five act play of seduction.

The cat is out of the bag: once you can meet the cost of accommodation, clothing and food, then more money adds only a little to one's wellbeing. Liz Hoggard, on the basis of her work on the television programme 'Making Slough Happy', comments that, 'Wealth is like health: its absence breeds misery, but having it doesn't guarantee happiness.' And she goes on to say, 'Chasing money rather than meaning in life is a formula for discontent.'[1]

Having a sense that one's life has meaning is the essential foundation for a sense of wellbeing. Interestingly, the research being undertaken by positive psychologists suggests that our capacity for wellbeing is not just to do with our genes and circumstances, but that there is vast scope for *intentional activities,* even when confronted by the direst circumstances.

History provides evidence of how faith practices can enable people – especially those in dire circumstances (including addictions) – to rise above those circumstances and engage in life-enhancing *intentional activity.* This is the challenge to pastoral care that early Methodism and early Salvationism pioneered to such good effect. They achieved this because, as positive psychologists now acknowledge, the ability to make sense of our actions within a larger frame gives vital motivation to embrace the intentional activity that enables us to resist being *victims* of troublesome circumstances.

Circumstances matter, but not as much as we think…

The work of positive psychologists suggests that circumstances matter, but not as much as we think. There is an inclination to cede too much potency to 'circumstances' in making sense of our lives, 'circumstances' have acquired a more potent status in our life script than is warranted.

Our inclination to overestimate the degree to which we are limited by circumstances may be due to what psychologists refer to as 'the focusing illusion',[2] i.e. 'Nothing in life is quite as important as you think it is while you are thinking about it.'

---

1 Liz Hoggard (2005) 'How to be Happy' (London: BBC Books) p. 64.

2 'The focusing illusion helps explain why the results of well-being research are often counter-intuitive. The false intuitions may arise from a failure to recognize that people do not continuously think about their circumstances, whether positive or negative– nothing in life is quite as important as you think it is while you are thinking about it. Individuals who have recently experienced a significant life change (e.g. becoming disabled, winning a lottery, or getting married) surely think of their new circumstances many times each day, but the allocation of attention eventually changes, so that they spend most of their time attending to and drawing pleasure or displeasure from experiences such as having breakfast or watching television… For example an experiment in which students were asked: (i) "How happy are you with your life in general?" and (ii) "How many dates did you have last month?" The correlation between the answers to these questions was –0.012 (not statistically different from 0) but when they were asked in the reverse order, the correlation rose to 0.66 with another sample of students. [By asking] the dating question first, this evidently caused that aspect of life to become salient and its importance to be exaggerated when the respondents encountered the more general question about their happiness.' From Kahneman D., Krueger A.B., Schkade D., *et al.,* 2006. 'Would you be happier if you were richer? A focusing illusion'. *Science, 312,* 1908-10. (Article available at www.sciencemag.org/cgi/content/abstract/312/5782/1908.)

Positive psychology, which has been energised by the work of Martin Seligman,[1] is based on research that suggests we are inclined to overestimate the impact of circumstances on our lives and *underestimate* the scope we have for 'intentional activity'. There are three things that have been identified as having an impact on wellbeing, as illustrated below.[2]

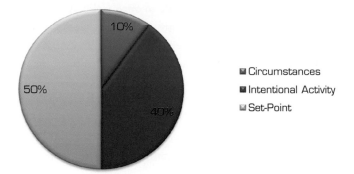

The set-point comes from our genes. Our genes play a significant part in whether we are upbeat or prone to gloom. This doesn't mean that those with gloomy genes can never be happy, just that when happy the gloomy genes are prone to pull us back to our 'set-point'.

The surprise is how little impact 'circumstances' have on people's wellbeing. Research suggests just ten percent. If we can get the motivation to engage in positive or meaningful intentional activities, circumstances associated with health, money, and even upbringing have a surprisingly small impact on wellbeing. So lottery winners are no happier one year after their win, and at the other end of the scale, people with paralysis are often not as unhappy as might be expected.[3]

This potent model suggests we are inclined to over-rate the impact of circumstances and underestimate the significance of our 'agency' (i.e. our ability to engage in meaningful intentional activities), and it is this that helps to account for the effectiveness of religious commitment and practice in coaching and sustaining change in people's lives.

Attitude matters

The commitment to follow Jesus in the way he lived his life, is a major contributor to empowerment which enables a sense of purpose to flourish. Embracing a faith commitment impacts on our attitude to our circumstances, and when our attitudes change so too do the micro-actions in which we engage.

Layard quotes Victor Frankl, who concluded from his experiences in Auschwitz that in the last resort 'everything can be taken from a man but one thing, the last of human

---

1 Martin Seligman founded the field of positive psychology in 2000. He directs the Positive Psychology Center at the University of Pennsylvania.

2 S. Lyubomirsky, K M Sheldon, and D Schkade (2005), 'Pursuing Happiness: The Architecture of Sustainable Change,' *Review of General Psychology*, Special Issue: Positive Psychology 9 (20: 111–31).

3 See the work of Andrew Oswald and Nattavudh Pawdthavee (Sept. 2005), 'Does Happiness Adapt? A Longitudinal Study of Disability with Implications for Economists and Judges' (Mimeo: University of Warwick).

freedoms – to choose one's attitude in any given set of circumstances.'[1] Becoming a Christian is about making an effort to choose one's attitude to one's circumstances.

Methodism and the Salvation Army

Rather than crushing the spirits of the new industrial proletariat, a case can be made that religious enthusiasm, and Methodism in particular 'may have helped the working men to face the challenges of the burgeoning industrial order, and others have added, may even have prepared them for a later socialism. Even Marxist historians were prepared to grant that Methodism had made many men "better rebels".'[2] To be a good rebel involves the capacity to resist the norms and sanctions on one's behaviour, it is, like revolution, the epitome of shaking oneself free from circumstances and opting for intentional behaviour, and the suggestion is that Methodism accomplished this amongst 'the anxious – the dislocated, the rootless, the disturbed.'[3]

There is one area where it is particularly difficult to step beyond circumstances, and this is in relation to addictions, where intentional activity consolidates or fuses with our circumstances. Addiction saps our best intentions, closing the door on other possibilities for life. But again history points to the ability of faith, and faith practices to help people break through the entrapping circumstances of addiction.

In 1865 the Salvation Army was co-founded by William and Catherine Booth. William was a Methodist preacher, and together they took the notion of Wesleyan holiness to 'the submerged tenth'. The movement spread rapidly, and was perhaps one of the earliest 'popular' global movements. It was a bold and innovative movement, seeking to engage with the poorest and most broken, often by chronic alcohol abuse. The Salvation Army achieved what today seems impossible:[4] to invite those broken and damaged by circumstances to positions of responsibility and leadership, that is to become sufficiently free of addiction to be able to embrace intentional activity.

In our culture which is dismissive of hierarchy and resentful of authority, the firmly hierarchical practice of the Salvation Army is easy to write off. Even if it did succeed in helping people to get free of addiction to alcohol and grinding poverty, the Salvation Army is dismissed because this was achieved at the cost of personal freedom, as people were recruited as soldiers and embellished with many of the trappings of the military, including the requirement to obey senior members. But this is to ignore some outstanding achievements in relation to intentional activity.

It may be apocryphal, but the witness of the woman who declares that 'I'd rather have my husband beat the Salvation Army drum than beat me!' is one of the early cries of the emancipation of women – and a description of transformation. The Salvation Army encouraged women as much as men into positions of leadership, and likewise those of African or Indian heritage. Whilst the Salvation Army might have modelled itself on a military chain of command, it also undermined the patriarchal power of

---

1 Cited by Layard (2005) *op.cit.*, p. 8, taken from Victor Frankl (1985), *Man's Search for Meaning* (New York: Basic Books).

2 Semmel (1973) *op.cit.* p. 4, Semmel's reference to the Hammonds is to Hammond, J.L. and B. (1918) *The Town Labourer*, 1760-1832 (London: Longmans Green) p. 287.

3 Ibid p. 7.

4 It could be said that Alcoholics Anonymous achieve this today.

the Victorian household,[1] and put into practice the Gospel teaching that we are all God's children, regardless of gender and ethnicity – a thoroughly transformational notion in that period.

So how now?

If mission is to be about transformation them perhaps it has to build-up our confidence in the economy of abundance – as much as we have invested in – and believe in the economy of scarcity.

We are so caught up in this pursuit of things that are on offer in the market that we find it hard to believe that there is also a reliable economy[2] of abundance. The tendency has been for the church – and others to assume that economy of abundance belongs to the realm of Heaven rather than earth.

And this brings us to Jesus. Jesus, through his death and resurrection rescues us from our sin, but Jesus also brings salvation to us through the way in which he lived his life. In his actions and teaching, Jesus shows us how we can participate in this reliable economy of abundance.

Jesus lived his life in a very distinctive way. This included:

- *Eschewing Power* – Being alert to how easy it might be for him to become powerful in the land. He seems to make a point of resisting the things that would lead to him becoming powerful in the world's terms. (Being powerful and being authoritative are not the same thing.);

- *Willing to risk being overwhelmed* – Always risking the possibility that he might be overwhelmed, not feeling he has to be in control all the time and being willing to take risks that might make the establishment people furious with him;

- *Subverting the 'status quo'* – Challenging the taken-for granted ways of doing things and understanding things, including religious practice;

- *Wide 'fraternal' relations* – Seeing our concern for others as going well beyond our own family or neighbours or 'tribe'. If God is our heavenly father all his children become our brothers and sisters;

- *Avoiding tit-for tat' behaviour* – Avoiding escalating differences and trying to get one's own back and have the last word – but also standing his ground;

- *Investing in the most unlikely* – The people whom Jesus chose were not the most obvious 'top team', in fact very often they were people whom others had written-off.

My thesis is straightforward:

---

1 See Lynne Marks 'The Hallelujah Lasses: Working Class Women in the Salvation Army in English Canada 1882-92' in Franca Iacovetta and Mariana Valverde (eds) (1992) *Gender Conflicts* (Toronto: University of Toronto Press) p. 67–118.

2 The word 'economy' can be traced back to the Greek word 'one who manages a household' (hmm... women's work?). According to Wikipedia, the first recorded sense of the word 'economy' was found in a work possibly composed in 1440, is 'the management of economic affairs', in this case, of a monastery.

When we muster an intention to do things like Jesus, i.e. to follow Jesus – even in the most modest of ways – we arrive at the portal into the economy of abundance, where virtuous processes flow and grace cascades;

By doing it like Jesus (even just a tad, and even just with the intention – because there is so much grace around) we trigger virtuous processes that gain momentum;

This relevance and transformational power of faith make it urgent to articulate and promote the resources at the heart of faithfulness that lead to human flourishing. And we need others to help us pass the test of public reason – it is not sufficient for our theologians or evangelists to simply assert the virtuous processes that faith sets in train.

But more than this, in our troubled times, the faiths have to forego investing and promulgating 'hard-to-believe' formulaic faith – which for post-modern and troubled times are so hard to believe that the come close to a fresh expression of... Gnosticism.

So there is a new evangelistic challenge – to enable people to weigh-up whether by following Jesus they can:

- Achieve a way of making sense of their lives;
- A means of sustaining virtuous intentional behaviour;
- Avoid judging some as deserving and some 'undeserving' (because of being beaten by their circumstances).

Wonsuk Ma

Mission as proclamation

Theological motivation for Pentecostal mission: a case of Mission as Proclamation

Introduction

Three Models of Mission

The three models of Christian mission have been around in various expressions for some time now, particularly in the last century: *missio Dei*; mission as transformation; and mission as proclamation. These three theological themes are initial findings suggested by data collected among churches and mission agencies in Britain and Ireland. The conference invitation further elaborates on each:

- *Missio Dei*: God is at work in the world and mission is essentially about following God's agenda and making it explicit.

- Mission as Transformation: Mission is in essence about transforming individuals and society with an emphasis on liberation theology, bias to the poor.

- Mission as Proclamation: [Mission is in essence the] proclamation of Jesus Christ as universal saviour.[1]

A couple of initial observations are in order. First, although it is never said, everyone understands that this is an oversimplification of the complex nature of mission theology and practice. Even some words in the brief explanations can easily be contested. Secondly, there is an underlying assumption in this continuum that the first represents the extreme 'left' and the last, the far 'right' (theologically and often politically). Thirdly, more pertinent to the present discussion, the continuum spans between the universality of God and the exclusivity of Christianity. *Missio Dei*, for instance, is not compatible with *Missio Christi*, as the former suggests universality of God's restoration, while the latter insists on the exclusivity of the Christian claim for salvation. While the very definition of mission is far from settled, so will be its theological basis and practical approaches. There is no doubt that this is a fundamental challenge as the Church plans to present a clear message of God's love and restoration to an incredibly diverse world.

---

1 'Speakers' Briefing Note' for BIAMS–Global Connections–Global Mission Network conference on 'Sinking Foundations: Why Mission Today?' (All Nations Christian College, UK, July 2009.) The order of the second and the third is adjusted.

The Task at Hand

My task here is to expand on the theological basis and practical outworkings of the third model: Mission as Proclamation. Although institutionally I represent a community which has pioneered various aspects of 'Mission as Transformation,' I suspect that my affinities to the Korean missionary movement and Pentecostalism may have led the organizers to assign me the study on 'Mission as Proclamation.' As I am theologically familiar with Pentecostalism, I decided to look at the Pentecostal mission theology and practice as an exemplar. It is assumed that readers are familiar enough with Pentecostalism.

While Pentecostalism can be defined and characterized in various ways, for this reflection I am taking a rather narrow scope of the global Pentecostal-charismatic family. Denominational Pentecostals or the first wave (or 'Classical Pentecostals') are more identifiable than Charismatics or the third category (sometimes called Neo-Charismatics), and for this practical reason, I am limiting my discussion to this group. They are doctrinally more coherent than the rest; they have been more articulate in their theology and spirituality than the others. But this comparison is only relative, and we need to keep in mind theological diversity that is present among classical or denominational Pentecostals, especially when they are transplanted in the global South.

Having argued for the availability of resources among classical Pentecostals, a challenge remains as much of the 'articulation' of their theology is embedded in songs, sermons, prayers and practices. The task of unearthing the assumed theological construct is never an easy task. Colorfully presented narrative preaching, for instance, employs nuances, illustrations and culturally interpretable symbols. The same message may be communicated in a radically different mode and language in a different socio-cultural context. This is, however, not to ignore an increasing number of scholarly researches and reflections.

Hermeneutical Roots of Pentecostal Mission Theology

Any theological investigation needs seriously to consider hermeneutical strategies of a particular group. Pentecostals' hermeneutical strategy influences how to read the scriptures and interpret their life towards their theological construct. Obviously much of Pentecostals' unique hermeneutical ethos was in development through the end of the nineteenth century. The following discussion is intended to be a brief presentation of key hermeneutical sources for Pentecostal mission theology.

Literalism

Pentecostals have maintained a notion that the more literally one takes the scripture, the more faithful one becomes to the word of God, thus the will of God. This led them to take all the narrative presentations as historical. Thus, denial of the historicity of any event recorded in the scripture is unacceptable. This is in part a reaction of conservative Christians against critical reading of the Bible, originating from the nineteenth century German scholarship, gradually spreading to Europe and North

America. Therefore, Pentecostals' firm belief in the supernatural work of God is based on their literalistic reading of the Bible. Another implication of their literalistic reading is the question of intent. The inclusion of a narrative pattern, according to them, has intent of normativity. Speaking in tongues as 'the initial physical evidence' of baptism in the Holy Spirit[1] is based on the recurrence of tongue-speaking in relation to the presence of the Spirit in the book of Acts. And this implication of Pentecostals' literalistic reading, such as 'snake handling,' has been hotly contested from without and within.

Restorational Impulse

As the twentieth century dawned, there is evidence of heightened interest in eschatology. One stream is the expectation of the early church restored with the manifestation of the spiritual gifts, particularly the supernatural kind found in 1 Cor. 11. Thus, healing houses and communities proliferated throughout North America, and not without controversy.[2] The expectation of prophecy was another. However, at the core was the outpouring of the Holy Spirit, out of which other spiritual gifts would flow. Camp meetings were a common annual feature for devout believers and their families to experience personal revival. The book of Acts was the most favourite book of the Bible, as it records the feat of the early churches and their Spirit-filled heroes. One of the most popular expressions among the late nineteenth century Holiness and early twentieth century Pentecostal believers was 'apostolic.' Countless Pentecostal periodicals and newspapers printed this word; and the dawning of the new century reinforced their eager expectation of the 'latter rain' to mark the end of the end time.

Participatory Process: Place of Community

The role of community as the locus of a hermeneutical process has been well recognized. Naturally worship is the main feature which provides religious experiences, theological formation and the shared process of theology-making. To begin with, Pentecostal worship, with not only singing and prayers and even preaching, is incredibly participatory in nature, often blurring the demarcation between the pulpit and the pews. One excellent example is the 'testimony' time, where anyone can be the 'main speaker'. This provides any member of the community with an opportunity to contribute to the corporate deposit of theology and also for the community to exercise the 'gift' of discernment, evaluation and shared ownership of the presented experience and its interpretation. This community is also the space where some spiritual gifts, such as prophecy or message in tongues, are exercised. For this reason, it is argued that Pentecostals indeed have a well-developed liturgical tradition, but it is, unlike the traditional ones, informal, spontaneous, oral, and often more than oral as

---

1 For example, the eigth of the (US) 'Assemblies of God Fundamental Truths' (ag.org/top/Beliefs/Statement_of_Fundamental_Truths/sft_short.cfm), accessed on 16 March 2010, reads, 'We believe…the initial physical evidence of the baptism in the Holy Spirit is "speaking in tongues", as experienced on the day of Pentecost and referenced throughout Acts and the Epistles.'

2 Vinson Synan, (2000) 'A Healer in the House? A Historical Perspective on Healing in the Pentecostal/Charismatic Tradition' *Asian Journal of Pentecostal Studies* 3:2, pp. 189-201. Also Allan Anderson, (2004) *An Introduction to Pentecostalism* (Cambridge: Cambridge University Press) pp. 30–3.

the whole body is involved in dancing, clapping and other movements.[1] At the end, Pentecostals have demonstrated a strong community-forming potential through the shared belief in and experience of the Holy Spirit.

The Role of Experience

Another important aspect of restorational thinking is the recovery of the dimension of religious experience. Unlike the Reformer's notion of the Holy Spirit as a shy member of the Trinity, Pentecostals, based on their reading in Luke-Acts, have re-profiled the Holy Spirit as the active player in the birth of the church, initiator of mission, and overseer of the spread of the gospel through empowerment.[2] Many experiences, whether supernatural or circumstantial, are all carefully initiated by the Holy Spirit. This has led Pentecostals into two important theological conclusions: 1) The Holy Spirit interacts with God's people through a wide range of religious experiences, including prophecy (Acts 11:22-23; 19:6; 21:9), dream and vision (Acts 9:10; 10:3), hearing voices (Acts 10:19; 16:9; 18:9), healing (Acts 3:1-8; 4:30), and the like; and 2) Such experiences not only enrich and embolden believers in their faith, but more importantly lead them into opportunities to witness to the risen Lord. It is true that this heavy weight on experiences and undue influence of experience over the Word has caused criticism. Nonetheless, with their literalistic reading of the Bible, religious experiences have a definite role in strengthening their sense of call and commitment to sacred vocation, as baptism in the Spirit (see below) will illustrate so well.

Theological Resources for Pentecostal Mission

It is already assumed that Pentecostal mission has had a strong emphasis on proclamation. Historically, the modern Pentecostal movement as an organized theological and spiritual tradition traces its origin in the nineteenth century Holiness movement of North America.[3] The fact that Charles Parham and William J. Seymour, the two most recognized Pentecostal 'fathers,' are Holiness preachers, illustrates this well. What is evident is that Pentecostalism came out of an extremely conservative stock of American Protestantism. Mission implications of four theological beliefs unique to Pentecostalism will be discussed.[4] To illustrate the beliefs and practices of early Pentecostals, reports published in *The Apostolic Faith* (*TAF*) of the Azusa Street Mission of Los Angeles (1906-1909) will be used. *TAF* is considered to be the most representative Pentecostal periodical of its formative years.

---

1 Walter J. Hollenweger, (1997) *Pentecostalism: Origins and Developments Worldwide* (Peabody, MA: Hendrickson), p. 47 traces Pentecostal oral, spontaneous and bodily liturgy to its African roots.

2 A pioneering work on this notion is Roger Stronstad, (2004) *The Charismatic Theology of St. Luke* (Peabody, MA: Hendrickson, 1984) and Robert P. Menzies, *Empowered for Witness: The Spirit in Luke-Acts* (London: T & T Clark).

3 I am well aware of arguments on multiple 'springhead' of the movement. For this reason, I used the qualifier, 'organized' theological and spiritual tradition.

4 On the contribution of pneumatology to Pentecostal mission, see Wonsuk Ma, (2007) "When the Poor Are Fired Up": The Role of Pneumatology in Pentecostal-Charismatic Mission', *Transformation* 24:1 (Jan 2007) pp. 28–34.

Baptism in the Spirit

This cardinal doctrine makes (classical) Pentecostals distinct from the rest of Christianity. Understood as an experience distinct from and subsequent to regeneration, belief in baptism in the Holy Spirit has caused a continuing debate between Pentecostals and Evangelicals. Based on the post-resurrection promise of the Lord that his followers would be baptized in the Holy Spirit, Pentecostals took it as a sign of the restoration of early church spirituality. Therefore, the reference to the 'latter rain' is fitting,[1] as it would restore the earlier experience, that is, the experience on the day of Pentecost (Acts 2). Although much has been written on the subject,[2] for the present discussion, three aspects of this belief will be explored with mission as proclamation in mind: experience, its interpretation and consequences.

As discussed above, Pentecostalism has brought back the significant role of religious experiences. Testimonies abound to the powerful impact of experiences loosely termed 'the baptism in the Holy Spirit'. Various life-changing stories are shared, although most North American classical Pentecostal churches insist on speaking in tongues as 'the physical and initial evidence'.[3] The sense of God's overwhelming presence is a common element of these experiences, as recorded in the first issue of *TAF*:

> **Proud, well-dressed preachers come in to 'investigate.' Soon their high looks are replaced with wonder, then conviction comes, and very often you will find them in a short time wallowing on the dirty floor, asking God to forgive them and make them as little children. It would be impossible to state how many have been converted, sanctified and filled with the Holy Ghost. They have been and are daily going out to all points of the compass to spread this wonderful gospel.[4]**

Speaking in tongues also brought tangible impact not only to the recipients of the Spirit baptism but also to those who witness them. It is no wonder that Pentecostalism spread like a wildfire. In fact, each issue of *TAF* has a substantial part of its pages dedicated to the reports of the spread of Pentecostal faith.

Such powerful experience is interpreted in various ways. First, as noted above, this was understood as a sure sign for the restoration of early church spirituality. Second, it shapes the self-identity of people who are called and commissioned to bring the news of salvation to the ends of the earth. Third, the experience is also interpreted as the enduing of power from above for witnessing in the context of Acts 1:8. Although classical Pentecostal denominations are divided between 'holiness' and 'non-Wesleyan' camps, the early Pentecostal literature made it clear that this is solely

---

1 The lead article of the second issue of *TAF* is illustrative: 'The Pentecostal Baptism Restored: The Promised Latter Rain Now Being Pours Out on God's Humble People', *TAF* 2 (Oct 1906), p. 1, cols. 1-2.

2 For example, the serious theological inquiry from a Pentecostal perspective by Frank D. Macchia, (2006) *Baptized in the Spirit: A Global Pentecostal Theology* (Grand Rapids: Zondervan).

3 Early testimonies are found in almost all the early Pentecostal periodicals of North America, and the best known among them is *TAF* of the Azusa Street Mission.

4 'Pentecostal Has Come: Los Angeles Being Visited by a Revival of Bible Salvation and Pentecost as Recorded in the Book of Acts', *TAF* 1 (Sept 1906), p. 1, col. 1.

for empowerment: 'The baptism with the Holy Spirit is not a work of grace but a gift of power.... The baptism with the Holy Ghost makes you a witness unto the uttermost parts of the earth. It gives you power to speak in the languages of the nations'.[1] Its biblical illustrations are often taken from Peter's bold preaching in Acts 2:14-40, and Stephen's courageous sermon in Acts 7:2-53. Last, especially at a popular level, baptism in the Spirit is understood to be the 'floodgate' of spiritual gifts including healing and miracles.

Consequences of this doctrine are evident in Pentecostal mission, often arguing that the pattern is found in the Book of Acts. The first is unbending commitment to mission. With a strong sense of calling to be witnesses 'to the end of the earth,' this revival movement quickly turned into a missionary movement. Heroic missionary achievements or passion, in spite of little or no training or support, is attributed to this sense of call. The second is zeal for preaching their 'full gospel.' In fact, tongue-speaking often functions as a reinforcement of this experience of call and empowerment. Some early Pentecostals even expected tongues to be a missionary language to bypass laborious language-learning.[2] Third, after the pattern of Acts, signs and wonders are expected in the context of mission. This power-orientation makes Pentecostals bold witnesses with claims of healings and miracles, albeit with many controversies surrounding them. The net result is the fast spread of the Pentecostal message and the expansion of the Pentecostal movement globally.[3] This pneumatologically-shaped missiology is well attested in a *TAF* report of an Azusa missionary in its early days:

> **A Pentecostal missionary has left for foreign lands, Bro. Thos. P. Mahler, a young man of German nationality. He has the gift of tongues besides the knowledge of several. He left here for San Bernardino. He may go by way of Alaska, Russia, Norway, Germany and to his destination in Africa. As our brother was leaving, Bro. Post spoke of his call and gave a message in tongues in regard to Bro. Mahler which he interpreted as follows: 'I have anointed this dear one with my Spirit, and he is a chosen vessel to me to preach the gospel to many, and to suffer martyrdom in Africa.[4]**

Prophethood of All Believers

This is closely related to the previous discussion on baptism in the Spirit. However, because of its significance in Pentecostal mission, a separate discussion is deemed necessary. This is almost a natural and logical outgrowth of the belief in baptism in the Holy Spirit. Peter's interpretation of the advent of the Holy Spirit on the day of Pentecost is important. In the Old Testament period, only a handful of leaders experienced the coming of the Spirit of God, such as the seventy elders (Num. 11), selected judges, first two kings of United Israel, and selected prophets. However, an

---

1 'The Enduement of Power', *TAF* 4 (Dec 1906), p. 2, col. 2.
2 'Russians Hear in Their Own Tongue', *TAF* 1 (Sept 1906), p. 4, col. 3.
3 A further exploration of its potential is found in Wonsuk Ma, (2005) 'Full Circle Mission: A Possibility of Pentecostal Missiology', *Asian Journal of Pentecostal Studies* 8:1, pp. 5-27.
4 'The Lord Sends Him', *TAF* 1 (Sept 1906), p. 4, col. 1.

eschatological expectation of the Old Testament is to break this exclusivity of the Spirit: everyone in God's community will experience the coming of the Spirit. This is the prophecy by Joel (2:28-9), which has its root in Moses' desire for the whole of Israel (Num. 11:29). This democratization of the Spirit is the gist of Peter's sermon in presenting the coming of the Holy Spirit on the day of Pentecost (Acts 2:16-21).

If anyone in God's community is baptized in the Holy Spirit, regardless of age, gender and social status, the calling, empowerment and commission for God's work is for every believer, thus, 'prophethood of all believers.' This theological paradigm should be understood within the context of Christianity in the West at the turn of the twentieth century. In spite of various expressions of 'every believer's prophetic call,' the dominant ministry paradigm among the established churches was clergy-oriented professionalism. Consequently, the clergy-laity divide was clearly established, and the new Pentecostal theology was a powerful challenge to the established norm.

The first evidence is the host of Azusa Mission missionaries who were laity, including many single women. The January 1907 issue of *TAF* published reports from 'Bro. and Sister Batman, Bro. and Sister Hutchins and Sister Lucy Farrow [who] sailed from England for Monrovia, Liberia, Africa'[1] and 'Mrs. Myrtle K. Shideler [who wrote] in New York on her way to Africa,'[2] among others. Particularly noted is the significant contribution of women in Pentecostal mission. Later this is expressed in Korea through the mobilization of lay women leaders in David Yonggi Cho's well-known cell group system. The second expression is found in mission networks, such as Youth With A Mission, which recruits, trains and mobilizes youth for mission. This is a radical expression of the liberation of ministry from the exclusive hands of elite clergy. Often advocating short-term missionary service, this movement and others have 'democratized' ministry and mission for every believer. Thirdly, an extension of this radical mission-thinking is the establishment and empowerment of, and transfer to, national and local leadership at the earliest opportunity. This paradigm was presented by Melvin Hodges, a Pentecostal missionary to Latin America, as a unique feature of Pentecostal missiology.[3] Undoubtedly this unique belief has made Pentecostalism the fastest growing religious movement in our day.

Eschatology

Early Pentecostals shared their eschatology with the late nineteenth century conservative pre-millennial orientation. The turn of the century provided a naïve expectation of the end of human history. Here is an example found in *TAF*:

> **All these 6,000 years, we have been fighting against sin and Satan. Soon we shall have a rest of 1,000 years.... We must go on to perfection and holiness, and get the baptism with the Holy Ghost, and not stop there, but go on to perfection and maturity. God has many things to teach us as we remain humble at His feet.**[4]

1 'Latest Report from Our Missionaries to Africa', *TAF* 5 (January 1907), p. 3, col. 1.
2 'Received Her Pentecost', *TAF* 5 (January 1907), p. 3, col. 1.
3 Melvin L. Hodges, (1963)*The Indigenous Church* (Springfield, MO: Gospel Publishing House).
4 'The Millenium [*sic!*]', *TAF* 1 (Sept 1906), p. 3, col. 3.

To this general sense associated with the beginning of a new century, the outpouring of the Holy Spirit was taken as a sure sign for the end of the end time, the last opportunity for the greatest harvest of souls before the return of the Lord. This created an incongruent theological system for Pentecostals, adopting the dispensational scheme of human history. With the fast closure of the church age, or the age of grace, the church is to be taken to heaven, before the return of the age where Jews are dealt with through tribulation. This formed the awareness of living at the 'five-to midnight' moment, giving them an extremely small window of opportunity desperately to save as many souls as possible as the 'latter day saints.' This eschatological consciousness made them extremely other-worldly oriented. Coupled with the religious consciousness of call and empowerment for witness, here we see the best ingredients for a significant mission movement. And that's exactly what we saw in the Pentecostal movement in the last one hundred years!

The Sept 2007 issue of *TAF* has the headline reading, 'In the Last Days: "And it shall come to pass in the last days, saith the Lord, I will pour out of My Spirit upon all flesh"—Acts 2:17.'[1] Although the reports under the heading are full of revivals in various places with little eschatological exposition, interestingly the same issue of *TAF* prints a song titled 'Jesus Is Coming,' the only one with full music throughout the two year publishing of the periodical. Its last stanza reads:

> **Jesus is coming! He's not far away!**
> **Jesus is coming! Jesus is coming!**
> **We'll care not to stay; the clouds are our chariots,**
> **The angels our guard; Jesus is coming!**
> **This truth is His word.**
> **Coming again, coming again,**
> **Jesus is coming, is coming to reign,**
> **The clouds are His chariots, the angels His guard,**
> **Jesus is coming, how precious His word.**[2]

The most important contribution of this eschatology to Pentecostal mission is the urgency of witnessing. It is assumed that 'one-way ticket missionaries' were strongly motivated by the eschatological urgency. It was not unusual that engaged young women broke off their engagements and left for their mission field.[3]

In spite of this powerful and positive contribution of this form of pre-millennialism with the expectation of the imminent return of the Lord, such clock-setting eschatology has to expire sooner or later. The gradual disappearance of eschatological messages from Pentecostal pulpits became evident as the movement now moves to the third generation. This coincides with the sudden surge of this-worldly

---

1 *TAF* 9 (Sept 1907), p. 1, col. 1.

2 'Jesus Is Coming', *TAF* 9 (Sept 1907), p. 4.

3 One example is Lillian Trasher who left for Egypt after breaking her engagement. She gave her life to caring for orphans and widows in Egypt until her death. See S. Shemeth, 'Trasher, Lillian Hunt', in Stanley M. Burgess and Eduard M. van der Maas (eds.), (2002) *New International Dictionary of Pentecostal and Charismatic Movements* (Grand Rapids, MI: Zondervan) p. 1153.

concerns, such as church growth, the message of blessings and health.[1] Fortunately, the dynamic motive of Pentecostal mission does seem to lie in the pneumatological interpretation rather than its temporal eschatological expectation, as the global Pentecostal movement has continued its growth even after the waning of Pentecostal eschatology.

Primacy of 'Soul' Matter

Pentecostalism has had all the crucial ingredients to become an unprecedented 'religion to travel,' well-evidenced in the exponential growth and spread all over the world in its wild diversity and creativity. Its evangelical heritage and the temporally oriented eschatology shaped Pentecostal missiology as being sharply focused on evangelism and church planting. The rise of a social gospel in the middle of the twentieth century may have further driven into the already narrowly focused attention. Mission impetus was also taken from the mission roadmap found in their favorite passage: '…from Jerusalem, all Judea, Samaria and (finally) to the ends of the earth' (Acts 1:8). Crossing geographical boundaries, therefore, has been part of Pentecostal mission paradigm. Many brilliant social programs, such as the well documented Mark Buntain's Calcutta operation,[2] have soul winning as their ultimate goal.

This, however, may reveal the Pentecostal understanding of humans, sin and salvation (or 'anthropology'). Every evil, be it personal or corporate, is traced to the sin factor, and traced back to Gen. 3 where a separation from God resulted in spiritual damnation, physical suffering, broken society, and cursed environment. The Pentecostal view of restoration, therefore, reverses the order, beginning with spiritual regeneration, and then personal (including at the physical level such as healing), communal (social) and even environmental, if the notion is conceived in a Pentecostal mission framework. Teen Challenge, the world-acclaimed Pentecostal drug rehabilitation program with over a 70% success rate, for example, is known for its strong emphasis on regeneration and even baptism in the Spirit.[3] In a similar vein, David Martin attributes the upward social mobility among Latin American Pentecostals to this paradigm: from an inner change to behavioral changes.[4] Recently systematic research was published on what is called 'progressive Pentecostals' who consciously engage in social issues, and this method is described as a 'one person at a time' approach. Albeit its criticism is for not confronting structural evil, its efficacy is well noted.[5] Another study by Sebastian Kim compares two radically

---

1 For example, Wonsuk Ma, (2006) 'Pentecostal Eschatology: What Happened When the Wave Hit the West End of the Ocean', Harold Hunter and Cecil M. Robeck, Jr. (eds.), *The Azusa Street Revival and Its Legacy* (Cleveland, TN: Pathway), pp. 227-242.

2 Calcutta Mercy Ministries, 'History' (www.buntain.org/about.html), accessed on 15 March 2010.

3 David Batty and Ethan Campbell, (2008) 'Teen Challenge: 50 Years of Miracles', *Assemblies of God Heritage* 28, pp. 14-21.

4 David Martin, (1990) *Tongues of Fire: The Explosion of Protestantism in Latin America* (Oxford: Blackwell).

5 Donald E. Miller and Tetsunao Yamamori, (2007) *Global Pentecostalism: The New Face of Christian Social Engagement* (Berkley: University of California Press), 182-83, 213-16.

different approaches to the issue of poverty in Korea: *Minjung* theology,[1] a Korean version of liberation theology, and the Pentecostal movement. He concludes that a long lasting impact to individuals and society has been made, not by the radical vision of Minjung theology, but by the transforming experience of Pentecostalism among the poor *Minjung*.[2]

Naturally 'revival' or 'renewal' is an important concept in Pentecostal thinking. The Pentecostal movement itself is often classified as a revival movement, with its impact to personal and communal transformation. The January 1907 issue of *TAF* opens with a headline, 'Beginning of World Wide Revival,' and reveals a glimpse of the Azusa Street revival:

> **The meeting went on till morning and all the next day.... Pentecost first fell in Los Angeles on April 9th [of 1906]. Since then the good tidings has spread in two hemispheres.... Wherever the work goes, souls are saved, and not only saved from hell but through and through, and prepared to meet the Lord at His coming. Hundreds have been baptized with the Holy Ghost. Many of them are now out in the field, and some in foreign lands, and God is working with them, granting signs and wonders to follow the preaching of the full Gospel.**[3]

As Pentecostal missiology matures, an argument seems to gain grounding that spiritual dynamism, evangelism, church growth and social service are not mutually exclusive. In fact, an increasing resource of a local congregation enhances social service and engagement, as demonstrated by, for example, the Yoido Full Gospel Church's engagement in public culture (through its daily *Kukmin* newspaper), reconciliation and unity (through the construction of a cardiac hospital in North Korea), and social service (through various non-governmental organizations and institutions).[4]

Conclusion

If this short study in any way leaves an impression that Pentecostals have finally unlocked the secret of Christian mission, the reality is exactly its opposite. In the name of God's kingdom and renewal, more church divisions were caused by this movement and unfortunately they have been part of its growth 'strategy'. Some of its serious blind spots, such as its eschatological expectation, have already been presented. While they are praised for their 'genius' creativity in contextualization,[5]

1 *Minjung* is a Korean word for the underprivileged mass who often live with grudges (*Han*). See Nam-dong Suh, (1983) 'Toward a Theology of Han', in Yong Bock Kim (ed.), *Minjung Theology: People as the Subjects of History* (Maryknoll, NY: Orbis Books), pp. 51-65. For a critical study between Minjung theology and Korean Pentecostalism, see Seyoon Kim, (1987), 'Is "Minjung Theology" a Christian Theology?', *Calvin Theological Journal* 22:2 pp. 262-63.
2 Sebastian C.H. Kim, (2007) 'The Problem of Poverty in Post-War Korean Christianity: *Kibock Sinang* or *Minjung* Theology?', *Transformation* 24:1 (Jan 2007), pp. 43-50.
3 'Beginning of World Wide Revival', *TAF* 5 (January 2907), p. 1, col. 1.
4 Young-hoon Lee, (2009)*The Holy Spirit Movement in Korea* (Oxford: Regnum Books), pp. 126-7.
5 Allan Anderson, (2007) *Spreading Fires: The Missionary Nature of Early Pentecostalism* (London: SCM) includes more than North American testimonies of early Pentecostal mission.

Pentecostals are also criticized for the ugly 'prosperity gospel'[1] and their extremely 'western' outlook and ethos. All in all, there is much to be reflected on and carefully studied.[2]

Classical Pentecostals also need to be reminded that they are the smallest components of the global Pentecostal-charismatic family, and yet with the most theological resources and institutions. And the western segment is not necessarily growing.[3] While it should continue its engagement in new frontiers of mission in the changing social context, it also suggests strongly that they have an empowering role to play to the rest of the Pentecostal-charismatic churches. It is good to note that the same church in non-western lands looks radically different from its North American or European 'mothers.' This seriously challenges their century-old theology and constantly institutionalizing ethos.

1 For various discussions, see Hwa Yung, (2004) 'The Missiological Challenge of David Yonggi Cho's Theology', in Wonsuk Ma, William W. Menzies, and Hyeon-sung Bae (eds.), *David Yonggi Cho: A Close Look at His Theology and Ministry* (Baguio, Philippines: APTS Press,), pp. 85-90; Wonsuk Ma, (2008) 'David Yonggi Cho's Theology of Blessing: A new theological base and direction', in Young San Theological Institute (ed.), *Dr. Yonggi Cho's Ministry and Theology: A Commemorative Collection for the 50th Anniversary of Dr. Yonggi Cho's Ministry*, 2 vols. (Gunpo, Korea: Hansei University Logos), I:179-200.

2 For suggested topics of Pentecostal mission for future reflection, Julie C. and Wonsuk Ma, (2010) *Mission in the Spirit: Towards a Pentecostal-Charismatic Missiology* (Oxford: Regnum Books) particularly Chapter 18 'Reflective Mission Practice: Suggested Areas for Pentecostal Mission Research'.

3 For example, the Assemblies of God, perhaps the largest global classical Pentecostal church, reports more than 63 million as its total adherents globally. However, the North American part numbers only 2.9 million or 4% in 2008. 'AGWM Current Facts and Highlights', Issue 1 (2009) (www.agchurches.org/Content/Resources/AGWMCurrentFacts.pdf) accessed on March 15, 2010.

Philip Knights

The Response of a Catholic to the Research Processes and Conference

The various strands and modalities of research undertaken by BIAMS, GMN and GC and the insights of the participants in the July Conference hold together many themes and have stimulated thought in several areas.

This paper is the reaction of one Catholic participant. It does not claim to offer any definitive Catholic response or to be given on behalf of the Catholic Church, the Bishops Conference of England and Wales or any particular Catholic mission agency or society. Rather it is a personal reflection drawn from one person who has been part of the research team and who was involved in the Conference. My own background has been in teaching the theology of mission in a Catholic Institution and of working for two or three Catholic mission agencies.[1] Therefore this contribution speaks from a Catholic context but its limitations and inadequacies are those of its author.

The starting point of the research was to examine whether or not the widespread academic acceptance of a theology within the umbrella of *missio Dei* was actually the driver for mission in Churches, agencies and mission societies within Britain and Ireland. The suspicion of the research team was that empirical research would highlight other drivers. Indeed the survey data and the interviews revealed that both a 'proclamation' model and a 'transformation' justice led model which in different ways began with the activities of Christians and Churches were more prevalent.

However, *missio Dei* begins with the activity of God. And even if the shorthand thematic orientation of *missio Dei* is not as dominant as some may think, nonetheless the theological frame of all Christian mission must be the relationship of God to the world. This sets the context for mission in which the Christian communities may act as agents of mission.

The Context: God and the world, cultures and persons

The Conference discussion brought to the surface several approaches to the presence and activity of God in the world: incarnational, Pentecostal, transformational and others. Within these discussions seemed to be implicit, although not always explicit, understandings of the relationships between nature and grace or, to put the same questions in a different frame issues concerning the theological status of the world and peoples and their cultures within the world.

---

1 The writer taught at the Missionary Institute London and worked for the *Catholic Missionary Society* which was transformed into the *Catholic Agency to Support Evangelisation*, whether that makes one or two agencies is an interesting semantic question. He is currently the Diocesan Director for the Diocese of Westminster for *Missio* the newly adopted name for the *Pontifical Missionary Societies*.

The dominant orientation of Catholic theological thinking of the second half of the twentieth century, at least that which is most prominent in missiological literature, may be associated with Karl Rahner SJ.[1] Without necessarily ascribing to all his philosophical anthropology or existentialist theology, his basic theological orientations of affirming the human person as a questioning being and of engaging with contemporary thought systems and a positive estimate of human cultures mean that we can recognise a loose commonality of views we may call Rahnerian. Hence writers including Vincent Donovan[2] and Walbert Buhlmann[3] may be considered missiologists in the Rahnerian mould. Certainly Gustavo Guttierez and other Liberation Theologians and Feminist theologians would acknowledge the influence of Rahner. (And yes, Rahner was without doubt the dominant theological thinker amongst lecturers at my old employer, the *Missionary Institute London*.)

However, it is apparent that more recently there has been a significant rise in what we may call neo-Augustinian theological thinking. The most notable and most influential member of this neo-Augustinian school being HH Pope Benedict XVI. However, even outwith Catholicism the 'Radical Orthodoxy' movement (albeit that that movement is partially from within Catholicism[4]) and others may be seen to be coming from a similar place.

Making comparisons can highlight differences more than similarities and it is important to notice that both the Rahnerian and *La Nouvelle Théologie* schools (the latter being perhaps the most significant progenitor of the contemporary neo-Augustinians) sought to move beyond the neo-scholasticism of the early twentieth century. In particular they both moved beyond the separation of the natural and the supernatural ends of humanity.[5] Nonetheless they differ as to whether contemporary culture is a partner or an opponent to the Christian tradition, or at least of lesser importance to that tradition. This is a tension that goes back as least as far as Aquinas and Bonaventure.[6] Commenting on tensions in the Second Vatican Council

1 For recent evaluations of Rahner see: Karen Kilby (2007) *The SPCK Introduction to Karl Rahner* (London: SPCK), Thomas O'Meara (2007) *God in the World: A Guide to Karl Rahner's Theology*, (Collegeville: Liturgical Press) Declan Marmion and Mary E. Hines (eds.) (2005) *The Cambridge Companion to Karl Rahner* (Cambridge: Cambridge University Press) and Patrick Burke (2002) *Reinterpreting Rahner: a critical study of his major themes* (New York: Fordham University Press). The last of these is most critical of Rahner and closest to what we shall call neo-Augustinian.

2 E.g. (1978) *Christianity Rediscovered* (London: SCM) – it is interesting to observe that this is undergoing something of a new following today amongst 'emerging church' proponents – and very Rahnerian (1989)*The Church in the Midst of Creation* (Maryknoll: Orbis).

3 E.g. (1977) *The Coming of the Third Church* (Maryknoll: Orbis), (1977) *Forward, Church!* (Slough: St Paul).

4 See Tracey Rowland (2003) *Culture and the Thomist Tradition* (London and New York: Routledge) for a trenchant criticism of Rahnerian affirmation of secular cultures and an explicitly neo-Augustinian agenda published under the Radical Orthodoxy banner. Dr Rowland herself is an Australian Catholic, whereas most of the Radical Orthodoxy school are English Anglicans.

5 See Paul McPartlan (1995) *Sacrament of Salvation* (Edinburgh: T & T Clark) p. 50f. McPartlan discusses this in relationship to the teaching of Henri de Lubac, perhaps *La Nouvelle Théologie* thinker *par excellence*. But similar understandings of 'pure nature' can be found in Rahner.

6 See for instance Aidan Nichols (1991) *The Shape of Catholic Theology* (Collegeville: Liturgical Press) p. 302ff on the medieval tensions between Thomists and neo-Augustinians. The contemporary debate, although having different points of disagreement is recognisably within the same pattern of argument.

and the underlying debates behind *Gaudium et Spes* and *Dignitatis Humanae*, Joseph A.Komonchak notes:

> At the risk of considerable over-simplification, one of these tensions might be described in terms of the traditional opposition thought to exist between 'Augustinians' and 'Thomists'. (I prescind here from the question of how fair this contrast is to either Augustine or Thomas.) Two questions characterize the presence of this tension at the Council. The first might be put in this way: Granted that we can no longer be content with the anti-modern neurosis of recent Roman Catholicism, what attitude should the church adopt before the modern world? And, if we are to look to our past for examples of the church's engagement with contemporary culture, which is most pertinent to our day: the great Patristic enterprise which led to the creation of the Christian intellectual and cultural world, or the great
>
> Thomist effort to meet, confidently and discriminatingly, the challenge to that world represented in the medieval period by the introduction of Aristotelian philosophy and Arab science?[1]

The debate at the Council was often seen in terms of *aggiornamento* or *résourcement*: between engaging with contemporary thought forms and patterns of meaning or renewal based upon drawing upon the biblical, patristic and liturgical traditions of the Church.[2] The Rahnerian approach would be decidedly in the former camp, the neo-Augustinian in the latter. As a rough rule the Periodical *Concilium* became the house journal for the former and *Communio* provided the same service for the latter school.

Consider the following distinctions:

Rahnerian	Neo-Augustinian
❏ Knit with grace	❏ Dualism
❏ Capacity to respond (or not) to grace Natural to the human	❏ Sin
❏ Universality of grace	❏ Rupture
❏ Particularity of human responses	❏ World something to be rescued from
❏ Inherent optimism about the world, cultures and persons	❏ Cultures to be redeemed
❏ cf Tillich & correlation	❏ Extrinsic optimism based on intervention of God into world, cultures and persons
	❏ cf Barth

---

1 Joseph A. Komonchak (2002) 'The Encounter between Catholicism and Liberalism' in R Bruce Douglas and David Hollenbach *Catholicism and Liberalism: contributions to American public philosophy* (Cambridge: Cambridge University Press) p. 86.

2 One significant account of these may be found in Joseph Ratzinger (1987) *Principles of Catholic Theology: Building Stones for a Fundamental Theology* (San Francisco: Ignatius Press) p. 134ff. The present Pontiff was a peritus at the Council and, of course has subsequently been an active shaper of the theological vision of the Church since the Council before and after his election as Pope.

Rahner was decisively 'integralist'. Indeed in the way he brings together nature and supernature his critics have claimed he naturalises the supernatural.[1] Certainly his understanding of human nature presumes an orientation to transcendence:

> **Our actual nature is *never* 'pure' nature. It is nature installed in a supernatural order which man can never leave, even as a sinner and unbeliever. it is a nature which is continually being determined (which does not mean justified) by the supernatural grace of salvation offered to it.**[2]

Thus it is impossible for Rahner to consider the human apart from grace and all that is human, including history and culture are knit together with grace. The capacity to respond or not to respond to grace is part of the constitution of humanity. All have a pre-apprehension of being (*Vorgriff auf esse*) which transcends the person and which is both an openness to the world and an openness to God whilst simultaneously the awareness of an emptiness, a lack which the person can only fill by reaching beyond self.

The consequence of these principles is to have a way of looking at the world and people in the world which starts with human questions and human experience. One may presume to discern the movements of God inherent within the movements of human hearts and human society. Although it would be wrong to draw too close a parallel, there may be seen here some parallels with existential theologians from outside Catholicism, not least Paul Tillich's 'method of correlation'.[3]

The neo-Augustinan presumption is very different. Whilst we should be careful of charging neo-Augustinians with being 'dualist', their manner of bringing together nature and supernature is to start with the Divine beyond the human. There is a consciousness of the distinction between God and the world. There is less a correlation than a rupture between God and the world. Whilst Rahnerian thinking does have a place of rejecting grace and therefore for the category of sin, one may be forgiven (excuse the pun) for thinking that this is the abnormal case. Neo-Augustinianism recognises sin as part of the normal human condition. There is a discontinuity between God and the world which must be bridged. The world is therefore something which needs redemption. The things of the world need the extrinsic intervention of God. Again, it should not be thought an exact parallel but one may see similarities here with Barthian neo-orthodoxy.[4] Compassion for the world into which God may irrupt, rather than identification with the world, would seem to be the engine of mission.

These two tendencies give us very different pictures of mission, the *missio Dei* and the mission of the Churches. The one has an intrinsic sense of God within the world leading the world to fulfilment; the other an extrinsic sense of the world as needing

1 See for instance John Milbank (1990) *Theology and Social Theory,* p.207 (Oxford: Blackwell) although the comment probably goes back to Hans Urs von Balthasar.

2 From *Theological Investigations IV* reprinted in Gerald A. McCool (1973)*A Rahner Reader* (London: DLT) p. 183f.

3 Paul Tillich (1978) *Systematic Theology I* (London: SCM Press) p. 59ff.

4 Interesting comparisons and differences may be found in lectures given by Hans Urs von Balthasar (a leading *résourcement*/neo-Augustinian figure) on Barth collected in Hans Urs von Balthasar (1992) *The Theology of Karl Barth: Exposition and Interpretation* (San Francisco: Ignatius).

saving. Of course one can see these as two sides of a single coin but it seems that they articulate different attitudes. The former, to use an unfair caricature of some *missio Dei* thinking, might suggest 'the world sets the agenda'[1]; the latter that the world needs to hear proclaimed God's agenda. In terms of this conference, the balance of the participants appear to lean towards the former tendency, however there have been significant and important voices more at ease with the neo-Augustinian perspective, especially as revealed from the surveys and interviews with local Churches.

Within the presentations there was a discussion of dystopia. Certainly it is clear that there must be some understanding as to whether we are encountering a dystopic world or promoting something more utopian. Does mission build on the inherent good or in a counter-cultural manner combat existing evil? It is probably best to understand ourselves between utopia and dystopia with both positive possibilities and destructive dangers before us. One of the tropes of Liberation Theology was to promote a vision of Utopia, the image of what should be challenging what is:

> **Those committed to integral Liberation will keep in their hearts the little utopia of at least one meal for everyone every day, the great utopia of a society free of exploitation and organized around the participation of all, and finally the absolute utopia of communion with God in totally redeemed creation.**[2]

Certainly all Christian mission must take seriously the flaws of what is and engage with it in the hopes of what could be and what should be. However, it must be noted that whilst in the early period of Liberation Theology there was a confidence in the shape of that Utopia, it would seem there is now a lesser clarity and greater fragmentation in considering what the elements of that Utopia might look like.[3]

It would seem that there are two related tasks for Christians in mission from the perspective of *missio Dei*: to celebrate what God is doing and to accept the challenge that God's will be done.

One of areas of discussion which arose at the conference but which was not apparent in the web search of agencies' mission statements, had not been fully considered in the research survey and did not feature significantly in the interviews was that of eschatology. It may be that Rahnerian/neo-Augustinian tension discussed here is an example of the already/not yet tension in eschatology. What is clear from the conversations in this forum is our need to be more explicit about what are the ends of mission: towards what εσχατον, τελοσ or τελοι is God working, and how and how far is that 'completion', 'end' or are those 'ends' realised in the Church or in the world? I am also minded to regret the absence of an orthodox voice in these discussions

---

1 As Dr Martin Conway rightly observed at the conference this was never the published opinion of the Uppsala meeting of the WCC in 1968, but the phrase has become associated with 1960s missional optimism about the secular world. See for instance the work of another Conference participant: Timothy Yates (1996) *Christian Mission in the Twentieth Century* (Cambridge: Cambridge University Press) p. 197.

2 Clodovis Boff and Leonardo Boff (1987) *Introducing Liberation Theology* (Maryknoll: Orbis) 94f. Cf Gustavo Guttierez (1973) *A Theology of Liberation* (London: SCM) pp. 46 and 213, and João Batista Libânio 'Hope, Utopia, Resurrection' in Ignacio Ellacuría and Jon Sobrino (eds) (1993) *Mysterium Liberationis* (Maryknoll: Orbis) pp. 716-28.

3 See for instance Ivan Petrella (2008) *Beyond Liberation Theology: A Polemic* (London: SCM Press).

given the Western norm of 'eschatology as an orientation' and the Eastern stance of 'eschatology as a presence' and implications this has for ecclesiology.[1] To borrow the maritime metaphors of one the conference speakers, it is not only that the 'Bark of the Church' may be seen as a different type of ship but there is also the question as to how the voyage, of whatever ship, is to be navigated and what kind of seas does she sail upon and what kind of port is she heading towards.

And that as an observation may lead us to consider in more depth mission and ecclesiology.

Missio Dei and Missio Ecclesiarum

Accepting as a given for the purposes of this reflection the principle of *missio Dei*, this still leaves us with the ecclesiological question of how the Church or churches are involved with the mission of God.

The first observation is to choose the plural title *missio ecclesiarum*. Whilst there may be some general or universal or even worldwide 'mission of THE Church'; even from the universalising habit of Catholicism that *missio ecclesiae* may be best seen in an eschatological context. The practice of mission in the present time is engaged in by local and particular churches. Indeed a global perspective on ecclesiology and an ecumenical perspective would both applaud the understand of the Church as communion of churches.[2] The *missio ecclesiarum* must be primarily concerned with what happens within local contexts. 'Global' links all three organisations hosting this Conference (In the title of Global Connections and the Global Mission Network and the strapline of BIAMS) yet the global can only exist as the collective expressed in a multiplicity of local situations.[3]

> **The one and unique spirit works with many and varied spiritual gifts and charisms, the one Eucharist is celebrated in various places. For this reason the unique and universal Church is truly present in all the particular Churches, and these are formed in such a way that the one and unique Catholic Church exists in and through the particular Churches.[4]**

That multiplicity of situations gives rise to a multiplicity of needs. One of the discussions in a small group concerned the situation of violent conflict in which working for reconciliation was a necessary and obvious response of mission. Much of the recent

1 See Paul McPartlan (2004) 'The local church and the universal church: Zizioulas and the Ratzinger – Kasper debate' in *International journal for the Study of the Christian Church*, Volume 4, Issue 1 March 2004, pp. 21-33.

2 See J-M. R. Tillard (1992) *Church of Churches the ecclesiology of Communion* (Collegeville: Liturgical Press).

3 Of recent interest in this field has been the public debate between the then two German Cardinals at the Vatican, Cardinal Walter Kasper (emphasising the importance of the local church) and the then Cardinal Joseph Ratzinger (emphasising the unity of the worldwide church). See Kilian McDonnell, O.S.B., (2002) 'The Ratzinger/Kasper Debate: The Universal Church and Local Churches', in *Theological Studies* 63: 227-50.

4 Extraordinary Synod of Bishops 1985, *L'Osservato Romano (English weekly Edition)* 16 December 1985) p. 7.

emphasis on Reconciliation and Mission comes out of those situations and their needs.[1] Clearly where obvious needs are apparent mission must necessarily respond to them. But what are the needs to which the necessary response is obvious in our time and in the various contexts for mission? Even if the world does not set the agenda, the course of mission must be in encounter with realities in the world.

This Conference meets the week after Catholics in England and Wales celebrated the feast St Peter and St Paul. In the homily preached by this writer on that Sunday the suggestion was made that 'the Church is ordered by Peter but ordered for Paul'. By which was meant that the structures of the Church and her internal coherence are there in order that the Church may reach out beyond her boundaries. Ecclesiology and mission are intimately and inextricably connected.

'[T]he Church on earth is by her very nature Missionary' (*Ad Gentes* 2) – asserted the Decree on the Church's Missionary Activity from the Second Vatican Council using explicit *missio Dei* reasoning. This was extended by Pope Paul VI in the Apostolic Exhortation *Evangelii Nuntiandi*:

> **Evangelizing is in fact the grace and vocation proper to the Church, her deepest identity. She exists in order to evangelize, that is to say, in order to preach and teach, to be the channel of the gift of grace, to reconcile sinners with God, and to perpetuate Christ's sacrifice in the Mass, which is the memorial of His death and glorious resurrection.**[2]

This last quotation explicitly affirms both the connection between mission and ecclesiology and the place of the Holy Eucharist in both.

Eucharistic ecclesiology, together with the overlapping sets of ideas of Communion Ecclesiology, has been an important element in contemporary understandings of the Church from Catholic, Orthodox, Anglican and ecumenical perspectives.[3] However, the label 'Eucharistic Ecclesiology' whilst pointing to a connectedness of these understandings may hide their diversity. Dennis M. Doyle, for instance, identifies at least ten strands which stand alongside and may even compete with each other.[4] Eucharistic ecclesiology is therefore qualified common ground.

---

1 See the papers of CWME Conference in Athens 2005, www.oikoumene.org/en/resources/documents/wcc-commissions/mission-and-evangelism/cwme-world-conference-athens-2005.html, the BIAMS Conference report Howard Mellor & Timothy Yates (eds) (2004) *Mission, Violence and Reconciliation* (Calver: Cliff College) and Robert Schreiter (1996) *Reconciliation: Mission and Ministry in a Changing Social Order,* (Maryknoll: Orbis)

2 *Evangelii Nuntiandi* 14

3 See Paul McPartlan (1993) *The Eucharist Makes the Church, Henri de Lubac and John Zizioulas in dialogue* (Edinburgh: T and T Clark) for a discussion of perhaps the two most influential voices in this field. For a discussion of how these concepts are played out in the official documents of the Catholic Church at and since the Second Vatican Council see John J. Markey (2003) *Creating Communion: The Theology of the Constitutions of the Church* (New York:New City Press). See *Mission-shaped Church* (2004) (London: Church House Publishing) p101 for a very brief Anglican synthesis of mission, ecclesiology and Eucharist. The *Special Commission on Orthodox Participation in the WCC* identified several issues connected with ecclesiology and Eucharist several of which need further resolution at forthcoming WCC assemblies. www.oikoumene.org/en/resources/documents/assembly/porto-alegre-2006/3-preparatory-and-background-documents/final-report-of-the-special-commission-on-orthodox-participation-in-the-wcc.html.

4 Dennis M. Doyle (2004) *Communion Ecclesiology* (Maryknoll: Orbis,)

Yet Eucharistic Ecclesiology may also be contested. What is central to some Christian traditions may be peripheral to others. Those who have strongly sacramental understandings of Church may misunderstand traditions who do not share their vision, and indeed be misunderstood themselves. Certainly the question was raised at the Conference about those outside explicit Christian believing and belonging who simply 'don't get it' when it comes to the practice of Eucharistic worship which may be experienced as exclusive and excluding.

'Worship and mission' was a topic of conversation, not least in some of the small groups at the Conference. If we can bear yet another Rahnerian allusion worship should surely be that which enables seekers to Hear the Word and which sends the Hearers of the Word into the world. Liturgy both gathers in the people of God and impels people into mission. There is therefore a double set of questions about worship and mission: how does worship gather in the world and people in the world into the Church and how does it send out those who are within the worshipping community?

Related to notions of Eucharistic Ecclesiology is to see the Church herself as a Sacrament, and indeed to understand her mission through sacramental imagery.

> **The Church, inasmuch as she is one and unique, is as a sacrament a sign and instrument of unity and of reconciliation, of peace among men, nations, classes and peoples.**[1]

Such a sacramental image does not simply describe the source, destiny and inner workings of the Church, it also orientates the Church to the world. The values of peace, justice, unity and mutuality which grow out of the Church's self-understanding are also a gift that the Church offers the world. There are circles of out-reach: God whose nature is love reaches out in love to include others in love. The Church is formed by that out-reaching love and because of it reaches out herself. Indeed we can say that the Church participates in the out-reaching love of God when she reaches out to the world. The Church is a beacon which reveals to people their true nature. It is as an effective sign of true humanity that the Church becomes both a location of transformed humanity and a symbol of transformed humanity. Just as all sacraments both point to and make present that which they signify, so the Church points to the unity and mutuality which is the truth and destiny of humanity and makes present that communion.

> **From this sacramentality it flows that the Church is not a reality closed in on herself. Rather, she is permanently open to missionary and ecumenical endeavour, for she is sent into the world to announce and witness, to make present and spread the mystery of communion which is essential to her, and to gather all people and all things into Christ so as to be for all an 'inseparable sacrament of unity.**[2]

---

1 Extraordinary Synod of Bishops 1985, Final Relatio *L'Osservato Romano (English weekly Edition)* 16th December 1985) p. 7.

2 Congregation of the Doctrine of the Faith 'Letter to the Bishop's of the Catholic Church on Some Aspects of the Church Understood as Communion' *L'Osservato Romano (English weekly Edition)* 17th June 1992 p. 8 §5.

Some other Catholic missiological streams

The previous two sections of this paper consciously developed themes raised at the Conference. However, it seems sensible, writing as a response from a Catholic missiologist to at least acknowledge some themes from contemporary Catholicism which were to some extent mentioned at the Conference but which may get obscured if not explicitly 'name-checked' here. That mission serves the world and changes the world is clearly an important stress for many Catholic missionary societies and agencies. A very brief web search of Societies of Apostolic Life, Congregations and Religious Communities engaged in mission reveals themes such as:

> ...working, in solidarity with the poor and the exploited earth, for justice, peace and the integrity of creation; promoting life-giving relationships between peoples of different cultures and religions;[1]

> We live together, usually, in small multi-cultural religious communities of MMM Sisters. We try to show God's love through a dedicated service of healing among people in areas of great need.[2]

> As an exclusively missionary Congregation, we seek to make common cause with the more unfortunate and disadvantaged of our world:
> * by proclaiming the Good News among peoples where Christ is unknown;
> * by fostering social development inspired by Gospel values;
> * by serving the Young Churches of Latin America, Africa and Asia as they grow and mature;
> * by bearing witness to the love of God for each and every human person by promoting the missionary vocation in all its many forms.[3]

The priority for most of the established missionary communities has clearly been in the area of mission which this Conference described as 'transformational': to make a difference to the lives of the poor, to be in solidarity with those in greatest need, to be advocates for the poor, to further 'integral human development'[4] and to promote justice, peace and the integrity of creation.

That important stress being rightly noted, it is also true that we can see a re-statement of a commitment to kerygmatic proclamation, especially in the case of the so-called New Communities and New Movements. This revived emphasis on proclamation is a major theme of the 'New Evangelisation' as it seeks to make good the late Pope John Paul II's call for an evangelisation 'New in ardour, new in methods and new in the means of expression'.[5] In particular this explicitly asserts

---

1 Columban Missionaries (www.columbans.co.uk).
2 Medical Missionaries of Mary:
   www.mmmworldwide.org/index.php?article=About_the_Medical_Missionaries_of_Mary.
3 Comboni Missionaries (www.comboni.org.uk/whycombonimissio.html)
4 Since the Conference the publication of the Encyclical *Caritas in Veritate* has underscored the commitment to integral human development.
5 See www.caseresources.org/evangelisation/evangelisation_newevangelisation.htm.

the need to proclaim the Good News in areas where it has already been proclaimed.[1] It is important to note the vitality, especially amongst young Catholics, of the new ecclesial movements and the commitment they have to proclamation. [2] Whilst there may well be some similarities between such New Movements and 'fresh expressions of Church' as experienced in the Churches of the Reformation I would suggest that whereas those fresh expressions are largely 'post-evangelical', the New Movements in Catholicism are largely 'post-Liberal' and in the terms with which this paper began are more neo-Augustinian than Rahnerian.[3]

The other significant strand of the practice of mission in contemporary Catholicism which should be mentioned is the revival of the Catechumenate and the approaches to Catechesis which are simultaneously, liturgical, personal and communal. RCIA (The Rite of Christian Initiation of Adults) has become the norm for how enquirers learn and seekers encounter the Church and further their journey of faith.[4] Certainly in terms of the experience of mission by Catholics in Britain and Ireland RCIA represents both the most common practice and may well prove to be the most effective driver.

Phase 2.2 – Philip Knights: A Catholic response

---

1 See, for instance, Ralph Martin and Peter Williamson (eds.) (1995) *Pope John Paul II and the New Evangelisation* (San Francisco: Ignatius Press).

2 See Michael A. Hayes (ed) (2006) *New Religious movements in the Catholic Church* (London: Continuum Publications).

3 See The Research Report of the Von Hügel Institute and the Margaret Beaufort Institute of Theology (2006)*Going Forth: An Enquiry into Evangelisation and Renewal in the Roman Catholic Church in England and Wales* (Cambridge) and Philip Knights (ed.) (2007) *Changing Evangelisation* (London: CTBI).

4 The writing of books in this field is close to inexhaustible but I would recommend (1998) *The Rite of Christian Initiation of Adults: A Study Book* (London: St Thomas More Centre), (1997)*The General Directory for Catechesis* (Rome: The Congregation of the Clergy) and other resources at www.rcia.org.uk/Resources/Books.html.
NB: All web addresses are as accessed in August 2009.

Paul Rolph

A personal response to a rich and stimulating conference

This is a personal response to what, for me, has been a rich and stimulating Conference. We have reflected on:

(i) Two related research projects – one local and the other national;

(ii) Mission as participating in the *missio Dei*;

(iii) Mission as proclamation of the Gospel;

(iv) Mission as transformation;

(v) A comparison of Edinburgh 1910 with Edinburgh 2010 and learned of the latest plans for Edinburgh 2010.

We have had opportunities to discuss and comment on the issues raised. My task now is not to cover all aspects of our Conference but to offer a personal response to what I have been hearing. I have also attempted to include as much of your group feedback as I can. I will provide the Steering Group with a fuller account of your written feedback at a later date.

The Two National and Local Research projects

Do these two research projects have clear and worthwhile aims?

All research must have clear and worthwhile aims. In the case of our two research projects their aims are similar. The national research has been designed to:

- contribute to a global conversation on foundations for mission leading up to Edinburgh 2010;

- help us to have a clearer understanding of the theological drivers for mission across a wide variety of denominations and agencies in Britain and Ireland at the beginning of the 21st Century;

- gain insight into how those theological drivers work out in practice;

- provide pointers to help us to identify key issues for the future.

The Nottinghamshire Case Study has very similar aims except, of course, it has a local focus and has collected the views of those who are ordained. Feedback from the groups suggests that you feel that these aims are clear and worthwhile. I agree.

Are these two research projects part of an on-going process?

There is a resounding 'yes' in answer to this question. We all know that well-conducted research depends on clear and worthwhile aims and that one's aims must build on previous research. Good research also offers reasoned suggestions for future work.

Research, then, is a continuous process and this is particularly true of these two research projects. Each project is a snapshot but if they are isolated from previous research and do not point to future research, the impact of each snapshot will be limited.

Are these two projects located within Empirical and Practical Theology?

Again my answer is 'Yes'. The two research projects are empirical in their approach. Both projects sit within the established field of Empirical and Practical Theology where an evidence-based approach is taken so that claims to new understandings can be made. On occasions I would engage in a debate over coffee where those colleagues of mine who are systematic theologians would 'pull the legs' of their colleagues who described themselves as empirical theologians. 'Empirical theology cannot exist' the systematic theologians would say.' Of course it can' came the reply, 'You do not understand the nature of empirical theology and what we do'. At times, in my university, such discussions could get nasty and those of us from other faculties, particularly from the sciences and social sciences, would try to calm things down. There are some profound issues here but I do not have time to address them.

Do these two research projects need to be based on a thorough literature search?

I am wondering very tentatively whether something of this debate between systematic and empirical theologians is there in some way in mission research since I can find very few published references to empirical research that relates to 'our' national and local projects. Both projects need to be based on a firm literature search – especially if we publish. *I should therefore be pleased to receive any references to empirical (and indeed any other systematic) research on the understandings of, and motivations for mission set within any part of the global church in, say, this century and the previous one.*

What are the strengths and limitations of the methodology employed in these two projects?

The advantages of a multi-method approach for collecting data in this type of research are manifold. It is well known that exclusive reliance on one method of collecting data is likely to lead to bias in one's findings. *Data collecting methods act as filters and are never neutral.* Feedback from the small discussion groups has reminded us, quite rightly, that research findings are much influenced by the methods used to collect the data. That is why (i) surveys, (ii) interviews, (iii) a website search and (iv) the involvement of participants at this Conference have been employed in our methodology. These methods complement and contrast with each other and so increase confidence in the findings. That is why we are using both qualitative and quantitative methods as well as two surveys: a national and a local one.

We were careful to provide each potential participant with details of our research project so that they could give (or withhold) their informed consent to take part. Care has been taken to conduct this research ethically.

I have also been impressed by the fact that the two research projects continue to complement each other – each has provided a comparison and a contrast with the other.

Those who are experienced in empirical research will know that research is 'messy'. Our best intentions are never matched by reality. The sample size is hardly ever as large as was intended. Some interviewees do not turn up – and so on. These two research projects did not escape the messiness of empirical research. The Steering Group is well aware that the findings of these projects must be limited, for example, by the size and nature of our sample of those who chose to respond to the surveys. Group feedback identified a range of limitations to 'our' methodology. Most of your criticism was leveled at the use of surveys. They are, you said, a blunt instrument, not popular and too restrictive in the responses available – and most of you reported on the concerns about the use of the word primarily!

What of the task of interpreting the primary data?

Both research projects have generated a huge amount of data and some straightforward ways of analyzing that data are being used. You saw the sort of analyses that Philip was employing when he used SurveyMonkey to attempt an early set of findings arising from your completed surveys. *But it is clear that the task of <u>interpreting</u> our primary data is our most challenging task yet.*

Could the survey be adapted into a teaching and learning resource?

We have heard from a number of respondents that completing this survey has enabled them to enrich their own understandings and practice of mission. I am convinced that here we have the potential of a significant teaching and learning resource. The survey will, of course, need to be adapted for this purpose. Some of the statements will need to be changed.

I have come across this before. Respondents have said to me that participating in my research has helped them to clarify their thinking on a particular topic and this has led me to adapt my survey (or whatever data collecting instrument I am using) into a teaching/learning resource.

Section 2: The three presentations

Bishop Michael's presentation on Missio Dei

I want to draw attention to Bishop Michael's last section. Here we were introduced to the three central emphases to which USPG is committed.

1. **The first is holistic mission.** Here is USPG's emphasis on the witness of scripture to the activity of God,
   - in creation,
   - through the saving acts of Christ,
   - and looking to the coming together of all things in Christ,
   that gives us an agenda far wider and deeper than either a crusading evangelism, or what might unkindly be called a social gospel. Those who fail to preach Christ AND those who fail to see Christ in the poor, have minimized the *missio Dei*.
2. **The second is USPG's commitment to the Church.** USPG works with the Church because they believe that it is an integral part of the *missio Dei* and

for them the Anglican Communion is a given – a gift from God. Therefore USPG plays its part in the Communion in the spirit of inter-dependence and mutual responsibility. It is necessary to recognise and respect the different and sometimes conflicting contexts in which USPG's partners are seeking to engage in God's mission.

3. **The third emphasis** guiding the future of USPG needs to be a dynamic spirituality which does not depend upon an institution or a book but from the love of the Father, incorporating us in the Son, through the power of the Spirit.

Wonsuk Ma's Theological Motivation for Pentecostal Mission – mission as proclamation

I want to highlight three issues that had great resonance for me.

1. I was much taken with a concept that was entirely new to me – The Prophet-hood of All Believers: the democratization of ministry and mission. We saw that this is linked to the establishment of local leadership at the earliest point possible. Has this something to do with the spread of Pentecostalism throughout the world? I want to reflect further on all that. There are, for me, important issues being raised here for other parts of the Church.

2. The Pentecostal strategy for social transformation impressed me. This was illustrated by' Teen Challenge' and their drug rehabilitation programme with such levels of success. I was the chair of a Christian Charity that worked among alcoholics and drug addicts for many years and so I know something of how demanding is the work among those addicted to alcohol and drugs.

3. I noted that the emphasis on proclamation in Pentecostal Mission includes caring for the poor. This goes further in that the sense of empowerment experienced by the poor and marginalized becomes a significant part of their identity. They see themselves as those who are commissioned and called by God. Although enriching and empowering, we were told that it can bring problems too.

Ann Morisy's presentation on Mission as Transformation

Ann described research that shows faith being linked to well being. We looked at the fraudulent narrative that money makes us happy and that, although circumstances matter, they do not matter as much as we think. We were reminded of the work of Martin Seligman in positive psychology which has emerged from the earlier disciplines of humanistic psychology or person-centred psychology. It was good for me to be reminded of these significant developments in psychology as I used to teach these areas to undergraduates training to be psychologists, teachers, social workers and other professionals. Ann went on to give us insights into early Methodism and the Salvation Army.

It was Ann's economies of abundance and scarcity that grabbed me. We are so caught up in this pursuit of things that are on offer in the market that we find it hard to believe that there is also a reliable economy of abundance. The tendency has been to assume that the economy of abundance belongs to the realm of heaven rather than earth. This brings us to Jesus who through his death rescues us from our sin, although Jesus also brings salvation to us through the way in which he lived his life. In his actions and teaching, Jesus shows us how we can participate in this reliable economy of abundance. And then we came to Ann's straightforward thesis, as she called it. *'When we muster an intention to do things like Jesus (i.e. to follow Jesus) – even in the most modest of ways, we arrive at the portal of abundance where virtuous processes flow and grace cascades'*. I will take that away from this conference and reflect further on the *'transformational power of faith so as to make it urgent to articulate and promote the resources at the heart of faithfulness that lead to human flourishing'*.

Kirsteen Kim's reflection on mission theology as seen in Edinburgh 1910 and to compare that with Edinburgh 2010; and to learn the latest plans for Edinburgh 2010

Janice and I attended the Study Theme One Conference in the Bossey Ecumenical Institute in Geneva earlier this year. I am highlighting issues that emerged during that valuable experience in Geneva as well as quoting from part of Kirsteen's presentation last night. Kirsteen makes it clear that to compare and contrast 1910 with 2010 and to do justice to all the issues would require a book.

So, one hundred years later, what is the theological worldview of Edinburgh 2010? Kirsteen answers this question with:

> This time theology is being addressed but the theology of the conference itself is not stated so again we need to read between the lines. First, we can deduce the theology of Edinburgh 2010 from its governance. Somewhat like Edinburgh 1910, Edinburgh 2010 was initiated by several (male) mission thinkers and mission executives from Northern European Protestant bodies, some of them in Scotland. They contacted the World Council of Churches to see if they planned to mark the centenary, since the original conference had led directly to the Council's formation. The WCC reaction was to involve itself in the planning but not to claim the centenary. So the WCC is just one of the twenty stakeholders, although it is contributing the largest funds. Edinburgh 2010 is therefore an experiment in a new kind of ecumenism. In the twenty-first century, the WCC is having to adjust the way it works to suit the reality of world Christianity. The reality is that the Protestant churches of Europe and the Orthodox churches around which the WCC was constructed no longer represent a majority of the world's non-Catholic Christians. Whereas in 1910 the cooperation of European denominations would have international repercussions because they were closely related to European states and they also controlled the churches on the mission field, the reconciliation of churches in Europe can no longer be expected to have much impact worldwide. The unity of Europe, to which the ecumenical movement made such a significant contribution,

has been achieved and the rest of the world no longer expects to be troubled by European wars. The daughter churches of Europe in the former colonies are now independent, many North American churches always had a mind of their own, and many more new forms of churches have emerged from multiple origins in different parts of the world. In view of this complex situation and of the impasse in Faith and Order discussions of organic unity, the WCC now see it has a role as a catalyst of wider unity, and this view informs WCC participation in Edinburgh 2010.[1]

Some concluding comments

1. These are some of the many issues that have emerged for me during the Conference as significant, surprising and challenging.
2. I am still pondering the question 'Can different approaches to mission live together and if so, how?
3. I am looking forward to the outcomes and findings of the two research projects so that we can gain further insights into what drives and what hinders mission.
4. I am keen to receive references to empirical research into areas close to the concerns of the two projects.
5. I am enthusiastic about being involved in plans for the next stage(s) of the research, including ways in which our survey may be adapted for a teaching/learning resource in mission studies.
6. I look forward to hearing more news of Edinburgh 2010 and to reading its publications.

---

1 Extract from Kirsteen's notes of her talk to us which she gave to me.

In-depth Interviews with local survey leaders

This research, carried out by Nigel Rooms, was intended to provide a comparative local and contextual study to support the national research in order to ascertain the theological basis for mission in local churches in Nottingham and Nottinghamshire at the beginning of the twenty-first century. [1] Data collection was based on interviews with selected church ministers who responded to the initial survey and were willing for further research to be conducted on their views. Dr Rooms conducted these interviews before the national interviews were undertaken and his conclusions were examined by the Mission Theology Advisory Group. His findings and experience were taken forward into the process for the national interviews which followed.

A key issue for the interviews was on what criteria to evaluate the theological positions of the churches. Dr Rooms used Bevans' and Schroeder's work on mission theological perspectives as detailed above and which could be expected to be present in the survey of local churches in Nottinghamshire. A key interview question was then developed to expose the position of the church/interviewee on the Bevans and Schroeder spectrum. Each interview explored with the respondent their stated five priorities for mission action in relation to their understanding of mission. The survey also identified the issue of mission as justice as one to explore in the interviews with a specific question.

Selecting the churches for interview

The initial survey was followed up by interviews with selected church ministers. These were identified on the following basis:

> … 48% of the respondents agreed to be interviewed – a total of 47 possible interviewees. Overall in the total sample of 98 there was a split of Anglican to non-Anglican respondents which Dr Rooms rounded up to 60:40. 16 interviews gave a substantial sample size and associated data. It was also necessary to go this high in order to have sufficient non-Anglican interviewees to make a comparison. About 30% of respondents agreed to the mission as justice question so Dr Rooms was looking for around 5 of the 16 interviews to be in this category.

He then filtered the respondents who agreed strongly or agreed with the justice question with those agreeing to be interviewed. This produced 2 Anglicans and 1 non-Anglican in the 'strongly agree' field and 7, 2 and 1 unknown in the 'agree' field.

---

1 The researcher in his professional role within the Diocese of Southwell & Nottingham is also interested in the missiologies of Anglican churches in the diocese and this may result in a separate internal study for the Diocese alone.

Since the 'strongly agree': 'agree' respondents were overall in the ratio of approx 2:3 he then needed 2 of three 'strongly agree's and three 'agree's. He also needed to keep the Anglican/non-Anglican ratio the same which meant one of each from the 'strongly agree's and 2 Anglicans (from 3 in total) in the 'agree's. These were chosen randomly where possible except in one case where he used local knowledge to distinguish someone whom he felt would be more in the justice category. This gave 3 Anglican and 2 non-Anglican interviewees – matching the overall ratio.

Of the ten remaining interviewees required these needed to be 6 Anglican and 4 non-Anglican. Dr Rooms filtered the 47 possibles for all those considered in the justice category above and then randomly chose the six Anglicans from what was remaining. On a random choice of the non-Anglicans he ended up with 2 Baptists and 2 Salvation Army so he changed one Salvation Army to the only Pentecostal that had agreed to be interviewed.

This initially gave a total of 15 interviewees: nine Anglicans and six non-Anglicans who were 2 Baptists, 1 Methodist, 1 URC, 1 Salvation Army and 1 Pentecostal. Because the Roman Catholic constituency were conspicuously missing, a Roman Catholic interviewee was added, making 16 interviews in total.

The interviewees were not filtered for gender but three of the nine Anglican interviewees were female coincidentally mirroring the approximate ratio of men to women clergy in the Diocese. There were no female interviewees amongst the non-Anglicans.

All were in 'sole charge' of a church/es, except the Salvation Army Officer who had a regional oversight role. Two of the Anglicans had additional oversight roles as Area Deans. All presented as White British (although this was not asked as a question) except for the Pentecostal who was originally from Pakistan.

Issues emerging from the Interview Data

Sixteen interviews were conducted on clergy who had responded to the survey.[1] The initial assumptions were that clergy do not fully represent the church and there is evidence that their views as leaders are in many ways 'ahead' of their congregations. The interviews confirmed our suspicion that the survey could be turned into an excellent tool for learning about mission and exploring mission ideas with congregations.

The following initial research conclusions and comments could be made from the interviews, which was done manually prior to confirmation by NVIVO analysis:

> **Most of my congregations are beginning to see this that we are in a missionary context in this country even in the little rural villages...**

- Clergy universally were convinced of the missionary task in Britain today and understand mission as the core purpose of the church, yet demonstrated a wide range of understandings about mission and an even wider range of mission actions. While we have no base line data from a previous age the research group suggests that this finding is significant since we suspect that until perhaps even 15 to twenty years ago the purpose of the church would

---

1   A detailed analysis of interview responses is given at Appendix K.

have been understood much more in pastoral rather than missionary terms. However the view that mission happens overseas and we simply give money for it still prevails in congregations, but is being addressed. This should raise questions for the mission agencies.

- Matthew 28:19-20 remained a key biblical driver and even 'default position' for the clergy's understanding of mission – across the traditions.

I would never ever want to disconnect mission from the core life of the church. It's not an add on, it's not something we do when we have finished fund raising or we've finished making our services nice...

- The institution of the church was both a driver and a drag on mission and there was evidence that mission can too easily be reduced to creating church growth to answer the issue of institutional decline.
- There was some receptivity of the idea of *missio Dei* amongst clergy, but only some. It was strongest amongst those clergy with greater oversight in their denominations –with a few sophisticated understandings of it including one which might be termed '*perichoretic*' mission. The majority of clergy, if pushed would still hold to the proclamation of Christ as their preferred position. A small number held to a pneumatological understanding of the *missio Dei*:

I mean we're the hands of Christ, but the Holy Spirit is the empowerer and facilitator, he paves the way, we look for where he's at work and then go and get stuck in...

- There was a fairly strong movement however to hold the different strands, threads or positions on mission together in a *holistic* way, which distanced itself from the dichotomies of the past. There was evidence then of some kind of 'paradigm shift' going on.
- There were real nuances and some resolvable tensions of belief and action about mission between what is continuous and discontinuous in the different approaches. Nevertheless real discontinuities did exist between the varying ideological stances especially around approaches to other faiths, the proclamation / justice question and the definition of who is a Christian or not – especially in rural communities.
- There was not much enthusiasm for mission as radical justice, political intervention and certainly not direct action. So we might ask whether describing ourselves as 'holistic' could be a kind of 'get out clause' when it comes to the prophetic voice in mission. Sometimes mission as justice was simply misinterpreted as being charitable.
- There was some evidence that mission activity is *not* connected to a deep understanding of the nature of God. A demonstration of any spirituality of mission was missing in some of the interviewees. The accusation that the church remains religious without being spiritual could therefore be said to be somewhat upheld.

In-depth interviews with national survey leaders

Mission can mean so many different things to different people...

Mission agency leader

As the third part of a triangulated study of national bodies eleven in-depth interviews were conducted between February 2009 and February 2010. The national interviews were conducted in the same constituencies that had completed the survey in phase two of the project, namely the Global Mission Network of Churches Together in Britain and Ireland, the Global Connections network.[1]

Relationship of the interview phase to the previous phases of the research

The purpose of the interview phase of the research was to explore in depth both the process and content of replies to the national survey. The research team was interested in the process participants undertook to complete the survey as well as what the replies revealed and the relationship between these two. In particular, the interview process made it possible to explore comments which had been made in the comment boxes on each page of the survey. The interview questions explored both of these areas using a template of questions devised by Dr Rooms (see Appendix G).

The most controversial aspects of the survey had been the use of terms such as 'primarily' and 'best' as qualifiers for the statements which pushed the participants towards a particular position. It was therefore useful to explore with interviewees how they had felt about responding to statements which contained these terms and whether they felt concerned about having to 'rank' issues of mission in this way. Equally it was necessary to explore further with respondents the nature of their theological understandings of foundations for mission which was at the heart of the Edinburgh 2010 research question. By enabling a more open and intensive discussion of key concepts and ideas, the limitations of the survey approach and its response system could be addressed. It was clear from comments on the survey that some respondents felt frustrated and also felt that, given the nature of theological language and concepts, the statements and responses could not easily be focused in a survey style. The need to put the survey statements in some sort of context and illustrate them with examples from experience could be tested in the interview process.

---

1 A detailed analysis of the four interviews conducted with members of Global Mission Network is given at Appendix J.

> We hold a spectrum of mission approaches and are trying to hold them together but projects may emphasise one or the other style or approach.
>
> *National denominational leader*

Method

The interview framework designed by Dr Rooms and intended also to be used in the national interviews was followed closely by one of the research team in their interviews but needed adaptation by the two interviewers.[1] The reasons for adapting the interview framework were that two of those interviewed in the national church and agency sample did not complete the survey themselves. One did not complete the survey because their predecessor had completed it. The other attempted to complete it as a denominational world mission team but they were unable to come to conclusions. Therefore the survey was passed to another senior member of staff for completion. This resulted in a methodological weakness, making it difficult to make detailed analysis in the same way or direct comparisons between the three parts of the sample. This focused on some difficulties with the process part of the survey. However, the exploration of theological aspects of the interview was conducted in similar ways.

Analysis of the interviews was carried out with broadly similar methods. Two of the interviewers recorded and transcribed interviews closely. The third interviewer recorded through note-taking on four occasions and through recording and transcribing with one interview. Data loss will be greater through the third method but sufficient data was preserved to enable conclusions to be reached.

The size of the sample overall (11) was sufficient to draw conclusions but could not claim to be representative of the entire range of churches, agencies and organisations sampled through the survey. Given this sample size, the conclusions drawn would need further research to hold sufficient validity to represent general trends.

Theological framework

The theological framework adopted throughout the interview process was also that argued by Bevans and Schroeder in *Constants in Context* and as explored by the speakers at the BIAMS conference.

It was difficult to identify previous available research that fed directly into this research and which would provide a context for understanding and analysing the interview data. The relationship between this kind of empirical research and mission studies was, interestingly, found to be distant. Such empirical research in mission studies as has been undertaken tends to focus more on the experience of missionaries in the field. Hence the theological framework for the interview phase was theoretical rather than empirical.

Issues emerging from the interview data

The nature of the representational role

All respondents were asked to answer the survey and participate in the interviews as *representatives* of their church or agency. We were less concerned with personal

---

1 For this reason detailed analysis in the appendices is restricted to those interviews which followed the designed template of questions. A summary analysis of the other interviews is included at Appendix I.

views. In reality however this was not easy to adhere to. The difference between personal views and organisational views were often blurred, though more so for the churches and less so for the agencies. The nature of many of the churches at local and national level is that they hold a simultaneously a number of different positions and approaches to complex theological issues. In effect this means that acting as a representative of a church cannot be easily equated with being a representative of an organisation that holds clear policy. Denominational Synods and Conferences do declare positions but these are often the result of compromises or a 'delicate balance' between different approaches that enable all views to hold together. This was the case with the churches in the national interviews.

With the agencies from the national samples (from Global Mission Network and Global Connections) it became clear that the majority of their spokespeople were able to say more confidently that they represented the views of their agency. One in particular said that their views were not accepted fully in the agency but they hoped the agency would move forward theologically. Issues about representation and speaking about mission on behalf of an organisation could be recognised across the sample. Others recognised that they had themselves learned or being moved to reflect, even 'grow' by the process of completing the survey and this had to be held in tension with the representative role.

We were therefore able to conclude from this data that churches and agencies work in very different ways and this is reflected in the way in which office holders attempt to integrate their personal views with those of the church or agency and represent them.

> **I was trying to do this on the basis of what the organisation would think. I expect there will be bias towards my personal views.** *Mission agency leader*

Potential of the survey for development as tool for mission education and reflection

There was agreement across the sample that whilst some had difficulty completing the survey it had been a valuable exercise that enabled reflection and theological engagement at a level beyond what was possible normally for individuals and teams. This led to a widespread view that the survey could be adapted for wider use as a learning tool in mission theology and practice. One interviewee commented that their organisation had a profile of the kind of people who would support their work and so a mission audit and reflection tool would be of benefit to agencies trying to reach a target constituency for support. This encouraged us to see the adaptation and refinement of the survey at a number of levels as a useful outcome of the project. It could be adapted for use as a learning tool in mission theology for use by ministerial and theological practitioners as well as local church members.

> **We probably don't reflect enough theologically. We are activist and concentrate on what we have to do rather than operate in reflective mode. We run around the same field instead of looking elsewhere – to the sidelines.** *National denominational leader*

Approaches to mission

The validity of the diverse nature of mission engagement was agreed upon by all interviewees. Mission is different in its expression in different places and this is the nature of its richness, versatility and adaptability. However, agreement on the theological *drivers* for Christian mission was more elusive. Of the three approaches outlined above from Bevans and Schroeder's work, proclamation proved to be the preferred model of the majority of interviewees in the local and Global Connections samples. The national sample of members of the Global Mission Network showed a clear difference in approach between the churches and the agencies. The agency representatives interviewed were able to articulate a coherent theology based largely though not exclusively on the *missio Dei* and liberating service. The churches, with their different role of holding the various approaches together were less likely to say one approach was more prominent than another. In one Roman Catholic agency interview *missio Dei* was the preferred approach but their work also included proclamation and liberating service. In this interview the agency representative did not want to associate with any form of proclamation that involved proselytism. A different Roman Catholic agency interviewee saw social justice as the filter for understanding God, so that empathy with those in need was a transforming (and therefore missional) experience.

Overall, we were able to determine from the interviews that whilst there was a high level of awareness of the *missio Dei* among the sample it could not be said to be the foremost driver of mission for the majority of the sample. There was little evidence of a spirituality of or in mission but the term 'holistic' was significant.

> **I would actually see the mission of God and Scripture as being two sides of the same coin.** *Mission agency leader*

Social justice and mission

It was in the relationship between mission and social justice that the biggest fault lines emerged between the various parts of the sample. The Global Connections sample which reflects the broad evangelical constituency expressed an enthusiasm for social justice, transformation and care of creation but did not understand these activities as mission in themselves. They understood such activity as the platform through which Christ's love could be shown and proclaimed. Mission activity was understood to be the setting or platform for proclamation. The word 'justice' for this constituency had a different resonance: only the return of Christ can bring true justice. In the Global Mission Network interviews, for the churches and agencies justice was seen as essentially equivalent to mission and was understood in itself as part of God's mission in the world. Both Roman Catholic agency interviewees showed there was a strong affirmation of social action and justice as mission as this strand runs throughout their ministry.

The interviews demonstrated that real differences in the understanding of mission exist between different parts of the sample and therefore across the range of churches and agencies in the UK and Ireland. These differences reveal an ongoing issue about what constitutes mission and how this is expressed in practice. An important question arising from this is: do these differences find tangible expression in mission practice and what does that mean for the way partnership is expressed and lived out? It was also important to note that a strong relationship between eschatology and mission was evident only in one group finding no expression in other parts of the sample. This particular fault line resonates across attitudes to the practice and outcome of mission and asks questions about the nature of the foundations for mission. Do drivers for mission begin in Christ's ministry and commission, or do drivers also resonate from God's future, as Christians are called to create the conditions for Christ's return? Understanding these issues helps to contextualise different attitudes to social justice and to the role and activities of Christians in mission.

> **The key thing has to be addressing injustice and poverty. So that people's lives are actually transformed and that is an expression of mission.** *Agency leader*

National and local interviews compared

In this third phase of the study, the results of the survey were interrogated more fully by in-depth interviews: 16.3% of the total of those completing the local survey were interviewed and 15.7 % of national survey respondents. Those interviewed therefore included national church and agency leaders and some clergy and ministers in the county of Nottinghamshire. All of those interviewed therefore were in some position of leadership, but their relationship to those within their organisations and churches, and their ability to articulate their understanding of mission was coloured, and in some cases made more difficult, by the office they held. For example, some from the national bodies identified a tension between their own views and those of their organisation, another found that the team which tried to complete the survey were unable to agree on a common view. Leadership in mission is therefore complicated by different kinds of relationships and responsibilities. In particular, the interview data from the local interviews suggested that the relationship between the local Minister and their congregations is not simply and clearly defined. Whilst the Ministers in the local survey expressed their understanding of mission the majority were also eager to say that their view was not necessarily shared by all in their congregation. It was likely that the Ministers were ahead of their congregations in understanding mission and theology as is to be expected given their levels of training, but this raises the question of where ordinary Christians, who live and work in the community, work out their own understanding of the foundations for mission.

The tension between mission and social justice was a particularly interesting theme, especially in the national survey where some of the people interviewed set out mission activity, including activity in pursuit of social justice as a platform for proclamation, tilling the field, so to speak. It is interesting to set this view in the context of Wonsuk Ma's paper, where the essential driver, through proclamation, is to create the conditions for God's reign to occupy the *now*. This range of mission possibility: creating conditions for God's action, proclaiming God's news, and transforming the human social environment, appear as different strands or entry points to a bigger mission picture in which all of these are understood to interact in some way. There was a distinct desire in both local and national interviewees to hold the different approaches through the term 'holistic mission.' Thus the survey responses showed, and the interviews confirmed, that particular strands, foundations for mission or perspectives on mission are not necessarily exclusive. In the local sample justice issues were also seen alongside proclamation though for many their congregations' understanding of justice was related to the broad range of development issues such as Fair Trade rather than challenging unjust political structures. Justice was seen as being part of mission alongside other approaches, again contributing to a more holistic picture of mission in operation in the world.

Some areas we identified for future research

Bible as driver for mission

The local survey in particular pointed to the Bible as providing foundational texts for mission, particularly Matthew 28:19–20. In view of the fact that this text also appears on websites, it would be interesting to explore how far certain Biblical texts not only provide inspiration but become hardened into drivers for mission activity.

Missio Dei *at congregational level*

Another issue for future research would be to test the receptivity of the concept of *missio Dei* in local congregations and to find out more about how congregations relate to the mission leadership provided by clergy. The survey could be used in by congregations in local churches, but it would require considerable adaptation to make it an easy tool to use for this purpose.

Mission and Social Justice

Another significant area for further study would be to examine more deeply the relationship between mission and social justice [1] and indeed the notion of 'justice' altogether. In particular, it would be useful to look for evidence that even if different churches and agencies at national and local level, across the denominations, have different entry points and drivers for mission, that they still cover common ground in the process of mission activity. Examining stories, for example might demonstrate that the 'difficulty' experienced by survey respondents in dealing with the word 'justice' is resolved by looking at what is actually done in the name of mission.

---

1 Currently being worked on by the Mission Theology Advisory Group.

Conclusions and outcomes

The Edinburgh 2010 study process asked us to look at the foundations for mission. To recap:

> **The task of this study group is to explore how a Trinitarian understanding of God as Father, Son and Holy Spirit relates to the theory and practice of mission; how the confession that God has a missionary identity impacts Christian witness; how a discernment of the Trinitarian God's inner relationships and love impacts ecclesiology, community life and society.**

In particular, we were asked to investigate a number of questions:

1. The relation of the Trinitarian nature of God to our understanding of Christian mission.
2. The relation of Christology to mission theology and practice.
3. The relation of the work of the Holy Spirit to mission theology and practice.
4. How does our understanding of the mission of the Triune God affect our ecclesiology and church practice?
5. What do we mean by salvation, present and future? What is its link to conversion, baptism and participation in the sacramental life of the church?
6. How does our understanding of salvation affect the way we do mission?
7. How does mission engagement affect our biblical hermeneutics and vice-versa?

In order to engage with these questions, we built them into the design of our research. The questions were principally addressed in the research through the theological statements in the survey and through follow up in the interviews. The papers presented at the BIAMS conference also provided considered responses to the questions for a more purely theological point of view and the interaction between them particularly gave insights into how our understanding of salvation can affect the way we do mission and its links to church (questions 4, 5, 6).

Questions 1, 2, 3 and 7 were also especially taken up by the survey and the in-depth interviews. We also took account of these questions in our analyses which highlighted particular issues concerning the foundations for mission.

We undertook this research in the four nations of the UK and Ireland by looking at three interlocking areas: website analysis, a survey covering topic areas suggested by the questions and in-depth interviews with some survey respondents. One of the interesting things we discovered was that the *process* was as important as the content. People were interested in the challenges presented by the survey and the opportunity it gave to reflect on what their church or agency thought or did. Consequently, one of the important outcomes of this research project has been to create three learning tools for churches or agencies interested in mission to use in website, mission audit or mission reflection. We hope that further and extended use of these tools will enable more data to be accumulated which will further elucidate the Edinburgh 2010 study process beyond the conference itself.

Conclusions against the task of the Study Process

Explore...how a Trinitarian understanding of God as Father, Son and Holy Spirit relates to the theory and practice of mission...

Our initial hypothesis about what the research would show in response to the Edinburgh 2010 questions was that public statements about mission by UK and Ireland churches, agencies and institutions do not necessarily match up with the mission practice, understanding and outworking of those same bodies.

Mission Language

The three parts of the study showed our hypothesis to be upheld. Mission is a word open to many interpretations, reconfigurations and different understandings. This meant that respondents often had difficulty *starting* with theological statement and suggested that some of the study process guidance questions have been asked the wrong way round. It is the messy praxis of mission that most often enables people to see more clearly how the theology works and also where the gaps seem to be. Further, asking people to apply theological principles to ideas of mission can lead to a difficulty with making sense of the vast diversity of what it all means in practice. We saw this not only in the sheer variety of material offered on mission-oriented websites, but also in the participants' engagement with the statements of the survey, where they wanted to wrestle with and argue about the possible interpretations of the wording. This is important, because it suggests that our language, including theological language about mission, tends to be limiting, even bundling God into a straight-jacket, while the diversity of God's action in the world is without limit and people everywhere respond to it even if they don't know exactly what it should be called or how it should be categorized. Yet words which suggest or imply *relationship*, people responding graciously to others, are strongly endorsed and these emerge as descriptors of mission. As such, this kind of language reflects the Trinitarian mystery of Father, Son and Holy Spirit, even if it is not set out as a theological statement. Further, this points to the interesting idea that there are other ways of describing Trinitarian understanding than the 'orthodox' or 'received' ways of doing so, and that mission is a particularly good generator of such descriptions.

Explore...how the confession that God has a missionary identity impacts Christian witness...

Missio Dei

Respondents at interview wanted to provide *contexts* for their responses and to tell stories from their experience and the experience of their churches or agencies which would illustrate those contexts. This means that there is no way to address the theologically oriented questions of the Study Theme in a vacuum. We might even go so far as to ask whether the foundations for mission have *any* meaning outside the lived experience of Christians working in the world alongside others, finding out what God is doing, and so the pictures of mission activity on websites and the messages they give out matter perhaps even more than statements of vision or of even of faith. This has theological implications, because if we assert that mission is *God's* mission, then we would also be arguing that God's mission has no intrinsic *human* meaning except in so far as it is entrusted to (all?) human beings and thereby becomes apparent and open to theological investigation in mission working itself out within the creation. Again, a photograph on a website or a snippet of story told by a mission worker can convey a great deal about the *missio Dei*, but it is very likely that web designers, and churches and agencies themselves do not necessarily realise how significant this can be.

What mission 'is' and what mission 'ought' to be

This embedding of theological drivers in human experience would further imply that mission activity of all kinds (including those primarily Christological and/or Pneumatological expressions which were described in the local survey interviews) can become conduits through which the *missio Dei* becomes operative. This raises interesting questions about the role of leadership in mission and also about the purpose and function of the Church in the outworking of *missio Dei*, and even more interestingly points to a tension, even a struggle, between what those leaders believe mission *ought* to be and what it actually *is*, a point noted in comments by several national and local respondents to the survey. What mission *ought* to be comes from an understanding of mission theology and is the prime constituent of the concept of *missio Dei*, what mission *is* comes from all of those working in diverse forms of mission, whether that be mission workers, the experience of reverse mission, or local congregations just getting round to Fair Trade initiatives.

Clearly, the closer 'is' is to 'ought', the more nearly the foundations and drivers for mission should match actual mission practice, but this was not true for any of the respondents. This was also highlighted by the way the three papers on 'mission as...' at the BIAMS conference so obviously complemented and interrogated each other and made the point about the difficulty of translating theological perspective into 'real life', whether it be working out how transformation happens in Ann Morisy's paper or making sense of an expected end-time that does not come in Wonsuk Ma's.

Public language about what mission is did not translate perfectly into what churches and agencies thought they were about and this requires creative solutions for the tension between what mission is and what it ought to be. In some cases this was 'solved' by thinking around more holistic views of mission which would tie public language or foundational biblical texts into the general messiness of mission activity. Any lag between the vision of local church leaders and the understanding of congregations could also be dealt with by looking for a more holistic understanding. For example, if congregations still think of mission just in terms of sending missionaries to foreign countries, then that could be contained within a more comprehensive view of mission held by the leader, rather than just becoming an anxiety for local leaders about out-dated concepts of mission. However, there is also potential, within 'holistic' mission for Christians to misuse the concept of *missio Dei*, calling all kinds of thing mission and blaming any damage on God, but the research showed willingness to think deeply and to reflect on complex mission issues and to struggle to answer honestly and with integrity.

The results of the research showed that in some ways there is clearly a creative and fruitful tension between 'is' and 'ought' and this is reflected in survey results from all three sets of data showing: a positive view of partnership, a generous view of people of other faiths, yet more confused response about how God works through others and who is really best equipped to share God's love in particular cultures. This tension is perhaps illustrated by a story from one of the interviews where the interviewee said that he wanted to become a priest to follow and be like a loved mentor but was told to tell the authorities who would examine his vocation that instead he wanted 'to save souls'….He asked what that meant and was told 'you'll find out'….

Explore…how a discernment of the Trinitarian God's inner relationships and love impacts ecclesiology, community life and society…

God and Church

There was an interesting tension too at local level where despite a hundred years of mission theological thinking and the absorption of mission experience and reflection on Christian engagement with other cultures and peoples, despite also, the experi-ence of reverse mission in the UK and Ireland, there was still a continuing feeling at local level that for congregations 'foreign' mission involves sending missionaries 'out there' and that involvement in such mission means supporting others, through the church, rather than becoming actively involved. Yet at the same time, clergy were on board with the idea of mission as a function of the Church and wanted to live the experience. They were aware that God was at work in the world, not just in the church and part of the mission imperative was to make that real for their congregations. This in itself showed that there has been an important positive shift in mission involve-ment and understanding for clergy over the last 20–30 years.

Consequently, despite public assertion of key mission language in vision and mission statements on websites, churches and agencies continue to struggle with what mission means in practice. They *should* struggle, because real life does not happen in neat theological packages. Foundations for mission were discerned in scripture (especially Matthew 28:19), and in mission theological 'lenses', but ultimately praxis carves out meanings for mission, like water flowing through rock. The different denominations and agencies each have their own unique channels, caverns and well-springs, as their websites demonstrate, but their paths are interestingly convergent, and even where they differ about perspective (for example about the relationships between mission and development) the research showed that they all move in the same direction in areas broadly covered by the five (six) marks of mission. This is shown by those survey responses where statements carried a large amount of general agreement. The final picture is one of creative diversity among the national churches and agencies, with local church leaders showing an outward-facing desire for mission across the denominations.

Because we discovered that the process was equally, if not more important, than the results of the research and because so many people had said they had found the process helpful, we decided to create three tools to enable others to use the process for themselves. Accordingly the outcomes of this research project have been a short document outlining some questions for discussion for anyone looking at design of a mission-oriented website; various adaptations of the survey for use by congregations, theological education, leaders – such as diocesan staff, and others interested in the mission foundations of their group or organisation; and a template of questions for more in-depth exploration of the issues and reflection on mission understanding and experience. We hope that these tools will help Christians and promote mission enquiry, audit and reflection. We ourselves learned a great deal about our own mission perspectives from undertaking the research and we hope others will too.

Websites visited in first part of website research

Pioneers – Action Partners   **www.pioneers-uk.org**

Aim International (UK)   **www.aimint.org/eu**

Arab World Ministries   **www.awm.org/uk**

BMS World Mission   **www.bmsworldmission.org**

Catholic Agency for Overseas Development   **www.cafod.org.uk**

Christian Aid   **www.christianaid.org.uk**

Christians Abroad   **www.cabroad.org.uk**

Christians Aware   **www.christiansaware.co.uk**

CMS   **www.cms-uk.org**

CMS Ireland   **www.cmsireland.org**

Church Pastoral Aid Society   **www.cpas.org.uk**

Churches Ministry Among the Jews   **www.cmj.org.uk**

Community of Christ the Prince of Peace   **www.newdawn.org.uk**

Community of Saint John   **www.communityofstjohn.btik.com**

Community of the Beatitudes   **www.the-beatitudes.org**

Cor et Lumen Christi   **www.coretlumenchristi.org**

Crosslinks   **www.crosslinks.org**

European Christian Mission   **www.ecmbritain.org**

The Faith Movement   **www.faith.org.uk**

Feed the Minds   **www.feedtheminds.org**

Franciscan Friars of the Renewal   **www.franciscanfriars.com**

Frontiers   **www.frontiers.org.uk**

Grassroots   **www.grassroots.org.uk**

IFES Trust   **www.ifesworld.org**

Intercontinental Church Society   **www.ics-uk.org**

International Nepal Fellowship   **www.inf.org/inf-uk**

Interserve   **www.interserve.org.uk**

Irish Missionary Union   **www.imu.ie**

Latin Link   **www.latinlink.org**

Leprosy Mission   **www.leprosymission.org.uk**

MECO   **www.aboutmeco.org**

Miles Jesu   **www.milesjesu.com**

Monastic Fraternity of Jesus   **http://monasticfamilyfraternityofjesus.**
                wordpress.com

Mothers' Union   **www.themothersunion.org**

Oasis Trust   **www.oasisuk.org**

OMF   **www.omf.org.uk**

Operation Mobilisation   **www.uk.om.org**

People International   **www.peopleintl.org.uk**

Pilgrims Community   **www.pilgrimscommunity.com**

SIM International (UK)   **www.sim.co.uk**

South American Missionary Society   **now part of CMS**

Tearfund   **www.tearfund.org**

USPG   **www.uspg.org.uk**

Verbum Dei   **www.fmverbumdei.com**

WEC International   **www.wec-int.org.uk**

World Vision   **www.worldvision.org.uk**

Websites analysed in-depth in Phase 1.2

Church Mission Society   **www.cms-uk.org**

USPG   **www.uspg.org.uk**

BMS   **www.bmsworldmission.org**

St Joseph's Missionary Society   **www.millhillmissionaries.com**

United Reformed Church   **www.urc.org.uk**

Methodist Church   **www.methodist.org.uk**

Church of England   **www.cofe.anglican.org**

Respondents by denomination: national and local

National survey[1]

Total started survey	**70**
Total completed survey	**68**
Anglican	29
Baptist	11
Black Led Church	5
Roman Catholic	10
Independent Evangelical	14
Interdenominational Evangelical	27
Methodist	13
Migrant led church	2
Orthodox	5
Pentecostal	7
Reformed	17

2 others did not respond to the question

Local survey

Total started survey	**98**
Total completed survey	**93**
Anglican	49
Baptist	6
Evangelical Lutheran	1
Independent Evangelical	3
Methodist	5
Pentecostal	7
Quaker	1
Orthodox	1
Roman Catholic	9
Salvation Army	3
URC	2
Anonymous	6

5 respondents did not answer the question

---

1 Respondents in the National survey could give more than one response.

Interviewees by denomination: national and local

National Survey

Anglican	4
Independent Evangelical	3
Methodist	1
Roman Catholic	2
URC	1

Local Survey

Anglican	9
Baptist	2
Methodist	1
Pentecostal	1
Roman Catholic	1
Salvation Army	1
URC	1

Tools for audit (1) – Questions on web design for mission related sites

Following analysis of a number of denominational and agency websites for their mission content, we have identified a number of issues which it might be useful to consider. These issues are focussed on mission, not any other areas or concerns which might be part of your site. This tool is an aid to discussion in the design and maintenance of sites which include mission as an important element, it is not a template for effective website design which should be discussed with those who have the appropriate skills and experience.

General

- Who is your site for? Is it for the general public, all Christians, members only or all of these? Will you have material for general consumption or private areas via login for your membership? Is there any crossover between the two such that the public might encounter images and text about mission that properly belongs to the in-group? If so, this might be off-putting. For example, your members might be very familiar with mission personnel and want to follow their news and pray for them. For the general public, these people are strangers and need introduction and explanation in order to empathise with them.
- Can people find your primary messages about mission easily? What will happen if people use a search box to look for mission related subjects? Will they be able to understand the search results and pick what they are looking for easily?

Text

- Do you want to use a strapline which sums up your interest, function or attitude to mission? How does that strapline relate to images on the page and your theology of mission? Is the strapline followed through with evidence? For example, if your strapline is 'transforming the world' will the user find evidence of transforming action and will there be images or stories from other parts of the world?
- Do you want your mission focus to be rooted in scripture? If so, what text(s) do you want to use and how does this relate to the content of the site? The general public may be unfamiliar with scripture and unable to make sense of it without any biblical or other context. How does your scripture come across as a driver for mission through interaction with other parts of the site?
- Do you want to root your site in a theology of mission? If so, what theological principles do you want to emphasise and where will people see these at work in other parts of the site? If you have foundational documents available, do the

statements in these documents match up to evidence on your site that these theological principles are appropriate for what you do? For example, if you have principles about conversion and change of life through mission, is there evidence of this on the site?

- Are your messages about your mission priorities clear? If you have questions yourselves about the relation between mission and social justice or mission and development, can you be sure that your site does not reflect mixed messages?

- Do you have ecclesiological principles that you want to relate to mission? If so, do your images and descriptions of church, clergy and laity support these principles? What other kinds of messages might be picked up by people who do not know very much about church?

Design

- Colour coding: do you have a signature set of colours which define your church or agency? Do you want to use colour to create paths or channels to guide readers through your site? If so do you have a mission-oriented path or channel which can be followed by enquirers?

- Social networking: do you have an appropriate range of ways for interested people to follow what you are doing? If you are likely to have a fairly static site which is not updated that frequently, social networking and blogging can help people feel they are in touch with what you are doing. How will you make sure that your primary mission messages are maintained in snippet narratives such as those used on Twitter?

- Images: what kind of images best convey your mission messages? What kind of ideas *might* be generated by your images? For example, if you have a number of images of your personnel involved with local groups from the developing world, could those images be construed as perpetuating old colonial models, patriarchal dominance, or making people from the developing world passive receivers of mission? If your images have limitations or are susceptible to multiple interpretations how will your text balance this and 'guide' the viewer to your intended message?

- What images will you choose to indicate your foundations for mission? Is the significance of those images only likely to be interpreted by Christians? If you want to attract support from the general public, what kinds of images speak most powerfully to non-Christians?

- Support: if your site wants to attract support and donations, how easy is it for people to do so and how does the site 'reward' people for their support? For example, how are people engaged and stimulated by the mission messages on the site? Can they feel connected to the leadership of the church or agency? Can they feel connected and involved with the activities of personnel? Are there stories or issues with which they can feel involved and feel they have made a difference to them? Are there interactive possibilities for supporters to react to the site?

Tools for audit (2)
Survey Template [1]

Introduction

Thank you for agreeing to take part in this survey of Churches and Mission Agencies. The purpose of the survey is to build a reliable picture of the theological understanding, motivation and practice of mission adopted by the Churches and Mission Agencies of Britain and Ireland at this current time. The results of the questionnaire will be used in the study process leading up to the 2010 Edinburgh Conference 'Witnessing to Christ Today' and at the conference itself. Individual responses will remain confidential though the results of the whole questionnaire will be used in presenting the research. The research is jointly sponsored by the Churches Together in Britain and Ireland Global Mission Network, the British and Irish Association of Mission Studies and Global Connections.

This survey concerns the theological understandings, motivation and practice of mission of the churches and agencies in the UK and Ireland. This means that we are asking you to record your responses to the statements below in your capacity as a representative of your agency. We are not asking for personal responses in this research. The questionnaire can be completed as a group exercise or by an individual.

Please submit any other literature that you feel will expand and clarify your responses with the questionnaire, for example, mission statements, strategy documents etc.

If you require further information on completing this questionnaire please contact Janice Price at janice.price@ctbi.org.uk

Please respond to all statements and indicate your level of response on the following scale.
– strongly agree
– agree
– neither agree nor disagree
– disagree
– strongly disagree

Survey being conducted by
Janice Price - Global Mission Network (GMN) of CTBI
Philip Knights - British and Irish Association for Mission Studies (BIAMS)
Martin Lee - Global Connections

---

1 Adaptations will be available on the CTBI website.
The introductory remarks were drafted at an early stage when a questionnaire was envisaged. In fact, since the resulting material used statements rather than questions, this material is referred to in this book as a 'survey'.

Mission foundations

1. Please answer these questions using the grading system indicated

	Strongly agree	Agree	Neither agree nor disagree	Disagree	Strongly disagree
Mission is primarily about bringing justice to the world	○	○	○	○	○
Christians have much to learn from other faith traditions	○	○	○	○	○
Mission is primarily about welcoming all people	○	○	○	○	○
Mission and development are inseparable	○	○	○	○	○
The kingdom of God transforms the world	○	○	○	○	○
Mission is primarily about the church taking the Gospel of Jesus Christ into the world	○	○	○	○	○
The kingdom includes the church but is wider than the church	○	○	○	○	○
Mission is best carried out in a particular culture by the people of that culture	○	○	○	○	○
God works through all people, regardless of their beliefs	○	○	○	○	○
Hospitality and openness to all are key aspects of mission	○	○	○	○	○
The priority for mission today is to proclaim Christ anew where people are drifting from previous Christian believing and belonging	○	○	○	○	○
Mission is relational and is best expressed through partnerships	○	○	○	○	○

Please add any relevant comments

Mission Foundations (cont'd)

2. Please answer these further questions using the grading system indicated

	Strongly agree	Agree	Neither agree nor disagree	Disagree	Strongly disgree
The heart of mission is the proclamation of the saving work of Jesus Christ and the call to repent and believe in Him	○	○	○	○	○
The church is, by its very nature, missionary	○	○	○	○	○
Mission, without social action, is not mission	○	○	○	○	○
The kingdom of God and the church are one, there is no separation between the two	○	○	○	○	○
God works primarily through Christians	○	○	○	○	○
The church is the herald of the Kingdom	○	○	○	○	○
Mission is about initiating people into the worshipping community	○	○	○	○	○
Proclaiming the Gospel is primarily about acting justly and loving neighbours, only using words if necessary	○	○	○	○	○
Mission is best expressed in a particular place by the people of that place assisted by Christian from other contexts	○	○	○	○	○
All faiths need to learn from each other as we share much in common	○	○	○	○	○
Verbal proclamation is essential to enable people to enter the Kingdom of God	○	○	○	○	○
Christians have little to learn from those of other faiths	○	○	○	○	○
The church is essential for mission	○	○	○	○	○

Please add relevant comments here

Mission Foundations (cont'd)

3. Please answer these further questions using the grading system indicated

	Strongly agree	Agree	Neither agree nor disagree	Disagree	Strongly disgree
Mission means confronting people with the consequences of sin	○	○	○	○	○
Mission, without proclamation, is not mission	○	○	○	○	○
For the church Mission is primarily about following God the Holy Trinity into the world	○	○	○	○	○
Mission addresses sin understood primarily as personal wrongdoing	○	○	○	○	○
Proclaiming God to the world is more important than improving peoples' lives in the world	○	○	○	○	○
God works through all people of goodwill	○	○	○	○	○
Mission challenges people to find salvation in Jesus or risk eternal condemnation	○	○	○	○	○
In a world of conflict mission must address reconciliation	○	○	○	○	○
Mission is best carried out in a particular place by Christians from any cultural background	○	○	○	○	○
Mission means telling people about the hope of heaven	○	○	○	○	○
Mission requires a call to repentance and new life in Christ	○	○	○	○	○
The church is the servant of the world	○	○	○	○	○
Development is an integral part of mission only if it helps people discover the Gospel	○	○	○	○	○
Mission partners entering contexts different from their own should undertake cross-cultural education and training	○	○	○	○	○
Proclaiming the Gospel is about using both word and deed to express God's love to all	○	○	○	○	○
Mission is enhanced by cross-cultural and world perspectives	○	○	○	○	○
The church is the sign and foretaste of the Kingdom of God	○	○	○	○	○
Mission is mainly about planting and growing churches	○	○	○	○	○
The yardstick of mission is its concern for the poorest	○	○	○	○	○

Please add relevant comments here

Mission Priorities

4. Please tick up to five of the following areas of work which indicate the priorities of your agency or church

☐ Advice and support

☐ Advocacy and campaigning

☐ Church growth

☐ Church planting

☐ Community building

☐ Development

☐ Education

☐ Emergency relief

☐ Environment

☐ Evangelization

☐ Evangelism

☐ Exchange visits

☐ Fundraising

☐ Health

☐ Inter-faith dialogue

☐ Long-term service

☐ Poverty alleviation

☐ Short-term service

☐ Support for existing Churches

☐ Theological Education

☐ Youth work

☐ Other (please specify)

Final questions

5. If you have any further comments about the priorities of your agency or church, please add them here

6. Please indicate the denomination your church or agency is linked to (more than one answer is possible)

☐ Anglican

☐ Baptist

☐ Black Led Church

☐ Catholic

☐ Independent (evangelical)

☐ Interdenominational (evangelical)

☐ Methodist

☐ Migrant led church (not denominationally affiliated)

☐ Orthodox

☐ Pentecostal

☐ Reformed

Other (please specify)

7. The survey is confidential and you will not be identified against your answers. However in order to ensure that we have a comprehensive list of those responding, please complete the information below.

Name of person completing survey:

Agency or church:

Email Address:

Local Survey – variation for Mission Priorities

4. Please tick up to five of the following areas of work which indicate the priorities of your agency

☐ Advice and support in the community (debt counseling)

☐ Advocacy, taking action and campaigning

☐ Church planting

☐ Community building

☐ Education / Schools Work

☐ Evangelisation

☐ Evangelism

☐ "Fresh Expressions" of Church

☐ Fundraising/giving for home mission / charities

☐ Fundraising/giving for overseas mission / charities

☐ Inter-faith engagement

☐ Overseas Exchange and Mission visits

☐ Pastoral care / Bereavement Care in the Community

☐ Work with the elderly / old people's homes

☐ Parent & Toddler Groups

☐ Open children's work

☐ Open youth work

☐ Other (please specify)

```

```

5. If you ticked advocacy, taking action and campaigning, which of these areas you are engaged in:

☐ Asylum Seekers and Refugees

☐ Environmental Issues

☐ Health

☐ Fair Trade

☐ Racial Justice

☐ World Development and poverty alleviation

☐ Other (please specify)

```

```

Tools for audit (3.1)
Ethical interview leaflet

Theological Foundations for Mission Research and Interview

Edinburgh 2010 is the global World Mission Conference taking place in Edinburgh from June 2–6, 2010 to mark the centenary of the seminal 1910 World Missionary Conference. Over 1200 participants from across the world are expected to attend. An international Study Process is underway in preparation for the 2010 Conference from which material will be presented at the conference.

Theological Foundations for Mission is the theme the British and Irish Churches and Agencies have been asked to consider. The Global Mission Network (GMN) of CTBI, the evangelical Global Connections and the British and Irish Association for Mission Studies (BIAMS) have agreed jointly to sponsor a research project seeking to take a snapshot of the theological understandings, motivation and practice of mission of the Churches and Agencies at the beginning of the 21st century. My name is Nigel Rooms and I am conducting a local church version of this research amongst Nottinghamshire churches to compare and contrast with the national research.

So far we have completed the survey phase and we are now conducting interviews – and you have been selected for one of these. **Thank you for agreeing to take part in this way.**

I am directing this local research and can be contacted at:

Dunham House, 8 Westgate, Southwell, NG25 0JL

01636 817231

email: nigel.rooms@southwell.anglican.org should you have any questions.

The information you give in the interview will be on the following basis:

- Your participation is entirely voluntary
- You are free to refuse to answer any question
- You are free to withdraw from the research at any time

The interview material will be kept strictly confidential. Individual results and excerpts from the interviews may be made part of the final research report and study paper, but under no circumstances will your name or any identifying characteristics be included in the work.

If you would like to receive a copy of the research report and study paper, please do not hesitate to say so at the end of the interview.

Dr. Nigel Rooms

18/12/08

Tools for audit (3.2)
Template for focussed interview questions

The survey could be completed by an individual or a group acting on behalf of their church or agency. Or the survey could be completed by individuals (such as a mission team or congregation members) as a basis for discussion and comparison of responses. The following questions could then be used either for focussed interviews for mission research or to facilitate group discussion of the survey in groups or teams.

Questions for focussed interviews with respondents

1. Was you who filled in the survey – and as yourself /yourselves or thinking about the position of the church as a whole?

2. I want to ask some questions about the process of filling in the survey so can you remember (have a look at your copy here it is…) …. What, if anything, did you find helpful about the survey?

3. What did you find difficult about the survey?

4. Where do you find your church's authority for (its engagement in) mission?

5. How did you react to the word 'primarily' in a number of questions?

6. How did you react to the question about the 'role of the Trinity'?

7. Did you want to respond positively to all statements carrying the word mission and if so, why?

8. Did some of the questions make you think more deeply about the issues in such a way as to affect some of the later questions? (*If yes, follow up by asking for examples….*)

9. Did you choose 'neither agree nor disagree' when you meant 'don't know'?

10. Can you tell me more about your choice of response to question x (to be decided on basis of responses from the survey)?
    The responses tend to fall into three understandings of mission:
    - Proclamation of Jesus Christ as universal saviour as essential to mission;
    - *Missio Dei* – God is at work in the world and mission is essentially about following God's agenda and making it explicit;
    - Mission as Transformation – transforming society, individuals etc with an emphasis on liberation theology, bias to the poor.

11. How would you describe the theological understanding of mission that characterises the church you represent? (*Compare this with their reported five priorities from the survey – how do these confirm or deny the stated theological*

understanding? Respondents may not wish to be fitted into these categories but range across two or more – this needs to be noted.)

12. What understanding of God underlies your church's approach to mission?

13. What do you feel about the relationship between mission and justice?

14. Finally, choose any specific or interesting responses from the survey which may not have been covered and explore them.

Appendix H

Survey Data

In the local survey, one respondent only answered questions 1–14 (the first page of the survey), and two others dropped out after question 29 (page two of the survey). These are recorded in the 'no response' column, but there is otherwise no significance in the lack of response to these questions.

	national	local	n+l	biams	all	no resp	rank
S1 Mission is primarily about bringing justice to the world							
strongly agree	6	8	14	5	19		5
agree	13	27	40	11	51		2
neither agree nor disagree	18	23	41	8	49		3
disagree	24	29	53	3	56		1
strongly disagree	9	11	20	0	20		4
S2 Mission is primarily about the church taking the Gospel of Jesus Christ into the world							
strongly agree	38	47	85	7	92		1
agree	24	41	65	7	72		2
neither agree nor disagree	4	8	12	9	21		3
disagree	3	2	5	4	9		4
strongly disagree	1	0	1	0	1		5
S3 For the Church mission is primarily about following God the Holy Trinity into the world							
strongly agree	30	19	49	9	58	1	2
agree	21	49	70	14	84		1
neither agree nor disagree	14	21	35	3	38		3
disagree	3	7	10	1	11		4
strongly disagree	2	1	3	0	3		5
S4 The Kingdom of God transforms the world							
strongly agree	49	55	104	17	121		1
agree	18	36	54	8	62		2
neither agree nor disagree	3	4	7	2	9		3
disagree	0	3	3	0	3		4
strongly disagree	0	0	0	0	0		5

	national	local	n+l	biams	all	no resp	rank
S5 The Kingdom of God and the Church are one, there is no separation between the two							
strongly agree	8	11	19	1	20	1	5
agree	12	19	31	1	32		4
neither agree nor disagree	12	23	35	1	36		2
disagree	20	34	54	16	70		1
strongly disagree	18	10	28	8	36		2
S6 The Kingdom includes the Church but is wider than the Church							
strongly agree	36	42	78	20	98		1
agree	17	41	58	5	63		2
neither agree nor disagree	10	7	17	1	18		3
disagree	7	7	14	1	15		4
strongly disagree	0	1	1	0	1		5
S7 Mission is best carried out in a particular culture by the people of that culture							
strongly agree	21	17	38	9	47		2
agree	31	42	73	9	82		1
neither agree nor disagree	12	26	38	8	46		3
disagree	5	12	17	1	18		4
strongly disagree	1	1	2	0	2		5
S8 Mission is best expressed in a particular place by the people of that place assisted by Christians from other contexts							
strongly agree	15	5	20	4	24	1	3
agree	29	50	79	17	96		1
neither agree nor disagree	18	31	49	4	53		2
disagree	6	11	17	2	19		4
strongly disagree	2	0	2	0	2		5
S9 Mission is best carried out in a particular place by Christians from any cultural background							
strongly agree	1	5	6	0	6	3	5
agree	11	16	27	5	32		3
neither agree nor disagree	19	41	60	13	73		1
disagree	32	33	65	7	72		2
strongly disagree	7	0	7	2	9		4
S10 The heart of mission is the proclamation of the saving work of Jesus Christ and the call to repent and believe in him							
strongly agree	38	46	84	10	94		1
agree	19	40	59	7	66		2
neither agree nor disagree	6	8	14	7	21		3
disagree	4	1	5	2	7		4
strongly disagree	3	3	6	1	7		4

	national	local	n+l	biams	all	no resp	rank
S11 Hospitality and openness to all are key aspects of mission							
strongly agree	32	30	62	9	71		2
agree	34	59	93	18	111		1
neither agree nor disagree	3	9	12	0	12		3
disagree	0	0	0	0	0		5
strongly disagree	1	0	1	0	1		4
S12 Verbal proclamation is essential to enable people to enter the Kingdom of God							
strongly agree	15	20	35	3	38	1	3
agree	30	38	68	7	75		1
neither agree nor disagree	13	19	32	10	42		2
disagree	9	19	28	7	35		4
strongly disagree	3	1	4	0	4		5
S13 Mission and Development are inseparable							
strongly agree	31	20	51	10	61		2
agree	19	47	66	12	78		1
neither agree nor disagree	11	15	26	3	29		3
disagree	7	11	18	2	20		4
strongly disagree	2	4	6	0	6		5
S14 Mission without social action is not mission							
strongly agree	31	20	51	10	61	1	2
agree	19	47	66	12	78		1
neither agree nor disagree	11	15	26	3	29		3
disagree	7	11	18	2	20		4
strongly disagree	2	4	6	0	6		5
S15 Development is an integral part of mission only if it helps people discover the Gospel							
strongly agree	1	5	6	1	7	3	5
agree	17	34	51	2	53		2
neither agree nor disagree	16	31	47	5	52		3
disagree	29	21	50	18	68		1
strongly disagree	7	4	11	1	12		4
S16 In a world of conflict mission must address reconciliation							
strongly agree	30	24	54	14	68	3	2
agree	34	63	97	13	110		1
neither agree nor disagree	5	5	10	0	10		3
disagree	1	3	4	0	4		4
strongly disagree	0	0	0	0	0		5

	national	local	n+l	biams	all	no resp	rank
S17 Proclaiming God to the world is more important than improving people's lives in the world							
strongly agree	5	3	8	1	9	3	5
agree	17	15	32	3	35		3
neither agree nor disagree	16	33	49	6	55		2
disagree	26	41	67	12	79		1
strongly disagree	6	3	9	5	14		4
S18 The yardstick of mission is concern for the poorest							
strongly agree	10	12	22	4	26	3	4
agree	22	37	59	16	75		1
neither agree nor disagree	21	29	50	3	53		2
disagree	15	15	30	4	34		3
strongly disagree	2	2	4	0	4		5
S19 All faiths need to learn from one another as we share much in common							
strongly agree	12	9	21	5	26	1	4
agree	17	44	61	16	77		1
neither agree nor disagree	21	20	41	5	46		2
disagree	14	16	30	1	31		3
strongly disagree	6	8	14	0	14		5
S20 Christians have little to learn from those of other faiths							
strongly agree	2	1	3	0	3	1	5
agree	6	16	22	1	23		4
neither agree nor disagree	17	17	34	3	37		2
disagree	29	49	78	15	93		1
strongly disagree	16	14	30	8	38		3
S21 Christians have much to learn from other faith traditions							
strongly agree	12	7	19	6	25		3
agree	30	49	79	19	98		1
neither agree nor disagree	16	24	40	2	42		2
disagree	10	13	23	0	23		4
strongly disagree	2	5	7	0	7		5
S22 God works through all people regardless of their beliefs							
strongly agree	17	17	34	7	41		3
agree	24	46	70	10	80		1
neither agree nor disagree	19	23	42	7	49		2
disagree	7	10	17	3	20		4
strongly disagree	3	2	5	0	5		5

	national	local	n+l	biams	all	no resp	rank
S23 God works primarily through Christians							
strongly agree	8	6	14	1	15	1	4
agree	24	22	46	7	53		3
neither agree nor disagree	22	27	49	7	56		2
disagree	11	40	51	10	61		1
strongly disagree	5	2	7	2	9		5
S24 God works through all people of goodwill							
strongly agree	10	9	19	6	25	3	4
agree	22	43	65	16	81		1
neither agree nor disagree	27	23	50	5	55		2
disagree	9	20	29	0	29		3
strongly disagree	2	0	2	0	2		5
S25 Mission without proclamation is not mission							
strongly agree	17	15	32	2	34	1	4
agree	21	40	61	7	68		1
neither agree nor disagree	20	22	42	8	50		2
disagree	10	19	29	9	38		3
strongly disagree	2	1	3	1	4		5
S26 Proclaiming the Gospel is primarily about acting justly and loving neighbours, only using words if necessary							
strongly agree	6	6	12	4	16	1	4
agree	14	40	54	7	61		1
neither agree nor disagree	21	26	47	11	58		2
disagree	21	18	39	4	43		3
strongly disagree	8	7	15	1	16		4
S27 Proclaiming the Gospel is about using both word and deed to express God's love to all							
strongly agree	49	53	102	19	121	3	1
agree	18	42	60	8	68		2
neither agree nor disagree	1	0	1	0	1		3
disagree	1	0	1	0	1		3
strongly disagree	1	0	1	0	1		3
S28 Mission addresses sin understood primarily as personal wrongdoing							
strongly agree	2	5	7	0	7	1	5
agree	20	30	50	2	52		3
neither agree nor disagree	18	29	47	8	55		2
disagree	24	28	52	13	65		1
strongly disagree	6	5	11	4	15		4

	national	local	n+l	biams	all	no resp	rank
S29 Mission means confronting people with the consequences of sin							
strongly agree	14	13	27	1	28	1	4
agree	27	28	55	6	61		1
neither agree nor disagree	13	27	40	12	52		2
disagree	11	24	35	4	39		3
strongly disagree	5	5	10	4	14		5
S30 Mission requires a call to repentance and new life in Christ							
strongly agree	28	25	53	4	57	3	2
agree	33	52	85	14	99		1
neither agree nor disagree	5	10	15	5	20		3
disagree	2	7	9	3	12		4
strongly disagree	2	1	3	1	4		5
S31 Mission challenges people to find salvation in Jesus or risk eternal condemnation							
strongly agree	11	15	26	2	28	3	4
agree	28	30	58	5	63		1
neither agree nor disagree	14	15	29	5	34		3
disagree	8	24	32	11	43		2
strongly disagree	9	11	20	4	24		5
S32 Mission means telling people about the hope of heaven							
strongly agree	21	16	37	1	38	3	2
agree	31	57	88	12	100		1
neither agree nor disagree	11	16	27	7	34		3
disagree	2	6	8	5	13		4
strongly disagree	5	0	5	2	7		5
S33 The Church is the sign and foretaste of the Kingdom of God							
strongly agree	31	25	56	7	63	3	2
agree	26	50	76	15	91		1
neither agree nor disagree	11	16	27	3	30		3
disagree	2	4	6	2	8		4
strongly disagree	0	0	0	0	0		5
S34 The Church is, by its very nature, missionary							
strongly agree	52	58	110	20	130	3	1
agree	13	27	40	4	44		2
neither agree nor disagree	4	11	15	1	16		3
disagree	0	1	1	2	3		4
strongly disagree	1	1	2	0	2		5

	national	local	n+l	biams	all	no resp	rank
S35 The Church is the herald of the Kingdom							
strongly agree	20	14	34	5	39		2
agree	41	65	107	12	119		1
neither agree nor disagree	8	14	22	8	30		3
disagree	0	4	4	2	6		4
strongly disagree	1	0	1	0	1		5
S36 The Church is essential for mission							
strongly agree	22	28	50	4	54	1	2
agree	30	43	73	14	87		1
neither agree nor disagree	10	17	27	6	33		3
disagree	6	9	15	3	18		4
strongly disagree	2	0	2	0	2		5
S37 The Church is the servant of the world							
strongly agree	21	23	44	7	51	3	2
agree	30	44	74	15	89		1
neither agree nor disagree	13	13	26	4	30		3
disagree	4	13	17	1	18		4
strongly disagree	2	2	4	0	4		5
S38 Mission is mainly about planting and growing churches							
strongly agree	4	2	6	0	6	3	5
agree	15	20	35	3	38		3
neither agree nor disagree	22	38	60	11	71		1
disagree	22	31	53	12	65		2
strongly disagree	7	4	11	1	12		4
S39 Mission partners entering contexts different from their own should undertake cross-cultural education and training							
strongly agree	45	33	78	18	96	3	1
agree	21	50	71	7	78		2
neither agree nor disagree	2	11	13	2	15		3
disagree	1	1	2	0	2		4
strongly disagree	1	0	1	0	1		5
S40 Mission is relational and best expressed through partnerships							
strongly agree	30	17	47	18	65		2
agree	30	50	80	7	87		1
neither agree nor disagree	9	23	32	2	34		3
disagree	0	7	7	0	7		4
strongly disagree	1	1	2	0	2		5

	national	local	n+l	biams	all	no resp	rank
S41 Mission is enhanced by cross-cultural and world perspectives							
strongly agree	43	30	73	15	88	3	1
agree	20	53	73	12	85		2
neither agree nor disagree	5	11	16	0	16		3
disagree	2	1	3	0	3		4
strongly disagree	0	0	0	0	0		5
S42 Mission is about initiating people into the worshipping community							
strongly agree	7	2	9	4	13	3	4
agree	27	46	73	9	82		1
neither agree nor disagree	22	29	51	11	62		2
disagree	11	17	28	2	30		3
strongly disagree	3	3	6	1	7		5
S43 Mission is primarily about welcoming all people							
strongly agree	13	16	29	3	32		4
agree	16	42	58	14	72		1
neither agree nor disagree	15	12	27	7	34		3
disagree	19	23	42	3	45		2
strongly disagree	7	5	12	0	12		5
S44 The priority for mission today is to proclaim Christ anew where people are drifting from previous Christian believing and belonging							
strongly agree	6	21	27	3	30		3
agree	25	38	63	10	73		1
neither agree nor disagree	24	32	56	8	64		2
disagree	11	7	18	5	23		4
strongly disagree	4	0	4	1	5		5

National interviews: GMN and BIAMS bodies

Churches and Agencies interviewed: Mission to Seafarers, USPG, The Methodist Church, The Church of Scotland, The United Reformed Church, Mill Hill Missionaries, CAFOD.

Seven Churches and Agencies were interviewed between March 2009 and February 2010 with the purpose of exploring further the ideas and understandings expressed in the Attitudes to Mission survey which had been completed earlier. Five of the interviews were conducted with the representative who had completed the survey and two with senior staff members who had not completed the survey. In one case, the senior staff member who completed the survey was on sabbatical leave and the other had left the employment of the agency.

Interviews were not conducted in a formal style but as a discussion about the experience of completing the survey which led to general discussion about the theology of mission in their church or agency. Analysis was done by reflection on the interviews by the interviewer.

Process of completing the survey

All representatives interviewed found the process of completing the survey both stimulating and challenging. Two of the church representatives first attempted to complete the survey as a staff team in the respective Mission Departments of major British denominations. Whilst valuing the process of attempting to complete it in this way it was not possible to find sufficient agreement across the staff team to complete the survey together. Interviewees expressed the reason for this as the diversity of views or approaches to mission among practitioners in their departments who often have considerable experience of working in the world mission field. In both cases the survey was referred to a senior staff member who completed it as a representative of the denomination. One denomination completed the survey at a meeting of the senior staff member and Chair of a Mission Board. They came to a compromise on contested areas and used the middle categories of the responses to express their view. They said that *'at times they were almost contradicting themselves but the response to the question seemed the obvious, natural response from our life experience.'*

The five interviewees who completed the survey themselves were divided on the use of words such as 'primarily', 'best' and 'most' in the questions. The senior representatives of the denomination who completed the survey as a pair found such terms helpful as they sharpened the issues and therefore pushed them into a more natural response. Two specialist Mission Agencies also found such terms helpful. The two denominations who attempted to complete it as a staff team found such terms unhelpful in the process.

All interviewees recognised the value of the survey as a learning tool both in the continuing professional development of their teams and for use with local churches after some modification in content and presentation.

Theological Expressions of mission

There was a clear divide between the way in which the Churches and Agencies expressed their theological understandings. The Agencies interviewed expressed a coherent theology whereas the Churches found it more difficult to articulate a theology of mission beyond the more general expressions such as 'mission is diverse.' One agency expressed their theology of mission in terms of always being 'through action' and cited Matthew 26 as the driving Scriptural force. Their theology of mission was bound up in the Gospels. They expressed the importance of context and justice to their work. However they had also changed their name in 2000 from 'missions' to 'mission' to indicate that all mission is one and it is God's reflecting the use of *missio Dei* thinking. The other agency interviewed saw their theology of mission as being relational, transformational and strategic. Relationships between the churches they work for and with in the world church as equal partners are expressed as historic continuity, funding, health and education. This was also the case for the Roman Catholic Mission agency interviewed. The Development agency interviewed emphasised the importance of work for justice within an ecclesial structure.

The approach of all the Churches interviewed was to hold together a variety of theological approaches to mission and to manage the complexity that this creates. One described this as '*a spectrum of mission approaches and trying to hold them together but projects may emphasise one or the other style or approach.*'

One church admitted that '*we probably don't reflect enough on theology…we are in activist mode rather than reflective mode.*'

Another church expressed the need to do theological and practical work on money and the need to look at issues of accountability through these lenses.

Conclusions

- All interviewees expressed the value of expressing their work theologically. As one said, '*we probably don't reflect enough theologically. We are activist and concentrate on what we have to do rather than operate in reflective mode. We run around the same field instead of looking elsewhere – to the sidelines.*'

- Though there was a high degree of awareness of the *missio Dei* among all those interviewed it was not acting as the overarching theological concept that governed practice. There was some evidence of convergence around the *missio Dei* though this was only articulated after prompting through a direct question. However one agency changed its name to reflect the belief that there is one mission which is God's. Two agencies expressly said that they saw their work as between the *missio Dei* and justice understandings. The denominations interviewed said that their staff and supporters would support a variety of approaches to mission and the denomination was able to encompass all approaches. Their understandings of God would be equally as diverse.

- Christian mission for the denominations and agencies interviewed is not a neat package of theological ideas that directly guide practice. The relationship between theory and practice is complex and sometimes contradictory. This raises the question of what the nature of the drivers are for their continued participation in mission and what the hoped for outcomes are. For some the drivers are about transformative relationships, for others proclamation of the good news of Christ and for others the search for justice.

- Does the holding together of different approaches to mission theology in the churches mean that theological reflection is less attractive and the focus becomes task orientated, particularly in a challenging financial climate where re-organisation and budget cuts are commonplace? For the agencies, working in the same very challenging climate, does the need to focus activities within a coherent theological framework become more necessary in order to maintain partnerships and stabilise the financial base?

National interviews: Global Connections

Summary

Seven interviews were conducted with mission leaders, of whom four were people from the Global Connections network who had responded to the survey. This summary relates to those four interviews. The process of selecting the interviewees was based on using those with different answers for some of the key questions in the survey based around the three models on which the survey was based on.

In seems that agency leaders all play a key role in the missiological development of their agency and stated that there was considerable similarity between their own views and that of the agency.

The agency interviews confirmed our hope that the survey could be turned into an excellent tool for helping mission agency staff reflect on their understanding of their task and to hep agencies tease out a better expressed missiology.

The following initial research conclusions and comments can be made from the interviews prior to a more detailed analysis:

- In general the agency leaders were committed to proclamation as a central or key part of mission, though Matthew 28:19–20 was not mentioned by any leader. However they did not like the use of the word 'primarily' even in questions which contained proclamation ideas.

- There was a fairly strong consensus that mission activity was varied and different expressions were all valid. So there was enthusiasm for social justice, social action, social transformation and creation care. However they were NOT seen as mission in themselves, but were activities through which Christ's love could be shown or proclaimed. The concept of mission activity being the context in which proclamation is done was emphasised and seems paramount. This activity and true mission divide came up repeatedly in one form or another.

- There was a range of views and understandings of *missio Dei*, with some unable to articulate it clearly. However for one leader this was clearly his preferred model, which for him led to mission being varied and creative, following God the Trinity in mission, rather than just proclamation.

- There was some variation around the understanding of how God works in the world and whether God can use people of other faiths and non-Christians as instruments of His mission. The church being the Kingdom of God seems to be the general position, though this needed further depth of questioning. Many surveys from those of an evangelical persuasion were more sceptical about whether and how God used non-Christians and this was borne out in the interviews.

- There are some real eschatological issues around the missionary task which was interpreted as proclaiming the gospel to all so that Christ can return. So, for example, while there was enthusiasm for social justice as an activity, there was little understanding of mission as justice as only Christ's return could really bring justice about.
- The view that the task of their agency was key in helping mobilise churches was expressed. Any development of the survey needs to take more account of the mission agency/local church divide in how questions are structured.
- There was some enthusiasm that with adaption the survey could be a useful tool to tease out some of the underlying theological drivers in mission. However there are some issues relating to some of the language and words used in the survey.

Detailed Analysis

Question 1: *Was the survey filled in as yourself or on behalf of the church?*
All said it was them, but that they tried to speak on the agency's behalf. However none had consulted others. One said that the agency was mainly activists, and they didn't really think about it.

COMMENT: An exercise to compare at different levels of an agency structure might be worthwhile.

Question 2: *What, if anything, did you find helpful about filling in the survey?*
Most had difficulty recalling completing as the interviews were conducted six months after the event. This is a flaw in the research. However people said it challenged you to think through issues. There was some discussion outside the interviews of it possibly being a tool they could use in their agencies.

COMMENT: There would appear to be evidence here that the survey could form the basis of an educational or developmental tool for agency leaders to help their staff and agency think about mission.

Question 3: *What, if anything, did you find difficult or unhelpful about filling in the survey?*
The only main issue was the use of the primarily, as it lead too a more negative answer than they wanted to give. For example, with the first question on justice, one person put strongly disagreed as he felt it was definitely not primarily about justice, though mission activity included justice.

COMMENT: There is some need to clarify words and meanings.

Question 4: *Where do you find your church's authority for its engagement in mission?*
The standard answer to this question was the Bible or the scriptures. However one leader also referred to the church in the location as being involved in giving permission. One qualified his comment with the statement – 'I find it in the mission of the triune God, in the nature of God, and only in scripture as an expression of God's mission'.

COMMENT: There was NO reference to Matthew 28 or the great commission. The scripture was the standard response, and only one referred to the missionary nature of God Himself.

Question 5: *How did you react to the word primarily in a number of questions?*
In general it was felt that this helped make a firm decision. However sometimes the qualifying word 'primarily' didn't quite fit, especially when the other words could have different meanings.

COMMENT: While people understood that the survey was trying to make them take up a position, most felt that it could lead to a variety of answers from people with similar positions, depending on whether one said disagree to the primarily or the issue itself.

Question 6: *How did you react to the question about 'the role of the Trinity'?*
The reactions were generally that people were pleased to see it there. All felt the Trinity is absolutely central to mission: 'Without the Trinity there is no mission'. However some questioned what was meant by the question – was He the initiator and well as the supreme missioner? Most showed little understanding of following the missionary, Trinitarian God into the world. Indeed that we could do this was questioned by one respondent as His understanding of Jesus' mission seemed to be only as coming as the supreme sacrifice. However for one this was the basis of his whole missiological understanding

COMMENT: Few agency leaders seem to have a well articulated understanding of the idea of following the missionary, Trinitarian God into the world.

Question 7: *Did you want to react positively to all the statements carrying the word 'mission' and if so, why?*
For mission agency leaders, this was not really a relevant question. However there was some debate on what was understand by mission, and whether with so much being mission these days, the word had been devalued.

COMMENT: None.

Question 8: *Did some of the questions make you think more deeply about the issues in such a way as to affect some of your answers to the later questions?*
In general most said that they filled it in without going back to make changes. However two interviewees stated that the survey had made them think. One used the opportunity to talk through the questions on the church and the Kingdom which had given him pause for thought that God's action is broader and surprising than the traditional evangelical view equating the kingdom with the church.

COMMENT: It seems the survey could be used to help people think through key issues, especially if an analysis tool was developed.

Question 9: *Did you choose 'neither agree nor disagree' when you meant 'don't know'?*
It had been used in several ways. This also varied from question to question. For

some, they were unsure of their answer. For others, they had problems with part of the wording again – for example the use of the terms 'mission means'. They felt mission included – but did not mean, and they used the neither agree nor disagree box.

COMMENT: The use of this term did not seem to cause a problem.

Question 10: *Can you tell me about your choice of response to question x (decided on the interviewer reflecting on the survey responses)?*
Not covered in the summary at this stage.

Question 11: *How does the respondent describe the theological position of the church they represent in relation to three understandings of mission:*
   1.   Proclamation of Jesus Christ as Universal Saviour;
   2.   *Missio Dei* – God at work in the world and the church's task to join in with that work;
   3.   Transformation, social justice, liberation theology, bias to the poor etc.

One respondent stated: 'I think the first category. I would not want to duck the need for personal repentance and reconciliation with God. I can see elements of mission where you could be doing something in mission without having got that across …. But the overall picture of mission cannot be without reconciliation with God.'

A second stated: 'I am also aiming for transformation in that sense. But really it is proclamation'.

A third: 'Sadly I don't think we have a theological position! We are committed to pragmatism, are roots are less theological, rather pragmatic. Our history is a pragmatic response to ….. So I suppose historically it sits in the proclamation area. I hope under my leadership we will move more to a *missio Dei* view.'

The fourth: 'Mission can only be mission if Christ is proclaimed.'

COMMENT: It is clear here that proclamation is the theologically underpinning for mission in the agencies interviewed, though one leader clearly wanted an awareness of the m*issio Dei* to be the agency's controlling basis for mission.

Question 12: *What understanding of God underlies your agency's approach to mission? In your opinion and experience, does the church constituency from which you come do enough thinking on the nature of mission?*
One felt that there was little thinking, and even the thinking was very confused. The agency was basically reactive to need and request. Another referred back to the scriptures as the sole place of the revelation of God, and all understanding came from there, where God sent His Son to die as saviour. That under-pinned all understanding of God. Another addressed the whole Trinity issue as key, but felt his agency was basically activists.

COMMENT: This question raised the whole issue that most mission agencies are activists, making the most of opportunities. Most spend little time in reflecting and contemplating any understanding of God who leads into mission?

Question 13: *What do you feel about the relationship between mission and justice?*
One leader was strongly supportive that mission by its nature was about justice and political, though he felt his agency would be horrified to hear him say it. At the other extreme, one felt that justice was all about God's justice. Most discussed again the issue of activity and mission.

COMMENT: This confirmed the conclusion that most saw a difference between missionary activity and mission itself.

Detailed analysis of local survey [1]

Question 1: *Was the survey filled in as yourself or on behalf of the church?*
The majority stated it was some of both of these – sometimes the length of service in a place influenced the ability to speak on behalf of the church. In one case, Geoffrey with over forty years as leader (with a particular model of leadership), stated that the church now 'follows the lead of the minister.' Several others were also clear that their personal views influenced the congregation's with Lee unsure whether they might be able to articulate their views in the way he could. James really only gave his own views as he was less than a year in post when surveyed. Only one interviewee, Luke from the Salvation Army was definitely speaking as a representative of the church, without much personal bias (except in the sense that he was a member of that organisation) – and he held a role slightly above direct church/congregational ministry.

COMMENT: It is clear from what follows that clergy/ministers are normally 'ahead' of their congregations when thinking about mission. We are researching 'foundations for mission' in the church and have chosen to interview ministers and we need to be aware of the biases that this approach introduces – we cannot simply equate clergy with church!

Question 2: *What, if anything, did you find helpful about filling in the survey?*
While a few could not remember that far back, the majority were positive about filling it in, some because they were actively involved in exploring mission questions with their congregations. In these situations it clarified thinking and reiterated priorities. For others it was reminder of such an exercise in the past. Several remarked on the comprehensive nature of the questions – covering as they did all aspects of mission – some noting that this was clearly the intention of the compilers. In the case of Martin the survey had actually enabled to him to start a new mission initiative in his church. In one case, Greg, the question prompted an important memory about the distinction made in some of the survey questions between gospel as word or deed which resonated with a real tension in his churches, or rather between himself and his largely rural congregations.

COMMENT: There would appear to be evidence here that the survey questions could form the basis of an educational or developmental tool for clergy and churches when exploring their views of mission.

---

1 Names have been changed to protect privacy. Comments are made by Nigel Rooms.

Question 3: *What, if anything, did you find difficult or unhelpful about filling in the survey?*

The interviewees were virtually unanimously negative on this question – not really finding anything difficult with the survey – perhaps just noting the repetitive nature of some of the questions and the need to think hard about some of the answers. One interviewee, Lee questioned what he felt was the either/or nature of some or even a majority of the questions which made them difficult to answer. He preferred to hold to a 'holistic' view of mission (more of this later).

COMMENT: The majority of responses here simply underline the conclusions made for question 2.

Question 3: *Where do you find your church's authority for its engagement in mission?*

This question is open and slightly ambiguous and the answers to it were very illuminating. Eleven of the sixteen respondents (69%) referred to 'The Great Commission' or Matthew 28 either at this point or later in the interview either explicitly or implicitly (by referring to discipleship). Nevertheless how this passage was used varied greatly – it could be taken in a Trinitarian direction by Lee, a classic evangelical position was offered by Geoffrey and a sacramental perspective by James. Perhaps surprisingly, Mike, the Pentecostal did not offer Matthew 28 at all.

Seven (44%) referred, either solely or in addition, to the church institution either investing authority for mission in the minister or through its structures and initiatives. A few of the interviewees were encouraged by further questioning to offer a biblical passage to add to their institutional answer, but this took some time. They had not heard the question as asking about Scriptural authority. One or two noted the ambivalent nature of institutional authority and how it could both enable and disable mission.

There were not really any other possible responses except perhaps for Lee who offered mission as the 'primary calling on all Christians through their baptism.' Other Bible passages were Johannine in nature, focusing on love of God and neighbour as well as Luke 4 and Galatians 3:28.

COMMENT: The ubiquitous nature of Matthew 28 here has to be important for the research question, not least because it seems to be an almost 'default position' or an instinctive reaction to the question for many. What is remarkable is that no-one responded with the idea that God is missionary in very nature therefore the church might follow. What is behind the institutional answers? Perhaps that general feeling that mission is an 'ought' which is required rather than a spontaneous response to the grace of God in Christ?

Question 4: *How did you react to the word primarily in a number of questions?*

Twelve out of sixteen interviewees positively affirmed the use of primarily. This was mainly because of the ubiquitous nature of mission and the need therefore to prioritise beliefs and actions within an understanding of it. As Tim said; 'it forced you to make a choice.' The was one interesting main exception, Lee who objected to the use of the word since he argued mission is holistic and it is not either 'this way or that way'.

COMMENT: it is arguable here that Lee has point which is worth making and perhaps directs us to the much more nuanced approaches that can be taken in 'late-modernity' as opposed to those harder positions argued for earlier eras.

Question 5: *How did you react to the question about 'the role of the Trinity'?*
Again an open question offers several possibilities and the respondents do fall into several noticeable categories. This question overlaps into the idea of the *missio Dei* because the survey question was about 'following God the Holy Trinity in to the world'. This particular emphasis needed explaining to some interviewees – most notably Elizabeth.

Of course all the interviewees understand the doctrine of the Trinity but a significant minority, it seems, have no use for it in understanding mission. Matthew reads the Trinity only in terms of the Holy Spirit – in fact in the interview as a whole he offers a kind of pneumatological understanding of the *missio Dei* where it is the Holy Spirit who is at work in the world. Geoffrey is only really interested in presenting Christ in mission. Mark finds the doctrine opaque ('what do we mean by it? [the Trinity]) and therefore he is not really interested in its usefulness.

On the other hand there is a strong understanding of the Trinity as a driver for understanding mission demonstrated in a further significant minority. Most strong on this is Lee who bases his whole missiological understanding and action on the idea. Luke also has a good grasp of the concepts and their usefulness. Bob has signed up to the idea for some time and has taught the ideas to his leadership team although he admits not every church member would be familiar with them. I believe it is significant for the research that all three of these interviewees held positions of oversight in their churches/denominations as well as offering different levels of pastoral ministry.

In between are all the other interviewees who display varying degrees of understanding and interest – there is perhaps more agreement overall with the importance of the Trinity than an understanding of the idea of the *missio Dei*. James is interesting as he wants to hold together the three persons in the unity of God and is concerned not to end up with three gods.

COMMENT: There is some real evidence here for the research question. It seems there is some kind of continuum or even 'adoption distribution curve' with regard to the receptivity of the idea of following the missionary, Trinitarian God into the world. The age of the interviewee and time interval since training may be significant, as well as the level of operation within the organisation.

Question 6: *Did you want to react positively to all the statements carrying the word 'mission' and if so, why?*
While this question is more closed than others in the interview there is very little disagreement with the basic premise that yes it is difficult to argue against being positive about mission in our current climate. It was heartening however to hear just how many, in fact virtually all the respondents understood mission as foundational or core to the church's task – it is the purpose of its existence (at least Mary, Luke, Lee, Tim,

Bob, Philip and Elizabeth). This seemed to be regardless of the tradition and focused on mission at 'home'. There were two caveats to this that quickly arose. First that in some congregations there is a vestigial understanding of mission which is that it is the work which the mission agencies undertake overseas. In fact Philip commented that since mission is now understood much more locally this is a reason why support for mission agencies can only further reduce. Second is the 'institutional drag' that some clergy feel prevents them from carrying out their core task in mission (Mary, Tim). An exception to all the other interviewees was Mike, the Pentecostal who seemed to want to use the word mission as 'missions' i.e. specific evangelistic events where preaching for conversions occurred.

COMMENT: I believe this confirms the 'sea-change' that has at least now almost fully occurred amongst the clergy that in Britain since the so-called 'Decade of Evangelism' in the 1990s – that we are in new missionary situation which is addressed by affirming the church's core purpose as mission. The self-understanding of the clergy is now 'post-Christendom.'

Question 8: *Did some of the questions make you think more deeply about the issues in such a way as to affect some of your answers to the later questions?*
About four or five of the interviewees agreed that this process of intensification may have been going on. A similar number simply could not remember that amount of detail at the distance of the interview from the moment of filling in the survey. (This was about the only point in the interview where the time distance really did affect the responses.) Others were clear that they answered all the questions spontaneously.

COMMENT: I am not sure anything that conclusive can be really be gleaned from this question.

Question 9: *Did you choose 'neither agree nor disagree' when you meant 'don't know'?*
This is, it seems to me a more subtle question than it at first appears and it elicited some subtle and nuanced responses. The question is where is the boundary between equivocation (not agreeing or disagreeing), not caring/or having an interest in the question or being genuinely ignorant of the answer to the issue presented? That is – do the interviewees display all these possible approaches to understanding the question?

About one third of the interviewees agree with the statement they were presented with in the sense that they genuinely didn't know the answer to the question. As Sarah commented; 'there may be people who have far more experience than I' – implying that such people would be able to answer the question one way or the other with their superior knowledge. Occasionally in this group there was also the idea that there may be no answer to the question anyway – so displaying a slightly different nuance to the idea of 'don't know.'

A similar sized group were able to develop this understanding of 'don't know' in the sense that they absolutely had thought about the question and in some cases quite deeply, but that took them to the equivocal point on the scale – it was not a 'don't know' at all, but a genuine 'agnosticism' on the question or else in some cases an effort to hold a both/and position. Others were between these positions or gave inconclusive answers to the question. There was little sense overall that interviewees had passed over any of the survey questions because they were too difficult or complex.

COMMENT: A simple first conclusion here is that there is real evidence that all the interviewees had interacted at some depth with all of the questions. Even those who really meant 'don't know' were saying so from a position of *knowing* they didn't know. The question also points up the nuanced nature of the possible positions that can be taken about missiological issues. In some of the responses there is genuine consternation at the need to hold together different and seemingly incompatible positions (e.g. Luke, Greg). Some interviewees are more at ease with having a position which can hold a both/and understanding rather than simply either/or. This of course may simply reflect the faith development stage (in Fowler's terms) of the interviewee. Nevertheless for the first time we come across the question of how far there are real incompatibilities and/or continuities between the various ideological stances/positions that can be taken in missiology.

Question 10: *Can you tell me about your choice of response to question x (decided on the interviewer reflecting on the survey responses)?*
We will look at this question at the end of this analysis when we take evidence from individual interviewees to add to the overall picture.

Question 11: *How does the respondent describe the theological position of the church they represent in relation to three understandings of mission?*

1. Proclamation of Jesus Christ as Universal Saviour;
2. *Missio Dei* – God at work in the world and the church's task to join in with that work;
3. Transformation, social justice, liberation theology, bias to the poor etc.

We will note all the responses to this question here as they are so important (the theological positions will be referred to as 1, 2 and 3):

- Matthew prefers a 'holistic' view of mission (uses the word twice) while offering a pneumatological version of the *missio Dei*.
- Mark declares his church to be firmly at 3 and himself mid-way between 2 and 3 (The church had moved from being Calvinist to liberal and pacifist during the 1930s and 40s.)
- Mary found herself partway between 2 and 3 while wanting to move on to 1 from that starting point. This was rather her personal view.
- Luke wanted to start with 1 but very clearly hold on to bits of 2 and 3. He uses the word holistic again and is aware of the concept of *missio Dei* but says it is not deeply rooted in the churches.
- Lee begins firmly in 2 while including 1 and 3, but *missio Dei* is definitely the starting point.
- Tim favours 1 first then 3 then 2 – he wants to emphasise Jesus as personal Saviour from his own experience and offer justice *for* others while not really recognising much role for the *missio Dei*.

- Geoffrey is firmly in position 1 as the church is the only body that is qualified and equipped to carry it out – others can deal with justice issues.

- Sarah has three concentric circles in her mind – 2 at the centre then 1 followed by 3. Proclamation and justice are still necessary.

- Bob is firmly in 2 but holds onto 3 and 1 (in that order) making three 'strands' – he calls 1 'journey into faith' rather than proclamation.

- James is clearly in 3 (personally) which 'puts you on the edge' with elements of 2 only.

- Martin has moved position in later ministry from 3 to 1 having a critique now of liberation theology as not sufficiently focussed on growth or conversion. He does not seem interested in *missio Dei* – even unaware of it.

- Greg again wants to hang on to all three, because of his life and ministry experiences, but if pushed will say 1 is most important above the others.

- Philip emphasises importance of all three but yet again if forced will hold on to 1, because that is his gifting – proclamation.

- Elizabeth – 1, 2 and then 3 in that order.

- Mark definitely 1, again offers a pneumatological version of 2 (in a previous question) and understands the importance of 3 while restricting it to mainly 'charitable works'.

COMMENT: It is clearly important here to note initially that 11/16 (69%) respondents want in some way to mention all three positions. Holistic seems to be an important word to several either explicitly or by implication. A question might be however are the different positions really that compatible? Where, if anywhere are the discontinuities?

Interestingly either when pressed or as a 'starting point' all the interviewees have a preferred position. The most, eight in all chose position 1, five position 2 and just two position 3. It is worth noting that these two were specifically interviewed on the basis that they had 'strongly agreed' to the mission as justice question. The interviews then confirm the survey results at this point.

It seems then there is some awareness of the *missio Dei* and while it is the controlling basis for mission for one or two and the starting point for others it is far from being a universal foundation for mission in the churches and amongst the clergy.

Question 11 continued: *Compare the five stated mission priorities of the interviewee with the stated view of mission*

All the interviewees are able to make significant connections between their understanding of mission and their top five mission action priorities. What is interesting is that in general there is little evidence of social and community interventions being made for the ultimate end of evangelism. Only Geoffrey really illustrates this phenomenon to any extent. Occasionally the evangelism/social action tension in theology is also played out in action as in the case of Luke in the Salvation Army.

The Anglican mission priorities are still to a major extent driven by the established nature of the church – so interaction with schools and church schools figures highly. Again there is evidence that churches are moving away from understanding mission as something that happens 'overseas' through missionary giving – though this still exists in some places.

What is also remarkable is the range of mission initiatives that are described by the interviewees – in what is a small sample of sixteen clergy there is an enormous amount of work going on – much of it for the 'common good.' Nevertheless drawing people into and becoming part of the Christian story is very much on the agenda of the churches.

Underlying the mission actions here is the general decline in church attendance which is a clear pressure on many clergy. It was difficult to discern how much of an influence this factor was on the actions but there is evidence in some of the interviews that there is real pressure felt to 'grow' the church.

COMMENT: This question is rather more difficult to analyse than the others [I wonder whether it might be possible to extract the text for this question only and subject it to NVIVO analysis?] If anything it at least confirms the findings of question 10 – that churches are not saying they are believing one thing and doing another.

Question 12: *What understanding of God underlies your church's approach to mission?*

This is a really helpful question as it repeats in a slightly different and more open way the earlier question about the Trinity. At least a third of the respondents are clear about their understanding of God but in very different ways – for Matthew it is the Holy Spirit at work and for Mark and Mary it is the incarnate God we meet and uncover at work in others. We know about Lee and James is offering a loving God exemplified by the cross – 'we [missionary priests] dig a pit for the cross' in the communities we are sent to.

However at least another third (five) interviewees found this question difficult to answer or gave an answer that didn't really refer to God but only repeated what they had said about mission. Only two gave a fully Trinitarian answer and while this was not required it was interesting that it was not the default position of most.

COMMENT: This is clearly a difficult area – there is little agreement across the interviewees on who the God of mission might be. Several are unable to articulate much at all about God. Why is this – are we simply pragmatists and activists, not really taking the time to reflect and contemplate our understanding of God who leads us into mission? What spirituality is there in mission?

Question 13: *What do you feel about the relationship between mission and justice?*

The response to this question was very varied. A couple of interviewees with a Christian Socialist background emerged on asking it (Matthew, James) and one or two who wanted to hold to justice as a vital part of mission (e.g. Martin). Others thought it was part of the whole, but only a part (Lee). Several equated justice with charitable giving or charity itself (Geoffrey, Mike). Elizabeth stated that it wasn't much of an issue in her context as it wasn't one of real poverty.

COMMENT: What is missing here is much sense (apart perhaps from Fair Trade and Trade Justice issues and some local interventions) that the church's task is to change the unjust structures of society. Is this because of the localness of church or that the theological foundations are not present to raise these issues over the horizons of Christians and clergy? Several interviewees focused on the importance of personal relationship with God which naturally militates against holding a quest for justice alongside other mission initiatives.

Question 10

Individual interviews and supplementary questions on particular issues in the survey answers....

Not every interview will be referred to here but it is worth noting at the end of this analysis the particularities of the individuals involved. They are not commented on directly as above but the issues raised are taken into account in the summary of the analysis at the start of this document.

- Matthew is a charismatic evangelical who describes himself as a 'pastor evangelist' having been trained for missionary work overseas but never realising that goal for medical reasons. He brings this missiological training to his ministry and demonstrates it in clear ways in the interview. As a charismatic he introduces the idea mentioned above of the pneumatological *missio Dei*, without of course using those terms, he puts it like this:

  > I mean we're the hands of Christ, but the Holy Spirit is the empowerer and facilitator, he paves the way, we look for where he's at work and then go and get stuck in...

- Mark: there are several things to note about this interview. First, as mentioned above, the legacy of pacifism and liberal theology passed down the generations of the church members (though how much longer it may last might be questioned). Second Mark reports a split with two members of the congregation who clearly held to position 1 for their missiology. Essentially this split is over Mark's and the church's understanding of mission as well as a specific issue around the idea of Inter-faith dialogue which distanced him from the neighbouring Baptist church these members had joined. Mark finds himself drawn into this area after studying it at Masters level and the church supports him positively in it such that he describes how he is active in it almost on their behalf.

  So the evidence here definitely points to incompatibilities and discontinuities arising from missiological positions.

- Mary: the only additional note here is about a mature, but non-growing church plant in her Parish which she describes suggestively as a religious community:

  > I always feel it as rather like and it's a funny sort of like evangelical way as something, a community, a religious community... it's about living together, praying together and all that, so it's community.

- Luke: there does seem to be a basic dichotomy running through this interview which could just be the classic evangelism/social action tension but seems more subtle than that since the interviewee is fully aware of the range of missiological positions including *missio Dei*.

- Lee, as we have noted above, argues cogently for a holistic view of mission versus what he refers to as the 'sixties' dichotomies of evangelism and social action. There is a sense in which he is developing an integrated, interconnected even *perichoretic* understanding of mission where the different strands overlap and interpenetrate each other:

  I think mission is core to what we should be as a church. So it's not just about Sunday services, it's equally as much about going out in mission with God. So I would never ever want to disconnect mission from the core life of the church. It's not an add on, it's not something we do when we have finished fund raising or we've finished making our services nice, it's an equally important part of the life of the church, it's having communion, praising God together, praying and mission it's all a part of that.

  I also asked Lee at the end of the interview about his views on other faiths since his survey answers to these questions stood out. He understood these questions as also coming from a 'previous generation.' He did not think we had much to learn from other faiths, given his understanding of the uniqueness of grace in the Christian tradition. This did seem slightly at odds with the rest of the interview, but perhaps a strongly bounded Trinitarian theology can be exclusive in this way.

- Tim remarks in a supplementary question how he is moving the church from an understanding of mission as giving to a hospital in Lesotho through USPG to seeing it as something that happens through the local church.

- Geoffrey is a cogent proponent of position 1 – that the task of mission is solely down to the church and the church alone. He makes a clear distinction in supplementary questions between the task of the church in mission which is proclaiming Christ and 'good works' all of which can be said to come from God:

  I was thinking there about the difference between mission, which is clearly the church's task and the work that humanists, secularists, people who claim to have no faith at all, nevertheless, do good work...

- Sarah has strongly agreed in the survey to questions about the importance of verbal proclamation and confronting people with the consequences of sin and she confirms this in the interview as being a 'biblical' approach.

  it's [mission] about telling people who Jesus is not just providing something that's a nice thing to do or say a social activity that actually doesn't have anything to do with the fact that we're doing this because we're Christians and we want people to know Christ.

This leads to her to proclaim Christ as she puts it in a Christingle service where 30% of the people 'we'd never seen in a church setting before.' It might have been interesting however to ask how many of these people actually thought they were 'doing church' by attending the service.

- James is unique amongst the interviewees as he has a high Anglican or catholic tradition and is a member of an order of missionary priests, the Society of the Holy Cross (SSC). So as noted above he has a sacramental view of Matt. 28 which directly affects the way he conducts baptisms in the parish. In supplementary questioning it became clear James did not like the language of sin but was nevertheless concerned to confront people with the cross. For James the church is also essential to mission as it takes the individual element away and provides accountability – like Geoffrey he has a very high view of church as a vehicle for mission. Nevertheless God can be at work outside the church it's just that from the standpoint of being inside the expectations placed on members are different. Later in the interview James shares a deep tension within himself because having accepted the authority of the church he must stay loyal to it – but this is not always easy as being a missionary priest takes him very often to the 'edge' of things. The support and accountability that the missionary order then provides for him is key to holding himself together within this tension.

- Martin had not strongly agreed with any of the statements on the survey which I checked out and he said it was perhaps more to do with his person after 30 years of ministry than anything he particularly believed. What was interesting though was an exchange we had about him disagreeing that the 'Franciscan' statement in the survey about mission as acting justly and loving neighbours only using words if necessary. He responds with a story which amounts to being 'evangelised' by a Muslim prison chaplain:

    > We both happened to go in on a Friday, ...he used to say 'you should be more up front about what you're about, I am, why don't you,' you know cause I was quite diffident about it initially. He was a Muslim coming into the prison life and Asif he used to challenge me all of the time and say, get out there, you know and sort of speak who you are to people and there's nothing wrong with that. I think probably I've learnt that from him.

- Greg: in a supplementary I ask him about his insistence on proclamation when the Kingdom is bigger than the church. He states than interesting tension for many protestants:

    > [quoting those 'outside' church] ... you don't need to go to church to be a Christian. Now that's technically in my mind true, you don't need to go to church to be a Christian. You need to enter into a relationship with God to be Christian. Now I like to think the church is significantly important

> in the process and in the discipleship afterwards and how you go in faith,
> but you know what I mean, there's a difference between entering into a
> relationship with God and church.

The question remains then what do we mean by the word Christian – especially in the rural context, this is clearly contested in Greg's mind. At the end of the interview the issue surfaces again with a background of church decline and the need for growth to survive:

> most of my congregations are beginning to see this that we are in a
> missionary context in this country even in the little rural villages, you
> know, you can no longer assume everybody is a Christian and even then
> *what is a Christian is the big question.* (My italics)

Int: what is it do you think that convinces them of that [need to be missionary]?

> when they see the long standing church members being buried and
> sent to the crematorium. They realise that if we don't do something this
> church ain't going to be here in ten/twenty years time.

- Philip clarifies his understanding of proclamation in a supplementary question that it doesn't need to be entirely verbal. He also disagreed with both God working primarily through Christians *and* through all people of goodwill He explains this by saying that clearly God is at work outside the church and in other faiths and that experience over a humanist funeral had made him nervous about the latter statement at the time. Interestingly this is much the same issue as that confronting Greg above:

> ...we had quite a few debates about humanists and the normal thing
> about I'm as much a Christian as anybody else because I'm good and I
> do good things and I suppose that's the bit I was, in a way, a bit nervous
> about, cause also many people come to faith and if we're honest the
> amount we sin we could hardly call ourselves good.

- Elizabeth, in some supplementary questioning, wanted to hold together both finding God at work out in the world and also taking Christ out in mission initiatives.

Later in the interview Elizabeth, when asked about the understanding of God which drives mission, tells a story about church growth and that being 'as good as it gets':

> ...there's also this sort of sense of mission is a sense of achievement
> in spreading the good news, but also in carrying something on that
> it will, you can then become like the domino effect that people will
> then teach other people who will then bring other people who will then
> bring other people, so it's that sense of achievement and when we had
> this confirmation a few weeks ago and people baptised in the morning
> and people confirmed in the afternoon ... there was a great sense of

celebration in the community and when I was talking to Paul who is our evangelist afterwards we were both saying this was actually as good as it gets, this is what we are doing this for.

- Mike: I asked a supplementary about Mike not agreeing with mission meaning confronting people with the consequences of sin and he clarified that the message is one of forgiveness not 'bringing fear in their lives.' We then had a discussion about church planting which seemed to be determined (i.e. whether it was right to plant or not) by contextual and attitudinal reasons on the part of the recipients alongside a reliance on the Holy Spirit to reveal the ultimate direction and decision. It is also worth noting again Mike's basic understanding of mission as 'missions' which occurs throughout the interview.